A Razor Wra

Born in Manchester in 1960, R. N. Morris now lives in North London with his wife and two children. *A Razor Wrapped in Silk* follows *A Vengeful Longing* and *A Gentle Axe* in a series of St Petersburg novels featuring Porfiry Petrovich, the character created by Fyodor Dostoevsky in *Crime and Punishment*. *Taking Comfort* was published by Macmillan under the name Roger Morris in 2006.

by the same author

A GENTLE AXE
A VENGEFUL LONGING

A RAZOR WRAPPED IN SILK

A St Petersburg Mystery

R. N. Morris

faber and faber

First published in 2010
by Faber and Faber Ltd
Bloomsbury House
74–77 Great Russell Street
London WC1B 3DA

Typeset by RefineCatch Limited, Bungay, Suffolk
Printed in England by CPI Bookmarque, Croydon

A CIP record for this book
is available from the British Library

ISBN 978-0-571-24115-6

2 4 6 8 10 9 7 5 3 1

For Gillian and Don

'I am convinced that hidden in his drawer is a razor, wrapped in silk, like that murderer in Moscow; he too lived in the same house with his mother and had wrapped a razor in silk to cut a throat with.'

From *The Idiot* by Fyodor Dostoevsky
(translation by Henry Carlisle and Olga Andreyev Carlisle)

September, 1870

1

The spinner's boy

Mitka looked up. He saw the high ceiling of the spinning-shop through a haze of cotton dust scored with countless lines of yarn. The dust was white, like snow but finer. It hung in the hot air, beneath the turning shafts that spanned the workshop and drove the machines. Incessantly moving, yet going nowhere, they held him entranced with a vision of infinity, presented as unrelenting monotony.

He could always taste the dust, always feel it, on him and in him, smothering him. Even in his parched dreams, even in the best of them, when he dreamt of her, and the great feeling took him over – even then, she came to him through a shifting white mist and fed him sweetmeats that tasted of cotton. And in those dreams, the throbbing noise that drowned out her tender words was the chiming clatter of the machines.

Was he dreaming now? The thought frightened him into a state of strained alertness.

He was crouched within the great jaws of the spinning mule. The mule itself, the movable frame which carried over a thousand spindles, or so Mr Ustyantsev claimed, was edging away from the fixed part of the machine. It drew the unspun rovings of cotton from the creel and stretched the fibres into the finest of prison bars. It was Mitka's job to watch for broken threads and tie up the ends, conspiring in his own imprisonment. Once the mule had completed its outward carriage, it would begin its return, walked home by Mr Ustyantsev as it wound in the threads it had spun. Mitka knew of children who, in falling asleep, had been caught in its inexorable bite, unseen by the machine operator. If they were lucky they'd lose a finger, ripped off in the blink of an eye. The hobgoblins and ogres of fairytales were nothing compared to the lurking terrors of the factory. His heart raced, like the bobbins on a double-speeder. He thought of Anya, the girl who had fallen into the driving belt. It had carried her round three times before they had managed to get her out, her screams mingling with the routine screech of metal. In the English foreman's arms, her body hung as limp as a sack of rags. Word got round later that every bone in her body had been broken. Mitka could never forgive Beck for the look on his face as he held her: a look devoid of pity or grief, showing only the contempt of an inconvenienced man. Anya had been ten years old, the same age as Mitka, and a foundling like him. This had been enough to bind them together, like two weak and ragged threads. Their friendship had not developed much beyond silent sympathetic glances and the occasional stolen word. But her eyes had always been the first he sought in the sting of any injustice.

Mitka craned his neck back to scan the taut threads over his head. Every muscle was tense and aching. He winced sharply as a spasm of cramp gripped his right calf. He longed to stand and straighten the leg, but couldn't, not yet at least. He closed his eyes over the pain. It could only have been for a moment, but it was a moment in which he allowed himself to luxuriate in the dangerous dream of lying stretched out on the hard floor beneath the cotton canopy.

He opened his eyes in panic. To his relief, he was still locked in his tight little squat. A thread had snapped while he had dozed. The loose ends trailed on the floor, one drawn away from him by the moving mule, the other gathering into a loose spiral as the rollers spewed more thread. Mitka moved quickly, tying the ends with dextrous fingers, taking secret pride in the speed with which he accomplished the task.

There was a clank as the mule reached the end of its track, followed by a whirring and grinding of gears as the machine adjusted to the next phase of the operation. Mitka grabbed the hand brush and swept the floor ahead of him as he retreated.

Out in the open, in the seemingly limitless expanse of the spinning-shop, there was just time to stand and stretch, to roll his shoulders and kick the cramp out of his leg, before he had to run round and duck into the now opening jaws of the machine opposite.

Bent into position once more, Mitka looked up at the haze of cotton dust scored with countless lines.

*

The steam whistle's blast announced the end of the shift. Mitka scurried out of his daily prison, as fast as a venting of pressure.

He came out into a choking fog that seemed, in the first shock, to be an extension of the cotton haze he had just escaped. But the air was cooler here, and the particles it bore, black and hard-grained. In the spinning-shop they kept the air hot as well as humid, for the sake of the cotton. The change of temperature set his teeth chattering. He had on a cap but no coat; was still dressed only in the clothes he worked in, the ragged cotton shirt, and drill trousers tucked into his boots.

Night was coming on and the lamps in the yard were lit. The dark, soot-laden fog absorbed any light it could and held it in a stifled glow.

5

It was unusually quiet for the end of a shift: disembodied footsteps, but no voices, apart from an occasional murmur or exhausted sigh. It was as if the fog sealed each individual worker off in a wad of solitude.

But the fog served Mitka's purposes. It would make it easier to slip past Granny Kvasova, who was even now waiting to shepherd the foundling children into the apprentice house. The thought of a place by the stove and a share of the communal bowl tempted him. But once inside the house there would be no escape. The door was locked on the children as soon as they stepped through it. He would miss that evening's class. He would not see *her*.

He called her Mother. All the children called her Mother, even the ones who had mothers of their own. Even the adult workers who attended the Free School called her Little Mother. She was the sweetest, kindest, most beautiful mother any of them could imagine.

She fed them dreams and hope, food for their souls not their bellies. He would gladly forego Granny Kvasova's cabbage soup for a smile from his Nourishing Mother. It was her image that sustained him beneath the immense veil of threads each day; the thought that he would see her, sit at her feet with the others as she told them the story of The Dead Princess and the Seven Knights, or taught them the words to *Kalinka*.

Mitka felt the towering presence of the Nevsky Cotton-Spinning Factory behind him. He did not look back. In the fog, its gigantic mass would be transformed into a vague, premonitory shadow of itself. But he knew that the blackened bricks were there, the filthy chimneys, the grimy windows, and he could not bear to turn his face in their direction, to acknowledge their hold over him with even a glance. Hated as it was, it pulled at him, like a weight of sorrow to which he was chained. He wanted to run from it.

Suddenly a soft orb of light appeared ahead of him, swaying high in the air. Someone had raised a lantern on a pole. He could see the flattened, drained form of Granny Kvasova and hear her croaking shout: 'Children, this way! Children! Granny's here!' In his exhaustion, he almost walked towards the summoning, drawn by habit, like a mechanised part returning to its housing. But now the fog was on his side. It gave him time to think, or at least to remember the Mother waiting for him in the schoolroom.

He gave the lantern a wide berth and left the old woman's cries behind.

A whiff of pipe smoke conjured forth the image of Uncle Pyotr, the gatekeeper. Portly and sly, he pretended to be a friend to the children, bestowing winks as if they were sugar crystals. But there was something about his eyes that Mitka never trusted, a cold watchfulness that belied his empty joviality. He had them call him uncle, though he was no more their uncle than the old Kvasova woman was their granny. The man's wheezing cough and high, almost falsetto voice sounded startlingly close, signalling both the way out and a final trap. If Uncle Pyotr caught him he was bound to hand him over to Granny Kvasova. Mitka would then have to plead to be allowed to go to school. She would inevitably deny him, while Uncle Pyotr chuckled as if it was all a joke. No doubt she would use the fog as an excuse, but the real reason would be because she sensed how much he wanted it. He had heard her arguments before, the same ones, more or less, retailed by Mr Ustyantsev: 'It will do you no good, filling your head with geography and nonsense. All you need to learn, young lad, is your place.'

But Mitka knew the place assigned for him only too well: between the yawning jaws of the spinning mule, beneath the cotton strands.

The gatekeeper appeared isolated by the choking blanket of grey. His bulky form came and went, like a figure in a nightmare, an embodiment of fear, partially glimpsed. Uncle Pyotr was warming his hands over a brazier, his greatcoat buttoned up against the raw air. He was sharing a joke with some of the men.

Mitka held back, so as not to be seen. But then he heard the heavy clomp of bark shoes, coming up behind him. Stepping to one side, he peered through the fog as a new group of men came into view. Judging by their grubby peasant shirts and kaftans, not to mention their wild beards and crude haircuts, they were unskilled workers, not long up from the country. There was a burst of sharp, unpleasant laughter as they drew level with the huddle at the gate. Mitka followed in their wake and ducked behind them, clearing the factory yard.

He could hear Uncle Pyotr teasing the country bumpkins: 'Careful you don't fall in the river, you lads. Mind, with those boats on your feet, you'll probably walk to the other side!'

His cronies provided a chorus of appreciative braying. Their smart, almost dandified city clothes, glimpsed by Mitka as he dashed past, marked them out as spinners.

The bleat of a barge's foghorn sounded from the nearby Bolshaia Neva. Mitka could smell the river and hear its lapping water, but not see it. It would be straight ahead of him. With Uncle Pyotr's facetious warning in mind, he turned sharply to the right.

He saw the glow of a street lamp ahead of him.

The boy experienced a giddy sense of liberation as he walked.

It was as if the fog had not merely masked but obliterated the factory. Softly, silently, and with infinite stealth, it had conjured away the great evil that loomed so high over his life, and weighed so heavily upon it.

But the fog also contained within it the promise of another life, the life he was walking towards, street lamp by street lamp.

In the fog, anything seemed possible; everything was equally real and unreal. An idea, a vision, a hope, had as much substance as a factory wall. And a voice, like the voice suddenly heard now, owed its existence to no one, to nothing but the fog. The voice of the fog was singing to him. His heart tripped as he recognised its song: *Kalinka*!

Her song, the one she sang to the children.

Kalinka, kalinka, kalinka maya . . .

The street lamps led him towards it.

Under the pine, under the green pine,
Lay me down to sleep . . .

The ghostly shapes of two feathered horses stood in the beam of a carriage lamp. Mitka couldn't see a driver behind the glaring light. The carriage itself glowed feebly from within, as if lit by the warmth of the voice that came from it.

Aida, Lyuli, Lyuli, aida, Lyuli, Lyuli,
Lay me down to sleep!

As Mitka approached, the door to the carriage swung open. The steps were already down.

Something new escaped with the voice. A scent – *her* scent? – of cleanliness and flowers. Now that he could hear it more distinctly, he began to believe it *was* her voice, and that his Mother had come ahead to fetch him.

Beautiful maid, dear maid,
Please fall in love with me . . .

9

He climbed into the song and into the scent. The carriage hardly registered his presence as the door clicked shut behind him. The voice of the fog gave a final muted chorus of *Kalinka, Kalinka, Kalinka maya*, then ceased.

2

An encounter with a gendarme

An ear-piercing shriek jolted Porfiry Petrovich from his reverie: the squeal of metal grinding on metal as the locomotive's brakes were applied. The train juddered to a halt. Porfiry looked out of the window of his third-class compartment through the slanting rain. They had pulled up alongside a cemetery. The sight of the damp headstones and moss-covered monuments was so in keeping with the melancholic cast of his thoughts that it seemed he had summoned them. However, he recognised it as the Volkovksy Lutheran Cemetery, just south of St Petersburg. He was nearing the end of his journey.

For the first time since he had boarded the train he regretted his economy. Lifting his head to scan the graveyard, he felt a sharp twinge in his neck, and then a second duller, longer ache in the lower right of his back. He realised that he had been holding the same position since leaving Tver, a good ten hours ago.

He closed his eyes on the grey, rain-soaked scene. The image of Zakhar's face came back to him. He remembered how it had seemed like the sculpture of a face, carved out of cork and covered with a waxy sheen. Strangely, in recollection, it seemed more real, more alive. He saw it just at the moment that his old servant had opened his eyes for the last time, showing whites tarnished with veins, a wan cloud dimming each iris. The eyes had swum with a desperate vitality, as the old man strained to lean forward to address a stream of inarticulate grunts to his former master.

It had been left to Porfiry to close his eyes. At the still warm touch of Zakhar's skin he had felt something steely enter him, like a shot of fortifying liquor.

He had picked up a bedbug from the dead man's wrist, crushing it between his nails in a small explosion of blood. Was this humiliating incident the only memory of his faithful servant that he would retain?

He remembered the words he had said to the ancient woman who was Zakhar's sister. 'He was a good man. I shall miss him.' But he had been thinking of another man as he said them, one long dead. For a moment he had once again been a grieving son, standing in need of consolation. Did that make the words a lie, the sentiment insincere? Or could the words apply to both Zakhar and his father?

Porfiry felt the train begin to move, but kept his eyes closed. He tasted again the smoke that had filled the tumble-down hut. He felt it tease the tears from his eyes, which he was forced to unclench.

The Lutheran church rang out the hour, its bell unexpectedly loud and resonant. Porfiry turned away and met the sympathetic and half-expectant gaze of a young man in a Swiss travelling cloak opposite.

'It's good to be home,' said Porfiry, knuckling away his tears.

The young man's face lit up. 'Oh yes!' he agreed, with an intense enthusiasm that seemed disproportionate to the platitude that Porfiry had uttered. 'That's precisely how I feel!'

There was something so sincere, and so open-hearted, about the young man's response that despite its naivety, it could not fail to cheer Porfiry.

The black bulk of the Putilov locomotive, idling after its exertions, continued to hiss and vent steam. The surplus vapour curled along the platform, as if seeking out individuals to enshroud and obscure, before rising to disperse beneath the girder-meshed vault of the Nikolaevsky station.

Porfiry Petrovich, laden with valise, stepped down from the train with the awkward skip of a man discovering himself to be heavier and more unwieldy than he had imagined. He screwed up his face at the itchy scent of machine oil. He then blew out his cheeks in a pantomime of surprise and scanned the platform with a distracted air. He pretended not to notice the unusual number of gendarmes, officers of the notorious Third Section of His Imperial Majesty's Chancellery, their bright blue uniforms lightly spotted with rain. They confronted the detraining passengers with scowls of importance beneath their kepis.

Some instinct drove Porfiry to stride into a shifting cloud. He enjoyed his brief concealment, although he had no reason to hide from them. It was a game without purpose.

When the steam cleared, he found himself face to face with an officer of the gendarmes – a very senior officer, judging by the sprawl of braid over his uniform. Porfiry noticed the oval badge of the Alexandrovskaya Military Academy of Jurisprudence on the right breast of his tunic. His heavily waxed moustaches stood out impressively beneath unexpectedly pink cheeks. There was a good humoured curve to his mouth, a wry, almost complicit smile. And yet his eyes narrowed in suspicion as he stared into Porfiry's.

'I know you.'

'Do you?' said Porfiry. 'It's perfectly possible. I am an investigating magistrate.'

'Porfiry Petrovich.' The officer smiled with self-satisfaction. 'That's right, isn't it?'

'Yes.'

'I can't remember your family name.'

'Most people simply know me as Porfiry Petrovich.'

'But you must have a family name?'

'Must I?'

'Don't tell me *you've* forgotten it, too!'

'I wouldn't be surprised if I had. It is hardly ever referred to. Certainly not in polite circles.'

'You are very droll. I remember now, you are known for that.' The gendarme pretended to be suddenly alarmed. 'But there must be other Porfiry Petroviches!'

'I am unlikely to be confused with any other Porfiry Petrovich. I am Porfiry Petrovich, the Magistrate. It suffices.'

'Porfiry Petrovich, the Magistrate. I will remember that, I'm sure.'

'And your name?' said Porfiry.

The gendarme held out a recriminatory finger, immaculately white-gloved. 'Oh, you don't get my name, if I don't get yours! You're not the only one who can play games, Porfiry Petrovich.'

The gendarme wagged his finger and moved away, still smiling. A moment later, his smile was gone and he nodded tersely to one of his junior officers.

'No sign,' reported the other man.

The senior gendarme looked back at Porfiry, who had set down his valise and was flexing the fingers of the hand that had been carrying it.

'We will wait for the platform to clear, then search the train.'

14

The gendarme kept his eyes on Porfiry as he gave instructions to his subordinate.

Porfiry's face lit up.

'Pavel Pavlovich! I was looking for a porter and I found a friend! Have you come to meet me?'

The young man, clean-shaven and wearing a bottle-green service overcoat, gave a nervous smile under the scrutiny of the gendarmes. He carried a loosely furled umbrella, from which he shook the drops. 'Yes, I have, Porfiry Petrovich.' Pavel Pavlovich Virginsky avoided Porfiry's gaze, as if he feared its penetrating capacity. 'Allow me,' said Virginsky, picking up Porfiry's valise with his free hand.

'That's very kind. It is not very heavy. Nevertheless, I am happy enough to relinquish it.'

'You must be tired. A trip such as the one you have undertaken affords no opportunity for refreshment.'

'On the contrary. After the funeral, I returned to Tver by steamboat. I sincerely believe that if I had endured another carriage ride I would have been jounced to pieces. At any rate, the river cruise restored me. The Volga is magnificent there. And there is something about the pace of water that soothes the soul. Even so, too much soothing and one gets bored. I am glad to be back in Petersburg.' There was something akin to hunger in the glint of Porfiry's eyes.

Virginsky cast an apprehensive glance over his shoulder. 'What did he want?' He spoke quietly.

Porfiry smiled as if he had been asked a completely different question. 'He wanted to know my family name.'

'Did you tell him?'

'It was just a silly little game we were playing. He would have been disappointed if I'd made it too easy for him.'

'Don't you worry that you might make an enemy of him?'

'He was quite charming.'

'That is when the Third Section is most to be feared. You know that, Porfiry Petrovich.'

'We are supposed to be on the same side, working together against the enemies of—'

Porfiry Petrovich became distracted by the sight of the gendarme detachment boarding the length of the empty train. They stormed it with the haste and vigour of an invading army.

'Doesn't it ever strike you, Pavel Pavlovich, that for a secret police force, gendarmes of the Third Section have a rather conspicuous uniform? I cannot help thinking that it would handicap some of their more clandestine operations.'

'We Russians do love our uniforms.'

'Do you know what they are looking for?'

'There is some intelligence about a known agitator – an exile to the mines in Petrozavodsk who has gone missing. It is feared that he is returned to St Petersburg.'

'And why are they searching this station? There are no trains from Petrozavodsk into here.'

'There are trains from Moscow, however. One in particular, the imperial train. It is the next one due on this very platform.'

'And in the meantime Count Shuvalov is taking no chances,' said Porfiry.

The two men cleared the platform in silence.

'It has come to something when the head of state is afraid to walk among his own people,' remarked Virginsky.

'The days are gone when all he had to fear was his immediate family.' Porfiry halted to survey the crowded station concourse. A step or two ahead, Virginsky stopped to wait for him.

The throng was fluid and restless. The families of the well-to-do jostled with those of tradesmen and middle-ranking civil servants, all returning from dachas of varying grandiosity. Despite the disparities of their summer residences, and regardless of whether they had travelled first or third class, their voices now mingled into an egalitarian hubbub. All moved in a single direction, animated by the same impatience, out towards Znamenskaya Square and the city that awaited them.

'Now then, Pavel Pavlovich,' continued Porfiry. 'Won't you tell me what this is all about?'

'What do you mean?'

'You. Here. At the station. Carrying my bag.'

Virginsky looked down sharply. 'There is someone I want you to meet. This person is waiting for us now in a hired *karet*.'

The information stimulated Porfiry into a spate of blinking. 'Waiting in a *karet*? But surely the proper place for any such interview is back at the Department? Unless this is to do with something other than our official duties?'

'Not at all. I was merely acting in the interests of efficiency, out of a desire to save time. My informant just now called at the Department. Having heard the details of the case, I felt sure that it would interest you. I knew that your train was due in. I proposed to my informant that . . . we should hasten together to meet you.'

Porfiry narrowed his eyes at Virginsky. 'I am very interested to meet this informant of yours. Where is your *karet*?'

Virginsky put down the valise and opened the umbrella, before leading the way out of the station into the light September rain.

3

Mother Nourisher

It did not surprise Porfiry to discover that Virginsky's informant was a young woman, whose face, though serious, was not
without a certain gentle allure. It was not the face of a great
beauty, rather one of quick intelligence and quicker sympathy.
She was dressed staidly, in a dark woollen overcoat of almost
severe plainness, in contrast to which her bright silver-grey
eyes startled: their gaze was steady, both trusting and inspiring
of trust. Her fine, oaten hair was pinned up beneath a simple
bonnet. She was not, Porfiry ventured to judge, Virginsky's
usual type.

The two men took the seat opposite her in the four-seated
karet as it lurched into movement.

'Maria Petrovna,' began Virginsky. 'This is the gentleman I
told you about, Porfiry Petrovich.'

'Good day to you, sir.' Her voice was firm and confident. She
had some experience, Porfiry hazarded, of a life outside the
drawing room. She thrust forward her hand almost manfully.
She was of good family it seemed, and yet by some miracle, her
upbringing had produced something more than an accomplished marionette.

'Maria Petrovna, I am delighted to make your acquaintance.'
Porfiry gave a small bow of the head as he took her hand.

'Please tell Porfiry Petrovich everything that you told me,'
prompted Virginsky. 'There is no need to be afraid.'

'I'm not afraid, Pavel Pavlovich.' She could not keep the impatience out of her voice.

Porfiry Petrovich pursed his lips to suppress a smirk at Virginsky's expense. *Oh dear, Pavel Pavlovich – that was a false step!*

'My name is Maria Petrovna Verkhotseva. You may have heard of my father, Pyotr Afanasevich Verkhotsev.' The disclosure was made factually, without boasting, her lack of constraint revealing the true privilege of her upbringing.

'I know of him.'

'I would be surprised if you did not.'

Porifiry allowed his head to fall forward with the bouncing rhythm of the *karet*.

'This has nothing to do with my father, except insofar as it has to do with me. Some people fear him. Some people hate him. To me, he is simply *Papochka*. I love him as a daughter. He has always been a good father to me, and my mother a good mother. I have wanted for nothing. Indeed, they gave me the most precious gift any parent can give a child: an education. They allowed me, encouraged me would be more the truth, to cultivate an independent mind. My father, you may be surprised to learn, has decidedly liberal views.'

'Why should it surprise me?' said Porfiry. He seemed distracted, more interested in the unfolding narrative of the city outside the *karet*.

'Some might hold that liberal views are inconsistent with his position as deputy head of the Tsar's secret police.'

'Isn't the Tsar a liberal?' Porfiry scrutinised each house and tenement building of the Moskvaya District for signs of change. It was as if he was looking into the face of an old friend re-encountered after years apart. 'I thought he was.'

'He *was*, perhaps. Once,' commented Virginsky, dryly.

'Like you,' continued Maria Petrovna, directing her discourse at Porfiry, 'I looked around me. Did I not have eyes in my head? I was not satisfied for their gaze to settle only on the surface of things.'

Porfiry turned a face of mild surprise towards her.

'I went inside the tenements.' It seemed almost as if she were rebuking him. 'I did not like what I saw.'

Porfiry nodded for her to go on.

'I decided to do something about it. But what could I, a mere woman, accomplish, even if I was the daughter of a powerful man?'

'Much, I would imagine,' said Porfiry, smiling.

'I trained to be a teacher. Using my father's influence, I gained admittance to the drawing rooms of the wealthy. I had connections of my own too. In addition to private tutors engaged by my father, my education had included a period at the Smolny Institute. Many of my friends from there had married appropriately. I will not say advantageously, for the advantages were mutually conferred. It was not a course I had chosen for myself, but I was happy enough to congratulate them on their good fortune. Especially if they were able to persuade their husbands to support my cause.'

'Your cause?'

'My plan, vision – dream. Call it what you will.'

'And it was?'

'To found a school. I wanted to share the gift of education that I had enjoyed with those less fortunate than myself. Many of the evils of society have their origin in the ignorance of the poorer classes. Eradicate that ignorance and you will eradicate the evils.'

'A noble aspiration,' said Porfiry, 'as befits an old girl of the Smolny Institute for *Noble* Young Ladies.'

'You're mocking me.'

'Forgive me. I didn't mean to. It is simply that one forms an idea of the type of young lady that the Smolny Institute turns out and, I am pleased to say, you do not conform to it. I did not realise that they had extended their curriculum to include either practical or political studies.'

'It is a mistake to indulge one's prejudices. The pupils of any institute are not a homogenous mass, but a congregation of individual souls, with varying interests and characters. As are the teachers. While I was there I was fortunate to come under the influence of a remarkable educationalist, one Apollon Mikhailovich Perkhotin. The seed of my aspiration took root in his classes.'

'What was his subject, may I ask?'

'Conversation.'

'Conversation?'

'Yes. He taught us how to converse.'

'I see.'

'It is not as simple a subject as you imagine. Not for girls who may find themselves moving in the highest circles of society, and who may be called upon to converse with all manner of individuals, from foreign heads of state to' – Maria Petrovna hesitated as she cast around for an appropriately contrasting exemplum – 'poets. It begins in etiquette and ends in ... well, who can say where any conversation may end?'

'Quite.'

'After I qualified as a teacher, I sought out Apollon Mikhailovich. He encouraged me in my scheme and advised me on educational matters. I was overjoyed when he consented to become a partner in my enterprise.'

'He left the Smolny Institute to work with you?'

'Not quite. His professorship at the Smolny had by then terminated.'

'Please continue.'

'Thanks to the generosity of our patrons, among whom we were proud to count the Grand Duchess Yelena Pavlovna—'

'The Tsar's aunt?' blurted Virginsky.

'Of course.'

Virginsky knitted his brows as he took this in. 'She is an interesting woman. A freethinker, it is said.'

'The Grand Duchess was greatly moved by the plight of foundling children, who not only grow up without the love of their mothers, but also are forced from an early age to work long shifts in factories. The law does not require our factory owners to make any educational provision for these children. Indeed, they expend only as much of their profits as is necessary to keep them housed and alive, which outgoings you may be sure are deducted from the foundlings' paltry wages.'

'Do you not need the owners' consent for the children to attend your school?' asked Porfiry.

'They are the owners of the factories, not of the children, though I concede you would not think so. However, the children find a way to get to us. Some of them travel far, on foot, to do so.'

'Where is your school?'

'We were able to secure suitable premises in the Rozhdestvenskaya District. It is only two rooms over an artisan's workshop, but it serves our purposes.'

'And how many pupils do you have?'

The swimming grey of her eyes settled on him; tears welled, adding to their brightness. Her face was flushed with feeling. A number of emotions seemed to be in contention: outrage, sorrow, disappointment, fear. But her gaze remained steadily fixed on Porfiry.

'That's just it,' she said, her voice if anything firmer than before. 'When we opened our doors, we had fifty-seven children and four adults. Far more than we had planned for, or could accommodate. However, we turned none away. Over the first weeks and months attendance grew, reaching a peak of over seventy children and about a dozen adults. That was last summer. In the winter, naturally, attendance declined. It was harder for the children to get to us. On top of that, the length of their shifts, which lasted from before daybreak till after nightfall, meant that what leisure hours they had were spent in perpetual darkness, which is inevitably debilitating and hardly conducive to study. However, in spring we enjoyed a resurgence in our numbers, which held, more or less, over the summer. Until several weeks ago, when I began to notice a gradual decline. I thought nothing of it. Attendance is not obligatory. That the children are able to come at all, even if just once, is a miracle. Who knows what effect even the briefest exposure to the schoolroom will have on their young minds? To see the wonder, the lively curiosity, awaken on their faces! Once that door is opened, the door to learning, you cannot imagine that it will ever be closed.'

Maria Petrovna broke off, distracted by the enamelled cigarette case which Porfiry was holding up expectantly. 'Forgive me for interrupting you, Maria Petrovna, but I fear we are reaching the point at which it is necessary for me to smoke.'

Virginsky and Maria Petrovna watched the lighting of the cigarette, which had a ritualistic formality to it. There was a practised crispness to Porfiry's movements, culminating in his eyelids quivering closed with an aesthete's sensuality at the precise moment of inhalation. 'I beg you to continue. You were talking about the decline in attendance.'

'Yes,' continued Maria Petrovna, somewhat nonplussed. 'As I said, I thought nothing of it. And then Mitka stopped coming.'

'Mitka?'

'Dmitri Krasotkin, an employee of the Nevsky Cotton-Spinning Factory. A foundling, ten years of age. All the children love to learn – really, they do! – but with Mitka it was more than that. It was something fiercer. A desperate need. He hung on my every word, picked things up so quickly. He showed a remarkable aptitude and I believe he realised that our little school offered him some hope of escaping his terrible life at the factory. It is back-breaking work they put them to, you know, and it's a tragedy to see a boy like Mitka, who is capable of so much, worn down by it. When he repeatedly failed to attend the school, I made enquiries at the factory. He had gone missing from there too. They assumed he had run away. Truth to tell, they cared little what had become of him and were only exercised insofar as his disappearance inconvenienced them and depressed their productivity. The foreman, an Englishman called Beck, whose Russian I could barely understand, pretended to believe that I had something to do with Mitka's disappearance. I also had an unpleasant interview with the old woman who supervised the apprentice house, who made such disgusting insinuations that I question her suitability to hold any position of responsibility over children.

24

'So troubled was I by Mitka's disappearance that I made enquiries concerning the other children who had ceased attending around the same time as he. Some had simply dropped out and I was relieved enough to discover them alive, though the conditions of their lives distressed me. However, there were two other children, Artur Smurov and Svetlana Chisova, the former a worker at the Nobel metal works, the latter employed by the Miller tobacco factory, who have also disappeared without trace, or so it seems. It was at this point that I decided to take my discoveries to the police.'

'I see. And what was their reaction . . . to your discoveries?' Porfiry stretched the question out with an ironic air of knowing what the answer would be.

'Indifference. Nothing was done.'

'You made a statement?'

'Well, yes.'

'A written statement?'

'Yes.'

'At which police station?'

'It was a station near the Nevsky Cotton-Spinning Factory. On Great Bolotnaya Street. I could tell that it was simply a matter of form. They filed the statement away without even reading it.'

'When was this?'

'It was last Friday.'

'That would have been the twenty-seventh. Thank you. That is helpful.' Porfiry drew on his cigarette and exhaled with a pained expression. 'I am afraid, Maria Petrovna, in my experience it is very difficult to find someone who does not wish to be found. Even here in St Petersburg, where we have City Guards every one hundred and fifty paces.'

'Why are you suggesting that the children do not wish to be found? Isn't it more likely that some harm has befallen them?'

'One mustn't always presume the worst, you know, even if it is a possibility. You yourself commented on the abject misery of their existences. How could they not wish to flee such horrors, especially now that you have opened their eyes to something better?'

The *karet* had come to a halt, signalling the termination of the discussion. The two horses shifted restively, the clop of their hooves tolling a despondent knell. Panic entered Maria Petrovna's eyes and seized her voice, raising it a good half octave: 'You are just like the police. You don't care.'

'I am merely trying to place myself in the position of one of these unfortunates. It is a fundamental technique of the investigator. If I were faced with a life of soul-destroying drudgery, I would do everything in my power to escape it.'

Maria Petrovna's voice, though still charged with passion, returned to its original pitch and firmness of tone. 'They have. Escape for them was the school. And that is why I know something terrible has happened to them.'

'Let us sincerely hope not.'

'Is that it? Is that all you will do? Sincerely hope? Are you not a father yourself?'

Porfiry gave a single slow blink. 'No, I am not. However—'

'But you were once a child?'

Porfiry tensed a smile.

'Do you not owe it to the child you once were to find out what has happened to my children?'

'We will look into it. You have my assurance.' Porfiry broke off and peered through the rain-spattered window. A single mass of heavy grey cloud seemed intent on absorbing the city with a cold and soulless greed. The building that faced him, distorted by the prisms of moisture through which he viewed it, appeared almost impossibly dilapidated. It was strangely familiar too, like the architecture of a dream. 'What street is this?'

'Stolyarny Lane,' answered Virginsky. 'We are back at the department.'

4

A scene at the Naryskin Palace

In a city of palaces, the Naryskin Palace did everything it could to assert its pre-eminence, shouldering out of the way its neighbours on the Fontanka Embankment. Built on a plot of land assigned to the first Prince Naryskin by Peter the Great, in gratitude for his services in the war against Sweden, it overlooked the river with a flamboyantly remodelled façade, a blushing pink celebration of Russian baroque.

The evening light exploded softly over it. The day had been clear and bright, a welcome break in the sullen dampness that had squatted over the city for the past week or so. This was autumn's other face, golden-hued and expansive, but all too briefly seen. The falling leaves had a brittle-edged crispness. There was a crunch, rather than a squelch, underfoot. But it felt like remission. To be shown their glittering city for a day only reminded the citizens of St Petersburg of what they were soon to lose, irretrievably, under the dark, endless months to come. They were days away from the first snows, and they knew it.

Maria Petrovna gazed up at the stone figures on the façade with some sympathy, seeing in their abashed poses a symbolic representation of her own uneasy relationship with the houses of the rich: that of the attached outsider. This was, after all, the world she came from, although the opulence and scale of the

Naryskin residence far outstripped that of her own or any other noble family's home.

But the Naryskin Palace was not so much a place to live as a declaration of self-importance. Ostentation was the guiding aesthetic, even in the private apartments, as if the Naryskins themselves were the ones who most needed reminding of their own wealth and status.

The rooms of the palace were rescued from an intimidating marble coldness by the crowds of portraits and busts purchased from the capitals of Europe at great expense. It was in the same spirit perhaps, to preserve his home from a devastating emptiness, that the current head of the family, Prince Nikolai Naryskin, occasionally threw open his doors, if not to the public, then to that section of the city's populace that is usually termed 'society'. It did not inconvenience him to do so. The palace had been planned to accommodate such gatherings. It housed a respectable concert hall, a grand ballroom, and even a theatre, which, though rather more intimate in scale, was nonetheless lavishly decorated.

Prince Naryskin was known to be an enthusiastic patron of the arts, as well as a generous supporter of a number of charitable causes. This evening it pleased him to host a gala of literary, dramatic and musical entertainments, to be held in the theatre, for the benefit of Maria Petrovna's school. It's true that there were some amongst his circle of acquaintances who questioned the worthiness of such a cause. The argument had been advanced that the inevitable result of educating the poor could only be increased criminality and unrest. A large attendance was therefore not expected, despite the considerable attractions: students from the St Petersburg Conservatoire were to perform a series of interludes devised by their young professor of composition; a number of celebrated authors were to read from their works; and, as a climax to the evening, the distinguished literary gentleman Prince Makar Alexeevich Bykov, recently returned from a prolonged stay in Switzerland, was staging scenes from his play *The Vanished Lover*. The theatrical performance was to be given added interest by the participation of Yelena Filippovna Polenova, whose engagement to Prince Naryskin's son Sergei had recently been announced.

So far, the only people gathered in the entrance hall seemed to be those taking part in the proceedings, to judge from the nervous expectancy turned upon Maria Petrovna as she entered. Almost immediately, something like disappointment transmitted itself through the assembly, leaving Maria feeling both aggrieved and at fault. But then she remembered that a highly important personage was rumoured to be attending. The Tsarevich himself had intimated in a letter to Prince Naryskin that he would find time to support the benefit, despite the fact that the cause of educating the masses could not be said to be close to his heart. His interest in the evening remained a mystery, though it was by no means certain that he would put in an appearance.

The atrium was the full height of the palace. A wide marble staircase, transposed from an Italian villa, swept away through a theatrical arch, upwards towards a highly ornate neo-classical ceiling. Most of those milling there appeared cowed by the grandeur of their surroundings, or perhaps by the imminent arrival of the distinguished spectator.

The one exception was the individual Maria recognised as Yelena Filippovna Polenova.

Maria was shocked by the quickening of her own heart. It

was seven years since she had seen Yelena and they had not parted on the best of terms. Maria could not claim that she was unprepared for this encounter: she had seen the programme in advance and noted the part of her former school friend. However, the idea of someone in the abstract is far more manageable than their presence in the same room.

She cast around for Apollon Mikhailovich. She was in the habit of referring to him as her rock. Perhaps she said it too often for it to seem quite sincere, and her mentor's smiles of self-deprecation had recently become tinged with embarrassment, as if he believed himself unworthy of the compliment. Apollon Mikhailovich never could stand flattery, or deception of any kind. When he had been their teacher at the Smolny, he had laid great emphasis on the distinction between deference and fawning. Genuine respect, he had argued, not only allowed honesty, it demanded it. He taught them that they should never be afraid to tell the truth to anyone, no matter how unpalatable the truth to be imparted. Given that he was addressing a classroom of girls, some of whom might reasonably expect one day to be married to – or if not, mistresses of – the most powerful men in the empire, the lesson was not without point. And of course, he taught by example: the respect he afforded them as young gentlewomen was characterised by a candour that was never brutal or spiteful, but neither was it compromised by self-seeking. He taught them the meaning of integrity, and the fact that he deemed them worthy of the lesson awoke in many of them, Maria Petrovna included, the first stirrings of social, and even political, consciousness.

Such was the man she sought out now, but without success. Perhaps he was there, she couldn't say. Her eyes only saw one person now: Yelena Filippovna.

31

In anticipation of this meeting, she had practised a few polite words thanking Yelena for her involvement in the evening. Perhaps she also imagined a brief kiss and the warm embrace of friendship renewed. Strangely, however, none of the words she had put into Yelena's mouth quite rang true, so that there was a stilted falsity to the projected exchange. She now realised that the point about Yelena was that she would always say and do the very thing that no one could anticipate. The realisation provoked a fluttering dread in Maria's stomach.

The cruellest imaginable thing that Yelena could do now, and therefore surely the most likely, would be to pretend not to remember Maria. Was it really possible that Yelena could bear a grudge after so many years? It little mattered that the grudge was not hers to bear. Yelena had always had a talent for putting others in the wrong. Knowing this somehow gave Maria the courage to face Yelena, and to bear with equanimity whatever construction she might place upon the past.

But before she could approach her, another young woman whose face was familiar to Maria interposed herself between them.

'I know you,' said the young woman. 'You're Maria Petrovna. You used to be Yelena's friend.'

Maria was slightly thrown by the abruptness of her manner. 'Yes.'

'Don't you remember me?'

'Of course I do . . .'

'Nobody remembers me. People only remember her. You didn't even see me when you came in, did you?' She made her self-deprecating remarks with a forced levity that did nothing to conceal her bitterness. 'You saw only her.' The girl who was speaking was handsome enough. The deep ultramarine silk of her gown complimented her pale complexion, though the fashionably tight-fitting dress did not sit altogether happily on her. She seemed to regret the boldness that had led her to choose such a plunging neckline, which left her pale shoulders and much of her bosom exposed. The usual adjectives of feminine attractiveness – such as pretty, charming – somehow did not apply to her. Her expression was not quite harsh, but it was sharpened by something that could have been hostility – or simply unhappiness.

'But I do remember you, Aglaia Filippovna,' insisted Maria.

Aglaia Filippovna smiled begrudgingly before narrowing her eyes in suspicion. She formed her mouth to speak but let it go.

The entrance hall was filling up. The performers began to relax, gratified to see their audience build. As they welcomed friends, the collective mood was transformed to one of excited volubility.

'Will you be taking part in the evening's entertainments?' asked Maria.

'I leave that to others.'

'It is very good of you to show your support, at any rate.'

'I hope that it will not be unduly tedious. Prince Bykov is rather too earnest to be amusing.'

'I believe his play, in which your sister has the leading part, addresses the woman question, as well as other important issues of the moment.'

Aglaia's voice sank to a murmur: 'You could not help looking at her even then, when you mentioned her. You always did have the most awful crush on her. Yelena used to laugh about it.'

Maria felt herself blush and bowed her head. She could not speak.

'You were not the only one. It's the same now, except that it is men who are her admirers.'

Despite herself, Maria cast a furtive glance in Yelena's direction. Aglaia's words seemed to be confirmed by the semi-circle of men now grouped around her sister; however, Maria could not be sure that it was admiration she saw in every face. She detected a kind of hunger in some of them, but a hunger conflicted by the dark emotions of hatred and fear. It was the kind of hunger felt by a man who knows the food he craves is poison to him. Only one man, an older gentleman with snow-white hair and imperial beard, gave the impression of being immune to her, and yet even his complacency was guarded, as if it held within it a secret store of desire. He seemed to be showing her off to the younger men. His smile was proprietorial. He watched their reactions avidly and seemed to take pleasure in the hold she had over them.

Yelena Filippovna was often described as a beauty and yet, to Maria, this hardly did justice to the extraordinary quality of her presence. It seemed that Yelena possessed a knowledge not granted to other women, and it was this, or the promise of it, that made her so desired by men.

'Go to her!' Aglaia's tone was angry and dismissive. 'I know you want to.'

'No. She despises me. Why should I want to expose myself to her contempt?'

Aglaia Filippovna seemed to consider Maria anew. 'That is the very thing you want. That is what they want, too. Weak natures such as yours . . .'

'You think I'm weak?'

'You will go to her, no matter what you say.'

'Who are those men?'

'The Seven Knights.'

'I beg your pardon?'

'You know the story, *The Dead Princess and the Seven Knights*.'

'The older man?'

'That is Bakhmutov.'

'He looks at her as if he owns her.'

'He did once. She is his to dispose of. You see Velchaninov, the fresh-faced youth with him?'

Maria looked at the young man. His cheeks shone with a babyish pink glow, and his hair was fair and silky, like an infant's. He was standing very close to Bakhmutov, inclining his head towards Bakhmutov's for a stream of confidences. All the time he kept his gaze on Yelena Filippovna, his eyes wide open in an expression that seemed to combine both naivety and greed.

'A pretty young thing, isn't he? And from a good family, though sadly impoverished. Fortunately, Bakhmutov, the eternal benefactor, bestowed ten thousand roubles on the young man. The only condition was that he take my sister off his hands.'

Maria's scandalised reaction must have been everything Aglaia had hoped for.

'You are very innocent.'

'As well as weak? No doubt that is a deplorable combination in your eyes.'

'It is unfortunate – for you. It doesn't matter much to me. You are wrong to condemn Yelena, by the way. She would have nothing to do with their little arrangement, once she found out about it – and so it fell through. But you know, things have not been easy for her, for either of us. We lost our parents, you know.'

'Yes, I know. It happened while we were at the Smolny.'

'Did Yelena tell you the details?' Aglaia asked with an unseemly relish.

'No. She never spoke of it.'

'Papa blew his brains out over some scandal at the department. The usual financial misunderstanding. Mama found the shame unbearable. And then there were the debts. It broke her. It wasn't long before she followed him, although her own chosen method of self-despatch was poison. She wrote a note saying that she did it for us, for Yelena and me.' The laughter that broke out of Aglaia was as startling as a wild animal breaking cover. 'Can you imagine? What she meant, I have no idea. And so we were left orphaned, friendless and without fortune. It was at that time that Bakhmutov began to take an interest in my sister. She saw him as her saviour.'

'That word does not seem appropriate to such a man.'

'You're looking at him as if you believe him to be the devil! He's just a man. But perhaps you have no experience of men.'

'Thankfully, I have no experience of men of his type.'

'Shall I introduce you?'

'Please don't.'

'He's very rich.'

'What's that to me?'

'Are you not trying to raise subscriptions for your school?'

'Nonetheless . . .'

'You cannot afford to allow your moral compunctions to stand in the way of your pupils' welfare. Money is money.

What matters is the use to which you put it, not from whence it comes.' Aglaia's cheeks glowed pink now, as if the exercise of cynicism invigorated her. She was almost panting for breath, baring her teeth, which for all their delicacy had a predatory form. Maria found herself fighting the urge to slap Aglaia, and the more she looked at her face, the stronger the urge became.

It was as if the thought called forth the deed, for the unmistakable sound of a hand striking skin was now clearly audible, bringing a sudden startling silence to the room. Maria instinctively looked towards Yelena.

Yelena's face was fired with outrage. A young Guards officer in a white dress uniform stood before her. Even with his head bowed, he towered over her; his inability to abase himself sufficiently seemed to add to whatever insult he was guilty of. He held his black shako in one hand, tucked back against the inside of his forearm, its enormous horsehair plume projecting stiffly like a miniature lance ready for the charge. His hair was dark, almost black, and he kept it long. It fell forward in two long bangs either side of his face, but failed to hide the patch of colour that blazed across his right cheek above his beard. Even allowing for the fact that anguish and embarrassment distorted his face, Maria could not help remarking on his ill-favoured features; she might have gone so far as to describe him as ugly. Even so, there was something compelling, something animalistic about his face, a barely controlled energy that seemed on the verge of breaking into wildness.

'My God!' cried Aglaia, finding voice at the same time as the rest of the room. 'She struck Mizinchikov!'

The officer deepened his bow and clicked his heels, then detached himself from the group around Yelena.

Maria saw Velchaninov's youthful cheeks flush even more

brightly, as if he had been the one struck. His ear now almost touched Bakhmutov's whispering lips. His eyes shone with an eager, unpleasant delight.

'It seems the drama has begun already,' said Aglaia, with evident satisfaction.

5

Entertainments

The scene between Yelena and the young Guards officer transformed the collective mood once more. The excitement tipped over into a wild nervous energy. Some people forgot themselves so far as to applaud, much to the disgust of Prince Naryskin. His long hair and large silk cravat marked him out as a liberal of the old school, one of the generation of the forties. But the hypertensive bulge of his eyes suggested that he was beginning to wonder if the conservatives had not been right all along. His wife, Princess Yevgenia Andreevna, sunken-cheeked and possibly consumptive, seemed particularly on edge. She could be heard insistently urging him to 'do something'. And, indeed, there was a general sense that something should be done, though the Prince was not alone in being at a loss to know just what.

The incident seemed to take on a significance greater than the personal, to be about something more than simply a fiery-tempered woman redressing an insult. In that slap, something had been unleashed, something ugly that seemed to have a bearing on them all. Yelena's dangerous glamour spread like a contagion.

Words were exchanged between Prince Naryskin and his son. It seemed that Prince Sergei was being directed to take his fiancée in hand. An anticipatory thrill set the assembly abuzz, for it was clearly felt that to do so would provoke further, perhaps greater, scandal.

All eyes were turned on Prince Sergei as he approached Yelena.

His words to her were not heard. But Yelena's laughter, the brittle laughter that was her last defence, crashed over them all like splinters from a fallen chandelier. For a second time, she had silenced the room. Those who had predicted a greater scandal were proven right. There was in this laughter, in its abandon, something far more shocking than a mere physical blow. What made it seem more callous still was that Prince Sergei was known to have a pronounced stammer.

Maria's impressions of what happened next were confused. She was certain that she saw the second blow, the one that fell with a dull knuckle-crack across Yelena's cheekbone; certain too that she heard Yelena's scream, and her terrible masochistic cry to Sergei: 'Yes, beat me! Beat me like a dog!'

But all this was engulfed in a greater commotion. Everything seemed to be happening in a dream, one pervaded by an atmosphere of violence and foreboding. Yelena, Prince Sergei and the officer Mizinchikov, vanished, to be replaced by other, even stranger figures. The entrance of the Tsarevich was announced. The next in line to the throne strode into the room with a premeditated swagger, but his over-bullish stare communicated an aggressive uncertainty, and although he was physically imposing, he possessed bulk rather than stature. He had the air of a man destined to be out of his depth. Maria recognised the sleek, watchful man accompanying him as Count Dmitri Andreevich Tolstoy, the Minister of National Enlightenment. His greater natural authority served only to diminish the Tsarevich further.

The unseemly hysteria of the gathering was turned upon the new arrivals. They, of course, could not comprehend what they had walked into; their confusion quickly turned to rage. Prince Naryskin ran over to soothe their affronted dignity, which only seemed to be aggravated by his intervention. For some reason, Maria felt herself to be the object of the three men's indignant gaze, as if she had been singled out for blame.

All at once, the press of people eased around her, as if it had been universally agreed to keep her at a distance. Aglaia Filippovna was nowhere to be seen. Maria did, however, at last catch sight of Apollon Mikhailovich. He was standing to one side with a preoccupied air, dressed uncharacteristically in a swallow-tailed evening suit. As always, the sight of him was calming. He seemed untouched by what had happened, as he teased away at his great shovel beard. Apollon Mikhailovich Perkhotin had a marvellous ability to cut himself off from his surroundings and remain focused on his mental processes. Perhaps he was preparing himself for his role in the forthcoming entertainments: he had taken it upon himself to open the proceedings with an extemporised talk on educational theory, which she had every confidence would be far more entertaining than the subject promised.

Prince Naryskin continued to keep her in his sight. Then, with a brisk nod in answer to something Count Tolstoy had said, he began to move towards her. All his earlier agitation seemed to have left him. His steps were precise and measured. She felt each sharp click of his heels resonate in the base of her skull.

'Maria Petrovna, I suggest we begin the evening's entertainment immediately.'

She nodded her agreement with relief. Maria sensed a kind of panic take hold of some of those around her. Performers suddenly remembered themselves and dashed off backstage.

This heightened the excitement of the others, prompting an unnecessary crush at the door leading to the theatre. Voices were raised.

Maria watched with dismay.

'Really!' said Prince Naryskin, his voice squeezed with exasperation. 'What is the matter with these people? They are behaving like children.'

'My children do not behave so badly,' said Maria.

'You have children?'

'The children at my school.'

This reference to the cause they were supporting did nothing to improve the prince's temper. 'This is what happens when you begin to educate the labouring classes.'

'With the greatest respect, Nikolai Sergeevich, I do not follow your argument. There are no members of the labouring classes here tonight.'

'But there are the classless ones, aren't there? The *raznochintsy*. The new *intelligentsia*. They do not know how to behave.'

'I do not believe what you say is true. There may be some among the music students and literary gentlemen who conform to your description. But as for the audience, I would say that they are from good families, for the most part.'

'There are Jews here. Financiers and industrialists. And their whores. New money.' The prince had his eye on the man Aglaia Filippovna had identified as Bakhmutov.

'Mr Bakhmutov is Jewish?' Maria watched as Bakhmutov approached the Tsarevich and Count Tolstoy. He addressed them with ease, familiarity even. They seemed to regard him with polite suspicion.

Maria glanced at the prince, his face touched by distaste. 'He may have converted to Orthodoxy but that was purely pragmatic. You might even call it a business decision. Like all his decisions.' The hint was edged with a precise bitterness. 'Where has that woman gone now?'

Maria remained neutrally silent.

'Let us hope that she has taken herself out of our lives for good.'

Her gaze spun instinctively towards where Apollon Mikhailovich had been standing but he was gone.

*

The theatre in the Naryskin Palace was decorated in a full-blown baroque style, giving it a comically stunted appearance. The tiny auditorium simply wasn't up to bearing the rampant encrustations of gilt mouldings and marble reliefs. One man, presumably never having set foot in it before, was moved to ridicule, declaring loudly: 'It's like a dwarf in a cavalry officer's uniform!' Maria thought of Mizinchikov. The remark seemed intended to bring the earlier incident to mind. It provoked widespread and careless hilarity.

Four boxes projected on either side, almost meeting in the middle. Maria couldn't help thinking that the theatre seats ought to have been scaled down. This was a toy theatre. Surely it was meant for children to sit in? The plush, adult-sized seats seemed intrusive, an effect that was exacerbated when they were occupied. The theatre made giants of them all.

The proscenium arch was oddly out of proportion. It was imposingly high, but severely narrow, as though squeezed in. The stage was concealed by layers of artfully hung crimson drapes, which on closer examination turned out to be a *trompe l'oeil* design painted onto a screen. Real drapes, of a similar colour, hung around the boxes, partially shielding the occupants from view. The impression made was of a multiple of stages, each capable of holding its own drama. Looking up, Maria saw a roundel painted into the white and gold ceiling, a depiction of *putti* looking down on the audience, as if they themselves were the spectacle.

The musicians hurriedly took their places in the cramped pit, keeping their elbows in and their instruments high. The volubility of the audience increased at their arrival. There was a brutal edge to the anticipation, which was not so much for them as for what would come after. No one said as much, but they were all waiting for the next appearance of Yelena Filippovna. The sound of the instruments tuning, the wavering note becoming quickly firmer, failed to quell the chatter. A few among the audience, Maria included, hissed for silence. The band waited to begin, their faces incredulous. Accepting that absolute silence was an impossible ideal, they took the decision to impose their music on the audience, whether they would have it or no. They played loudly and wilfully, which was precisely what was needed. Something in the music, something new and until now unheard, startled the audience into listening. As the band played, the painted screen covering the stage was raised upon an arrangement of real drapes identical to those depicted on the rising screen. Maria felt that perhaps the mood was turning and the evening might be salvaged. When the piece was over, the applause was slow in coming, as if the audience needed a moment to absorb what they had heard, but when it came it was enthusiastic, excessively so.

They are *like children*, thought Maria. *They go from one extreme to another.*

The house lights were extinguished. A flurry in the curtains culminated in the appearance of Apollon Mikhailovich. He was not a tall man, a little under average height in fact, but on that tiny stage he attained the stature of a giant. His eyes twinkled with a benign but compelling light. Maria began to relax, sensing the confidence and control in his presence.

His bass voice boomed out, filling the auditorium effortlessly: 'My friends – and I hope I will not be accused of presumption in addressing you all thus –' he cast a sly, mischievous glance up towards the imperial box. 'But by your presence here tonight, you all – each and every one of you – declare yourselves friends of education. And may I say that any friend of education is a friend of mine!' The quip was well judged. It found favour with the democratically-inclined members of the audience, without causing offence to the conservatives. Even the Tsarevich, known to be the most unthinking of reactionaries, could not fail to be disarmed by the crinkles of good humour in Apollon Mikhailovich's face.

Now that face became suffused with feeling. 'My name is Apollon Mikhailovich Perkhotin. I stand before you as a humble teacher. No – more than that – as a *humbled* teacher. And what I have been humbled by is nothing other than . . .' He broke off, with a natural storyteller's sense of the dramatic. His glittering eyes cast their gaze this way and that over the audience, drinking in their expectation. ' . . . my pupils. Yes, that's right – children! For what could be more humbling than a child . . . who, of his own volition, without enforcement or encouragement, overcomes every obstacle, risks even punishment and abuse, to come before a teacher and demand, "Teach me!" What could be more inspiring?'

The audience responded to the rhetorical question with murmurs of approval.

'I am proud and honoured to stand before you now as the teacher of such children. My friends, now it is your turn to be proud, your turn to be honoured. Yes! Be proud!' His eyes widened as he encouraged them to open themselves up to that emotion. 'Be honoured!' he insisted. There was some embarrassed laughter now. Apollon Mikhailovich smiled and nodded, acknowledging it. Then the smile snapped from his face. A sudden intensity burned in his eyes. 'By your presence here tonight . . .' The words came in a forceful staccato. He stabbed the air on each syllable with two fingers of his right hand. He had transformed himself into a demagogue, holding the pause beyond the dramatic, stretching it into a breathtaking chasm. ' . . . You have shown yourselves to be the friend of these children. And I know you are not the men and women to turn your back on your friends. You are, after all – we all are – Russians!'

The diverse political strands of the audience were united by this appeal to nationalism. They roared their enthusiasm and stamped their feet in approval. Apollon Mikhailovich bowed humbly, then turned to push his way through the barrier of velvet.

The stage was clear for the first of the literary gentlemen.

This was Karmazinov, an established and once celebrated author who had fallen out of favour with the younger generation for his negative portrayal of a 'new man'. Tall and broad-shouldered, he cut an impressive figure, physically at least. The whiteness of his hair and beard glowed, giving him a distinguished if prematurely-aged appearance. But there was a diffidence to his expression, a timidity even, that diminished him.

Blinking in the limelight, he was barely able to look directly at the audience, preferring either to stare loftily over their heads, or to keep his gaze fixed on the sheets of manuscript in his hands. His voice was soft, and failed to carry even in that auditorium. It was not long before cries of 'Speak up!' were replaced by others even less encouraging.

Maria could bear it no longer. She sprang to her feet and turned on the audience. 'Quiet! Show some respect!' The shock of her intervention, and her undoubted school mistress' manner, had the desired effect. She turned to Karmazinov, who looked as dumbfounded as the chastised audience members. 'You sir, continue – but speak up, I beg you.'

He did as he was directed – indeed, what else could he do?

It was now possible at least to understand what he was reading, and perhaps it would have been better if his voice had remained inaudible. For the poems he had chosen were altogether too romantic, too painfully sensitive, for the modern taste. Suddenly people remembered why no one read Karmazinov any longer. It was not that the poems were badly done – Karmazinov had always been acknowledged to be a fine writer – it was just that they seemed superfluous. He was felt to be a man who had had his day and now they were impatient for him to clear the stage.

Strangely, Karmazinov seemed to share this sentiment, and was as relieved as anyone when he came to the end of his reading.

The applause, apart from Maria's strenuous clapping, was perfunctory and brief. Karmazinov fought his way through the complicated drapes, which conspired to prolong his humiliation.

And so the evening progressed. The musical interludes were on the whole more enthusiastically received than the readings. One young writer bucked the trend, winning favour by reading a series of crude lampoons of well-known literary figures including, in an outrageous exhibition of bad form, Karmazinov. However, the audience still appeared cowed by Maria's earlier rebuke. Occasional warning glances from her were enough to keep a lid on any further unpleasantness. There was no doubt, though, that the prevailing mood of impatience only increased as the entertainments wore on.

At last the curtains parted on a scene from Prince Bykov's play, and the audience readied itself for the imminent reappearance of Yelena Filippovna. Indeed there was some disappointment that she wasn't present from the outset.

The narrow stage appeared crowded by the disposition of props and actors upon it. A young man in a Bukhara dressing gown lay sprawled across a chaise longue. Another young man, more formally dressed, was seated at a writing desk, pen in hand. A third man, evidently a servant of some kind, stood to one side. In a gesture of great irony, this part was taken by the epicene Prince Bykov himself. A more unlikely manservant it was impossible to imagine. He performed his part with relish, even though all he had to do was take a letter from the young man at the desk and quit the stage.

The two actors left on stage delivered their stagnant lines without conviction. It took some time to understand that they were discussing the disappearance of a young lady with whom the young man on the chaise longue was in love. The audience became more enlivened and engaged at this, sensing that this would be the part taken by Yelena Filippovna. But still the interminable exchange of platitudes ground on.

Then suddenly the dramatic genius of Prince Bykov seemed to show itself at last. A piercing off-stage scream cut short the stodgy dialogue. The actors' performances were transformed. They became, in a word, authentic. The two men were hanging on what would happen next as much as any member of the audience. And when Aglaia Filippovna burst out from the wings, one arm extended back as she pointed at an unseen something, they gave the most truthful portrayals of shock ever seen on a St Petersburg stage.

The *coup de théâtre* came when Aglaia cried out: 'She's dead. My sister's dead. He's killed her!' Her eyes spun upwards, filling with white. A kind of wave went through her as she fell. Her arms and head rose, as if resisting. But the ultramarine dress that had sat so uneasily on her pulled her down, as though it were made from some impossibly heavy material.

The two actors stood frozen to the spot. No one knew what to do next or how to interpret what had happened.

Maria could not get out of her mind the image of Aglaia's eyes at the moment before her collapse. There was something so raw, so intimate, something almost obscene in that exposure, that she knew it could not be an act.

'Help her! Somebody help her!' She was on her feet again. Her words released the two actors from their suspended state. They rushed to Aglaia Filippovna. Unable to rouse her, one called for a doctor while the other communicated urgently with stagehands. The curtains came together and the painted screen descended.

The audience broke into uproar.

6

White camellias, a red thread, and seven rings

Porfiry Petrovich looked down at the body of the young woman. She was frozen in an angular pose. Her arms retained the tension with which they had been lashing out at the last moment, acutely bent at the elbows and wrists, fingers splayed to grasp life as it leeched from her. Her head was sharply skewed to one side, as if in the throes of angry denial. She lay half on her side, her body cork-screwed. It seemed she had died writhing to lift herself out of the swamp of blood that encircled her.

As always in these circumstances, Porfiry's gaze was drawn to the wound. Of course, his interest was professional, but it occurred to him that his choice of profession might have been influenced by a need to confront such sights. Or perhaps it was a profoundly human compulsion, little more than the vulgar urge to gawp at the scene of an overturned carriage. He had merely elevated morbid curiosity into a calling. The morose cast of his musings could be excused by the fact that he had been wrenched from uneasy dreams of his father by the frantic hammering of police officers sent to rouse him. Usually when he dreamt of his parents, the mood of the dream was joyful. These were dreams of reunion that he did not want to end. The simpler familial relationships of childhood were restored and there was only love between them. Whatever complications there had been in life were blissfully forgotten. But this night's dreams were shot through with an obscure sense of guilt that he couldn't shake off, but was reluctant to probe.

Undoubtedly, Zakhar's death had something to do with it.

It was almost as if he took solace in the wound.

It was a deep, neat incision across the full breadth of her throat. The pumping force of life had burst through it, pushing the severed flesh apart. The front of her dress was sodden, the black silk heavily darkened in a sweeping arc that extended below her midriff. Her blood drenched the Turkish rug on which she lay, obscuring the rich reds with its muddy cast. Porfiry saw the wound as a second mouth, its inert lips slightly parted as if it were trying to tell him something. But it spoke only blood.

The body was in a small, windowless room in the basement of Naryskin Palace, close enough to the tiny theatre to serve as a dressing room. Three narrow, elaborately moulded doors on one wall gave onto a wardrobe, which Porfiry had already discovered to be hung with dusty clothes. As far as he could tell from a cursory examination, they were male clothes. The room was furnished with a dressing table, which was cluttered with the accoutrements of stage make-up. Next to it was a small table bearing a wash basin and jug. The water appeared fresh and unused. There were a number of burning candles on both surfaces, adding to the light provided by a hissing gas lamp mounted on one wall. There were two mirrors: one over the dressing table, and another, full length and gilt framed, mounted on the wall opposite the wardrobe. An embroidered screen closed off one corner of the room, with a small sofa placed in front of it. All this was enough to give the room a cramped air.

A bouquet of white camellias, still in the florist's wrapping, lay on the sofa. The card read: 'I will always love you, M.'

His gaze still fixed on the wound, Porfiry breathed in deeply. The air was perfumed, though the flowers of course gave off no scent. But Porfiry could discern the smell of the butcher's slab, the dark odour unstoppered by violence.

The door opened but he did not look round. He knew by the other's patience that it was Virginsky.

'It is a long time since those were fashionable,' said Porfiry, at last looking up from the dead girl. In answer to Virginsky's quizzically gathered brows, he gestured vaguely at the flowers. 'Who is M, I wonder?'

'An officer of the Preobrazhensky Regiment, by the name of Mizinchikov, was seen to have an argument with the dead woman – Yelena Filippovna Polenova. She slapped his face. Several witnesses saw him running away from this room shortly after the dead woman's sister, Aglaia Filippovna Polenova, raised the alarm. All the witnesses testified independently to the fact that Mizinchikov's uniform was spattered with blood.'

'Spattered?'

'Yes.'

'That is the word they all used? Independently?'

'Not necessarily. I am providing you with a digest. You may read the witness statements in full, of course.'

'And what does . . . this officer Mizinchikov have to say for himself?'

'Captain Mizinchikov is not available to be interviewed.'

At this unsurprising information, Porfiry raised his eyebrows showily and blinked his consternation. 'I understood that the owner of the house – Prince Naryskin, is it not? – had the doors of the palace secured to prevent anyone from leaving before the police arrived.'

'It seems that Captain Mizinchikov had already effected his escape.'

Porfiry sighed. 'That is very tiresome of him and will not help his cause when finally we catch up with him. I trust we have put out a description of him. Exceptionally tall, dark-haired, bearded, not particularly good-looking . . .'

'How did you know?' Virginsky's tone was suspicious rather than amazed.

'You did say he was an officer of the Preobrazhensky Regiment?'

'Yes.'

'Have you not observed the practice amongst Russian Guards regiments of selecting recruits according to certain physical attributes? The Semyenovsky Regiment, for example, is known for fair hair and good looks. Whilst the men and officers of the Preobrazhensky tend to be exceptionally tall and dark-haired individuals with beards. I believe they are generally held to be the least handsome of the regiments, by those who notice such things.'

'I see. I had never noticed. I am not much interested in military affairs.'

'You should be, Pavel Pavlovich. There are sixty thousand soldiers garrisoned in St Petersburg, making every tenth inhabitant a soldier. If one takes an interest in St Petersburg – as our work demands we must – one must therefore take an interest in military affairs. A passing knowledge of the city's regiments will aid you considerably in your duties. I presume you have dispatched some men to Kirochnaya, 35. That *is* his address, is it not?'

'So I have been informed.' There was a flinch of annoyance from Virginsky.

'Naturally. It is the address of the Officers' House of the Preobrazhensky. Of course, he won't be there. Even so, I imagine we will at least find some of his fellow officers, who may or may not be able to shed light on his whereabouts.'

Porfiry was peering into the large mirror with his head angled back, evidently to allow himself the best possible view of the interior of his nostrils. 'I wonder who else the prince has allowed to absent themselves.' Porfiry was now tentatively fingering a row of transparent whiskers growing out of the top of one ear. 'When a man reaches a certain age he finds himself faced with an abundance of hair in places he had not expected it.' He angled his head down to examine the pale stubble that covered his bulbous skull, and pursed his lips in satisfaction. 'And a dearth of hair in those places he might reasonably hope for it.'

'I did not take you for a man too much concerned with his own appearance, Porfiry Petrovich,' remarked Virginsky with a sly smile.

'Oh, it is not on my own account, you understand,' threw out Porfiry casually, bending forward to scrutinise something on the surface of the mirror.

'Not on your own account? Do you mean to say—?'

'I wonder what *that* is,' murmured Porfiry absently, before turning his back on his own reflection. Virginsky took his superior's place before the mirror and frowned as he scanned its surface, looking for whatever had caught Porfiry's eye.

'What do you think he meant by it?' said Porfiry, opening one of the wardrobe doors. The sight of the discarded clothes, still exactly as before, reminded him that he had already looked inside. He sniffed the air in the wardrobe suspiciously, then closed the door and prowled the room like a caged animal.

'Who? By what?' Virginsky reluctantly gave up his examination of the mirror to keep a watchful eye on Porfiry.

'M. By giving her camellias. White camellias.'

'Some ladies like white, others prefer red.'

'There is a special significance to the red ones, I believe.'

'Yes, but that is a signal for the ladies to give to their admirers.'

Virginsky's remark drew Porfiry up sharply. He looked down at the card. 'Brilliant, Pavel Pavlovich. Quite brilliant.'

'I beg your pardon?'

'Could not the card equally be read as being addressed to M, as from him? Could it not be her protestation of undying love to him?'

'Possibly.'

'As well as an advertisement of her sexual availability. Ironic, is it not? She announced herself free from menstrual blood, only to be drenched in fatal blood.' Porfiry caught a knot of uncertainty tightening Virginsky's brows. 'You're not convinced? But it was your idea.'

'I cannot honestly take credit for it.'

'The original *dame aux camelias* was a prostitute, was she not?'

'A courtesan.'

'A high-class prostitute. But a prostitute nonetheless. Perhaps that was the significance of the flowers, if they were as we originally thought, a gift from M to her: you are a whore but I will always love you.'

'You think the flowers are important?'

'I think the flowers are here. In the same room as a dead girl. What was she? Some kind of actress?'

'No, not really. This was an amateur affair.' Virginsky paused a moment before going on with uncharacteristic diffidence: 'Porfiry Petrovich . . . Maria Petrovna is here.'

'Maria Petrovna? The charming young lady whom I met yesterday?'

'Yes.'

'What a remarkable coincidence.'

'I do not like to hear you say that, Porfiry Petrovich. I know you do not believe in coincidence.'

Porfiry said nothing.

'However, it is not so strange,' Virginsky went on. 'This evening was organised as a benefit gala for her school.'

'I see.'

'Prince Naryskin – the Naryskin family – is one of those connections she has made through her father.'

'And what of Yelena Filippovna?'

'What of her?'

'Did Maria Petrovna know her?'

'Yes. I believe so. They were at school together. At the Sm—'

'Smolny Institute,' finished Porfiry. 'How very interesting.'

'You do not think Maria Petrovna had anything to do with this?'

'Do I not?' Porfiry Petrovich met Virginsky's anxious expression with a bland face and much blinking.

'Will you wish to speak to her?'

'I hope that I will have that pleasure before too long.'

'She is very tired. She has already given a full statement to me.'

Porfiry Petrovich gave no answer to this, or none that Virginsky could understand. He merely rubbed the tops of both ears now with the tips of his index fingers while staring blankly into his junior colleague's face.

*

Pavel Pavlovich Virginsky knew better than to press the point. He had been working with Porfiry Petrovich for a little over two years now and had become as skilled at divining his superior's moods as at executing any of his more formal duties as a junior investigating magistrate. He knew that Porfiry Petrovich's famous capriciousness was an essential part of the mysterious process by which he solved his cases. To attempt to curtail his eccentricity would be futile; as inconceivable as forbidding Porfiry his cigarettes. Certainly it was infuriating, as a colleague, to be on the receiving end of the old man's puckish behaviour. He really ought to be able to confine such tricks to his dealings with suspects and, at a pinch, witnesses; regrettably he was not. At first it had amazed Virginsky how willing others in the department, including otherwise hard-line police officers, were to tolerate Porfiry's individualism, which, he had noticed, had become more extreme over time. Perhaps there were those who were only waiting for the celebrated investigator to fail. And then all the resentments that had built up over the years, the procedural irregularities, the wounded dignities, the nurtured humiliations, not to mention the ill-judged pranks – all this would be remembered and used against him. His downfall would be swift and irrevocable, Virginsky feared. Everything was permitted, or certainly a lot was overlooked, so long as Porfiry's record as an investigator remained impeccable. Virginsky wondered how many failures it would take before the tide turned against him and the chorus of his enemies was heard to cry: 'You have gone too far this time, Porfiry Petrovich.'

Virginsky watched as the subject of his thoughts with a loud groan lowered his rotund form into a squat beside the dead woman.

'I'm getting too old for this, Pavel Pavlovich.'

Virginsky was startled by the pronouncement, which seemed uncannily in tune with what he had been thinking.

Porfiry grunted as he re-arranged his legs. The difficulty of the manoeuvre provoked a fit of giggles which, given the proximity of a corpse, struck Virginsky as shockingly inappropriate.

'Yes, this is not the occupation for an old man.'

'You are not old, Porfiry Petrovich.'

'Nonsense. I am old. And getting older. I am staring retirement in the face. Perhaps I should get out sooner rather than later, while my reputation is still intact. Why, whatever is the matter, Pavel Pavlovich?'

'It is nothing . . . I . . . I was only wondering . . . How do you do it, Porfiry Petrovich?'

'How do I do what?'

'It seems almost, sometimes, as though you are able to read minds.'

'So you were thinking that I am over the hill?'

'No, not exactly. I was thinking that you have had a long and singularly successful career as an investigator.'

'Diplomatically put, but it amounts to the same thing. I am yesterday's man. While you are tomorrow's. Besides, I have had my share of failure, although I do not look upon it as such. Even failure serves a purpose. We learn from it.' Porfiry

Petrovich bent over the dead woman, almost pressing his face into the gash at her throat. 'Damn these tired eyes. Look at me. I have to get so close to see in focus. Of course in so doing I block out the light.'

'Perhaps you should consider spectacles.'

'I am not a vain man, Pavel Pavlovich. However, I do not think that spectacles will create the right impression.'

'But surely it is more a question of practicality than image?'

'In this occupation, the two are more closely related than you imagine.' Porfiry was now engaged in moving his head along the dead woman's torso, rocking side to side from his pelvis in a mechanical linear motion.

'What about a magnifying glass?'

'I prefer to have nothing between my eye and the object I am observing. The curvature of a lens distorts reality. The surface distracts us with its glints and motes. Ah, now, when one is looking with the naked eye, however old and defective, one finds things like this!' Porfiry pinched at the dead woman's dress and lifted his hand away. Virginsky could see a fine trail of red drawn trembling through the air.

'What is it?'

'A thread, I believe. A red silk thread.'

'How did it get there?'

'You have an undoubted talent, Pavel Pavlovich, for asking the pertinent question.' Porfiry sat upright and held the thread high. It was now completely detached from the body. 'Tell me, did you discover anything interesting about the mirror?'

'There are a number of smears on it.'

'What number?'

'Four.'

'Thank you. Four smears. I appreciate your precision.'

After a moment's thought, Virginsky added: 'They are red. Most likely blood, I should imagine.'

'Most likely?'

'It seems a not unreasonable supposition.'

'And what conclusion do you draw from this not unreasonable supposition?'

'That someone has wiped the mirror . . .'

'Go on.'

'Clean of blood.'

'Yes. It would appear so, if your not unreasonable supposition proves to be correct. Wiped clean. With what, I wonder?'

Virginsky looked around sharply.

'Perhaps in the wardrobe?' suggested Porfiry. 'I thought I smelled something in there.'

Virginsky opened the first of the wardrobe doors. He thrust a hand into the hanging garments to part them, moving them along the rail one by one. Next he groped along the bottom of the wardrobe. He repeated the procedure through the other two doors. His movements were brisk and eager, as if he believed the energy of his search would be enough to produce what he was looking for.

In the base of the wardrobe were two large drawers. The first drawer was stiff and came out slowly. It appeared to be empty. When it was extended half way, Virginsky reached inside and ran his hand along every surface, probing the corners with his fingers.

'Empty,' he confirmed, pushing the drawer in with difficulty.

The second drawer had a smoother action, and came out without any resistance. It contained several items of pressed linen.

Virginsky closed the wardrobe and turned to Porfiry. His face was crestfallen.

'Nothing? I must have been mistaken about the smell. Ah well . . . and so, Pavel Pavlovich, if the mirror was wiped clean, then we must presume that whatever was used to wipe it has been removed from the scene of the crime.'

Virginsky nodded hesitantly; the gesture indicated doubt rather than agreement.

'Did anything else strike you about the smears of what is, most likely, blood?'

Virginsky was unable to call anything to mind. He watched in painful silence as Porfiry Petrovich wound the thread around his thumb. When the action was completed, Porfiry turned his gaze on Virginsky with a look of mild inquisition. 'What shape do they make?'

'They make the shape of the letter M,' said Virginsky, quickly consulting the mirror.

'The letter M, indeed.'

'Rotated forty-five degrees on its axis.'

'Thank you. Of course it could be a coincidence. If one were to wipe a looking glass, especially in haste, one's hand would naturally describe a series of Ms.' Porfiry mimed the action he was describing in the air. 'Although one could just as easily wipe in a circular motion, in a series of Os.' He changed the pattern of his mime. 'Remind me, do we have any suspects whose names begin with O?'

'No.'

'Just one, whose name begins with M?'

'Yes.'

'Thank God I have you with me, Pavel Pavlovich, to remind me of these essential details.'

Porfiry took hold of the dead woman's right hand and turned it, repeatedly examining the palm and back. 'She struck him, you said? The officer?'

'Yes.'

Porfiry moved the hand slowly, as if in rehearsal of a slap. 'It must have hurt.'

'Why do you say that?'

'The ring on the middle finger is turned so that the stone protrudes inwardly – in the direction of the slap. It is a large and rather pointed cut ruby. There appears to be . . .' Porfiry held the dead hand closer to his face, as if he were intending to lick the palm. 'Something . . . it could be blood . . . on the tip.' He now held and scrutinised each finger separately, paying particular attention to the fingernails. 'There is not the usual sign of resistance. It seems death came quickly and stealthily to her, perhaps in the guise of a friend.' He turned his attention to her left hand, which he held and turned as he had the other. 'Three rings on the right hand, four rings on the left, including what looks like an engagement ring – a cluster of diamonds – on the third finger.'

'Yelena Filippovna was recently engaged to Prince Sergei Nikolaevich Naryskin.'

'I see. She also wears a thumb ring on this hand, a gold ring embossed with what appears to be a double-headed eagle.'

'The imperial symbol,' supplied Virginsky, his excitement barely contained.

'The emblem of the house of Romanov, it is true,' said Porfiry, with determined weariness. He laid the hand down and looked into the dead woman's face. All the faces of the dead held the same fleeting secret, and the longing that he felt when he gazed upon them was to share in it. All the dead looked out from her eyes. This was their time, while death was still fresh, before corruption had taken hold: their opportunity to lay their claims upon the living. 'Did I ever tell you about my father, Pavel Pavlovich?'

'No.'

'He was a mining engineer, you know.'

'I did not know.'

Porfiry Petrovich looked for his father in the dusk-tinged turquoise of her eye.

'He was murdered.'

'Good God.'

'Who found the body?'

Virginsky was momentarily thrown. 'This body?'

'Of course.'

'As far as we can tell, she was found by Aglaia Filippovna Polenova.'

'The sister of the deceased?'

'That is correct.'

'I am puzzled by your uncertainty. As far as we can *tell*?'

'Yes. We are not able to take a statement from Aglaia Filippovna.'

'She has disappeared too?'

'Not exactly. She fell into a dead faint, from which it has been impossible to rouse her. We may surmise that she discovered the body because it was she who raised the alarm and because of the severity of her reaction to her sister's death. The shock of discovery seems to have unhinged her.'

'Are you really suggesting that some of the horror of such an event may be absorbed by a previous viewing? So that if she were not the first to see it, she would not have been so shocked?'

'No, simply that if someone else had got to her sister first they might have prepared her. Besides, no one else has come forward.'

'I see. Where is she now?'

'She has been taken to a guest bedroom here in the palace.'

'You will ensure that we are notified as soon as she recovers consciousness.'

'I have already seen to it.'

'What about this blood-spattered officer, Mizinchikov? Who saw him running away?'

'A number of servants.'

'Number?'

'Two.'

'A small number.'

'I have also taken a corroborating statement from one Ivan Iakovich Bakhmutov.'

'I see. And did any of these witnesses remark on the presence of a bloody cloth about Captain Mizinchikov's person?'

'No. But we did not know to put the question when we interviewed them.'

'Isn't it something that we might reasonably expect them to remark upon, even without prompting?'

'I suppose so.'

'And so, let us see where we may get to merely through an accumulation of suppositions. Let us suppose that the mirror was wiped clean of blood. That act must have produced a bloody cloth. However, we can find no bloody cloth in this room; therefore it must have been removed from the scene.

Captain Mizinchikov was seen running away from the scene of the crime, but he was not seen to have about him any such article – or at least no one remarked upon it. What may we conclude, provided that the first of our suppositions is correct, of course?'

'That someone else carried the bloody cloth from the room.'

'That is one possible conclusion, Pavel Pavlovich. Another is that Captain Mizinchikov secreted the bloody cloth about his person somehow. Perhaps the marks that witnesses inter-preted as spatters of blood, were in fact evidence of blood seeping through from the inside of his tunic. He hid the offending article inside his clothes, only to have it reveal its presence in this way.'

'That is hardly the most effective method of disposing of it, as it only succeeds in drawing unwanted attention to him.'

'True, but we have to accept that the murderer was under intense pressure at this time. He may not have been thinking rationally. Individuals in these situations often improvise from one panic-stricken moment to the next. This is fortunate for the investigator, for it is while they are acting in this way that criminals make mistakes. At any rate, I fear that we will not be able to draw any definite conclusions just now.'

Porfiry was once again staring at the wound on Yelena Filippovna's throat. It drew his face towards it, as if it exercised a peculiar magnetism.

'Porfiry Petrovich!'

Virginsky's sharp warning brought him upright. 'What is it?' Porfiry's voice was thickened with tiredness.

'Are you all right? It seemed as though you were about to pass out.'

'I was looking into the wound. You have to look into the

wounds, you know.' Porfiry Petrovich held an arm out towards Virginsky. The younger man pulled him to his feet. 'You will kindly enquire of Prince Naryskin if there is a room that may be put at our disposal.'

7

The beautiful coffin

They were shown into a cork-lined study with a highly polished parquet floor. A massive ornate mantelpiece carved from beech towered over them; on either side of it shutters, also made of beech, inlaid in the same herringbone pattern as the floor, were spread like giant wings across two great windows. The furniture was all of a darker wood. A heavy circular table in the centre of the room had four empire chairs placed around it. There was a wooden easel bearing a Japanese sketch of a woman washing her feet.

The door closed on them with a discreet clash of wood. They were left alone with the smell of beeswax.

'It's like being shut up inside a marquetry box,' said Virginsky.

'Or a beautiful coffin,' said Porfiry. 'I think it will serve our purposes adequately.'

*

Porfiry Petrovich looked up suddenly from Virginsky's note-book. 'Prince Bykov! The play they were performing was by Prince Bykov!'

'What of it?'

'I have met Prince Bykov. He was involved in the case which first brought you and I together, Pavel Pavlovich. But you would not have met him.'

'No, I would not. Being confined in a police cell, I met very few people, other than my guards and interrogator.'

'*The Vanished Lover*. My goodness! How very bold of him.'

'I don't understand.'

'A very special friend of the prince's vanished in real life.'

'I see. The play is autobiographical.'

'Only up to a point, I imagine. I see that the part of the vanished lover was to have been played by Yelena Filippovna. The prince's vanished friend could not have been played by her, or any woman.' Porfiry paused, then added with a heavy, almost comical wink: 'Prince Bykov was educated at the *Cadet Corps*, you understand.'

'He is a homosexual? The *friend* was another man? Is that what you are saying?'

'Good grief, Pavel Pavlovich, since when did you develop such a lamentable taste for the explicit? Is it not enough to say that he was educated at the Cadet Corps and leave it at that?'

'Are you suggesting that everyone who comes out of the Cadet Corps engages in the kind of degenerate practices you refer to?'

'Not at all. But if I say *educated at the Cadet Corps* with an unusual emphasis, whilst winking significantly, surely it is enough for you to pick up the hint?'

'But you wink so often that it is hard to say when it is done significantly and when it simply occurs as the result of some neurological spasm.'

'Neurological spasm? I do not suffer from spasms, neurological or otherwise. However, I cannot help it if I am beset by an excess of significance in my professional life, which necessitates a higher than average rate of winking.'

'And blinking.'

'Ah now, the blinking is something different. The blinking is an involuntary physiological function. We all do it, even you, Pavel Pavlovich. I have no control over that.'

'You have control over everything you do, Porfiry Petrovich.'

'My, how you do exaggerate my abilities, Pavel Pavlovich.'

'Do you wish to interview this Prince Bykov?'

'Not formally. I may have a friendly word with him if the occasion arises. I am interested to know how he has fared in the years since last I saw him.'

Virginsky fixed Porfiry with a stare that bristled with astonishment.

'Why are you looking at me like that?'

'Do you think it wise to be seen on friendly terms with such a man?'

'Why would it not be?'

'You have admitted that you know him to be a homosexual.'

'What are you suggesting? That I am in some way imperilling myself? I am sure that Prince Bykov will be able to control himself in my presence.'

'Do not make jokes about this, Porfiry Petrovich. Consider your position as a magistrate. Homosexuality is against the law, as you well know. By consorting with a known homosexual, you are in effect consorting with a criminal.'

'I won't be *consorting* with anyone!'

Virginsky's head rocked backwards, as if buffeted by a wave of incredulity.

'I am surprised at you, Pavel Pavlovich,' continued Porfiry. 'As one of the new men, as a man of the future. Does the golden future you envisage hold no place for men such as Prince Bykov?'

Virginsky did not answer. Porfiry went back to studying the statements. 'I will talk to this Bakhmutov first. Will you kindly arrange it, Pavel Pavlovich?'

'I will send a *politseisky* to fetch him.'

*

'Ivan Iakovich Bakhmutov?' said Porfiry dubiously. The young man with ruddy cheeks and blond hair whom Virginsky had just admitted was not at all what Porfiry had expected from the notes.

'Ah – no. I am his private secretary, Ardalion Gavrilovich Velchaninov.'

Porfiry glared at Virginsky in bemusement.

Virginsky addressed Velchaninov sharply: 'My orders were for Ivan Iakovich to come here himself. The magistrate needs to talk to him in person.'

'Yes, yes indeed. But he sent me to find out what you need to know. If I could take a list of your questions to him, Ivan Iakovich would be very happy to supply you with all the answers at his soonest convenience. By tomorrow lunchtime at the latest. Ivan Iakovich feels it would be a better way to proceed. He really is ready to go home now, and does not feel that any purpose would be served by your interviewing him tonight. He really is most, most *tired.*' Velchaninov shook his head to emphasise his point. 'It has been a shattering experience.'

'No no no!' cried Porfiry, slapping both hands down on the table. 'That is not how things are done. You may be at his beck and call, but we are not. Bring him here.'

'I fear he may already have left.'

'*Im*-possible! I gave orders that no one was to leave.'

'Yes, but, as I'm sure you understand, Ivan Iakovich is a very important person. Your orders, I'm sure, were not intended to include everyone.'

Porfiry's mouth gaped in disbelief. He turned to Virginsky. 'Pavel Pavlovich, what are we to make of this?'

Virginsky shrugged.

'How could he have left?' Porfiry's incredulous rage closed down suddenly into a look of vicarious cunning. 'Unless . . . he *bribed* someone?'

'I . . .' Velchaninov thought for a moment before replying: 'I cannot comment on that accusation, except to say that I am sure Ivan Iakovich will deny it in the strongest possible terms. Furthermore, unless you have evidence to back it up, sir, whoever you are, I suggest you retract it.' Velchaninov spoke without looking at Porfiry, almost swallowing back his words as he uttered them, so little conviction did he have in them.

'I am Porfiry Petrovich, the investigating magistrate in this murder enquiry. If I find that your master has bribed one of my policemen, be assured that I will not hesitate to bring the full force of the law down on him. That is how things are done now.'

'There is a possibility that he may not have left, after all,' said Velchaninov. 'I will see if I can find him.' He ran from the room.

'What *do* you make of that?' Porfiry demanded of Virginsky.

Virginsky pursed his lips. 'The rich and powerful have long considered themselves above the law in this country. It is a difficult habit to break. It will take more than a few judicial reforms. And, of course, they always have their lackeys.'

'Would he do whatever his master asked of him, do you think?'

Virginsky raised his eyebrows, acknowledging the peculiar significance of the question. 'I do not believe that Bakhmutov has left already. He was testing the waters, I think. If you had gone along with his little proposal he would have taken himself off. Young Velchaninov will be able to produce him in surprisingly quick time, I dare say.'

A second knock at the door proved the perspicacity of Virginsky's words. Porfiry treated him to a wryly appreciative smirk. 'Come in.' He winked at Virginsky as he snapped out the command.

Porfiry turned his attention on the man who had entered. He gave no sign of being at all contrite, but strode in with his head high and his lavish white mane falling back on his shoulders. Though his hair was long, his beard was precisely groomed in the style of Napoleon III. It was the decisive finishing point on a compelling face: its sharpness complemented that of his aquiline nose and somewhat disguised the unusual fleshiness of his lips. He met Porfiry's gaze with an unflinching directness.

'So *you* are Ivan Iakovich Bakhmutov? How good of you to condescend to see us.'

'It is my pleasure, I'm sure.' His voice was a resonant bass. 'One's duty is always a pleasure when one is a loyal subject.'

'Please be so good as to sit down. This need take no longer than it will,' said Porfiry.

'I beg your pardon? I didn't quite follow what you just said.' Bakhmutov's mask of absolute confidence slipped momentarily. He regarded Porfiry with a look that suggested he did not know whether to make of him a fool or a rogue.

'It was really quite simple. Sit down. There is a seat. Sit on it.

Unless ... you have a problem with haemorrhoids? I have suffered from them myself in the past, so I do sympathise.'

'No, I do not have that problem, I am happy to say.' Bakhmutov pulled out a chair hesitantly.

'Then you are very lucky. A man of your age must be prone to any number of inconvenient ailments. There is your legendary tiredness, for example.'

Bakhmutov was still standing, his hands on the back of his seat. 'Did you call me here solely to make a fool of me?'

'Please don't ask such tempting questions. I called you here because I am conducting a murder enquiry. I urge you to sit down. I have some questions to ask you.'

'I have already given a statement to him.' Bakhmutov nodded slowly towards Virginsky as he took his seat.

'Yes, I have read that statement, and still find I have some questions to ask you. This is not unusual. It happens from time to time. One might even say frequently.'

'It is very tiresome for those concerned.'

'One becomes accustomed to it.'

'I was thinking of myself.'

'Ah, yes, of course. That is only natural.' Porifiry Petrovich lit a cigarette and considered Bakhmutov's face. There was something sealed-off, almost steely, to his bearing. A contained power lurked behind the slackening skin, still blotched with summer colour; and yet, at the same time, there was no doubt that the source of that power was shaken.

Porfiry blinked, then looked down and re-opened Virginsky's notebook. 'You said in your statement that you saw Konstantin Denisevich Mizinchikov, an officer in the Preobrazhensky Guards . . .' He made a show of reading from

73

the statement in front of him: ' . . . *running away*. Those were your words. Running away.'

'Yes.'

'How is it possible to tell that a man is running away, as opposed to simply running? Could he not just as plausibly have been running towards something as running away from something else? Perhaps he was running to get help.'

'If he was running for help, why did he push past me and ignore my urgent enquiries?'

'Ah, forgive me. That information is not in your statement. Pavel Pavlovich, did you fail to take down everything this gentleman said?'

Virginsky rippled his brows over the sudden sharpness in Porfiry's tone but did not answer.

Turning to Bakhmutov once more, his tone softer again, Porfiry continued: 'Would you care to add it now? I understand how these things can be forgotten, or overlooked. Here . . .' Porfiry pushed the notebook across the desk towards Bakhmutov. He uncapped a reservoir pen, which he offered to the other man. 'You can write it underneath the main statement and initial it. There is space.' Bakhmutov made no move to take the pen. 'Have you not used a reservoir pen before?'

'I . . . Lena is dead. Do you not understand?'

'Did you know the deceased?'

'Lena . . . Yes.'

'In what capacity?'

Bakhmutov pursed his lips before replying: 'We were friends.'

'I see. Well then, it is a terrible shock. I understand. I am not a monster.' There was a strange stifled noise from Virginsky which drew questioning glances from both Porfiry and

74

Bakhmutov. Porfiry blinked out his surprise and continued. 'I will write it for you if you prefer – but you must tell me what to write, and initial it yourself, of course.'

'Lena is dead, damn you. Why are you wasting time with all this talk of pens and writing?'

'These things are important, I assure you. Such details may be crucial. In any trial, the existence of an accurate written testimony, taken near the time of the crime, may decide the case. May I write that Mizinchikov pushed past you?'

Bakhmutov grunted his consent.

'And ignored your urgent enquiries?'

Bakhmutov formed a fist and held it to his lips. He hooded his eyes and nodded.

'Thank you. Now, if you would be so good as to . . .'

Bakhmutov signed the addendum with a deep sigh.

Porfiry snapped the notebook to, as if closing a trap, and pocketed the pen. 'Did you know Mizinchikov?'

'I beg your pardon?'

'I'm sorry, did I not speak clearly? I asked whether you knew Mizinchikov. I mean, was he known to you before tonight? Perhaps that is what you didn't understand.'

'I do not . . . understand . . . your tone.'

'My tone?'

'Your tone is impertinent.'

'Forgive me. I too am tired. You see, you are not the only one who can be tired. I am merely trying to get through this as quickly as possible so that you may go home. So that we may all go home.'

'But this is not necessary. As I have said, I have already given my statement to your colleague.'

'Which, regrettably – as we have discovered – contains some

75

omissions.' Porfiry stabbed the black leather cover of Virginsky's notebook with his index finger repeatedly.

'The main point is clear enough,' insisted Bakhmutov, calmly, almost complacently. 'He had blood all over his tunic.'

'Ah yes, the blood. Tell me, did you notice whether Captain Mizinchikov was carrying anything?'

'Such as?'

'I don't want to suggest what he might or might not have been carrying. Suffice it to say that I have in mind a reasonably noticeable article.'

'No, I saw nothing. Just the blood on his tunic.'

'You are quite insistent on that detail, I see.'

'Does it not signify his guilt?'

'It's true, things do not look good for Captain Mizinchikov.' Porfiry once again split open Virginsky's notebook and turned the pages, as if looking for confirmation of something. 'That is his rank, is it not?'

'I believe so.'

Porfiry closed the notebook and looked up. 'So you did know him before? You put in your statement that he is an officer of the Preobrazhensky Regiment. You must have known that much about him.'

Bakhmutov considered a moment before answering: 'Yes.'

'Another friend?'

'An associate.'

'An interesting distinction. Do you mean to say you had business dealings with Captain Mizinchikov?'

Bakhmutov gave a heavy, reluctant nod, as if it cost him a great deal to do so.

'May I ask, what is the nature of your business?'

'I am a financier.'

'A money-lender.'

'Do you mean to be offensive?'

'Certainly not. Do you not lend money?'

'I raise money for companies and individuals, on a some-what larger scale than is suggested by *money-lender*.'

'You had lent Captain Mizinchikov money?'

Bakhmutov gave a noise which could have been of assent.

'How much money?'

'I cannot remember.'

'The debt was an old one?'

Bakhmutov regarded Porfiry with a look of weary con-tempt. 'No.'

'I see. But, presumably, given that you do not lend money on a small scale, it was for a considerable amount of money.'

'Presumably.'

'You must indeed be a very wealthy man, Ivan Iakovich.'

'I, or rather my bank, lends money to a great number of clients. The details are kept at the bank's headquarters. I do not have the figures to hand now. Naturally. I do not go about armed with my bank's book-keeping ledgers.'

'Do you remember why Captain Mizinchikov needed the money?'

'I do not inquire into those aspects of my clients' affairs.'

Porfiry widened his eyes sceptically, then blinked flutter-ingly as if to say, 'Now, come come . . .

'Presumably,' Bakhmutov conceded, 'as is quite common with Guards officers, he found his salary was unequal to his expenses.'

'Presumably. A pity there was not an older and wiser friend to advise him, in a fatherly way, about the need to moderate his habits and modify his expenditure.'

'In my experience, such cosy chats serve little purpose. When a man is set upon his own destruction, there is little one can do to prevent it.'

'So one may as well finance it?'

Bakhmutov eyed Porfiry narrowly. He seemed to be about to say something but thought better of it.

Porfiry's face was serious as he studied the glowing tip of his cigarette. 'What was Captain Mizinchikov's particular weakness? Gambling?'

'Women. Or rather, a woman. She will not torment him any more. He has made sure of that.'

'Yelena Filippovna?'

'Yes.'

'Had you lent her money?'

'I . . . no.'

'You seem unsure.'

'I have never lent Yelena Filippovna a single kopek.'

'Do you expect that Captain Mizinchikov will be able to repay his debt?'

'*Lena is dead!*' Bakhmutov shouted out his refrain. 'What do I care about his debt now?'

'You do not expect him to.'

Shockingly, Bakhmutov laughed. It was a harsh, cynical sound, mirth without compassion.

'Presumably he has collateral?' pressed Porfiry.

'He stands to inherit a tidy fortune. However, I know his father. In his dotage, he has become a very moral gentleman. Do you not often find it is so? He was once as dashing a rake as his son. But now, as death approaches, the old man has rather gone in for religion. And morality.' Bakhmutov said the words almost distastefully. 'He will not wish the estate to go to a murderer, especially if it will only be used to pay off the costs of his dissolution.'

'To whom will the Mizinchikov fortune go if Captain Mizinchikov is cut out of the will?'

'There is a cousin, a nephew of Mizinchikov's father. But I have never met him. He resides in Moscow, I believe. He would be the next in line.'

'From what you are saying, Mizinchikov would not seek refuge with his father?'

'Certainly not.'

'What about this cousin?'

'I could not say.'

'Is there anyone to whom Mizinchikov might reasonably present himself for protection?'

Bakhmutov turned to Virginsky. 'Why is he looking at me in that way?'

Virginsky considered his answer for some time. At last he said: 'It is important that we find Mizinchikov.'

'Of course! But I find his insinuations insulting. What have I to do with this sordid crime? It was merely an accident that I saw Mizinchikov when I did. It could just have easily been someone else. I wish now that . . .' Bakhmutov broke off and licked around his teeth as if to clean away an unpleasant taste.

'What do you wish? Now?' Porfiry's tone was distracted. He once again had Virginsky's notebook open and was skimming through its pages.

'Nothing. It doesn't matter.'

'There is no explanation in your statement . . . if we may call it a statement . . . no explanation as to why you were not in the theatre. Were you not enjoying the show?'

'The behaviour of the audience was appalling. I was going to warn Yelena Filippovna, to advise her against going on.'

'I see. You are very protective of her.'

'Naturally. She is my friend. I have her best interests at heart.'

'What time was this by the way?'

'Some time after eight o'clock, I believe. I remember looking at my watch at about eight o'clock.'

Porfiry closed the notebook and looked up. 'You walked out of the performance?'

'Yes.'

'Did anyone see you leave the theatre?'

'I really cannot say what others did or did not see.'

'Very good. I like that in a witness. It is very meticulous. You were here with friends?'

'Yes.'

'Presumably your friends noticed your absence?'

'One would like to think so.'

'May I have their names?'

'Why? They have nothing to do with any of this.'

'Even so, I would like to speak to them. Perhaps one of them will be able to shed some light on Captain Mizinchikov's whereabouts.'

'I shared a box with my private secretary, Ardalion Gavrilovich Velchaninov.'

'We have met that gentleman already.'

'And with my friend and business associate, Baron von Lembke.'

'The industrialist?'

'Yes. He is also on the board of my bank. I am of course on the friendliest of terms with Prince Nikolai Naryskin, our host for the evening, as well as with his son, Prince Sergei. They were not, however, in my party tonight.'

'Of course.'

'Other friends of mine who attended include Count Dmitri Tolstoy . . .'

'Count Tolstoy is here?'

'And Tsarevich Alexander.'

'The Tsarevich too! My goodness. You did not tell me you had taken a statement from the Tsarevich, Pavel Pavlovich!'

Consternation tightened Virginsky's brow. 'I did not. Nor from Count Tolstoy. They were not among the witnesses I interviewed.'

'How strange,' said Porfiry. 'They must have made their exit before Prince Naryskin sealed his doors. Or perhaps the good prince felt it his loyal duty to spare them the tedium of an investigation.'

'I am also on the very best of terms with the Tsar himself,' put in Bakhmutov.

'Heavens! The Tsar was here?'

'No, no. That is not what I said. I merely wished you to understand that I count the Tsar amongst my friends.'

'I understand! How could I fail to understand? Clearly I understand.'

'Then there is no need to labour it.'

'I merely wished you to understand that I understood. That your meaning *was not lost on me!*'

'I take it then that we are finished here.' Bakhmutov placed his hands on the table, in preparation to rising.

'Very nearly, Ivan Iakovich. There is just one other aspect of the evening's tragedy that is not yet clear to me.' Porfiry once more opened Virginsky's notebook.

'Why do you keep fiddling with that blasted notebook? Open, closed, open, closed . . . ! Can you not decide once and for all whether you wish to consult it or not?'

Porfiry met Bakhmutov's exasperation with astonishment. 'I do beg your pardon. It is the nature of this work. One thinks one has grasped the essentials of a case only to discover there is some aspect of it that . . . eludes one's understanding, after all. You were on your way to see Yelena Filippovna?'

'Yes.'

'You did not know at the time that she was dead?'

'Of course not! What an absurd question!'

'Yes, but you may be surprised how often the absurd intrudes into my investigations.'

'That is no doubt because you are an absurd man.'

Porfiry gave the impression of thinking seriously about what Bakhmutov had just said. 'After Captain Mizinchikov had pushed past you, ignoring your urgent entreaties, what did you do?'

'You know very well what I did. It's all there in that little book.'

Porfiry gave a sharp nod of appreciation before consulting the notebook. 'You then saw Aglaia Filippovna, the deceased's sister.'

'That is correct.'

'This was where?'

'She was coming out of the dressing room.'

'It was at this point that she screamed?'

'Yes.'

'She screamed upon seeing you?'

'I suppose you could put it like that.'

'That is what I don't understand. Why she screamed then.

Would it not have been more natural for her to scream when she discovered her sister dead?'

'I really cannot say. She was in shock, clearly.'

'You then went into the room and saw Yelena Filippovna's body for yourself?'

Bakhmutov closed his eyes and nodded.

'Was there anyone else in the room?'

'No.'

'You searched the room?'

'I did not.'

'You did not look behind the screen?'

'No.'

'A pity.'

'It did not strike me as necessary.'

'At any rate, you saw no one else between your encounter with Captain Mizinchikov and meeting Aglaia Filippovna?'

'There were servants about, I believe.'

'How many?'

Bakhmutov now opened his eyes and looked at Porfiry with a kind of stunned bewilderment. 'I really cannot say. I did not count them.'

8

In the red drawing room

Prince Naryskin the elder felt the heat on his face as the fire in the red drawing room flared, tongues of orange licking greedily over the small bundle of letters he had just fed into them. The paper edges crackled and disintegrated. Multiple layers of words, written in her unexpectedly regular hand, were briefly revealed and quickly consumed. It seemed that the last remnants of her personality were contained in the strokes and whorls of ink, and that this was a further destruction of her, a second more final murder. He watched the fine black smoke curl and rise from the letters, her soul set free; he felt it in his eyes, drawing tears, and tasted it in his throat, its harshness somehow welcome.

The fine red silk ribbon around it was the last part of the bundle to catch. Wielding the fine tongs with dangerous clumsiness, Prince Naryskin piled burning coals over the flimsy ashes, burying this last vestige of what had passed between them.

'F-father?'

The prince stood sharply. 'What?'

'It looked like you were . . . b-burning something,' observed his son, suppressing his stammer by slowing down his words. He closed the door behind him as noiselessly as he had opened it.

'It was nothing. I was just stirring the coals.'

'With the . . . t-tongs?'

'Does one not?' The elder prince bent and replaced the guilty object on the stand.

His son crossed the red drawing room to join him at the European-style hearth. He peered suspiciously into the heavy marble frame, then picked up the poker and stirred the coals himself, as if to demonstrate how it was done.

'I find it strangely comforting,' said the elder prince, to his son's curved back.

'Why do *you* need c-c-comforting?'

'Perhaps I was thinking of you.'

The younger prince straightened. 'Those magistrates are looking for you. I have them outside.'

'Did we not give them a study in which to conduct their investigations?'

'It seems they cannot be c-c-contained there.'

It was a moment before the elder prince replied: 'Where is your mother?'

'She has taken to her bed, I believe. The evening has placed a very g-great strain upon her nerves.'

'Of course.' The elder prince fell into a contemplative silence.

'The . . . magistrates?'

'Very well. Show them in.'

'Prince Nikolai Sergeevich,' said Porfiry as he and Virginsky were admitted by Prince Sergei. 'Why did you not inform us that the Tsarevich and Count Tolstoy had been here this evening?'

'I did not wish to confuse you.'

Porfiry's face flushed almost as red as his surroundings. 'That is very considerate of you. I might say a little too considerate. I regret that you allowed them to depart before the police arrived.'

'It is inconceivable that I should detain a minister of state. It is beyond inconceivable that I should detain the Tsar's son. Their presence here need not concern you. They have nothing to do with your investigation.'

'Why was the Tsarevich here? His political position is well known. I do not see him as a natural supporter of such a cause.'

'The wellbeing of all his future subjects is naturally close to his heart.'

'So he was here as a benefactor?'

'What other capacity could there be?'

'I wondered if he had an interest in any of the performers. Yelena Filippovna, for example.'

'Your line of questioning is impertinent,' said the elder Prince Naryskin.

'And insulting,' added the younger.

'But I am afraid it is necessary, and permissible. Under the new laws, even the Tsarevich could be brought before a court to testify.'

'Preposterous.'

'I am surprised, sir,' Porfiry confided to the elder prince. 'I would have taken you for a supporter of the Tsar's reforms.'

'And so I am, but I had not imagined that it would be used as a means to harass one's friends.'

'It is not a question of harassing. However, if we are to fulfil our duties as investigators, we must be permitted to ask what questions we will of whomsoever we wish.'

'Surely you have asked all the c-c-questions you need?' cut in the younger prince heatedly. 'All you have to do is c-c-catch Mizinchikov and then you will have your murderer.'

'No doubt. But to investigate a crime properly one must understand what led up to it, which requires us to take statements from everyone involved.'

'But the Tsarevich is not involved.' The elder Prince Naryskin charged his assertion with absolute authority. 'And it is nothing short of treasonable of you to suggest that he is.'

'His presence here involves him.'

'Then, sir, I say that he was not here, and whoever says that he was is a liar.'

'Ivan Iakovich Bakhmutov says that he was here.'

'All you need to know about that man is that he was born a Jew. He has changed his name and his religion. Burnstein, that's his true name. Can you trust such a man?'

'He describes himself as a friend of the Tsarevich's.'

'Nonsense. The Tsarevich would never be on friendly terms with a Jew. You know that.'

'You will swear, under oath, that the Tsarevich was not here?'

'Of course.'

'But you just admitted to me a moment ago that he was!'

'Be careful what you accuse me of, sir. A magistrate may be stripped of his office. And then he is just a man. It becomes a case of one man's word against another's. And indeed, of a gentleman's word against a Jew's.'

'I have a feeling you are about to tell me that you count the Tsar amongst your closest friends.'

'Of course. That goes without saying.'

Porfiry turned to the younger prince. 'Prince Sergei Nikolaevich, allow me to express my deepest condolences. Please believe me when I say that I shall devote all my energies and all the resources at my disposal to apprehending the murderer of your fiancée.'

'M-m-mi-zinchikov.'

Porfiry inclined his head respectfully. 'The questions I ask may be painful, but be assured that they are framed only with that purpose in mind.'

'It will not bring her . . . back.'

'Why – do you believe – did Captain Mizinchikov kill Yelena Filippovna?'

'I c-c-cannot say.'

'Jealousy perhaps? Was he in love with her too?'

'His . . . way of loving . . . was not . . . not . . . civilised.'

The answer prompted Porfiry to look again at the younger prince. 'Had she given herself to him?'

'How d-dare you suggest such a thing!'

'How long had you been engaged?'

'We announced our engagement two . . . days ago.'

'Two *da-a-ays* ago?' Porfiry drew out the word in a sing-song. 'Forgive me. Before that she was . . . unattached?'

'We were very much in love.'

'But she had other lovers.' Porfiry did not frame it as a question. It was a private thought voiced.

'I must protest!' put in the elder Prince Naryskin. 'Have you come here with the express purpose of driving a knife into the open wound of my son's grief?'

'No,' answered Porfiry almost thoughtfully. 'Rather, my purpose is to learn the truth. Before two days ago, Yelena Filippovna was not engaged to your son. I wish to know if she was amorously involved with anyone else at that time.'

'M-m-mizinchikov,' spat out the younger prince. 'She was engaged to Mizinchikov. She broke it off to become engaged to me.'

'One day she was engaged to Captain Mizinchikov, the next day she was engaged to you?'

'Yes.'

'Thank you. You see, it was painful but necessary. Now I am able to understand more clearly why Captain Mizinchikov might have killed Yelena Filippovna.'

'What difference does it make why he did it? He did it. That's all you need to know.'

'A jury may need to know more, however,' concluded Porfiry with a strained bow.

*

'These skin-deep liberals are worse than the reactionaries.' Porfiry's remark, made under his breath as the door to the red drawing room closed behind them, drew a look of surprise from Virginsky. Before he could reply, however, the door re-opened and the younger Prince Naryskin followed them out. The rigours of the evening showed in his face, which had a rawness to it, as if it had been struck repeatedly. His eyes, though, seemed possessed of a cold resolve.

He closed the door carefully and drew himself upright.

'This is where it g-gets you.'

'I beg your pardon?' said Porfiry.

'My father's . . . liberal ideas. He is regretting them now. The Tsar is to blame for much. His insane and unnecessary reforms . . . he has opened a Pandora's . . . box.'

'There are many who share that view, I believe.'

'The labouring c-c-classes need flogging, not education.'

'You were not yourself a supporter of Maria Petrovna's school?'

'I allowed myself to be ... *p-p-persuaded* to lend my support.'

'By whom?'

'Lena. She was at school with Maria Petrovna. Although she had not seen her for many years, she had followed her philanthropic ... c-career. I believe that she saw it as a way of making amends, to involve us all in supporting this project.'

'For what did she have to make amends?'

'I don't know. For her life, perhaps. It was strange. This seemed to be a ... *c-c-cause* very ... c-close to her heart, although she was reticent about renewing her a-c-c-quaintance with Maria Petrovna. She seemed to want to work behind the scenes.'

'Although tonight she was to have taken the leading role on the stage, was she not?'

'Yes, well, that was d-different. She always did love theatrics. As for this evening, I was against it ... from the beginning. I knew it would end ... b-badly.'

'But surely you did not know it would end with Yelena Filippovna's death?'

'She had asked for it.'

'Good heavens, Sergei Nikolaevich! Think what you are saying! Can you be serious?'

'I mean it c-c-quite literally. In fact, she demanded it. She asked me to k-k-kill her. Two days ago. And when I refused, when instead I asked her to marry me, she ... she must have made the same demand of M-m-mm ... of him.'

'Mizinchikov?'

'She was a troubled and unhappy woman. I ... foolishly ... be-believed I c-c-could make her happy.'

'She wanted to die?'

'It was the only freedom left to her.'

'I don't understand. Why do you say that?'

'She was a woman.'

'But not all women are driven to desire their own deaths.'

'Not all are as c-c-consummately . . . logical as Lena.'

'She sounds to have been an extraordinary woman. But tell me, why did you not say this just now?'

'I did not want my father to n-n-know. He has always been against my engagement to Yelena. It has been his c-c-custom to blacken her name to me. I did not want to allow him this final triumph.'

Porfiry angled his head sharply as he considered the prince. He gave a slow nod. 'I see. Yes. I think I can understand that.' To Virginsky, he added: 'Pavel Pavlovich, can you understand that?'

Virginsky gave a dismissive grunt.

'We are all sons,' said Porfiry, finger-drawing a loop in the air to link them. 'Now tell me, how is her sister – Aglaia Filippovna, is it not?'

'The doctor has sedated her. It is important that she rests.'

'Her testimony will hold the key to this case, it is clear.'

'I only hope that the shock has not destroyed the balance of her mind. She was not the most stable of individuals, even before this.'

'I take it that the family have been informed? She should have her mother with her,' said Porfiry. 'Perhaps it would be as well for us to talk to the parents?'

'There is no family. Their parents are both d-dead.'

Porfiry rocked backwards as he took in the information. 'Tragedy upon tragedy. We shall leave her to her physic-induced oblivion. It is perhaps the last peace she will know in this world. Pavel Pavlovich, I fear that there is little more we can do here tonight.'

'What about the rest of the witnesses?'

'Everyone from whom we have taken a statement may be allowed to go home.'

'You do not wish to cross-examine them yourself?'

'I am content to rely on the statements you and others have taken.' A terse impatience accelerated Porfiry's words. And then he was left all at once stooped and exhausted. 'There is a limit to the suffering one can endure in a single day.'

9

A repellent curiosity

The audience and performers were held together in the candy box theatre. Most had been interviewed once by now and were impatient to be gone.

A stale bodily smell hung in the room. As Porfiry entered, he saw a woman spray cologne from an atomiser to dispel it.

At his side, Virginsky drew himself up in preparation to addressing the room. 'Ladies and gentlemen,' he began. 'Would those of you who have already been interviewed please take a seat on the left hand side of the auditorium and those of you yet to be interviewed on the right.' Virginsky indicated the relevant directions with clear arm gestures. 'Once I have confirmed that I have your statement, you may go.'

This announcement was met with a mixture of ironical cheering and despondent jeers. It prompted a flurry of movement, the crowd's weariness temporarily dispelled by the novelty of having something to do.

As the witnesses moved about, Porfiry scanned the auditorium and was surprised to see the man he was looking for dressed in the garb of a butler, sitting on the edge of the diminutive stage as if it were an upturned crate. He regarded the activity around him with a bored detachment. The unexpected servant's livery was not the only change that had come over him. The slight, boyish man had filled out into a barrel-shaped figure. His face too was fuller and fleshier. Whereas once it had appeared smooth and unnaturally youthful, it was now so deeply lined that the effect was equally unnatural. There was still something childlike about his features, but he looked like a child who had aged prematurely, through some strange disease. He held a cigarette in an ebony holder, and watched, engrossed, as the swirls of smoke rose and drifted from its burning tip.

'Prince Bykov?'

The prince looked up vacantly, the tedium of the night instilling a glazed stupefaction into his face. The sight of Porfiry galvanised him. He sat up sharply. Something like panic flashed in his eyes. 'You?'

'Yes.'

'What are you doing here?'

'I am the investigating magistrate. A woman has been murdered. Of course, you know that.'

'How could I not. She ruined my play.'

'That was very thoughtless of her.'

'Oh, yes, I know. I shouldn't say such things. It is callous and unfeeling of me. But I am an artist. I make no apologies for that. Artists are above the norms of morality.'

'It is very dangerous of you to make such admissions to a magistrate.'

'Surely you do not suspect me of involvement in this lurid crime? To begin with, there is the question of *taste*.' Prince Bykov screwed his face into a wrinkled clump of disgust. 'Besides, I was on stage at the time.' The prince held his arms outstretched to indicate his costume. 'I might also say that I had no motive. Indeed, I had every motive to keep her alive, at least until the end of my play.'

'And then?'

'Oh, I would happily have murdered her then. Yelena's beauty was extraordinary. But her talent was rather less than average. And her temperament, frankly, appalling. The last few weeks have been a torture for me.'

Porfiry smiled indulgently. 'I was interested in the title of your play. *The Vanished Lover*. I wonder, did you ever go to Switzerland?'

Prince Bykov gave a start, then looked the magistrate up and down with a new interest. Somehow what he saw seemed to relax him perceptibly. 'You have a good memory, Porfiry Petrovich. I did indeed go to Switzerland.'

'And did you find . . . what you were looking for?'

'No. And so, I am back in Petersburg.'

Porfiry smiled distantly and nodded. 'Your friend – Ratazyayev . . . that was his name, was it not?'

'Again, I congratulate you on your memory.'

'Whatever became of him, I wonder?'

'I have no idea. He vanished from my life without a trace. I have given up looking for him now.'

'When you stop looking for something is often when you find it.'

'Is that a proverb?'

'No.'

'It should be.'

'However, they do say wild ducks and tomorrow both come without calling.'

Prince Bykov snorted smoke appreciatively. 'Yes, a wild duck. That's Ratazyayev all right.'

Prince Bykov's smile became wistful. 'The thing is, I no longer wish to find him. I certainly do not wish him to head my way. A bird may be known by its flight, you know. He flew

. . . away.' Prince Bykov made a fluttering sweep with the hand that held the cigarette, trailing smoke. 'And so, by that act of his, for the first time, I truly knew him.'

The pain this knowledge had entailed filled the prince's eyes with moisture, and Porfiry found himself blinking in sympathy, although his own eyes were, he was sure, quite dry.

*

As he was leaving the theatre, Porfiry caught sight of Maria Petrovna deep in conversation with the shovel-bearded man to her right. They were sitting with those who had already been interviewed, but she seemed in no hurry to leave. She left it to others to clamour around Virginsky, demanding to be released. She looked up as Porfiry approached. Her face lit up in recognition and perhaps even pleasure. Porfiry had the impression she had been waiting to speak to him. She rose from her seat, squeezing out along the row. The shovel-bearded man gave Porfiry a look of passing curiosity.

'I did not expect to see you again so soon, Porfiry Petrovich.'

'Nor I you, Maria Petrovna.'

'This is a terrible business.'

Porfiry nodded gravely.

'Naturally, I will do whatever I can to help.'

One or two people watched them with half-aroused interest, latching on to any novelty as a relief from their boredom. Porfiry sensed their attention. 'Perhaps you would care to step outside?'

They entered the dimly lit corridor.

'May I ask you about Yelena?'

The name sapped Maria Petrovna's face of energy and colour. Her eyes shot downwards. 'Poor Yelena. It's so horrible.'

96

'You were good friends?'

'I had not seen her for many years. But we were once close.'

'I am very sorry. Death is always difficult to bear, but the death of one so young, under such circumstances, it touches everyone.'

'Her fiancé must be devastated,' said Maria.

'Yes, I am sure.'

'When I saw him, he appeared strangely calm.' Maria Petrovna's voice became distant.

'Do you know the officer concerned? Captain Mizinchikov?'

'I had never seen him before tonight.'

'And what of Ivan Iakovich Bakhmutov?'

'I do not know that man at all.'

'Can you shed any light on Yelena's relationship with Captain Mizinchikov?'

'No, I'm sorry. As I said, it is many years since we last spoke. I regret – I greatly regret – that I did not get the chance to speak to her tonight. I only know what Aglaia Filippovna told me.'

'You spoke to Aglaia Filippovna?'

'Yes.'

'When was this?'

'Before the performance. At the time of the terrible scene in the entrance hall.'

'Ah yes. The slapping.'

'Yes.' Maria Petrovna's face was pinched with disapproval.

'Aglaia Filippovna spoke about her sister?'

'Yes. She said that the man called Bakhmutov had once kept her as a mistress and that she was his to dispose of as he wished.'

'I see. Certain things are beginning to make sense. I thank you, Maria Petrovna.'

97

'Porfiry Petrovich?'

'Yes?'

'May I see her?'

Her eyes oscillated wildly, as if seeking escape from the prospect she had just voiced.

Porfiry tried to calm them with his own gaze. 'I do not advise it. Do you want your abiding memory of her to be as she is now, or as she was when you were friends? She has been brutally attacked. These sights have a way of etching themselves on the soul. You are tired. Go home.'

'You don't understand. There are things I have to say to her.'

'She cannot hear you. Go home. Kneel before the icon and pray for her soul. Give your words to God. He will pass on your message.'

'You are a believer?'

'Yes,' said Porfiry.

'Even with these sights etched on your soul?'

'I have to believe. If I did not, I would go mad.'

'But what if belief is itself a form of madness? There is no logic in it.'

'On the contrary, it is supremely logical. It is the only thing that makes sense of . . . of everything.'

'How did he kill her?'

'Her throat was . . . cut open.'

'Yes. That's what people are saying. Was there a lot of blood?'

'Yes.'

'You must let me see her. Spare me the torment of imagining this!'

'To see it is a greater torment.'

'You have seen it.'

'My profession requires me to.'

'And my love ... requires ... me ... to,' echoed Maria Petrovna, though her final words were almost swallowed by her sobbing.

*

Porfiry led her down to the room. Neither spoke. Once, Maria Petrovna reached out and touched a wall, as if to convince herself of the reality of what she was experiencing.

They descended by a back staircase. Porfiry had a vertiginous sense of disaster. He tried to make his steps as quiet as he could, to make himself weightless, as if he believed he could float away from this.

He had no wish to see the dead woman again. However, he realised that he would have to watch Maria Petrovna as she confronted her friend. He wanted to witness the transformations wrought in her face. The recognition of this repellent curiosity created an invisible force of resistance against which he had to push.

A door as bland and blank as any other faced them as they reached the foot of the stairs. A *politseisky* stood to one side, the only indication of anything untoward.

'She is here?'

Porfiry nodded.

Maria glared at the door with starting eyes; her hand shook as she reached for the handle.

'You do not have to go through with this,' said Porfiry, grasping her careening hand in his.

She looked down at his protective hold. A smile, small and faltering, flickered on her lips. Then she looked into his eyes, her gaze pleading and urgent. 'Let me see her.'

*

Her cry shamed him. High, like a wheeling bird, it was the inarticulate voicing of flesh crying out to flesh, her throat opening without the intercession of thought, beyond consciousness, knowing only the need to voice.

He watched her face, as he had known he would. He watched and mentally recorded the rippling fluctuations of her horror and her suffering. He told himself that it was right that she should have someone with her as she endured this, some living person to reassure her that life triumphs over death. But it felt like a platitude. The thought came from somewhere: *that life should triumph over death is no consolation to the dead.* Then he remembered that other life, the eternal life that comes after death, and marvelled that he had forgotten something so important, so central to his being. He had declared himself a believer but minutes earlier. But was it merely a pretence, empty words, another piece of play-acting?

He held out an arm to steady her. She clutched at it with both hands, like a bird clawing food. But instead of lifting him into the air, she pushed down with all her weight. His arm shuddered with the effort of keeping her upright. He had to shift position or she would take them both down. He stepped towards her, into her collapse, and held her with both arms around her body. Her head was on his shoulder, rolling in a strange, infinitely soft motion of denial. She clung on to him. He could feel the quivering spasm of her chest against his own. At some point their breathing became synchronised. He was very aware of the heat of her body.

Eventually, the burden of her physical weight eased, and a different weight replaced it. He felt it in his face and in his chest, a weight of longing and loss. They drew apart, their heads bent, each scrupulously avoiding the other's eye.

The door swung open with a rude, intrusive force. Porfiry and Maria hastened to increase the distance between them.

'Ah, Porfiry Petrovich, there you are.' It was Virginsky. He held before him a black military hat, with a chain chin-strap and an extraordinarily long plume standing irrepressibly upright. As he took in the presence of Maria, and the quickly changing configuration of their bodies, his eyes contracted with suspicion. 'One of the men found this,' he said at last. 'Outside.'

'A shako,' said Porfiry.

'It's Captain Mizinchikov's,' said Maria. 'He was holding it earlier. When Yelena struck him.'

Porfiry took the hat and turned it in his hands. The name MIZINCHIKOV was sewn into the lining. 'It would appear so. Apparently, he abandoned it in his haste to flee the palace. Possibly also to make himself less conspicuous.' He handed the shako back to Virginsky. 'Take it back to the bureau. But first we must see to it that Maria Petrovna is escorted safely home. Can you assign a *politseisky*?'

'No, there is no need. I shall take a cab. No harm will come to me,' protested Maria.

'You have had a terrible shock. I know how hard it is to bear these things.'

'Then why did you put her through it?' demanded Virginsky, his face flushed with unexpected heat.

Porfiry met the accusation with a look of mild hurt.

'Pavel Pavlovich, I asked to see Yelena,' said Maria. 'Porfiry Petrovich tried to prevent me.'

Porfiry hung his head and shied away from Virginsky's sceptical scrutiny, as if he was unworthy of Maria's defence.

'I see,' said Virginsky. He nodded slowly while he calculated what his next words should be. 'Then . . . I . . . apologise,' came eventually.

Porfiry winced at the stilted tone. 'We shall say no more of it.' He fled the room with his head down.

10

At the Officers' House

The knock, when it came, was not the one Afanasy had been expecting. At the time, he was sprawled on the sofa, one arm inside Captain Mizinchikov's left boot. His other hand worked blacking into the leather with a soft rag. A pipe was clamped between his teeth, filling the room with the thick, scented fug of smoking tobacco.

Both 'his' officers were out for the evening and he did not expect them back until the small hours. This perhaps explained the liberty he took in polishing boots in the officers' sitting room.

Despite his lolling pose, Afanasy was in a hurry to complete his evening duties, eager to have them out of the way by the time he heard Olga's muted tap on the felt-lined apartment door. It was a sound that managed to be at once playful, timid and teasing. By now she would have put the little ones to bed, and her husband would be out of the way, off on one of his benders. Vanya, the *dvornik*, knew to admit her with a discreet wink, no questions asked. He was a good sort, that Vanya.

Afanasy had distractedly been aware of some kind of commotion, a hammering on the street door, voices raised, the stamp of boots on the stairs, but his attention had been directed inwards. He had a lot on his mind. It seemed Olga had recently developed a guilty conscience regarding her feckless husband.

She had threatened to break off their relationship altogether, only relenting when he had promised her more of the gifts – jewellery, silverware, money – with which he had won her affections in the first place, but which had not been forthcoming in recent months.

Times had been hard. His generosity to her depended much on the combined good fortune and gullibility of 'his' officers. But both Captain Mizinchikov and his co-lodger Staff-Captain Herzenstube had suffered extended runs of bad luck at the gaming tables of the Officers' Casino, and so there had been little point touching them for funds. Afanasy had never resorted to open theft, though he did not scruple at lying, having invented for his perfectly healthy and unsuspecting mother a vague but life-threatening disease. Like any good Russian son, he wanted the best for his mother. But the best medical care was inevitably expensive and he was periodically overwhelmed by doctor's bills he had no hope of paying. Fortunately, Captain Mizinchikov and Staff-Captain Herzenstube were also both good Russians sons, and it cut them to the quick to see their loyal and hard-working orderly in such a desperate predicament through no fault of his own, but through filial devotion – the noblest of sentiments.

He sincerely hoped their fortunes would change tonight, for he didn't know how much longer he could count on ensuring Olga's fidelity with promises alone.

These thoughts were interrupted by the explosion of raps on the apartment door. The harshness of the noise startled him. It sounded as though some hard metallic implement was being employed, with the intention of breaking down the door.

No, this was not Olga.

His heart was pounding as he leapt to his feet, one arm still plunged into the boot. Hesitating only to take courage from a glance at the St George's cross of the regimental banner, with its inscription 'Awarded for conspicuous valour in the Battle of Kulm, 17th August, 1813', he ventured into the corridor, holding his booted arm out in front of him, as both a shield and a weapon.

The violent rapping had ceased. Now the cry was raised for him to 'Open up!'.

The face that he saw as the door sprung open took his breath away. It was hardly a face at all, more like an unfinished model executed by a poor craftsman. In places the skin was unnaturally smooth, and glistened with a lurid pink hue; in other places it was pitted and ridged. The mouth was a slit, the enlarged nostrils seemed almost to swallow up what there was of a nose. But the most unsettling feature was the eyes. As Afanasy stared into them, a shiver of revulsion passed through him. The lids were stretched taut and were without lashes. It seemed that it would have been impossible for them to blink, at least not without causing the possessor of this unfortunate face some discomfort. This gave the eyes a strange fixity of expression. In them burnt a constant fire of rage and resentment, as if those eyes held the world responsible for the disfigurement around them.

'Where is Mizinchikov? We have a warrant for his arrest.' The effort of barking these terse demands distorted the face into a sinewy, flushed knot.

'He's not here.' It was only now that Afanasy took in the grey uniform and the kepi, beneath which sprouted strands of unruly red hair. He noticed too the silver-bossed walking stick in the police officer's hand. Two other policemen crowded at his shoulder, together with a gentleman in a frock coat. The latter seemed notably ill at ease and shifted distractedly, as if he was in a hurry to be elsewhere. 'What's this about?' asked Afanasy.

'I'll ask the questions.' Then, as if to prove his point, the officer with the disfigured face said, 'What do you mean by brandishing that boot at me?'

Afanasy looked down at the boot on his hand and shrugged. 'I was just cleaning it.'

The officer raised his walking stick and placed the tip against Afanasy's chest. He held it there for a moment before thrusting it sharply forwards, forcing Afanasy to take a step back. He then lurched past him into the apartment, opening every door he passed.

'Search every room,' he barked over his shoulder. The two policemen rushed in like a small swarm, disappearing together into the first of the rooms, Afanasy's own.

'You won't find him in there!' protested Afanasy. 'You won't find him anywhere. He's not here, I tell you.'

The gentleman in the frock coat, who was hanging back diffidently on the landing, cleared his throat to signal his presence. 'I say, Lieutenant Salytov, sir, if you'll not be needing me any more . . .'

The disfigured officer withdrew a folded paper from his uniform and turned sharply back towards the man. He shook the paper open in one hand. 'Sign here and you may go.'

The gentleman in the frock coat stared at the hand that gripped the paper. The skin on the back of the hand was hairless and utterly without texture, as smooth as molten wax. 'I don't have anything to write with,' he said at last.

'You!' Lieutenant Salytov snapped at Afanasy. 'Fetch pen and ink.'

'There are writing implements in Captain Mizinchikov's room. At his desk. I will gladly show the gentleman . . . and your honour, too.'

Salytov paused to consider the suggestion. The moment trembled with unpredictability. 'Very well. Lead the way.'

Afanasy extricated his arm from the captain's boot, which he placed upright on the floor.

Captain Mizinchikov's room was behind the third door. In the light from the corridor, it appeared small and well-ordered, its Spartan furnishings no doubt facilitating tidiness. Afanasy retrieved a candle from a shelf and lit it, revealing a few faded prints of battle scenes on the walls, together with a monochrome portrait of the Tsar. There was an icon of St George in one corner. A small writing desk was crammed in beneath the black square of the window, its green leather surface cleared of papers. At the rear of the desk, three pens sprouted from an ivory pen stand decorated with the double-headed eagle of the Romanov crest.

Lieutenant Salytov pointed to an oil lamp hanging above the desk. 'Light that too.'

In the spreading glow of the lamp, he took a moment to scan the room, stooping slightly to peer beneath both the desk and the bed. He then satisfied himself that Captain Mizinchikov was not hiding amongst the uniforms in the wardrobe. At last he laid the piece of paper on the desk and nodded abruptly at the man in the frock coat.

The gentleman put on a pair of dusty, smeared spectacles in wire frames and squinted at the document. 'What exactly am I signing, may I ask?' He smiled a tense, appeasing smile.

Lieutenant Salytov exhaled his impatience. 'It is merely to indicate that you have witnessed a search of these premises –

the apartment of Captain Mizinchikov, at the Officers' House of the Preobrazhensky Regiment, Kirochnaya, 35 – at the time and date specified . . .'

'There is no time or date indicated. And no address given, either.'

'Don't worry about that. We will fill in those details later. The important thing is that you testify that force was not used. The police freely admitted. That any evidence offered in court as a result of this search was indeed found here. So on and so forth. It is all there in black and white. All you have to do is sign.'

'You have completed the search then?'

'That doesn't matter. Just sign it now and we finish the search after you have gone.'

'But what if you break something after I've gone.'

'That won't happen. The sooner you sign, the sooner you can go about your business. Whatever that may be,' Salytov added with a distasteful sneer.

'Perhaps I should make a note that I left before the search was completed?'

'That will only get you into trouble.'

'With all respect, Lieutenant Salytov, does this not rather make a mockery of the whole system? I mean to say, why go to the bother of bringing a civilian witness along if you are not going to require him to . . . *witness*?'

'This is the way it is done. Let me assure you that you have discharged your duty as a citizen here tonight. There is no reason to detain you further. All that remains is for you to sign the statement and you may go.'

There was a crash from the next room.

'Should we not . . . ?' began the civilian witness, pointing vaguely in the direction of the noise.

'No.' Lieutenant Salytov's voice was chillingly calm. It was far more menacing than any amount of bluster.

'In that case, it's probably for the best if I leave you to it.' The witness took up a pen. 'I'm sure you know what you're doing.' He stooped over the desk and signed with a flourish. He nodded once and was gone without a further word. His pounding footsteps could be heard as he threw himself down the stairs.

Lieutenant Salytov pocketed the document and pulled open a small drawer in the desk. A flash of colour caught his eye: crimson, glistening garishly. For one absurd and shocking moment he was convinced that the drawer was filled with blood. But as he pulled it to its full extent, he saw the brilliant red was contained within a narrow rectangle. He realised that it was some sort of cloth; the sheen suggested silk, which his touch confirmed. The silk glided under his fingers. He could feel that there was something wrapped inside it, something weighted and hard, that gave the silk around it shape. Salytov pulled back the loosely folded material, revealing a cut-throat razor, the blade closed inside a nacre handle.

Salytov wrapped the razor back in the silk and pocketed it. He turned his attention to the other contents of the drawer, a bundle of letters tied up with a ribbon, also of red silk. He untied the ribbon and watched the letters spring apart, as though they couldn't abide each other's company.

At the thump of boots behind him, Salytov almost guiltily removed his hand from the bundle.

'No sign of him,' one of the policemen announced.

'I told you,' said Afanasy.

Salytov said nothing. His hand returned to the letters. He lifted the first one and read.

I have never loved you, any more than I have loved any man. I have tried on the idea of loving you, as I might a dress. But it did not fit. I could not walk freely. I was not myself. You might even say the idea of loving you clashed with my complexion. Console yourself with the knowledge that I do not love Naryskin. The idea of loving Naryskin is absurd. Naryskin is absurd. But the idea of marrying Naryskin is not absurd. Naryskin is a Prince. I have always dreamed of marrying a Prince. The fact that he is rich is also in his favour. If only you had been richer, I might have married you. If you had been richer, you would not have sullied yourself and insulted me by that shameful act. Poverty cannot but be shaming.

Of course, it is horribly cruel of me to confide this to you, of all people. I do it so that you should know the character of the woman who has betrayed you, so that you might feel less torment at my betrayal. I do it out of kindness and generosity. I do it to set you free. Consider yourself to have had a lucky escape.

You may also consider that you have brought this on yourself. How could I love you now?

In the same spirit, let me inform you that I have tried on the idea of loving many men, and none of them suited. Be under no illusion, as with you, so with them. That is to say, I gave myself to them completely. One cannot try on the idea of loving a man without trying on the man. You must know by now that it pleases me to express myself in such crude

'What shall we do now, sir?'

Salytov swallowed thickly and put the letter back with the bundle. 'No wonder he killed her, the whore.' He looked at the letters distastefully. 'There are some letters in this drawer. Gather them up and bring them back to the bureau.'

'You can't take them. They're Captain Mizinchikov's private property,' cried Afanasy. But the cold glare of Salytov's eyes drained the conviction from his voice even before he had finished his protest.

11

An extraordinary meeting

Bakhmutov saw the tramp on the corner of Nevsky Prospekt and Yekaterininsky Canal. He had just breakfasted and was looking out of his dining room window to gauge the day, prior to going down for business. The sight of a destitute would not normally have engaged his attention, but this man was staring fixedly at the bank as if he had some business with it. The beggar's overcoat hung off him in ragged strips; only the turned-up collar was intact. There was something pathetic about the way the man's head sank down into the flimsy band of cloth, the only protection against the weather that his old coat still had to offer. The man also wore a soft cap, pulled down as far as possible. It was almost as if he believed his head was the only part of him worth preserving.

A carriage passed between the beggar and the object of his attention. When it had gone, his gaze shifted up to the top storey window from which Bakhmutov looked out. Bakhmutov instinctively shrank from the man's accusing eyes.

'The poor will always be with us,' he murmured to himself, pulling the drape in front of him. But he knew that there was something more personal in the beggar's challenging look.

*

For a wealthy man, Ivan Iakovich Bakhmutov lived almost frugally in the four-roomed apartment he kept above his bank.

He maintained only one servant, for example. However, this was occasioned by an unwillingness to share his private life, any more than was necessary, with people who might conceivably come to bear a grudge against him. Tittle-tattle was the poor man's weapon against the rich, and it was a powerful one.

If his own apartment was furnished comfortably rather than extravagantly, the public rooms of the bank evinced a discreet commitment to the aesthetic of wealth. The marble-clad walls breathed affluence from their mineral pores. Art hung over the marble, huge canvasses within massive gilt frames that hinted at the gold locked away in the vaults. This was a business calculation on Bakhmutov's part. He had argued successfully to his board that such expenditure was necessary to inspire confidence in a financial institution.

The back room of the bank, the counting house, was more functionally done out. The clerks' stools were not upholstered in watered silk, nor were their desks carved from mahogany. But they served their purpose well enough.

Velchaninov looked up and greeted his employer with a wincing smile. Bakhmutov gave a slight nod to acknowledge the other man's solicitude.

'Baron von Lembke is waiting for you, sir.'

Bakhmutov wrinkled his mouth distastefully. 'Ardalion Gavrilovich, there is a disreputable individual loitering outside the bank. Some kind of tramp. Kindly see to it that he is moved along.'

'I shall see to it myself, Ivan Iakovich.'

'No. That will not be necessary. Get one of the doormen to do it.'

'Very well, sir.'

Bakhmutov nodded to himself in satisfaction as his secretary sprang off his stool.

In the boardroom, von Lembke sat alone at the far end of the long oval table. Placed in front of him was a silver tray bearing a pot of coffee and two small cups, together with some pastries. The aroma of the coffee was overpowered by the cigar that von Lembke had just lit. At Bakhmutov's entrance, von Lembke began to pour the coffee. 'You're late.' Baron von Lembke was a man of bulk and yet there was something essential about his size. It was impossible somehow to imagine him being reduced to anything less than he was. There was a hard-boiled quality to his physique, though perhaps this was suggested by the utter baldness of his head. He held a cup out to Bakhmutov without looking up. Bakhmutov took the cup and walked to the far end of the table.

'Late? Well, what do you expect after last night?'

'I was not late. And I was there.' Von Lembke had a way of barking out his words as if he were evicting them. 'Here at ten o'clock sharp. And I do not have the advantage of living over the premises.'

'It has been a terrible strain. I did not sleep at all.'

'Terrible business. Terrible *for* business, too. For the bank.'

'I fail to see the business implications,' said Bakhmutov irritably as he took the seat at the opposite end of the table. 'It is a private tragedy.'

'It's a scandal! No banking house wishes to be associated with a scandal. Reputation is everything. Confidence comes from reputation.'

'But the bank is not associated with the scandal. There is no connection between what has happened and us.'

'Don't be naïve. She was your mistress.'

'*Was*. But no longer.'

'You continued to take care of her. She lived in the apartment you provided. You put a carriage at her disposal.'

'I was not so rash as to have the bank crest on the side of that carriage.'

'Nevertheless, your name is linked to hers.'

'But not in the financial pages, surely?'

'Investors . . .' Von Lembke took several deep puffs from his cigar, as if the smoke fuelled his irascibility, 'don't just read financial pages.'

'I refuse to accept there is a financial aspect to this.'

'There's a financial aspect to everything. You know that the Moscow Merchants and their propagandists are always whipping up public opinion against us.'

'Us?'

'Outsiders. You, a Jew. Me, a foreigner.'

'I am not a Jew. I am a Christian.'

'In their eyes, you are a Yid. Always will be. You are Iakov's son. Me, I'm no foreigner. I'm as Russian as you. But I have a foreign name. That's enough for them.'

'Your friends in the finance ministry will not back them. Which means the Tsar will not tolerate it. The Tsar is a father to all Russians.'

'Don't put your faith in this tsar. He lost heart after the reforms. They were meant to make everyone love him. Instead, they start taking potshots at him. We can all go to hell as far as he is concerned. And the next tsar – a real Jew-hater. Friend of the Slavophiles. Their campaign against foreign money – he's on their side. Russian industry in Russian hands, that's what they say. This affair gives them another stick to beat us with.'

'I don't see how.'

'The decadent, sensualist Jew. Corrupter of Russian virgins.'

'But I am not a Jew, I tell you.'

'So, you do not deny the other charge.' Von Lembke gave a smoky chuckle. 'They are talking about founding a bank of their own. A Russian bank.'

'This *is* a Russian bank. It has a Russian name on the plaque.'

'The Tsar has already given his approval.'

'Well, let them. There is room for another bank.'

'And what if our Russian investors transfer their deposits to them?'

'That will not happen. Our clients are our friends. Besides, we have reserves. And our loan business is turning over a good profit. We are a well-run bank.'

'Owned by a Jew and a German.'

'What's wrong with that? The Finance Minister himself is a German. The Tsar surrounds himself with Germans.'

'Public opinion is turning against the German influence at court.'

'I care nothing about public opinion.'

'Then you are a fool. At least be thankful we don't have a French partner. However, if our aristocratic friends decide they prefer to pay interest into Russian pockets . . .'

'My pockets are Russian. This suit was tailored here in St Petersburg!'

'This is no laughing matter. The situation is grave.'

'Our friends will not desert us.'

'And our enemies? What if Mizinchikov was put up to it by our enemies?'

'You're being absurd. Mizinchikov loved her. He didn't kill her because someone told him to. He killed her because she rejected him.'

'I don't know anything about that. I don't pretend to under-stand love.'

'You, but even you . . .'

'Business. That's what we must concentrate on.'

'I agree, up to a point. However, I fear there is nothing we can do.'

'Not true. We must bring a Russian in. A true Russian. Not a Yiddish convert. An old Russian. Get a proper Russian name on the plaque. That'll carry some weight.'

Bakhmutov sipped his coffee without commenting on von Lembke's proposal.

12

The story of a love affair

The following day, Porfiry Petrovich awoke to a sluggish depression. An obscure sense of guilt infected him, no doubt the emotional ripple of a dream he could not remember. He had overslept. Stabbing his arms into his dressing gown, he hurried from his bedroom into the main room of his private apartment. His depression sharpened into annoyance when he saw the table had not yet been laid for breakfast.

'Zakhar!' Immediately he realised his mistake. He slumped into a seat, his elbows on the table, face in his hands. Only the chiding tick of the grandfather clock disturbed the silence of the apartment.

He heard the door to the kitchen open. There was a rattle of pots.

'Begging your pardon, sir, but Zakhar . . .' It was Katya, her voice strained to its usual unnaturally high pitch, in the way of so many Russian peasant women.

'I know.'

He heard her put the tray down heavily.

'Will there be anything else?'

Porfiry looked up, as though surprised by the question. She was the cook whose services he shared with the other residents of the apartments provided by the department, for the most part magistrates and senior police officers and their families. She prepared food for him every day, the food which Zakhar brought to him, but it was a long time since he had laid eyes on her. She had aged. He remembered her as a strong bustling woman, agile, despite her weight. She had filled out even more and there was an arthritic stiffness to her movements now. Though her face still shone with health, there were deep lines scoring the ruddy glow.

'Thank you, no.'

She nodded and left with a haste that saddened him. He half-raised an arm after her. The apartment was cold and gloomy; the chill of autumn had taken possession. The stove had not been lit. But it was not simply on account of the unlit stove that he regretted her departure. He wished he had been able to talk to her of Zakhar.

The drapes were still open from the day before. He had not drawn them himself and there was no one else to do it. The windows were flat planes of grey, through which a meagre light seeped. Porfiry did not have the will to look out at the raw, damp day. He felt the saturated moisture of the air in his chest, and dwelt for the moment on the rattle and wheeze of his breathing; a precise dread of the inevitably worsening weather, of the inescapable winter ahead, entered him.

What saved him from complete lethargy was the desire for a cigarette.

Three cigarettes later, there was a knock at the door of his apartment. The intrusion seemed to set off a coughing fit, which served as his greeting to Virginsky, who pointedly wafted the fuggy air and frowned his bemusement at the sight of Porfiry in his dressing gown.

'Are you unwell, Porfiry Petrovich?'

'Perfectly well, Pavel Pavlovich,' said Porfiry as he at last poured himself a cup of coffee. The cold bitter liquid caught at his throat and merely renewed his hacking fit. He sat down to absorb it.

As Porfiry settled back in his chair, drawing a splayed hand across his face, he caught the indulgent amusement now in Virginsky's eye. 'What are you smiling at, Pavel Pavlovich?'

'You remind me of Oblomov.'

'How can you possibly say that! Oblomov is nothing like me!'

'Goncharov describes him wearing a dressing gown just like yours.'

'Nonsense. His is more oriental.'

'Well, it's a dressing gown. He wastes away the day in his dressing gown.'

'This is nonsense. I am a man of action. Not a lethargic wastrel consumed by ennui and indecision.'

Virginsky contented himself with a sceptical pinching of his lips.

'I am surprised at you, Pavel Pavlovich. You of all people should know that when I am sitting still and smoking a cigarette, I am never simply sitting still and smoking a cigarette. I am at work, active. My mind races. The very thing I am not, however, is an Oblomov.'

'Oblomov is a very lovable character. The Russian reading public took him to their heart.'

'I am not lovable, Pavel Pavlovich. Not by any means. If I were lovable, then . . . there would be someone here, a loving creature, loving me.' There was no self-pity in Porfiry's voice as he offered this opinion. If anything, there was a triumphant delight in his own logic.

'But I thought there was someone. Last night, you hinted . . .'

'What on earth are you talking about?'

'I was sure . . . Perhaps I was mistaken.'

'No doubt. I will see you in my chambers in ten minutes.'

'Very well.' Virginsky nodded and turned to go. At the door, he hesitated and added: 'I thought you would be interested to know that Aglaia Filippovna regained consciousness.'

'Excellent.'

'But only briefly.'

'What do you mean?'

'She is in a coma now.'

'I don't understand.'

'I think it would be best if you spoke to her doctor yourself. I cannot explain it.'

'I am most eager to speak to him. An eagerness which I shall act upon . . . imminently, if not immediately.' Porfiry took out another cigarette and lit it.

Virginsky had the door open now, but a further thought detained him. He seemed unsure whether to express it.

'Is there something else, Pavel Pavlovich?'

'It just occurred to me. Wasn't Oblomov's servant called Zakhar?'

Porfiry considered the burning cigarette as he rotated it between thumb and forefinger. A full inhalation and exhalation later, his gaze once again concentrated on the cigarette, he at last said: 'Go.' He did not look up as Virginsky left his apartment.

*

A little under half an hour later, Porfiry was seated at the desk of his chambers, his face razor-nicked and the bottle-green frock coat of his civil service uniform flecked with ash at the cuffs and dandruff at the shoulders. He smoked in silence as he again read through the witness statements taken at the Naryskin Palace.

'Any news of Captain Mizinchikov?' he asked at last, without any expectation in his voice.

'According to his orderly, he did not come home,' answered Virginsky from the brown sofa, its artificial leather cracked and threadbare. 'Lieutenant Salytov found no sign of him at his apartment. He did, however, find this. In a drawer in Mizinchikov's writing desk.'

Virginsky rose and crossed to Porfiry's desk to hand him the parcel of red silk, which he had been holding back, apparently for the pleasure of giving it to him.

Porfiry took the mysterious parcel with a puzzled and vaguely recriminatory frown. He felt its weight before placing it on his desk to unwrap it. 'I see. How interesting.'

'You will notice the colour of the silk,' said Virginsky.

'Do not fear. The colour of the silk is not lost on me.'

'It is frayed at one edge. A number of threads are loose and some almost detached.'

'Yes. I have noticed that too.'

'It is curious, is it not, that this razor should be wrapped in a material consistent with a thread found on the body of a woman whose throat was cut?'

'Curious is not the word.'

'Of course a man may possess a razor merely to shave himself. But why keep it in the drawer of a writing desk? Moreover, Captain Mizinchikov is not a clean-shaven gentleman. But perhaps he had simply put the razor away in a drawer in expectation of the day when he would take up shaving again.'

'But this is not the murder weapon, Pavel Pavlovich,' declared Porfiry with quiet, almost weary, emphasis.

Virginsky seemed deflated. 'How can you be so sure?'

'Let me put it another way, if it is the murder weapon, then Captain Mizinchikov is not the murderer. I believe you said just now that the captain did not return to his apartment after leaving the Naryskin Palace – is that not correct?'

'Yes.'

'Well then. How could he have murdered Yelena Filippovna with this razor and then placed it in his drawer? Are we to imagine that he stole into his own apartment without being seen by his orderly? And if that is the case, then one is obliged to ask the rather bigger question, *why*? It is usual, in my experience, for murderers to *dispose* of murder weapons – preferably in places where they will never be found, or at least in places where they cannot be associated with them. It is not usual for them to take them home and put them in a drawer for the police to find.'

Virginsky let out a defeated sigh. 'So the razor is irrelevant?'

'Of course it is not irrelevant. It is very relevant. It is a great triumph to have found it. Was anything else discovered in this drawer?'

'These.' Virginsky removed from a pocket the bundle of letters, which were once again tied up with the ribbon. Again he received a recriminatory spring of the brows from Porfiry. 'They are letters to him from Yelena Filippovna.'

'Are they indeed?'

Porfiry took the letters from Virginsky and untied them. He flicked through them and saw from the dates that they spanned a period of about a year, although by far the majority of them had been written and sent within the last two months. Then he settled down to read them through.

What emerged was the story of a love affair, or rather a story of desire, seduction, manipulation, disillusionment and rejection. It was hard to tell whether there was love involved, on either side. On the side of the party who had no voice in the narrative, Mizinchikov, his love could only be inferred, along with the pain he must have suffered, and his brief, rare, but surely intense, moments of joy. Was there ever a moment in the story when Yelena Filippovna had loved him? Certainly she seemed to profess it on occasion, though in a careless or even conflicted way.

If I do not proclaim my love for you in every line that I write – as I know you would have me – it is not because I do not love you, but rather because I naturally baulk at such a tedious task. I am a grown woman. You must believe that I love you, as much as I am able to love any man.

To the besotted Mizinchikov, 'you must believe' might have read as a passionate entreaty. To Porfiry's objective eye, it had about it a little too much of a command. Similarly, the qualification 'as much as I am able' could be taken two ways: it could be joyously expansive, an indication that her love for Mizinchikov was bounded only by her capacity to love, which after all might be infinite; or, far more likely, it was an admission that she was incapable of loving any man, including him.

In the earlier correspondence, she certainly held out the possibility of loving him, though her preferred tone, after the first few highly formal letters, was flirtatious. She was more comfortable promising physical intimacy than emotional equivalence. Porfiry identified the point at which their relationship was consummated. A letter dated the twenty-eighth of July spoke of the heights of ecstasy to which he had taken her. It also spoke of Mizinchikov's 'skilful swordplay'. She declared that she eagerly awaited being 'sweetly stabbed' by him again. No doubt such passages gratified his male pride. No doubt they were intended to.

Soon after, her letters began to talk of their engagement and something approaching a sense of hope entered her tone. *I look forward to the day when you and I will be one in law and before God, and this time of tribulations will be at an end.* At times, however, a note of resignation could be detected. *We deserve one another. There is no one else for each of us. And so we must learn to be content with one another. Perhaps the fire of passion does not burn as it once did. What of it? I cannot live my life in a conflagration.*

But later in the same letter, she reproached him for his want of feeling. *You do not love me any more, admit it. Admit it so that we may be free of one another. Is that not what you want?* And a few lines later: *Forgive me. I am a foolish woman. I know you love me. I have never doubted that.*

Then came the final letter, in which she suddenly and irrevocably put the matter beyond either hope or doubt. *I have never loved you*, she had written, along with the barely mitigating proviso: *any more than I have loved any man.*

Something had brought a new clarity to her understanding of her feelings. Something that Mizinchikov had done. *You may also consider that you have brought this on yourself. How could I love you now?*

'What did he do?' wondered Porfiry, as he laid the last letter down on his desk, his eyes fixed on her words. 'What was this shameful act that *sullied* him and *insulted* her?' After a moment's silent reflection, he turned to Virginsky, who made no attempt to provide an answer.

Porfiry lit a cigarette. 'I begin now to understand the razor.'

'You do?'

'I do.'

'Then could you explain it to me?'

'As I have said, this razor is not the murder weapon. No, it is the tangible symbol of a possibility, perhaps of an intention. Or perhaps, by keeping this razor next to her letters, he was in fact, in some way, preventing himself from killing her. It was a kind of talisman to him. As long as he kept the razor in the drawer, she was safe. But if he took it out, he knew he would kill her.'

'This is proof of premeditation.'

'Go on,' encouraged Porfiry.

'He put the razor next to the letters at the precise moment when he decided to kill her,' Virginsky ventured. 'And of course, he had another razor with which he committed the actual crime.'

'Why did he want her dead, though? Because she had jilted him?'

'It would appear so.'

'If he couldn't have her, no one could. Let alone the absurd Naryskin.'

'Yes.'

'A crime of passion?' Porfiry put the question with narrowed eyes.

'I do not believe you can call it that. A crime of passion, as I understand it, is a crime committed in a sudden rage. The result of an intense and overwhelming emotional upheaval. There must be no opportunity for reconsidering or turning back. If the letters provoked Mizinchikov to murder, he had ample time to reflect as he travelled to the Naryskin Palace. This was not done in the heat of the moment. As we have discussed, the presence of the razor in the drawer, next to her letters, indicates a certain degree of premeditation. "This is what I will use against the woman who has rejected me" – that is what it says. We must assume that he went there armed with his second razor, fully intending to use it. And that he bided his time until he had the opportunity to put his plan into action.'

'But is it not possible,' countered Porfiry, 'when an individual is overtaken by such a destructive passion, that "the moment" may last for some considerable time, its heat maintained for hours, days even? If we do not call it a crime of passion, we may talk of diminished responsibility. They act without reason, without planning, without strategy. They are compelled. A force more powerful than them takes them over. And while they are in the grip of this compulsive force, they can think of nothing else. It is hardly a question of thought. They become the act itself. All their will, emotion, energy – their very soul, in short, is channelled into one moment, one fatal transgression. Certainly they do not think beyond the execution of the act. And once they have crossed over from intent to execution, once they have made the transgression, and they find themselves standing in the aftermath of their crime, they are to a large extent baffled, lost – even bereft. For not only have they been deprived of the compulsion that gave shape and purpose to their existence, but also they have lost the person they once loved more than any other. Put simply, they have no reason to live any more. Can we wonder that such criminals often go on to take their own lives, or passively surrender to their fate? They have nothing else to live for.'

'I do not dispute your construction of his mental state,' conceded Virginsky. 'Although it occurs to me that we are both forgetting Prince Sergei's testimony, that Yelena Filippovna wanted to die and indeed solicited her own death.'

'Then how are we to explain the mirror?' asked Porfiry, suddenly dismayed.

'The mirror?'

'Someone cleaned the mirror.' Once again, Porfiry drew the shape of a large M in the air. 'Why did he go to such trouble to cover his tracks? What did it matter to him? Indeed, how could he have mustered the required presence of mind?'

'Yes, I see.' Virginsky nodded thoughtfully. 'By your account, he should have simply waited for the police – or killed himself on the spot.'

'What if Captain Mizinchikov is in fact innocent? Then perhaps his flight can be adequately explained by panic. He was fleeing the prospect of a false accusation. An unwise and regrettable decision on his part, but that I suppose is the nature of panic. Tell me, Pavel Pavlovich, did you notice any blood on the floor beneath the mirror?'

'No.'

'Neither did I. However, it is reasonable to assume that the liquid soaking her dress and the rug beneath her body was blood. Logic therefore suggests that she was killed where she lay. Which means that she cannot also have been killed in front of the mirror. Assuming the smears on the mirror *are* blood, how did they get there?'

Porfiry lapsed into silent thought, as though unable to answer the question he himself had posed.

Virginsky seemed hesitant to break the silence. He offered his explanation tentatively: 'The murderer placed a bloody hand on the mirror ... and then, noticing the mark it left, attempted to wipe it clean – perhaps with the sleeve of his tunic? That would explain why we were not able to find a blood-soaked cloth, and why no one was seen carrying one away from the room.'

Porfiry seemed enlivened by the suggestion. He nodded in excited approval. 'Having committed this terrible deed, he felt compelled to confront himself. Looking into his own eyes and seeing for the first time the eyes of a murderer, he is overcome by an unbearable horror. His legs buckle and he falls forward, reaching out a hand to hold himself up.' Porfiry mimed the action he described, his eyes wide with vicarious horror. He suddenly frowned in dissatisfaction. 'But why bother to wipe clean the relatively small amount of blood on the mirror, when there is copious blood on the rug, about which he can do nothing?'

'Because the blood on the mirror appears to him as a sign of his guilt. It is his hand that has left the mark.'

'And if the murderer is indeed Mizinchikov, he subconsciously signals his guilt...' Porfiry described the letter M with one hand. 'Whilst his conscious mind attempts to eradicate all trace of it. Yes, I find your theory very interesting, Pavel Pavlovich. It is at least psychologically coherent.'

'Thank you.'

'It is vital that we find Captain Mizinchikov. Vital for him, I mean. If our reconstruction of events is correct, his soul must be burdened by this terrible crime. More than burdened – tortured. His soul is in conflict with itself. We must give him the opportunity to confess. We must arrest him for his own salvation. I fear what he may be driven to, left alone with his guilt.'

'He must know that we are looking for him,' observed Virginsky.

'Yes, and a man in a blood-spattered dress uniform will be conspicuous. The first thing he will try to do is change his clothes. He had an opportunity to do so at the Naryskin Palace. You noticed the clothes in the wardrobe?'

'Yes, but he may not have realised they were there.'

'Indeed. Perhaps, however, we should postpone further speculations until we have a clearer idea what the substance on the mirror is. Has Dr Pervoyedov been alerted?'

'I understand that he wished to visit the scene of the crime. There is every chance that he is there now.'

'Then let us join him,' said Porfiry, slapping both palms decisively on his desk as he rose. 'While we are at it, we shall pay a visit on the invalid, Aglaia Filippovna, thus killing two hares with one shot.' He gave Virginsky a challenging look, as if to say, *Does your Oblomov kill two hares with one shot?*

13

Sanguinary expectations

A fine white mist rose off the Yekaterininsky Canal, as if it were generating obscurity. The vague silhouette of some vehicle, rattling over Kokushkin Bridge without lights, came towards them at speed. It turned out to be an empty *drozhki*, which Virginsky hailed at the last moment, almost as it was upon them. The driver stood swearing as he reined in his horse. Porfiry Petrovich almost threw himself into the frail cab, which shook under his weight. As always in a *drozhki*, it was a tight squeeze for the two men, and they sat with Porfiry's arm around Virginsky back.

'Will you wish to interview the Tsarevich?' asked Virginsky, once the horse had settled into its stride.

'Why should I?'

'Because he was at the Naryskin Palace last night.'

'Was he? I thought Prince Naryskin said otherwise.'

'You did not believe him?'

'The powerful create their own truth, which they are able to impose on the rest of us. It is left to us to adapt our truth to theirs.'

'You cannot be serious, Porfiry Petrovich!'

'I would expect that the Tsarevich has by now left Petersburg. Whilst I am perfectly at liberty to request his return, only the Tsar may command it. Before I petition the Tsar, let us first find Mizinchikov. Let us also speak to Aglaia Filippovna, if we are able.

If those enquiries prove fruitless, then we reserve the right to extend our investigation to include ministers of state and, indeed, heirs to the imperial throne.'

'Are you not concerned that you are shaping your investigation around the rank of your witnesses?'

'No, though thank you for voicing that concern. I feel confident that if the Tsarevich had any information to impart concerning the death of Yelena Filippovna, he would have wasted no time in coming forward to volunteer it.'

Virginsky gave a half smile. 'And yet last night you rebuked Prince Naryskin for allowing him and Count Tolstoy to leave.'

'Did I? I don't remember.' Porfiry let his head loll back and closed his eyes. 'There is nothing quite like riding through the mist in an open *drozhki*, do you not think?'

But Virginsky did not answer.

*

At the Naryskin Palace, Dr Pervoyedov stared into the dressing room mirror with a fixed frown, as though dismayed by his own reflection. And well he might be: his hair stood up in untameable clumps and his plaid overcoat had clearly seen better days. No doubt it was the overcoat of a busy man, but that consideration did not mitigate the obscure horror it inspired in all decent people. His face was bland and unprepossessing, distinguished only by the flush of high colour that often occupied it, the result of Dr Pervoyedov's unfortunate propensity for tardiness, which he sought to rectify by constantly rushing between appointments. It might be said against him that he had two great faults. The first was that of taking on too many duties; the second, that of fulfilling them too conscientiously. Narcissism, however, was clearly not one of Dr Pervoyedov's faults, and so Porfiry Petrovich thought it was reasonable to assume that something other than his mirror image had caught his eye.

'So, you have found the smears, Dr Pervoyedov!'

'Yes indeed, Porfiry Petrovich,' said Dr Pervoyedov, addressing himself to the magistrate's reflection. 'Yes indeed.'

'And what do you think they are?'

'Goodness, Porfiry Petrovich! What can you mean by such a question? Are you asking me to hazard a guess?'

'I would not dream of it.'

'I am glad to hear it. *Ve-ery* glad to hear it.'

'We – that is to say, Pavel Pavlovich and I – wondered if it might not be blood.'

'That does not surprise me, Porfiry Petrovich. The nature of your work must encourage such sanguinary expectations.'

'And your work does not?'

A good humoured smile kinked Dr Pervoyedov's face in the mirror. 'I make a point of suppressing expectations of any kind. Expectations are not consistent with a scientific outlook.'

'A scientist is as capable of entertaining expectations as the next man. He merely calls them by different names.'

'Is that so?'

'Theories. Hypotheses. What are they if not expectations?'

'But we always put them to the test.'

'Good. That is what I want you to do with our . . . what was it you called them?'

'Sanguinary expectations.'

'Are you able to confirm whether the substance smeared on the mirror is blood or not?'

'Not simply by looking at it, Porfiry Petrovich. There is, as far as I know, only one reliable test for the presence of blood –

133

spectral analysis, as described by Sorby. You may know that it was used successfully in the Briggs murder case in London some years ago.'

'I had read about it in one of my journals. I would not have asked you to do it, if I did not think it possible.'

'Really? That is very considerate of you, I must say. Very considerate indeed. I will need to collect a sample and take it back to my laboratory.'

'Are you able to do that now?'

'If you wish.' Dr Pervoyedov retrieved a scalpel and a circle of filter paper from his bag. He folded the paper to form a cone, which he held close to the mirror, beneath a section of one of the smears. 'The substance, whatever it is, has dried.'

'That is consistent with the behaviour of blood upon oxidisation, is it not?' asked Porfiry.

Dr Pervoyedov gave no more than an ambiguous smile in answer to this.

'So tell me, Dr Pervoyedov, what do you make of our cadaver?'

Dr Pervoyedov turned from the mirror to consider Yelena Filippovna. 'She is a beauty. Or rather, was.'

'Is such an opinion consistent with the scientific outlook?'

'I dare say not. Will I be required to conduct an autopsy?'

'I have yet to discuss the case with the *prokuror*. As you know, it will be his decision. In the meantime, I suggest we arrange for the body to be removed to the Obukhovsky Hospital morgue. Would that suit you?'

'Very much so.'

'I would also ask you to conduct your spectral test on a substance I detected on one of her rings. The large ruby ring

134

on her right hand, the one turned inward. I have sanguinary expectations regarding it.'

'It would be my pleasure.'

'Now, Pavel Pavlovich, shall we visit the invalid? Perhaps it would interest you to accompany us, Dr Pervoyedov?'

'What is this?'

'Aglaia Filippovna, the dead woman's sister,' supplied Virginsky. 'She succumbed to a nervous attack last night, which has rendered her unconscious. She revived briefly this morning, but according to the physician attending her, she has sunk into a coma. She is here at the palace.'

'And how do you expect to interview a patient in a coma, Porfiry Petrovich?'

'She may come round. In the meantime, I have some questions I would like to ask her doctor. Your presence would be invaluable.'

*

Aglaia Filippovna's hair lay in a loose black halo over the pillow. There was an eggshell fragility to her head. Her skin seemed as thin as rice paper. Apart from where it veiled her eyes with purple shadows, it was pallid to the point of transparency. Her lips were slightly parted, which gave her face an ugly, unguarded expression. Her body lay as neat and unmoving as a pencil beneath the covers, arms pressed close to her sides, legs together.

The room was in semi-darkness; the drapes were partially drawn, allowing a torpid grey light to intrude without conviction. A fire had been lit in the grate, and its reflected glow filled and enlarged the bedroom, dancing in restless shifts across the ceiling.

A woman on the wrong side of middle age stood by the bed looking down at the invalid with appalled fascination. The woman was so stationary that she appeared almost to be a waxwork. It was conceivable that she had once been beautiful, but she was a long way from her heyday now. Her face had a sunken, sour expression, as if she were sucking on a bitter pill. Her dress was very dark, and in the gloom appeared black, or to have been sewn from a fabric of shadow. She did not look up when Porfiry and the others came into the room.

'Madam?'

Slowly she lifted her head and revolved her eyes heavily towards Porfiry.

'Madam, I am Porfiry Petrovich, the investigating magistrate.'

She met this information with a disappointed nod. Her eyes went back to watching Aglaia Filippovna.

'I take it you are the lady of the house, Princess Naryskina?'

A slow blink seemed intended to confirm this supposition.

'I wonder, madam, if we might be permitted to talk to the doctor who is responsible for the young lady's care.'

Princess Naryskina turned to the nurse who was seated by the bed and released her with a prolonged sigh. The nurse hurried from the room with almost unseemly eagerness, as if she could not wait to be free of that torpid gaze.

'Dr Müller is at this moment in the kitchen, enjoying the cook's hospitality.' Princess Naryskina's voice was deep for a woman's. She spoke with her chin against her collarbone, so that her words seemed choked out. She did not meet anyone's eyes as she spoke. Perhaps once, her evasive glance had passed for coquettish shyness. In a woman of her maturity, it seemed suspect.

They waited in silence, Porfiry keeping his eyes on this interesting specimen of aristocratic womanhood, watching her with a lively smile.

At last, an elderly and rotund German, who had obviously spent a lifetime enjoying the hospitality of cooks, presented himself with patient equanimity. The dramatic circumstances of his patient's sudden decline barely disturbed the essential stolidity of his character. He spoke slowly in a heavily accented and lulling monotone. It seemed that upon waking from her first sedated sleep, Aglaia Filippovna had become agitated. Pressed for details of this agitation by Dr Pervoyedov, he described a whole range of extraordinary symptoms, including uncontrollable laughter alternating with equally uncontrollable sobbing, muscular spasms, compulsive wringing of the hands, inarticulate shouting and the voicing of obscenities, all of which he catalogued under the general heading of hysteria. He also revealed that Aglaia Filippovna had ripped off the nightshirt with which she had been provided and run naked through the corridors of the palace. She had once again found her way on to the stage of the now empty theatre only to collapse in exactly the same spot she had the night before. Relieving her bladder where she lay, she had then suffered a seizure which the good Dr Müller had diagnosed as epileptic. He had naturally administered potassium bromide in solution; however, the patient had suffered an unfortunate reaction to the drug and had fallen into a bromide coma. This at least gave the nurse the opportunity to clean her, and, with the assistance of some of the servants, to return her to her bed.

'Does the patient have a history of epilepsy?' asked Dr Pervoyedov.

'Not known.'

'Is there epilepsy within the patient's family?'

'Not known.'

Porfiry ventured a question: 'When do you expect her to regain consciousness?'

'Not known.' It seemed to Porfiry that Dr Müller took unwarranted satisfaction in being able to give the same answer.

'Would you permit me to examine your patient?' asked Dr Pervoyedov.

Dr Müller assented with an economical nod of the head.

Dr Pervoyedov peeled open the first of her eyes, revealing a purer turquoise than that of her sister. He bent his head close to hers and gazed into the small startling circle of colour. The eye stayed open when he took his hand away, and failed to track the finger that he moved in front of it. He repeated the examination on the other eye, with the same result. Next he pulled down the covers and lifted a frail arm. After feeling her pulse, he laid the other arm down with delicate precision, as if it were vital that it be replaced in exactly the same position.

'More. There is more – to see.'

The abrupt bark of the elderly German doctor was startling enough. But when he pulled down the covers in a single and surprisingly energetic sweep, the effect was positively shocking. He did not stop there. He grabbed the lace-trimmed hem of Aglaia Filippovna's night dress in fingers that now seemed obscenely thick and coarse and yanked it up, high above her waist, exposing her slightly parted legs and pubic hair. Her skin gleamed in the half light.

She did not stir. Her unblinking eyes continued to stare straight ahead. For a moment, no one spoke.

'I notice it when she naked. See.' Dr Müller pointed to a

criss-cross of lines running up the side of her left leg and continuing past her hip to stop at the side of her abdomen.

'What are they?' came Virginsky's hoarse whisper.

'Scars,' answered Dr Pervoyedov. Dr Müller nodded vigorously.

Now that it had been said, Virginsky could see that the lines were cut into her flesh and that they were red. Some of them appeared fresh, glistening crimson against the pallor of her skin. They brought to mind fine threads of silk laid across marble.

'Who did this?' Virginsky's question was shot through with resignation. At that moment, he hated Porfiry Petrovich, for it was Porfiry who had forced him to confront it all, the surface scratches, the gaping wounds, the mangled flesh and bone, the erupted blood. He could almost believe that Porfiry took pleasure from it.

'She did it to herself.'

Virginsky flinched away from Porfiry's voice, as if there was something in it that he could not face: the realisation of his own injustice. There had been no hint of pleasure in that voice, only boundless compassion.

'Cover her up,' commanded Porfiry. 'And close her eyes.'

Virginsky felt a surge of relief. His hatred for Porfiry Petrovich had passed.

Porfiry looked up at Princess Naryskina, and Virginsky followed his gaze unthinkingly.

She had not moved. However, the energy that might have gone into movement had instead intensified her unnaturally fixed stare, as it feasted on the network of wounds.

139

14

Fathers and sons

Prince Sergei Nikolaevich Naryskin watched the departure of the magistrates and their disreputably shabby doctor from the window of his study on the first floor. He saw Porfiry Petrovich glance back at the palace, his face drawn and colourless. Some instinct drove the prince to step aside from the window so as not to be seen. And yet he felt that the magistrate's penetrating gaze had detected him. The three men stood for a moment in conference, Porfiry Petrovich all the time looking up at the prince's window. Finally, he nodded once and they moved on into the grey drizzle.

Prince Sergei was about to turn away when a lacquered carriage drawn by two feathered greys clattered into the Fontanka Embankment. He recognised the crest on the door as that of Bakhmutov's bank, a commercial rather than familial crest. Of course – the man had no family. The carriage pulled up. One of the footmen, impeccably liveried in dove grey, jumped down to see to the steps. He opened the door and handed down Bakhmutov himself, who wore an astrakhan-trimmed coat loosely over his shoulders, a concession to the seasonal inclemency. He too looked up at the palace, as Porfiry Petrovich had done, though Bakhmutov's face was lit by determination, and even a glint of cunning. This time, Prince Sergei made no attempt to conceal himself, but met the moneylender's gaze with a defiant stare. He would not be put to shame in his own home. Why was Bakhmutov here? If it was to offer his condolences, he did not want anything to do with them. And he found it hard to believe that his father, who had his own reasons for hating Bakhmutov, would have had any cause to welcome him today.

Bakhmutov released himself from this eye contact with a sneer of contempt. He disappeared beneath the prince's window. The jangle of the visitors' bell presaged his intrusion into the sealed, silent interior of the palace.

Prince Sergei now turned his gaze on the bust of Kutuzov that he kept on a fluted pedestal. He saw reproach in his hero's blank, eternally unblinking eyes.

'What would you have me do?'

But the stone lips refused to offer either comfort or advice.

*

In the red drawing room, Prince Naryskin stood with his back to his guest, staring into the fire. Bakhmutov had shrugged his overcoat into the hands of a footman and was revealed to be wearing a black morning suit, his usual apparel for a business day. The prince was dressed for the department, in his bottle green frock coat and medals.

'What do you mean by coming here?'

'Am I not permitted to make a social call on friends?'

Prince Naryskin pinched his lips against the answer that was pushing to get out. He contented himself with saying, 'What do you want?'

'How is Seryozha?'

'Prince Sergei Nikolaevich is naturally devastated by the death of his fiancée under such ... shocking circumstances.'

'Naturally. And yet . . .' Bakhmutov put a hand to his neatly trimmed beard. 'He knew what he was . . . exposing himself to. He knew the history. It was a brave man who took that on. Or a fool.'

'You dare to call my son a fool!'

'No no no! You misunderstand me. He was not the fool. Mizinchikov was the fool. Your son's actions betokened great nobility of soul.'

Prince Naryskin did not see the smile that accompanied this soaring eulogy. He stared in silence at the dancing flames.

'Tell me.' A cold, wheedling note had entered Bakhmutov's voice. 'Did your son know . . . everything? Did he know about your . . . ?'

'Of course not.' In the transmutations of the fire, Prince Nikolai saw again the eager flare of orange that had consumed her letters. 'And he will never know. What do you take me for?'

'And now – if he discovered the truth now?'

'It would destroy him.'

'But a man . . . could it not be argued, has a right to know the truth, in a general, philosophical way of speaking?'

Prince Naryskin turned on Bakhmutov. 'So! That's what this is about! You've come to blackmail me.' The fury suddenly fell from his face, to be replaced by a bitter despair. His voice cracked. 'What could I have that you would want? I'm in your pocket as it is!'

'Once again, you misunderstand me, Nikolai Sergeevich. I am with you in this. We are as one. Seryozha must never find out. This affair is hard enough for him to bear as it is.' Ivan Iakovich Bakhmutov drew himself up, and puffed out his chest. He articulated his next words slowly, with an almost sadistic clarity. 'If he found out that his father had once been his dead fiancée's lover, who knows what it might do to him?'

'Be quiet!' Prince Nikolai narrowed his eyes suspiciously at Bakhmutov. 'What are you up to, you snake?'

'I want – if I may be said to want anything – I want to be your friend.'

Prince Nikolai gave a grimace of pain. 'I don't understand.'

'It is simple. I will be your friend. And you – in return – will be my friend.' Bakhmutov's tone suddenly hardened. 'There will be no more of this "Snake!", no more of this "Jew!", no more of this contempt. You will acknowledge me as your friend. As your equal.'

'You don't know what you ask.'

'I know what I give. A friend would never betray a confidence. But a man who is not your friend, a man whom you have made your enemy – who can say what such a man might do?'

Prince Nikolai looked Bakhmutov up and down, as if considering him for the first time. A smile curled on Bakhmutov's lips, which was not mirrored on the prince's.

Bakhmutov held out his hand. 'Come now, friend.'

At last the prince raised his own hand, stiffly, slowly, as if he were lifting a tremendous weight. Bakhmutov seized the hand with the one he had extended, while his other arm stretched possessively around Prince Nikolai's shoulder, pulling him to him. His smile now was one of satisfaction.

*

On the other side of the ornately moulded double doors of the red drawing room, Prince Sergei Nikolaevich Naryskin snatched his hand back from the gold handle as if it had

143

suddenly grown white hot. But the handle was only a little warm, no warmer than the palm of his hand. Admittedly, his palm was drenched in sweat, and that sweat, he saw, had dimmed the lustre of the metal.

He looked at his hand and then looked back at the tarnished door handle, as if he had lost something precious in the contact of flesh and gold.

*

All the available resources of the St Petersburg police force were mobilised in the hunt for Captain Mizinchikov, but to no avail. A watch was kept on his apartment, and his known friends and associates were monitored, including fellow officers of the Preobrazhensky Regiment. An interview with the suspect's father confirmed Bakhmutov's assessment of the relationship between father and son. As far as General Mizinchikov – a thin, scooped-out man who smelled of cloves – was concerned, his son could 'go to the devil', and if he had already, it was a source of neither surprise nor regret to him. He assured Porfiry that he would waste no time in notifying the authorities, should he hear from his son. His eyes as he made this promise were cold and steady, suspiciously guarding even the pain over which he held himself hunched. Porfiry recognised the miser's ruthlessness; and the miser's gift for cherishing bitterness. He did not doubt that General Mizinchikov would be as good as his word. He felt a stirring of sympathy for the fugitive.

'You have a nephew in Moscow, I believe.'

'I have several nephews, in Moscow and elsewhere. Not to mention nieces. My sisters were notoriously fecund.'

'I would be grateful if you could supply us with the names

144

and addresses of these family members, so that we may extend our enquiries to include them.'

'I shall do better than that. I shall write to them all, commanding them to deny quarter to the criminal. If they wish to expect anything from me, they will follow my example and summon the police the instant he presents himself.'

'I . . . am grateful to you. Even so, I would appreciate the names and addresses. And if there is one cousin to whom Konstantin Denisevich is particularly close, perhaps you could indicate that on your list.'

'Ah, that would be Alexei Ivanovich,' said General Mizinchikov, after a moment's reflection. 'Those two have been firm friends from childhood, though two more opposite characters, it is difficult to imagine. Alyosha is thoughtful, sober, considerate . . . What he sees in my reprobate son, I cannot imagine.'

'You have only the one son?'

'Regrettably, my first born son died in infancy.'

'I'm sorry. And no daughters?'

'No. And now I consider myself to have no son either.'

Porfiry was taken aback by the force with which the general made this assertion. 'Do you not have any residue of fatherly feeling towards Konstantin Denisevich? After all, we do not know for certain that he is this woman's murderer.'

'He has deserted his regiment. And brought dishonour on the family name. If he did not kill her, he should have stayed to make his case. He can expect nothing from me.'

'You will disinherit him?'

'He has forced me to it.'

'May I ask in whose favour you will change your will?'

'It will go to the oldest of my nephews, Alexei Ivanovich.'

'I see. Now, sir, if I may trouble you for the list. It will help us greatly if we are able to take it away with us.'

*

'*There* is a murder waiting to happen,' said Porfiry carelessly, as they descended the gloomy staircase of the Gorokhovaya Street apartment house.

'Are you serious?' said Virginsky.

'Either that or he is the greatest argument for Captain Mizinchikov's innocence.'

'I don't understand.'

'If Mizinchikov really is a murderer, then why he has not long ago dispatched such a father must surely baffle us. It can only be because he has not yet got round to it. Even such placid and indisputably loving sons as you and I, whose fathers are – or were – by comparison paragons of paternal virtue, even we must have felt at times the provocation to parricide. What son has not? How much more strongly must a man in whom the homicidal propensity is already awakened feel it?'

'I wonder that you can be so flippant, given what you have said about the circumstances of your father's death.'

They reached the ground floor and stepped out into the drizzle-soaked gloom. 'I did not kill my father, if that's what you mean.'

'I did not mean to suggest that you had.'

Porfiry said nothing. They stood on the front steps considering the bleak prospect before them without enthusiasm. The mist seemed to sap their will to action. Porfiry's voice came thickly, his words directed to the mist: 'My father was a good man. In many ways, an extraordinary man. He had a gift. I think I told you that he was a mining engineer. His gift, however, had nothing to do with that, and in many ways stood at odds with his professional outlook, which you could describe as highly rational. He was an exemplary scientist, except in one particular.'

'Go on,' prompted Virginsky.

'He was able to heal people. Perhaps he was what we would call a faith healer, though he never referred to his gift in those terms.' Porfiry started walking, taking the first turning into Sadovaya Street. It took Virginsky a moment to catch him up.

'Indeed, he hardly ever referred to his gift at all, certainly not in polite circles. It was almost as if it embarrassed him. It seemed to undermine everything that he had spent his life building up. He feared, I think, that if his superiors found out about his gift, it would be the end of him professionally. He never spoke even about his faith, but I am convinced he was a believer, otherwise how would he be able to do it?'

Virginsky did not attempt an answer.

'I know, I know,' said Porfiry, meeting a point that had not been raised. 'That begs an interesting question. Would God choose to work His miracles through a non-believer? Indeed, would that not produce more compelling evidence of his existence, at least for the non-believer concerned? But I ask you, is God really in the business of proving or disproving his own existence?'

'You know my opinions on the subject of God.'

'At any rate,' continued Porfiry, as if he had not heard Virginsky's terse interjection, 'my father could not fail to believe in his own gift, however inconvenient and possibly even frightening it was for him to do so. People would come to our house, peasants for the most part. They would present themselves at the tradesmen's door. My father would have them come in, take them to his study and sit them down. He would talk to them quietly and calmly. And at the end of ten minutes' chat about the harvest, or the frost, or whatever new-fangled machinery their master was intending to introduce, he would lay his hands on their afflicted area, and they would go away somewhat eased in their pain.' Porfiry gave a chuckle. 'He was deeply loved. Many hundreds came to the funeral, all the old peasants whose stiff joints he had loosened. He knew his limitations and that was his secret.' After a pause he added: 'It's difficult to live up to such a father.'

'I'm sure he was proud of you.'

'No. I am sure that he was not. And I don't blame him. At the time of his death, I was not a son to be proud of. I was young, a student of law like you once were, at the university here in Petersburg. I was living beyond my means. You could say I had fallen in with a bad lot, or perhaps I was the bad lot others had fallen in with. At any rate, I spent my leisure time in expensive dissipation. My letters home were a constant stream of reproaches, relieved only by selfish and manipulative demands for money.'

Virginsky cast a quick sidelong glance at Porfiry but said nothing.

'There was one among my fellows who happened to come from Pinsk, which is near to my home village of Dostoeve. I would not say he was a friend of mine. It was merely the accident of originating from the same region that threw us together. He was a strange individual and it was unnerving to be in the same room as him, especially alone. He had a way of looking at you and not looking at you at the same time. But more than that he awoke a powerful frisson of unease in me, almost a revulsion. Perhaps this was my own debased version of my father's gift in operation. My father traced his family to

Siberia, you know. Sometimes it amuses me to imagine a tribal shaman amongst our ancestors.'

'I have no doubt of it,' said Virginsky wryly.

'This fellow student of mine was the son of the local priest and had heard about my father. He seemed fascinated by my father and would often ask me questions about him. To my shame, I saw this as an opportunity to vent my spleen over what I saw as my father's unjustified parsimony. "So your father is a wealthy man?" he would ask. "Oh, yes. He has pots of money," I think I may even have replied.'

Virginsky bowed his head, tactfully silent.

'Well, something unpleasant happened at the university, a disciplinary matter, and he was expelled. He returned to his home village. Soon after, he made a point of seeking out my father. He pretended some affliction, knowing this would gain him admittance. But it was he who laid hands upon my father. He strangled him. I imagine that as he tightened his grip around my father's neck he demanded to know where the money was hid. He may even have said something like, "I know you have money. Your son told me."'

'You don't know that.'

'Well, there was no money. My father's fears concerning his career had proven true. His superiors, learning of his healing activities, had presented him with an ultimatum. Give up the charlatanry, as they termed it, or give up his position. Of course, there was more to it than disapproval of his miraculous gift, which they claimed brought the department into disrepute. Professional jealousy played a part too. My father tried to stop, he really did. But the people kept coming to him, and how could he turn them away? This was the excuse his enemies needed and he was relieved of his post.'

They had come to Stolyarny Lane. The corner of the department building was like the prow of a ship breaking through the mist. The two men instinctively halted beneath it, allowing Porfiry to finish telling his story.

'His dismissal had occurred months before the visit from my murderous fellow student. My father had not informed me of his change in fortune, out of pride, or perhaps for fear of worrying me. When I returned for his funeral, I found the letters I had written placed neatly in a drawer in his study. I was never able to ask his forgiveness. I stole them away and burnt them, in my shame. The boy who had killed him was easily caught and quickly confessed. It was not about the money, not really. His fascination with my father had crossed over into a dangerous obsession. He believed, or so he claimed, that my father's gift came from the devil and that a voice had told him to kill him. As is often the case, he seems to have been driven by a whole range of motivations, some of which contradicted others. He was exiled to Siberia, ironically the source of my father's powers, and has no doubt grown old in a labour camp.'

There was a moment of silence. Virginsky's expression, though, was strained with impatience. There was evidently something on his mind. 'Porfiry Petrovich, what did you mean earlier when you talked about your own version of your father's gift?'

'I can always tell.'

'What?'

'The killers. As soon as I meet them. I experience the same frisson. It was like that with the student Raskolnikov. Of course, being a rationalist like my father, I do nothing until I have gathered the evidence.'

'You once suspected me of murder.'

'Did I?'

'You arrested me.'

Porfiry looked up at the department building. 'Shall we go inside? We have work to do.' It was a moment before he led the way inside.

*

In the days following, autumn took hold in earnest. The shifting mists that chased along the canals became bolder. They filled the parks and avenues with a weightless flood, and bound the days together under a fine mesh of monotony. The city was concealed in layers of lace. Another city took its place, a city of imagined buildings and inhabitants, of voices disembodied from their speakers, of footsteps without feet, of ghostly carriages and phantom houses. This was a city in which secrets loomed larger than palaces, in which an unaccustomed licence was suddenly at large. It was now possible to smoke in the street without provoking a policeman's reprimand. This was a city, in short, in which anything was possible. Whatever man could imagine, for good or evil, could take shape in the St Petersburg fog.

Aglaia Filippovna continued to drift in and out of a coma, almost as if there were some link between her and the fog, as if the fog were claiming her for one of its own. On one occasion, alerted to her return to consciousness, Porfiry and Virginsky hurtled dangerously through the enshrouded streets to the palace on the Fontanka, but by the time they got to her, Aglaia Filippovna was in the throes of an epileptic seizure.

Princess Naryskina was once again in attendance. Indeed, it seemed as though she had not moved from her position by the bed. Her gaze was lit by the same static energy, which seemed to feed off the spasms and distress of the invalid.

It seemed to Porfiry that the disease was another, stronger being that had taken possession of Aglaia. He thought of a dog he had once seen shake a rat to death in its jaws. He imagined the disease as an invisible predator, and the poor frail girl as the prey caught between its teeth.

After the fit had passed, she slept, under the weight of a tremendous exhaustion. She came to briefly an hour or so later, but Dr Müller forbade them from mentioning the death of Yelena Filippovna, for fear of provoking a further attack. She seemed to have no recollection of the events of the night of the benefit gala and spoke of her sister in the present tense, as if still alive.

'Where is Yelena? Why does she not come to see me?'

'You must rest now.'

Aglaia Filippovna wrenched herself upright, then fell back more exhausted than before. She closed her eyes and they thought that they had lost her again. But her hands fidgeted convulsively on top of the counterpane. She enclosed the thumb of her right hand inside the fist of her left and twisted her hands against one another, as if she were turning a screw at the base of her thumb. Her voice throbbed faintly, her lips barely moving. 'Yelena is to be married, you know.'

'Yes.'

'To her dashing officer of the Guards. Captain Mizinchikov.'

'I think you are mistaken, Aglaia Filippovna.'

Dr Müller shook his head warningly at Porfiry.

'It is all arranged. He has no money but she loves him. Love will find a way. I am happy for her.' Still she kept up the twisting motion with her hands. Then suddenly they fell lifelessly apart. The smile froze on her lips and slackened into a curve of enervated distaste.

'Aglaia Filippovna?'

They got no more out of her that day.

*

Prince Sergei was waiting for them in the corridor outside Aglaia's room. Or at least he appeared to have been waiting. The possibility came readily to Porfiry's mind that he had been eavesdropping. He had the skulking disposition of an eavesdropper.

'How is she?'

'She remembers nothing,' said Porfiry. His face was grave, even forbidding. A single blink sealed his thoughts as he scrutinised the prince. 'She believes her sister is still alive.'

'W-would that she were!' His flitting gaze chased along the moulded curlicues of the wall, before coming back to settle on Porfiry. 'Aglaia Filippovna will have to be told.'

'Dr Müller advises against it, for now at least. Her constitution is very delicate. She has been able to take in very little nourishment between her bouts of unconsciousness. And her epilepsy exacts a terrible toll on her.'

'But she c-cannot live out a *lie!*' There was an unexpected force to his protest. 'How are we to maintain such a pretence? What if she asks to see Yelena? What if she insists?'

'It will not be easy. But neither will it be indefinitely. Dr Müller will notify us when he considers that she has regained strength sufficiently to be told the news. In the meantime, she needs to rest. Is it convenient for her to stay here at the palace?'

'Of c-course. We would not have her taken anywhere else. We will ensure she is well c-c-cared for.'

'That is very . . . kind of you.'

'It is no more or less than our c-Christian duty. Besides, she is my sister-in-law. That is to say, she would have been, if Yelena and I had married.'

Porfiry thought of the words Yelena had written to Captain Mizinchikov.

I do not love Naryskin. The idea of loving Naryskin is absurd. Naryskin is absurd.

'She asked you to kill her, but you refused. Instead you asked her to marry you.'

'Yes.'

'And she accepted your proposal, willingly, with a free heart?'

'Of c-c-course!'

'But still she prevailed upon Captain Mizinchikov to kill her?'

'Either that or he k-killed her out of jealousy. She had rejected him in my favour.'

'She rejected him as a husband but chose him as a murderer. Who should be jealous of whom, I wonder?'

'I don't understand.'

'She chose *him* to carry out this momentous deed!'

'But she had asked me to do the same. I had no c-cause for jealousy on that account, although I must say, I find your . . . argument c-c-convoluted and repugnant.'

'I am sorry if this line of enquiry offends you. However, this is an unusual situation, to say the least. A murder victim who solicits her own murder. Did she ask any other men to kill her, do you know?'

'You really are an outrageous individual.'

'Perhaps she was as promiscuous in her desire to die as she seems to have been in her desire for physical intimacy.'

For a moment it seemed that Prince Sergei would strike Porfiry. In the end he let out a fragmented groan of denial.

'The signal honour that she conferred upon you, in asking you to kill her, was surely debased in your eyes by the fact that she made the same request of Mizinchikov.'

'Honour? What k-k-kind of honour is it to be c-called upon to k-k-kill the woman one loves?'

'Let us say privilege, then. A murder committed under such circumstances would be no common murder. It would itself be a declaration of love. She had set the ultimate test. Perhaps one could say that you were not up to it and Captain Mizinchikov was.'

'If so, I am glad that I failed her in that.'

'Naturally.'

'I do not see what you aim to achieve with this unpleasant c-c-questioning. Are you suggesting that I am in some way involved in Yelena's death?'

'Not at all. I am merely trying to understand the situation fully. Do you believe that Captain Mizinchikov loved Yelena?'

'She certainly did not love him.'

'That is not what I asked. But even so, how do you know?'

'She . . . told me so.'

'I see. In a letter, by any chance?'

Prince Sergei flushed but did not answer.

'But he loved her? May we establish that?' insisted Porfiry.

'In his own c-crude and brutish way, yes.'

'If so, and if he did kill her at her request, how could he bear to go on living? Surely the only way a man, a passionate man – am I to take it that is what you mean by crude and brutish? – the only way he could bring himself to c-c-contemplate such a deed was if he had also resolved upon his own destruction, or should I say self-destruction?'

'Do you mock me, sir?'

'Mock you?'

'You affected to stammer.'

'I assure you I had no intention of . . . you must forgive me. If it's true, I am mortified.'

'Your c-c-colleague will c-confirm what I say.'

Porfiry turned to Virginsky in desperate appeal. 'You did *seem* to stumble over a consonant, Porfiry Petrovich.' The younger magistrate winced apologetically but could not disguise his enjoyment of Porfiry's discomfiture.

'If indeed that is true, then believe me that it was out of sympathy and not a desire to mock. It was an unconscious slip. The mind plays tricks on us. My mind is especially prone to do so. I meant nothing by it at all. Except . . .'

'Except what?' demanded Prince Sergei.

'Except perhaps, in my mind, I was merely registering the particular consonant that most commonly causes you difficulty. My mouth, perhaps, betrayed my thoughts. There is no more significance to it than that.'

'But why think it in the first place?'

'One cannot always curb the direction one's thoughts take. I will also say in my defence that I was conscious of a desire to smoke. Distracted by the need and yet feeling myself unable, here in the palace . . . Well, when I am not able to smoke I find that I have a tendency to do absurd things. I am a deeply absurd person. Without the mitigating influence of tobacco I would be even more absurd.'

'Why do you say that? Why *absurd*?'

'If I have unwittingly given offence again, I apologise. I couldn't have known. How could I have known?'

'How c-could you have known what?'

'That she mocked you. Your stutter. That she called you absurd.'

'Why do you persecute me like this? I am not her k-killer. Mizinchikov is her k-k-killer.'

Porfiry hesitated a moment before replying: 'Ah yes. Captain Mizinchikov. Is it possible, do you think, that he might have refused to kill her in the same way that you did? That such a refusal also prompted from him a proposal of marriage? Perhaps he too hoped to save her from herself by marrying her.'

'Now you accuse me of a want of originality!'

'And so, because he would not kill her willingly, perhaps she saw the need to goad him into killing her. Could it be that she saw her engagement to you in that light?'

'Have you any c-c-conception how offensive that insinuation is? That she would c-consent to be my wife merely to provoke another man into k-k-killing her!'

'Perhaps she was playing you and Captain Mizinchikov off against each other. Ultimately, we may suppose that she did not care who killed her. In the same way that she did not care whom she married.'

'How do you dare to presume such things?'

'It is my unfortunate duty to presume far worse.'

'Your duty, sir, is to find Mizinchikov and charge him with the murder of Yelena Filippovna. He is of c-c-course a deserter from his regiment now. That is enough, surely, to c-c-confirm his guilt.'

'Confirm? I don't know about that. It certainly would be better for Captain Mizinchikov if he came forward to clear his name. But then again, perhaps he is unable to come forward. If he is the romantic gentleman I take him to be, it is not out of the question that he has taken his own life by now. He may not have done it immediately after killing Yelena. Perhaps he was overwhelmed by panic, and fled. Only later did he realise the full enormity of his crime. That is to say, the significance of the crime to him. Life, his life, no longer contained the woman he loved, even as an object of his hatred. How could he endure that?'

'I c-c-cannot answer for c-Captain Mizinchikov. You had better find him and ask him yourself,' said Prince Sergei pointedly.

15

The injured detective

'What are you doing, Porfiry Petrovich?'

'I'm carrying the samovar in.'

'Yes, I see that you are doing that,' said Nikodim Fomich. The Chief Superintendent's astonishment had turned to bewilderment. 'I only wonder *why* you are doing it.'

'Because there is no one else to carry it in for me.' Porfiry placed the steaming samovar down heavily on his desk. It rattled dangerously and seemed about to topple. Porfiry instinctively reached out a hand and carelessly touched the hot metal urn. He immediately gave a sharp cry of pain.

'What on earth is the matter now?'

Porfiry shook the damaged hand, then held it tightly at the wrist, as if he could seal off the pain. 'I burnt it on the samovar.'

'Here, let me see.' Nikodim Fomich, although several years younger than Porfiry, automatically lapsed into a fatherly role towards him. 'My wife always puts grated carrot on burns.'

'Nonsense.'

'At the very least, some cucumber juice will take out the heat.'

'It's nothing, Nikodim Fomich. And kindly remember I am not one of your children.' Porfiry snatched his hand away.

'You need someone to look after you, Porfiry Petrovich. You remember Varvara Romanovna?'

'Varvara Romanovna?'

'Come now, Porfiry, she was your bridge partner at the dacha this summer. She was very taken with you, as well you know.'

'The corpulent widow?'

'My goodness, Porfiry Petrovich, have you looked at yourself recently?'

Porfiry screwed his nose up over his burn. 'I try to avoid it.'

'I can understand why. However, as your friend, I am obliged to tell you that you are past your prime.'

'Thank you, friend.'

'The days of your bagging a young, beautiful bride are sadly long gone.'

'Please be assured, Nikodim Fomich, I entertain no such hopes.'

'Just as well.'

'But just because I am not capable of bagging – as you so delicately put it – a young, beautiful bride, am I therefore obliged to settle for an old, ugly one?'

'Varvara Romanovna is not ugly!'

'No. That was unkind of me. And her charms, for the right man, will prove irresistible. However, I fear I am not that man. The inclinations of the heart cannot be forced, Nikodim Fomich. Now, was there some official purpose to your visit? Or are you here solely in the role of match-maker?'

'Have you made any progress in the case of the murdered society belle?'

'Really, Nikodim Fomich! *The murdered society belle*? You have been reading too many newspaper accounts.'

'Indeed so. The newspapers are full of it. And frankly, they are portraying us as fools.'

'Until we are able to talk to the missing captain, there is little hope of making progress in the case.'

'Ah yes, the missing captain.'

'We have contacted colleagues in Moscow and elsewhere, requesting that they interview and monitor a number of Captain Mizinchikov's relatives. We are especially interested in one Alexei Ivanovich Zahlebinin, a cousin of Mizinchikov's with whom he is on particularly friendly terms. This Zahlebinin denies having seen him so far and has given assurances that he will report his cousin's appearance, should it occur. I trust the police surveillance of Mizinchikov's St Petersburg associates continues?'

'Yes, of course.'

'It would greatly assist us also if we were able to take a meaningful statement from Aglaia Filippovna.'

'Do you think she witnessed her sister's murder?'

'That would certainly account for the extremity of her reaction to it.'

'Am I to take it that you regard her reaction as excessive, Porfiry Petrovich?'

'Who can say? Grief takes many forms. And it was certainly an excessive crime.'

'We should not be surprised that it has wrought such destruction on a delicate feminine constitution.'

Porfiry looked at his friend sharply. 'Are you implying that her constitution must necessarily be delicate because it is feminine? Feminine *ergo* delicate?'

Nikodim Fomich became momentarily flustered. 'I, well . . . is that not the case, Porfiry Petrovich? I mean, are women no longer delicate? Is that then the resolution of the woman question?'

'Surely you and I have encountered, in the pursuit of our duties, women whose constitutions, and indeed sensibilities, are very far from delicate.'

'But look at the severity of Aglaia Filippovna's collapse . . . Surely that is in itself a cogent argument for the delicacy of her constitution.'

'I believe that is known in logic as a circular argument.'

'I don't know anything about that. At any rate, news has reached me of a communiqué from the very highest quarters. As a result of which, the Prefect of Police is keenly desirous that progress should be made. To put it bluntly, Porfiry Petrovich, he is looking for an arrest.'

'*Gr-ahh!* I am afraid my hand is beginning to throb most vehemently. I believe I have some dandelion lotion in my apartment. You will forgive me, Nikodim Fomich, while I administer to my injury.'

'Are you by any chance running away from this conversation, Porfiry Petrovich? I shall await your return.'

*

When Porfiry returned to his chambers, holding aloft an untidily bandaged hand, he found that Nikodim Fomich had been joined by the police clerk Zamyotov.

'There is someone to see you. A young lady. She does not have an appointment. However, she insists that she is a friend of yours.' Zamyotov tilted his head back in a display of scepticism.

'A claim which we may easily verify, Alexander Grigorevich. Please show her in.'

Nikodim Fomich raised both eyebrows enquiringly and watched the door with interest. A moment later, Maria Petrovna came through it.

Porfiry was aware of Nikodim Fomich watching him closely as he greeted the young lady, which made his welcome more stilted than it otherwise might have been. He sensed an unexpected coldness in Maria Petrovna, as if she too felt similarly constrained. He craved her gaze, just a flash of her brilliant eyes in his direction, for him alone, but she withheld it. He wondered if it was not so much the presence of Nikodim Fomich as the recollection of how they had parted, and with what emotion, that inhibited her.

He saw that she held a copy of the *St Petersburg Gazette*, which seemed to act as a further constraint on her. She appeared uncertain what to do with it, yet it was clear that she had brought it with some purpose. She cast sharp, almost wary glances at Nikodim Fomich as she fumbled with it.

Porfiry was attuned to her unease. 'May I introduce Nikodim Fomich, Chief Superintendent of the Haymarket District Police Bureau.'

'Pleased to meet you, Nikodim Fomich. Perhaps you know my father, Pyotr Afanasevich Verkhotsev?'

'Our two departments from time to time engage in joint endeavours.' An edge of wariness crept into Nikodim Fomich's usually affable tone.

Maria Petrovna relaxed enough to smile. 'And the rest of the time, regard one another with mutual suspicion. I know how it is.'

'Not at all!' But Nikodim Fomich's uneasy smile belied his words.

'Please sit down, Maria Petrovna.' Porfiry gestured with his damaged hand towards the brown sofa. 'Perhaps you would care for some tea?'

Maria Petrovna did not sit down. 'No, thank you. I did not come here for tea.'

Porfiry absorbed her abruptness with a pained smile. 'Nikodim Fomich?'

'As you have gone to so much trouble, I will take a glass with you.'

Porfiry looked uncertainly at the samovar. 'Ah. I seem to have forgotten something.'

'What?'

'The tea liquor. Zakhar always took care of such things.'

'Please, Porfiry Petrovich, do not trouble yourself any further.'

'It will only take a moment.'

'No, no. You must attend to your guest . . .'

Porfiry hesitated. Then bowing stiffly to Maria, he said: 'You have remembered something concerning Yelena Filippovna?'

'It is not that.' Maria's voice hardened with remembered grievance. But her eyes tracked his bandaged hand and she frowned. 'You have hurt yourself?'

'It is nothing.' Porfiry could not keep a small flicker of pleasure from his lips. Neither could he resist a proud, vindicated glance at Nikodim Fomich. He was somewhat put out, however, by the carelessness with which Maria accepted his demurral.

'Have you seen the *Gazette*?' She thrust the paper forward. The hardened, unmistakably aggressive tone had returned to her voice. 'Yelena Filippovna's murder is turning you into something of a celebrity, Porfiry Petrovich.'

'That's hardly fair, Maria Petrovna. Nikodim Fomich and I were just talking about the newspaper reports. They are far from flattering. Was I not charged with *bumbling incompetence*?'

'No, that was me,' said Nikodim Fomich. 'You were *ineffectual*. Really, these journalists . . .'

'Thank you, Nikodim Fomich. I confess I only glanced at the piece. However, such articles are helpful when we are trying to locate a suspect. They serve to alert the public. After all, the Gazette is extremely widely read. There is a description of Captain Mizinchikov, I believe? And do we not also call for him to give himself up? All that is standard procedure in such cases.'

'You are also quoted as saying that you are. . .' Maria Petrovna scanned the front page to read in an accusatory tone, '*devoting all my energies to the single imperative of finding Miss Polenova's murderer.*'

Porfiry blinked uncertainly. His mouth contracted into a questioning shape. 'Is that not what you would have me do? I understood she was your friend.'

'And what of Mitka?' Her voice rose sharply in pitch. 'Can you tell me how your enquiries into Mitka's disappearance are progressing? Will you, I wonder, have energy remaining to devote to that?'

'Who is Mitka?' asked Nikodim Fomich.

'I see you have not even deemed it necessary to discuss the case with the Chief Superintendent.'

'Forgive me, Maria Petrovna. The murder of Yelena Filippovna has proven unusually distracting, I admit. And a murder is necessarily given precedence over a missing persons case. The presence of a dead body does have a galvanising effect on policemen.'

'Particularly when it is the body of a beautiful woman with society connections,' said Maria bitterly.

'Hers was a conspicuous death, certainly,' said Porfiry. 'There is considerable pressure on us to bring the case to a swift and satisfactory conclusion. A killer is at large.'

'And how many more children will have to go missing before you take Mitka's disappearance seriously?'

'I repeat, who is Mitka?'

'Mitka is a boy,' said Porfiry, 'a factory worker and a pupil at Maria Petrovna's school. He has gone missing. He is one of several children from the school to have gone missing. Maria Petrovna fears that the children may have come to some harm.'

'I see,' said Nikodim Fomich. 'Then we must look into it. Have you discussed the case with Prokuror Liputin?'

'I intend to raise it at our next meeting.'

'I am glad to hear it, Porfiry Petrovich. As a father, crimes against children trouble me greatly.'

'With respect, Nikodim Fomich, we have yet to determine for certain that a crime has been committed. You know how it is with missing persons.'

'Nevertheless, as agents of the state, we stand *in loco parentis* to all the children of the empire.'

'You do not need to remind me, Nikodim Fomich.'

'So,' insisted Maria Petrovna. 'What do you intend to do about it?'

'Well, Nikodim Fomich?' said Porfiry. 'Whom can we spare, bearing in mind the Prefect of Police's exhortation?'

'What about Pavel Pavlovich?' put in Maria. 'I feel sure that if you were to assign him to this investigation, he would pursue it with the greatest of diligence.'

Nikodim Fomich considered the suggestion. 'Of course, it's not for me to say. He does not work under my authority. What say you, Porfiry Petrovich?'

'Yes, by all means.' Porfiry's answer came distractedly. There was a hesitant catch in his voice.

'You will direct him, of course,' said Nikodim Fomich, as if to appease him.

Porfiry Petrovich appeared not to have heard. He was lost in an extended fit of blinking, at the end of which he flashed the mildest of recriminatory glances towards Maria Petrovna. He could not deny that he was disappointed she had not asked for him.

*

WANTED: EXPERIENCED AND DISCREET MANSERVANT FOR SOLITARY GENTLEMAN. APPLY IN WRITING TO CHIEF CLERK, DEPARTMENT FOR THE INVESTIGATION OF CRIMINAL CAUSES, HAYMARKET DISTRICT POLICE BUREAU, STOLYARNY LANE. REFERENCES REQUIRED.

'What is this?'

'The wording,' said Alexander Grigorevich Zamyotov, with his accustomed terseness.

'What wording?'

Zamyotov sighed heavily as he snatched the slip of paper back from Porfiry. 'The wording for the advertisement that is to run in the *St Petersburg Gazette*. Situations Vacant. Domestics, Male. Nikodim Fomich authorised me to place it. He says that it is widely read, even if it is written by kikes. And he asked me to solicit your approval of the wording.'

'Nikodim Fomich said nothing of any advertisement to me.'

Zamyotov's eyes bobbed upwards, just stopping short of rolling.

'May I see it again?'

Zamyotov clicked his tongue and handed the paper back.

'I fail to understand why you have so particularly described me as a *solitary* gentleman.'

'It is to assure the applicant that his duties will not be onerous. You are not married. You do not have a family. You are one, single, solitary individual. The needs of a solitary gentleman are necessarily rather more limited than those of a family man.'

'Why is it necessary to give this assurance? Are we not thereby likely to attract lazier applicants?'

'You do not want to put people off.'

'But *solitary?*'

'It describes your situation accurately, I think.'

'I see.' Porfiry handed the paper back forlornly. 'When will the advertisement appear?'

'If you approve the wording, I will take it to the newspaper office myself today and it will run in tomorrow's edition. Nikodim Fomich is keen to find a suitable person as soon as possible. He is concerned that your unsettled domestic arrangements are distracting you from the efficient execution of your official duties.'

'He has said nothing of the sort to me.'

'I take it you are satisfied with the wording?'

'Delete solitary.'

Zamyotov sucked air through his teeth. 'If you insist.'

'I do.'

'Will you wish to interview the applicants?'

'I am far too busy for that. I shall leave it to you. I will meet with your selected candidate and, provided he meets my approval, the position shall be his.' Turning his attention to a case file, Porfiry added in an undertone: 'How difficult can it be to hire a servant?'

Zamyotov tilted his head into a look of affront, then turned sharply out of the room.

16

The factory children

The gatekeeper at the Nevsky Cotton-Spinning Factory deflected Virginsky's enquiries with an impervious shrug. His eyes carefully avoided the young magistrate's, though there was no doubt he took in everything about his interlocutor with a sly, sidelong watchfulness. He was inordinately preoccupied in tending the precarious glimmer of his clay pipe, with which he produced industrial quantities of pungent smoke. It was as if he saw this as the foremost of his duties, from which he could not be distracted, and for which he was confident of a handsome reward. He stood in the wooden lodge at the entrance to the yard, possessing it with a wide stance and a portly, padded body; behind him, a number of massive keys were hung on numbered hooks, their weight and scale attesting to the importance of his office. His head was sunk low into the collar of his great coat, as if it was making ready to withdraw completely into the worsted carapace should the questioning get too sticky.

All of a sudden, for no reason, he gave a high, wheezing laugh, devoid of humour. 'Yes, I know that one. But you won't find him around here, *your honour*.' He gave the respectful address an unnecessary emphasis. His eyes glinted coldly. 'He's done a bunk, has that one.'

'Thank you. I am aware that Mitka has gone missing. I'm

trying to ascertain what has become of him. When was the last time you saw him?'

'The last time I saw him? There's no good asking me a question like that! How can I be expected to know when the last time I saw him was? Though I can remember the first day I didn't see him.' The gatekeeper's high-pitched laughter broke down into a fit of coughing. Tears of delight at his own wit trickled from his eyes.

'Very well, tell me about the first day you did not see him,' said Virginsky flatly.

'It was a foggy day, you see. Or rather, you didn't see. I didn't see no one, hardly, that day.' After a long pause, the gatekeeper added, his sarcasm not in doubt this time: 'Your honour.'

'A foggy day. Very droll. But the date? Can you remember the date?'

'I couldn't see my hand in front of my face so there was no chance seeing the almanac.'

'Approximately how long ago would this have been? A week, two weeks, one month?'

'Yes, that's right, your honour. A week, two weeks, one month.'

'I have to tell you that your answers are not at all helpful.'

'I'm not too keen on your questions, if it comes to that.'

'A child has gone missing. Are you not concerned to help us find him?'

'That one's no concern of mine. I knew he would come to no good.'

'Why do you say that? Was he a trouble-maker?'

'He had the makings of being a trouble-maker, let's put it like that. He was filling his head with nonsense, that's what he was doing.'

'You're talking about the school he was attending?'

'What need had he to attend school? What good would it do *him*?'

As he considered the question, Virginsky looked away from the gatekeeper, towards the towering presence of the factory. The day's light was crystal-sharp, and in its stark autumnal glare, the factory's most oppressive aspect was revealed to be its drabness. It seemed to absorb whatever light was cast upon it with a sullen greed, giving nothing back, only the dense dark smoke puffing relentlessly from its chimneys. Virginsky found his answer in the prospect. 'What good, do you say? It might get him away from this place.'

'Well then, what's the fuss about, your honour? I mean to say, if the point of book-learning was to get him away from here, then it seems to have succeeded tremendously.'

'You're a clever fellow.'

'Yes, and I haven't had no book learning. I picked it all up myself.'

'I congratulate you.'

The gatekeeper grinned complacently.

'Where exactly was Mitka employed in the factory?'

'He worked for Oleg Sergeevich.'

'Who is this Oleg Sergeevich?'

'Ustyantsev. The spinner.'

'And where will I find this spinner Ustyantsev?'

'In the spinning-shop, I should think.'

'Will you take me there?'

'I cannot leave my post.' The gatekeeper sucked self-importantly on his pipe, to remind Virginsky of the vital work he had to do there.

'I shall make it worth your while.'

'If I leave my post I shall lose my post, and nothing you can give me will make that worth my while. You'll have no trouble finding Oleg Sergeevich. Everybody knows him. Mind, I would warn you that he will not take kindly to your intrusion. Oleg Sergeevich is a piece worker. He won't appreciate you taking him away from his work, not unless you intend to compensate him.'

'It is his civic duty to talk to me, as it is yours.'

'If you rely on that, then I wish you luck.' The gatekeeper at last granted Virginsky the privilege of his gaze. His eyes were narrowed almost to points, as if he were squeezing the life out of whatever vision came into them.

*

What struck Virginsky first was the noise. It was a resistant force that he had to walk into and through; it possessed and defined the room he had entered far more than anything else in it. There was a raw energy to it. It attacked his ears, took over his body, and drowned out all his other senses. The machines screeched like angry demons, their spinning parts whirling with the frenzy of the possessed.

The agitation of production was everywhere: the particles of white dust that filled the hot air danced and trembled in its vibrations; in fact, it was easy to believe they were particles of noise.

The rows of machines, mysterious in their purpose, solemnly tended by their human ministers, daunted him. This was a world he had not glimpsed before. That so much energy and unswerving concentration, so much hard metal and speed, should go into the production of fine cotton thread, was somehow both inspiring and shaming. He had the sense that he was staring into the future. He felt it drain the hope from his heart at the same time as he acknowledged its allure.

A man in a checked suit and bowler hat, evidently some kind of foreman, shouted something incomprehensible into Virginsky's face. Virginsky shouted back the name Ustyantsev. The foreman replied with further shouts. It was a moment before Virginsky realised he was being asked, in bad Russian, 'Who are you?'

He shouted back, 'Magistrate.'

He was led between two rows of clattering machinery, some parts of which were pent with such violent force that it seemed that they would fly apart at any moment; or that the whole suite of machines would break loose from the bolts that fixed them to the floor and spin like massive seed pods into the air, to disseminate their monstrous din.

The man he was led to was dressed in a loose white shirt, with a garishly patterned waistcoat open over it. He wore his hair long, swept back from a face that could have been aristocratic, for all the arrogance of his expression. He was slowly walking a moveable frame of spinning bobbins away from a squatting, thread-spewing bulk, with the patience of a man leading an animal. There was a yelled conference between the foreman and the spinner, the details of which were lost to Virginsky. The outcome was a dark, suspicious glance in his direction.

An upward nod from the foreman invited Virginsky to draw near.

'Ustyantsev?' shouted Virginsky.

The man walking the frame confirmed his identity with the most minimal of nods, his eyes darting all the time along the lines of thread stretched across the widening jaws of the machine.

'Can you stop the machine?' Virginsky pointed at his ears and gave a wince of distress. His request and the gesture went ignored. 'I need to talk.' He nodded energetically. 'And hear!'

The spinner gave a shrug that indicated eloquently how little this concerned him.

'Mitka,' shouted Virginsky, stepping backwards to keep pace with the spinner's progress. 'You know Mitka?'

'Mitka's gone.' The spinner's reply was clear enough.

'What happened?'

'Let me down, the bastard.'

'Let you down? How?'

'Ran off.'

'Where? Where'd he go?'

Ustyantsev shook his head, his mouth set in a non-committal down-turn. 'Dunno.'

'Any ideas?'

The moving frame clanked as it reached the outward extent of its track. There was a slight lull in the noise of the machine, or at least a modulation of its frequency which seemed to hold out the promise of a more sustained conversation. However, Virginsky was distracted by the appearance of a small boy who darted out from under the vast skein of threads. Ustyantsev launched himself at the boy and landed a heavy blow across the side of the head. His face as he returned to the frame was defiant and grim.

'Why did you do that?' demanded Virginsky.

'Keeps them on their toes.'

'Do you not consider that they might work with more enthusiasm and effectiveness if you treated them more kindly?'

Ustyantsev's expression was one of brutish incomprehension.

'You are a working man yourself. Does it not shame you to oppress your fellow labourers? Especially as they are children?'

'How dare you call me a labourer? I am a spinner, I'll have you know.' Ustyantsev's affront was genuine.

'Can I speak to the boy?'

'The boy?'

Virginsky looked around but the boy had disappeared.

'Be my guest,' said Ustyantsev with a malicious grin.

'Will you call him out?'

'No.'

'You expect me to get in there?'

'He's not in there. He's in this one now.' Ustyantsev turned to the machine opposite. 'Mark you, if you distract him from his work and a single thread wants tying, I shall beat him mercilessly. And you shall not stop me.'

'I see. Very well. In that case, I shall wait till the end of his shift.'

'You'll have a long wait.' Ustyantsev turned his back on Virginsky and began to open the machine up. The noise, once again, was deafening.

*

By the time the whistle blast heralded the end of the morning shift, Virginsky's legs were aching. His throat and lungs were clogged with cotton dust. A film of sweat lay between his skin and his underclothes. He was worn out and he had done nothing but stand and wait. To be fair, he had not been entirely idle. He had been monitoring the abuses perpetrated by the spinner against the boys in his employ, entering the number and severity of assaults into a notebook. This had failed to inhibit Ustyantsev. Far from it: as soon as he noticed what Virginsky was about, he seemed to increase the frequency of his attacks, flaunting his brutality with a perverse pride. It even occurred to Virginsky that the spinner might be acting in the misguided belief that he would gain his approval by such displays.

Released by the whistle, the boys came out from under the machines as dazed and hesitant as uncaged rats. Habituated to hold themselves hunched, and to walk with a flinching gait, they readied themselves for further blows. None came. It seemed that Ustyantsev refrained from such exertions during his lunch break.

Virginsky beckoned to the boy he had spotted earlier. The boy shied away with an instinctive suspicion of authority, deferring instead to Ustyantsev. The spinner tilted his head in a minute gesture of permission. With a heavy shuffle, and head bowed, the boy presented himself to Virginsky.

'What's your name, son?'

'Pasha.'

'I am Pasha too! Pleased to meet you, Pasha.' Virginsky shook hands with the boy. He flashed a glance towards Ustyantsev, who was watching them with a sullen glower. 'He treats you pretty roughly, that fellow.'

'Mr Ustyantsev's a good boss.'

'Good?'

'There's worse.'

'I dare say, but . . .'

The boy looked up, his eyes wide with questions. Then a weight of disappointment settled on him, bowing his head back down. He had looked for something in Virginsky and not found it.

'Do you know Mitka? The boy who used to work here?'

'He's gone.'

'Yes, I know. Do you have any idea where he might be?'

The boy shrugged and shifted his feet unhappily. 'Please, sir.'

'Yes?'

'I have to go now. I'll miss my lunch.'

'Can I come with you?'

Puzzlement rippled across the boy's face.

'I wouldn't want you to miss your lunch.'

'There won't be none for you.'

'That's all right. I . . . don't want to eat anything. I just want to talk to you, and perhaps some of the other children.'

'I only have half an hour.'

'We'd better go then.'

The boy's eyes widened in alarm, as his confusion spiked into fear. He looked Virginsky up and down uneasily.

'There's no need to be afraid. I'm a magistrate. Do you know what a magistrate is?'

The boy shook his head forlornly.

'It's a gentleman who looks into things. At this present moment I am looking into why Mitka disappeared and where he might have gone. I need you to help me.'

'I shall have to ask Granny Kvasova.'

'Who is Granny Kvasova?'

'She looks after us at the 'prentice house.'

'Well, that's very good of her. She sounds like an excellent woman. May I meet her?'

The boy nodded, the twist of a smile at last flickering onto his lips. 'She gives us our lunch.'

'Well, what are we waiting for? Lead the way, my friend.'

The boy's shrug took Virginsky back to his childhood. He had seen precisely such a shrug animate the shoulders of his school friends when he was Pasha's age, and had felt its jounce in his own. It was a shrug of fellowship and good humour, a shrug of acceptance and understanding. It was the way you met a world you little understood and were powerless to control, not so much a gesture of indifference or resignation, as a recognition of kinship. He smiled as he followed Pasha through the factory.

Around them the machines idled like predatory beasts feeding. It would not be long before their hunger for production was re-awakened.

'Was Mitka your friend?'

The same shrug jerked Pasha's shoulders and Virginsky realised that there was another aspect to it that he had not acknowledged: it was a way of expressing things for which the child had no words, that perhaps would always remain beyond words. But it was capable of nuances even so, almost as much as any verbal language.

'Did you go to the school with him? You know that Mitka went to school?'

Pasha shook his head fiercely. 'Granny Kvasova told us that Satan would get us if we went to that school.'

'I can assure you that that's not true.'

'She says the lady teacher is a witch who consorts with the devil.'

'Does she indeed? Well, I know the lady teacher and I can tell you she's not a witch.'

Pasha looked unconvinced. 'Did Satan get Mitka? Granny Kvasova says he did. She says the lady teacher lay with Mitka and then fed him to Satan, her husband.'

'That really is the most outrageous lie!' cried Virginsky. 'You don't believe her, do you?'

The shrug now had a different meaning. It seemed steeped in wilful ignorance and left Virginsky depressed.

*

The apprentice house was a low, brick-built outhouse, on the other side of the yard but still within the precincts of the factory and beneath its sprawling shadow.

So this had been Mitka's home, thought Virginsky as he crossed the threshold. They entered through the canteen, a large open room arrayed with benches, the air thick with the vinegary smell of cabbage soup. The floor was bare, the boards gaping and grubby, soft wood crumbling away; walls of white-washed brick.

Pasha's face fell immediately. The other children, about fifty in number, of varying ages, were already seated, clustered around a series of communal bowls from which they spooned their meagre nourishment with competitive haste. He dashed away from Virginsky and forced his way into a circle of backs. His intrusion was not resisted, merely met with distracted resentment. Virginsky knew he had lost him.

A settled stupor possessed the diners, though whether of exhaustion or hunger – or both – Virginsky could not say. No one spoke. The clatter of cutlery was eloquent enough. There was none of the wheeling liveliness and laughter that is usually found when children congregate. They spooned the soup into their mouths with determined concentration, the same kind of concentration they applied to their tasks in the factory.

None of the children paid him any attention, though his presence was noted by the one adult in the room, a bonneted woman with the scrawny head of a turkey, who stood guard over the children. She wiped her palms combatatively on a filthy apron and began to move in his direction.

Virginsky gave a distant bow and stepped forward to meet her halfway. 'You must be Granny Kvasova. Pasha told me all about you.'

The woman gave him a sharp look that set her dewlap trembling. 'And who might you be?' Her voice was high and piercing.

'I am Pavel Pavlovich Virginsky. A magistrate. I am investigating the disappearance of a boy who was until recently employed at the factory, and indeed may still be considered an employee. Dmitri Krasotkin. I presume you know him?'

'You had better speak to Oleg Sergeevich about him. Mitka worked for Oleg Sergeevich.'

'Yes, I am aware of that. I have already interviewed that gentleman. I wish to speak to you now. Mitka lived here at the apprentice house?'

Granny Kvasova's head twitched in what may have been a nod of assent.

'Under your care?'

'That's right.'

'It's a lot of children for one person to look after.'

'I have help. But they ain't too bad. They're good children. Always behave themselves.'

Virginsky glanced around. 'They seem too exhausted to do otherwise. Were you not concerned when Mitka went missing?'

'He always was a wilful one.'

'Did you report his disappearance to the factory management?'

'I told Oleg Sergeevich.'

'And the police?'

'The police have better things to do than chase runaways.'

'Runaways? The boy was not a slave here, I hope. He was free to leave.'

'Exactly. He was free to leave. And he did.'

'Were you not afraid for his safety?'

'I dare say he can look after himself.'

'Why did you spread malicious rumours about the young gentlewoman who runs the school Mitka attended?'

'Malicious? Who says they're malicious?'

'You called her a witch, I believe.'

'She came round here, poking her nose where it wasn't wanted. I could see right through her. Godless and depraved, she is. That's why she was after Mitka. She likes them young.'

'Are you aware there are laws to protect people from such slander?'

'Slander, is it?' The woman's voice rose to a pitch at the limit of human hearing. 'I saw the way she looked at the children. Licking her lips. I sent her packing, I can tell you.'

'I advise you to curtail such vile allegations or you may find yourself in deep trouble.'

Granny Kvasova's face contracted in distaste. However, she seemed to take in Virginsky's threat. She calmed down enough for her voice to drop several tones to a more comfortable register. 'A friend of hers, are you?'

Virginsky noted the malice in her cold eyes. 'I am here as a magistrate, on official business.' He looked about him dismissively. 'This place . . . what kind of a home life do you provide the children here?'

'It's a roof over their heads, warm grub in their bellies. A bed to sleep in.'

'Where do they sleep?'

'You want to see their beds, do you?' There was something unspeakably disgusting about the intonation with which she managed to invest the question.

Virginsky looked away from the woman, suppressing an impulse to strike her. The children were beginning to rise from their hurried meal. 'I repeat, I am a magistrate. I am investigating the disappearance of a child who was in your care. The more I can learn about his life before he went missing, the better our chances of finding him.'

'I don't see how looking at his bed will help.'

'I have not come here to discuss my methods with you, old woman. Show me where he slept, before I haul you in and charge you with obstructing a magistrate in the execution of his duties.'

'There's nothing much to see, I tell you,' said Granny Kvasova, undaunted.

'Nevertheless,' insisted Virginsky.

The children were now filing out to return to work, each one enclosed in his or her own morose silence. They were not like children, but like shrunken adults, already worn down and defeated by the treadmill of their existence. What was most shocking to Virginsky was the blankness of their expressions. He saw no trace of the outrage or horror that they should by rights have displayed at the prospect of the afternoon ahead of them. In one or two, perhaps, there was a look of puzzled awe, as if they were struggling to comprehend the mystery of their lives. But that may simply have been the expression their faces naturally fell into when they were exhausted.

'You will show me the sleeping quarters. Now.'

Granny Kvasova clicked her tongue and took her time. She led Virginsky through a door in the side wall of the canteen, directly into a dormitory. The beds, such as they were, consisted of a series of long wooden platforms, subdivided by partitions. Each of the sleeping booths created by this arrangement was numbered, and furnished with a coarse grey blanket. As there was no space separating each 'bed' from its neighbour, the children had nowhere to put any personal belongings. Indeed, it seemed doubtful that they possessed any. Worse still, there was no space for them to simply be. No chairs to sit in. No floor to play on. The room was severely purposed. You came into it, found your booth, and fell into it to sleep the sleep of the physically exhausted.

It was cold but airless. The accumulated smells of humanity, or their ghosts, stirred resentfully at this unwonted daytime intrusion.

'Which was Mitka's bed?'

'What difference does it make? Someone else has it now.'

'He has been replaced?'

'Of course.'

'Even so, show me where he slept.'

Granny Kvasova approached one of the booths and bowed grimly at it. Virginsky rubbed his chin as he contemplated the empty space. In truth, he did not know what he was looking for. He wondered what Porfiry Petrovich would do, without reaching any definite conclusion. He realised he had only insisted on seeing the bed because he had been goaded by the old woman's obstructiveness.

He tried to imagine Mitka curled up on the bed. Of course, he had no idea what Mitka looked like. Instead, an image of

Pasha, the boy he had spoken to that morning, flashed momentarily before him.

'Are all the children who live here orphans?'

'Yes, we get them from the Foundling Hospital.'

The woman spoke of them as if they were a commodity, just another raw material to be processed in the factory.

'What kind of a life is this for children?'

'It's not so bad. It keeps them out of trouble. How would they live if they were not here? Ask yourself that. By thieving and whoring, you can be sure.'

'Not if they were educated.'

'Educated! A lot of good it did Mitka!'

'Why do you say that? Do you know what became of him? And no more of your scandalous lies, madam.'

'Dead in a ditch, I shouldn't wonder. That boy doesn't have the sense to keep himself from falling in the canal. He wouldn't survive a day outside here.'

'Perhaps not. Perhaps he preferred one day of freedom to a lifetime of this.'

'If that's what her school taught him then it did him no favours.'

Virginsky continued to stare at the tiny space allocated to Mitka to sleep in. Even the boy's dreams, it seemed, had been confined and restricted.

'Have you seen enough?' squealed Granny Kvasova. 'Do you know where to find him now?' she added sarcastically.

Virginsky shook his head. 'At least I know what he ran from.'

17

The beggar's song

The following day a sluggish grey fog hung deliberately in the air, as if generated by the city to impede his investigation. Virginsky kept his head bowed as he burrowed into it. The moisture took possession of the urban spaces, forcing the human inhabitants off the streets. It brought with it a sense of spreading hopelessness. The squares and broader avenues were desolate because of it.

He began with the hospitals. There were three children's hospitals in St Petersburg, the Elizaveta, the Nikolai and the recently completed Prince of Oldenburg's. The Nikolai was the closest to the bureau, with the Elizaveta about one and a half *versts* further on along the Fontanka, on the opposite side of the river. Midway between those was the Alexander Municipal Hospital, at which he also made enquiries. The Prince of Oldenburg's Hospital was a long trudge east, on Ligovsky Prospekt in the Liteynaya District, at the far end of Nevsky Prospekt.

None of the hospitals he visited had any record of admitting a boy called Dmitri Krasotkin, or any child of Mitka's age or description, on or around the estimated date of Mitka's disappearance.

Virginsky stood on the top step at the entrance to the Prince of Oldenburg's Hospital, somehow built as a neo-classical palace; its architect had obviously been more intent on asserting his patron's nobility than serving the function of the building. But the pungent chemical smell that still lingered in Virginsky's nostrils suggested that its doctors were familiar with the latest developments in surgical cleanliness.

The fog was as impenetrable as a gauze bandage around his eyes.

As so often with Virginsky, his emotions expressed themselves in thoughts of a vaguely political cast. His frustration led him to conclude that the very names of the hospitals served to remind the sick how much they owed to their imperial and aristocratic benefactors; so that the practice of philanthropy was seen to be just another weapon in the armoury of oppression. Medical care was in the gift of the autocrat and his friends. And instead of justified rage, this stirred a craven gratitude.

He had learnt to keep such thoughts to himself. But now, as the cold fog smothered him in its obscurity, he felt emboldened to cry out: 'Sweep them all away!' He accompanied the cry with an appropriate sweep of his arm, unseen by anyone but himself. Almost immediately, after only a single pulse of numb silence, the low rumbling throb of male laughter came back at him. Virginsky felt his face flush, even though there was no reason to assume the laughter had been directed at him.

He strained to listen and peered into the soft grey fuzz that filled the air. The laughter gave way to singing, or rather a tuneless baritone drone: 'Save your soul. Give alms to save your soul. Pity a poor sightless sinner. I'll pray for your soul if you give me a crust. If you haven't a crust, I'll settle for a kopek. If you haven't a kopek, I'll settle for a rouble. If you have no rouble, gold will do. Give alms to save your soul.'

At first, the voice was right beside him, as though the singer was chanting the words directly into his ear. But he realised that that was just a trick of the fog. The beggar was ahead of him, below, on the street.

With every step down he had the sense that he was stepping off the edge of a cliff into nothing.

'I lost my sight in the service of the Tsar. God save the Tsar! God save his soul. I pray for the souls of all who give alms. Heaven awaits those who give alms.'

As Virginsky moved towards the voice, he saw a soft white figure through the drifting mist. As he approached, the details of the man's appearance became clearer. He was dressed, Virginsky realised with a flash of astonishment, in a white tunic, half of a Guards officer's dress uniform. The tunic was grubby now; even so, Virginsky saw the rust-coloured stains, now muted by the layers of filth over them. Virginsky looked into the man's face. It too was filthy, but for all that, it was a surprisingly handsome face, or once had been: the remnants of his looks were being swallowed up by the bloated effects of dissolution. He could have been aged anywhere between forty and sixty. His hair was long and matted. His eyes oscillated wildly in their sockets, searching desperately for a point of focus in their darkness.

'You there!' Virginsky held out an arm to catch hold of the man as he ran towards him. He could have sworn the beggar looked straight at him. His eyes were strangely compelling – enough so to give Virginsky pause as he closed in on him. In that moment, the beggar turned on his heels and broke into a run. Virginsky's hand grasped the mist.

Virginsky gave chase. He kept his eyes fixed on the tunic, which appeared strangely insubstantial. It flickered in and out of focus, subject to the shifting density of the fog. As Virginsky closed the gap between them, the tunic gained solidity, almost within his grasp now. The other man seemed to stumble. Then suddenly the flash of white flew up into the fog-filled air, like a kite snapped up on the wind. For an instant, Virginsky half-believed the beggar had taken wing. He came to a halt and craned his head. Something white plummeted out of the infinite greyness, as if regurgitated. It fell flat onto the pavement, a sprawl of fabric.

Virginsky bent down to retrieve the discarded officer's tunic.

18

The fourth Robert

Prince Naryskin surveyed the interior of the bank with a proprietorial gaze. He nodded approvingly at the artworks hung on the walls. A huge canvas depicting classical ruins in a romantic landscape caught his eye, provoking an onset of aesthetic salivation. He recognised it as the work of Hubert Robert, and believed it would go well with three similar paintings by the same artist in his possession (albeit purchased with money he had borrowed from this very bank). The painting before him showed the skeletal structure of a dilapidated amphitheatre, golden in the light of a dying sun. The few isolated human figures were dwarfed by the great stone remains, which stood to remind them of the vanity of human ambition. It answered his soul's craving for an irrevocable solitude. Sometimes he believed that it was only the presence of other people, with their inconvenient desires and clamorous demands, that prevented him from being happy.

At any rate, the room was so in keeping with his taste that it seemed almost to be an annexe to his palace on the Fontanka.

Perhaps his satisfaction was premature, as he had not yet signed the papers that would make him a director of the bank, adding the name Naryskin to those of Bakhmutov and von Lembke. He made a mental note: it would be better for all if it simply became known as the Naryskin Bank. What was the point of bringing in a genuine Russian aristocrat if they did not then exploit the association to the full? However, it was certainly a more pleasant sensation to enter the bank as a prospective director rather than in the humiliating position of a spendthrift in need of funds.

Prince Naryskin looked with less approval on the pink-cheeked young man approaching him with a fawning smile. He recognised him as the one on whom Bakhmutov had attempted to settle Yelena. It struck him as an insult that Bakhmutov had sent this individual to greet him; but then again, Bakhmutov's own person was hardly more pleasing to him.

'Your Excellency, Ivan Iakovich and Baron von Lembke await you in the boardroom. May I take your hat and coat?'

Prince Naryskin did not deign to look at the young man. He handed over his beaver and allowed his velvet top-coat, trimmed with a sable collar, to be peeled from him without any acknowledgement of the courtesy.

'This way, Your Excellency.'

*

Prince Naryskin was gratified by the alacrity with which Bakhmutov and von Lembke rose to their feet. The German was puffing on a fat cigar. His eyes narrowed greedily as he took in the prince. An unexpectedly tiny pink tongue lapped out to moisten his lips.

Bakhmutov's posture was more relaxed, though affectedly so. He gave the impression that his suavity was something he could turn on, or off, at will.

'My friend!' Though seemingly casual, and warmly welcoming, his choice of greeting was deliberate and pointed, reminding the prince of Bakhmutov's claims over him. To reinforce this he pulled the prince to him in a prolonged embrace, which von Lembke ogled with a sly grin. Prince Naryskin shuddered as he was held by the banker. The venal toady who had greeted him was bad enough, but to be pawed and petted by this Jew, while the fat German licked his lips as if he were a particularly tasty morsel of bratwurst, was more than he could endure. He would make them pay, that was for sure.

Released from Bakhmutov's grip, Prince Naryskin's agitation was eased by the sight of a bottle of champagne cooling over ice. Next to it, three crystal flutes had been placed in readiness on a silver tray.

Bakhmutov followed the direction of his gaze. 'This is a great day.' He nodded to a waiting lackey. 'We must celebrate.'

The lackey stepped forward, his white-gloved hands grappling with the wire around the neck of the bottle.

Prince Naryskin felt an intense craving for the champagne. Even so, he had the presence of mind to object: 'But we have yet to iron out the details of our arrangement. Perhaps we should postpone the celebrations until everything is agreed to our mutual satisfaction. The devil is in the detail, they say.' His smile snapped into place as he fixed Bakhmutov with a challenging look.

However, the champagne cork popped, and the lackey hastened to catch the foaming spillage in the first of the flutes.

'Prince is right,' barked von Lembke, with his characteristic terseness. 'Detail first.'

'Yes, yes,' said Bakhmutov impatiently. 'However, I am confident we will be able to arrange things in a way that we all will find highly satisfactory. Let us first drink a toast.' He took his glass from the salver and waited for the others to do the same.

'To Prince Nikolai Naryskin, and the great family of Naryskin of which he is the wise and noble head.'

Although they were meant to flatter, Prince Naryskin found the words strangely offensive: impertinent, in fact, coming from Bakhmutov's mouth. 'That's all very well,' said the prince, nevertheless sipping his wine. 'But I have some demands.'

'Demands! My friend!' Bakhmutov beamed, as though in making demands Prince Naryskin was paying him the warmest compliment. 'There is no need to make demands of your friends, when you know that your friends will freely give you everything you desire.' Bakhmutov gestured expansively around him with his free hand. 'This will be yours, all this, your bank, as much as it is ours. How do you like it?'

'It will serve.'

Bakhmutov chortled as if the prince had uttered a great witticism. 'And the paintings! Did you notice the paintings?'

'I did. One in particular . . . a landscape by Robert.'

'I know the one. It is yours! We will have it packed up and taken round to Naryskin Palace this very day. A small token of our measureless esteem.'

'A gift? There will be no strings attached?'

'Merely your signature on the titles we have drawn up.' Bakhmutov indicated some papers on the boardroom table.

'It will certainly go well with the three other works by the same artist that I own already.' But the thought of his Robert collection reminded the prince of less pleasant considerations. 'What of the outstanding debt I owe to the bank? What will become of that?'

'Well, once you are director, it could be said to be a debt you owe to yourself,' said Bakhmutov cheerfully. 'Which is an interesting position to be in.'

'Could it not be cancelled?'

'That is precisely the kind of bold and innovative thinking that we will value once you are signed in as a director,' said Bakhmutov enthusiastically. More cautiously he added: 'It is certainly a possibility. However, as I am sure you will understand, it is something that will have to be put to the board. But as the board consists in us, your friends, I can foresee little to prevent you achieving the outcome you desire.'

'You would do that for me?'

'Why should we not? For I feel sure that you would do the same for us, *your* friends.'

'What do you have in mind?' asked the prince, suspiciously.

'In fact, it would be truer to say that you would be doing it for yourself, because as a director of the bank, whatever is in the bank's interest is in your interest too.'

'What would you have me do?'

Bakhmutov met Prince Naryskin's darkly anxious enquiry with a deflective smile. 'Why discuss it now? This is a celebration. The appropriate time to go into these matters fully will be at the next board meeting. I hope and trust we will have the honour of your attendance.'

Prince Naryskin downed the rest of his champagne. He was not used to drinking in the morning. Something shifted within his perception of the room, a slight swimming of reality. His unease began to lift. He felt the situation simplifying. 'I could have the Robert? It could be hanging in the palace today?' Suddenly it seemed as though that was all that mattered.

*

'And what if he finds out it is a fake?' demanded von Lembke as he and Bakhmutov crossed the foyer of the bank, having seen a decidedly tipsy Prince Naryskin into his carriage. As the painting in question was being lifted from the wall, Bakhmutov paused to study it with a smile of deep satisfaction. He gave no indication of having heard his partner's question.

19

The colours of blood

Dr Pervoyedov stood back from the bench, his gaze fixed on the spectroscopic eyepiece attached to his microscope. A curved brass arm clasped a small circular mirror, as though holding it up for examination. It gave the eyepiece an air of raffish inquisitiveness, which was enhanced by a metal kiss-curl at the top of the instrument's rectangular face. Dr Pervoyedov smiled to himself at the ingenuity of the device. The mirror, and the slit towards which it was directed, allowed a spectrum of natural light to be viewed by the observer along-side the spectrum created by the sample to be inspected, so that any significant discrepancies would be more easily detected.

Outside, the first snow of the season was struggling to distinguish itself in a murky fall of sleet. The natural light in the pathology laboratory of the Obukhovsky Hospital was meagre. To compensate, Dr Pervoyedov had placed a kerosene lamp before a parabolic reflector, to direct light down towards the stage of the microscope.

The material taken from the mirror had dissolved in cold distilled water, which did not rule out its being blood. The scrapings had been brown, consistent with oxidised blood, and the resultant solution had taken on a pale pink colour, the freshness of which again suggested blood. Residues of brown oil-based paint, for example, or dye, would not have reacted in that way. A drop of this solution was now between glass slides held by the frame of the microscope.

Squinting one eye closed, Dr Pervoyedov stooped to place the other against the brass eyepiece. His field of vision was flooded with shimmering strips of colour, contained within an infinite vault of black. There was always something miraculous in the moment when the truth of a theory was revealed in a startling, living experience. White light is made up of all the colours of the spectrum: his mind had always been capable of grasping that fact. But now his soul was bathing in it. He gazed into the vibrant strips of colour, each one both irrefutably bold and tantalisingly insubstantial. The colours existed somewhere he could never reach.

As he adjusted the lens, bringing the bands of colour in and out of focus, he was able to identify the two distinct spectra. The spectrum on the right, cast by the unfiltered light from the mirror, was clear. In the spectrum on the left, two dark bands jumped out at him immediately, one running through the green strip, the other where the green met the yellow. Dr Pervoyedov consulted Chapman's article in the *Lancet* of June, 1863. There was a monochrome figure that endeavoured to represent the seven colours of the spectrum. Two thick black lines cut across the diagram, and although they did not look exactly like the soft-edged bands of negation that he had seen, they were in the same relative positions on the spectrum. This was blood. Arterial blood.

Dr Pervoyedov removed the slide from the microscope stage. He then lifted a test tube containing a thin pinkish solution from a rack. He drew off some of the liquid with a pipette and allowed a drop to fall on to a second glass slide.

This time he saw a single, broader, softer beam of darkness, again cutting across the green band, close to the yellow. He finely adjusted the screw that controlled the lens and the single dark strip separated into two distinct absorption lines with a fuzz of green between them.

The pattern corresponded to a second diagram in Chapman's article. The solution made from the material taken from Yelena Filippovna's ring was also blood, but venous blood, rather than arterial.

Dr Pervoyedov again looked through the spectroscope eyepiece to confirm his interpretation. He had succeeded in giving Porfiry Petrovich what he expected – exactly what he had expected, he shouldn't wonder.

*

'It would have been better, Pavel Pavlovich, if you had brought the man and not the tunic.' Porfiry Petrovich stood at the window of his chambers, looking out at a bleak, sleet-filled sky. He turned to face Virginsky with a woeful expression. 'Or better still, the man *and* the tunic.'

Porfiry lifted his bandaged hand. The dressing was loose and grubby, in places even stained with ink. With his free hand, Porfiry attempted to tighten it, but the cotton strip unravelled in his fumbling fingers. Porfiry shook it loose from his hand, causing a wad of gauze to fall on the floor. He picked this up and examined it. Blowing the dust off, he turned it over and placed it again on his hand. Clasping the end of the bandage with his thumb, he began winding.

Virginsky watched with a mixture of fascination and horror.

Porfiry bound the hand slowly, straining the bandage to keep it taut, and pausing after every turn to check that the dressing was holding its shape. At last he reached the end of the bandage, to which he gave one last sharp tug before folding it under one of the tightly bound edges. As soon as he let go, the dressing returned to its earlier laxity. Porfiry let out a despairing sigh. 'What were we talking about?'

Virginsky said nothing but looked resentfully across at the tunic, which was draped over Porfiry's desk. Even without a Guards officer in it, the article succeeded in attaining a certain swagger.

'Ah yes, the man in the white tunic. Of course, it was not Mizinchikov,' continued Porfiry blithely, again beginning to re-bandage his hand. 'A fugitive from the law – and a deserter to boot – would not draw attention to himself in such a way. Singing for alms, you say?'

'It was not Mizinchikov,' confirmed Virginsky with a display of impatience. 'This man was older than Mizinchikov. And from the look of him, had been living rough for quite some time. Years, I would say. It's strange, beneath the grime, he had surprisingly regular features. In his time, I expect he was capable of cutting quite a figure. He had the face of an actor – of a leading man gone to seed.'

'Really? How interesting. And his hair? What colour was his hair?'

'Difficult to tell. It was very dirty.' Virginsky was staring at Porfiry's dressing as he said this.

'Dark?'

'No. It was the colour of dirty straw.'

'So, an ageing, once good-looking man with blond hair. No, that does not sound like a young officer of the Preobrazhensky Regiment, does it?' Porfiry let out a wheezing chuckle. 'The likelihood is that Captain Mizinchikov exchanged clothes with this beggar soon after making his escape from the Naryskin Palace. We are looking for a beggar, Pavel Pavlovich. Or rather, a Guards officer in a beggar's garb.'

'There is no shortage of beggars in St Petersburg.'

At that moment, the clerk Zamyotov, in his usual manner, barged in without knocking. Virginsky was relieved to have some other object upon which to focus his gaze. 'A communiqué from the Obukhovsky Hospital.' Zamyotov held the buff-coloured envelope out towards Porfiry from the doorway, making no effort to cross the room to hand it to him. Virginsky took it from him and opened it.

'Dr Pervoyedov writes to inform you that the substance taken from the mirror is indeed blood.'

'I see,' said Porfiry, striding from the window to take the letter, his preoccupation with the bandage forgotten. 'Arterial blood, no less. Whereas the blood on the ring is venous.'

'Is that significant?'

Porfiry mimed slashing his own throat. 'Arterial.' He then slapped himself on the face. 'Venous.'

'So the blood on the mirror is hers, most likely. And the blood on the ring is his. Just as we suspected.'

'It would seem so. And now it occurs to me, Pavel Pavlovich, that it would be expedient to have Dr Pervoyedov apply his new contraption to analysing the stains on the front of this tunic.'

'What else could they be but blood?' said Virginsky. 'They certainly look like blood.'

'Do they? Could they not equally be soup? Or rust? Or red wine?'

'No, not red wine,' insisted Virginsky, with almost petulant force. 'That is not the colour of red wine. Neither is it borscht.

And although they are rust-coloured, they could not be rust. Whatever caused these stains was liquid when it hit the tunic. The most likely explanation is blood. But as you say, Dr Pervoyedov will be able to confirm it.'

'Yes. And shall we take bets on whether it is arterial or venous?'

'I am not a gambling man, Porfiry Petrovich,' said Virginsky, his cold disapproval on the edge of self-righteousness.

'Pity.' Porfiry seemed to notice for the first time that Zamyotov was still lurking by the door, like a porter waiting for a tip. 'Was there something else, Alexander Grigorevich?'

'He's here.'

'Who is here?'

'The new man. Your ... *servant*. I have interviewed the applicants. My recommendation is waiting to see you.'

'I see.' Porfiry looked down at the louche, seedy sleeve around his hand. 'Yes. Perhaps now would be as good a time as any to see him.'

Zamyotov was gone from the room before Porfiry had finished the sentence. A moment later, a young man with pomaded hair came in. He was dressed in a respectable enough jacket and clutched a well-brushed black bowler in both hands. One of his eyebrows appeared to be permanently arched, which gave his face an ironic expression. This seemed, however, to be due purely to an unfortunate disposition of features, and could not be held against him. Porfiry made a conscious effort to overlook it. He could not, however, ignore the small nick in the man's left earlobe, evidence of a piercing.

'Good day,' said Porfiry, taking the individual in with a nod. 'And you are?'

The young man was looking around Porfiry's chambers with a quick, hungry eye. When he caught sight of the stained tunic, a jolt of excitement shook his head back perceptibly. Remembering himself, he gave Porfiry an enquiring glance. It was a look to which his asymmetrical eyebrows were especially suited. A moment's thought produced the name: 'Svyatoslav. You may call me Slava.' After a further hesitation, he added, 'Your honour.'

'Slava, very good. Your full name?'

'Svyatoslav Andreevich.'

'Svyatoslav Andreevich – *ye-es*?'

'Svyatoslav Andreevich Tushin.'

'Thank you, Svyatoslav Andreevich. And what experience do you have as a gentleman's gentleman?'

Slava seemed a little taken aback by the question, as if it were the last question he had expected. 'I have given my references to the other one,' he said in some irritation, pointing vaguely out of the door.

'I'm sure they are satisfactory. I merely wished to talk to you about it. To chat, one might say. Your previous employer was . . . ?'

'Count Drozdov.'

'Count Drozdov. A titled gentleman, goodness. I am afraid that working for a lowly public servant such as myself will be something of a step-down for you.'

'I don't mind.'

'That's just as well. And why was your employment with Count Drozdov terminated?'

'He hanged himself. Out of shame. You must have read about it in the *Gazette*?'

'I don't remember.'

'You would have remembered if you'd read it. The account was brilliantly done.'

'I see. One question occurs to me . . .'

'What was he ashamed of?' supplied Slava quickly, his superior eyebrow jumping even higher.

'I have no wish to pry into that.'

'I would have thought that would have been of interest to a man like you.' Slava again cast an eager glance around the room. 'Given your occupation, I mean to say.'

'It is of no interest to me whatsoever. I merely wonder how Count Drozdov was able to supply a reference when . . .' Porfiry allowed the sentence to trail off delicately.

'He wrote it before he did himself in.'

'That was indeed considerate of him. One might even say excessively considerate.'

'I could see the way it was headed. The scandal affected him badly. For a man of honour like that, there was only one way out. I took the liberty of troubling his Excellency for a reference, just in case my suspicions were borne out by events, as sadly they were.'

'And that was very perspicacious of you.'

Slava shrugged. 'And not a moment too soon. I got it off him the very day he put the halter round his neck.'

Porfiry cleared his throat. 'By whom were you employed before Count Drozdov?'

'Before Count Drozdov?'

'Yes.'

'Prince Shch.'

'That is an unusual name.'

'It was not his full name, of course.'

'Would you care to confide his full name?'

'It was a long time ago,' said Slava carelessly.

'And what happened to Prince Shch? Not another suicide, I trust?'

'He died of a wasting disease.'

'How unfortunate. I hope you were able to extract a reference from him before the ultimate moment?'

'The disease took several years to run its course. I was prepared.'

'I confess, I am almost afraid to take you on, Slava. I fear what may become of me. Do you have any former employers who are still with us?'

'Before Prince Shch, I was a waiter. At a well known restaurant near Nevsky Prospekt. It is still in business, I believe, though no one will remember me there now. It was . . .'

'A long time ago, I know,' said Porfiry. 'Now then, do you have any questions of me?'

'Are you any nearer finding Yelena Filippovna's murderer?'

'I meant regarding your employment. I see you are a devoted reader of the *St Petersburg Gazette*.'

'Of course.'

'That aspect of my life will be of no interest to you. You will work for me in a private capacity. Mostly in my apartment, though at times you will be called upon to serve me here in my chambers.'

'I am to be employed, then?'

'It is not yet decided. I thank you for your time. You will be informed of my decision by letter.'

'He said the position was mine, if I wanted it.'

'He?'

'The other one.' Slava repeated the vague hand gesture that went with this designation for Zamyotov.

'We will have to see about that,' said Porfiry dismissively.

Slava made one last effort to win the magistrate round. 'I have some theories of my own, you know,' he said abruptly. At Porfiry's flash of interest, he added enticingly: 'Regarding Yelena Filippovna.'

Porfiry again began to unbind the dressing on his hand. 'How interesting. Perhaps you would share them with us.'

'Porfiry Petrovich!' The objection came from Virginsky. 'This is hardly appropriate.'

Slava crossed to Porfiry. He took the loose end of the bandage from him and pulled it tight. 'In cases like this, one always has to ask, who stands to benefit?'

'*Cui bono?* But who could possibly benefit from the death of a young girl?' Porfiry watched the wrapping take shape around his hand with satisfaction.

'It is well known that the financier Bakhmutov wanted her out of the way. He was prepared to pay his secretary Velchaninov a small fortune to take her off his hands. That fell through because of her quite reasonable scruples. Needless to say, Bakhmutov saw them as unreasonable, and highly inconvenient.'

'But that doesn't make sense. Prince Naryskin was about to marry her. Voluntarily, I believe.'

'Was he?'

'Their engagement had been announced.'

'Yelena Filippovna Polenova was a notoriously fickle woman. Only a few days before her engagement to Prince Naryskin she had broken off an engagement to the Guards officer Mizinchikov.'

'You seem to know an extraordinary amount about the life of Yelena Filippovna.'

'I take a natural interest in all these cases. That is why I could be especially useful to you.' There was a ripping sound as Slava pulled at the end of the bandage to split it. He tied the two halves firmly around Porfiry's hand. 'There would be no need for any extra consideration.'

'You are an intriguing individual, I will grant you that,' said Porfiry, examining the tightly bound dressing.

'You cannot seriously be intending to employ him!'

Porfiry turned his gaze on Virginsky with some surprise.

'You cannot allow your servant to become involved in official investigations.'

Slava pursed his lips, in an admirable display of self-restraint.

'And besides,' continued Virginsky, 'his theory is patently absurd. It is the typically convoluted theory of an amateur. It ignores the obvious. Mizinchikov's flight. The blood on his tunic. The letters. The razor found with the letters.'

'The razor? Yes,' said Slava. 'They mentioned that . . .'

'In the *Gazette*?' wondered Porfiry.

'I have a theory about the razor,' confided Slava.

'Really!' said Virginsky with exasperation.

'Please,' invited Porfiry.

'I think the razor was put there,' revealed Slava.

'Of course. It must have been.' Porfiry's tone was subtly mocking.

'By someone else, I mean.' Slava's answer showed that the satire was not lost on him.

'I see. That is an interesting theory. And who, do you think, put it there?'

'I have my suspicions,' was all that Slava would say.

Porfiry bowed, acknowledging his delicacy.

'Is this the blood?' said Slava, crossing to Porfiry's desk to examine the tunic more closely.

'Put that down,' snapped Virginsky. 'You have no authority to touch that.'

Slava held on to the tunic and looked to Porfiry for direction. Porfiry nodded slightly for him to do as Virginsky had said. Only then did Slava place the tunic down.

Virginsky clicked his tongue in disgust.

Porfiry looked again at his neatly bound hand. There seemed to be a hint of despondency in his expression now, as if he regretted that he no longer had cause to meddle with the dressing. He looked uncertainly at Slava and then at Virginsky. The two men were hanging on his next words.

'It would do us all good to have someone to keep us on our toes, I think.'

'But Porfiry Petrovich . . .'

Porfiry shot Virginsky a minatory glance. 'Now, Pavel Pavlovich, you can make yourself useful to me by delivering this tunic to Dr Pervoyedov and awaiting his findings.'

'Am I not supposed to be working on the case of the missing boy?'

'What case is this?' Slava's eager enquiry was met with an even sharper look of warning.

20

A vile traffic

'Pavel Pavlovich, what an unexpected pleasure!' Dr Pervoyedov eyed the brown paper package under Virginsky's arm with a covetous gleam. 'Do you have something for me there?'

Virginsky avoided the doctor's eye. Indeed, he avoided looking around the pathology laboratory at all, but kept his head bowed, staring fixedly at his feet like a sullen adolescent. But he could not avoid breathing in the formaldehyde-laden air. That pungent smell brought to mind the first time he had set foot in Dr Pervoyedov's laboratory at the Obukhovsky Hospital. His feet then had been clad in the boots of a dead man, charitably supplied to him by Porfiry Petrovich.

For an instant, Virginsky felt again the vertiginous lurch to which he had succumbed on that occasion.

'He wants you to examine this for bloodstains.' Virginsky handed the package over to Dr Pervoyedov, who pulled at the string like a child with a Christmas present. 'We believe it to be the tunic worn by the murderer of Yelena Filippovna. He wants to know whether it is arterial or venous blood, if indeed it is blood at all.'

'I imagine he does.'

Dr Pervoyedov studied the stains on the front of the regimental tunic, at one point holding it close to his nose and inhaling. There was one roughly circular burst of rust colour in the middle of the double-breasted facing. It had a dense nucleus about the size of a ten kopek piece, which decayed into a wide areola made up of finer spots. A second stain, a narrow, elongated trail around eight inches in extent, also haloed with spatter, descended from the first at an angle.

'Interesting,' said Dr Pervoyedov. 'Very interesting. Has Porfiry Petrovich offered any opinion regarding these stains?'

'I believe he is confident that they will prove to be blood. For some reason, he seems to be in doubt as to whether they are arterial or venous. He wished to enter into a wager over it.'

'A wager!' cried Dr Pervoyedov delightedly. 'That is very like Porfiry Petrovich, and to me it suggests that he is in no doubt at all. If I were you, I would not take him up on it.'

'I have no intention of doing so. I do not gamble. Besides, I dare say we are both of the opinion it is arterial. Such a spray of blood would only occur when an artery is severed. And we know that her throat was cut. The bet is pointless.'

'You may be right. May I cut a swatch from it? It will aid precision.'

Virginsky pinched his lips dubiously between thumb and forefinger.

'First I will make a sketch to show the position of the stains. I will then be able to correlate my samples to reference points on the drawing.'

'Do whatever is necessary, only do it quickly. He has told me to await your results. He little realises that I have other duties to attend to, though they are duties that he himself assigned to me.'

'Am I right in thinking that a certain frostiness has entered your relations with Porfiry Petrovich?' Dr Pervoyedov withdrew some sheets of paper and a pencil from a drawer in the bench. 'I do not believe you have once called him by his name this morning.'

'I swear that man is becoming more eccentric by the day.'

'Good heavens!' Dr Pervoyedov laid out the tunic flat on the bench. 'I find it hard to credit that there was any distance left for him to travel in the direction of eccentricity.'

'His latest aberration is to hire a most unsuitable individual as his valet.'

'But surely that is a private matter?' Dr Pervoyedov squinted at the tunic as he made the first tentative lines on paper. 'With all respect, Pavel Pavlovich, I do not see what it has to do with you.'

'You do not understand. This individual wishes to involve himself in the business of the department. He has theories!'

'Theories? Oh dear. We do not need more *theories*.'

'And Porfiry Petrovich, who by rights ought to send the man away with a flea in his ear, indulges him by listening to these theories.' Virginsky noted with annoyance the chink of amusement on the physician's lips. 'I swear he does it to provoke me. "We all need someone to keep us on our toes," he says. Looking at me, of course. He is punishing me. That's why he sent me here this morning.'

'My goodness!' Dr Pervoyedov's face opened in mock alarm. 'It grieves me to be the instrument of another man's punishment.'

'No – I didn't mean that.'

'But why should he wish to punish you?'

'I don't know. Possibly because I allowed the man wearing this tunic to escape.'

'I see. That *is* . . . regrettable. You might have had your murderer, Pavel Pavlovich.'

'No, it was not our suspect. It was just a tramp. Possibly one who had found the discarded tunic. Or maybe Captain Mizinchikov had given it to him, in exchange for the tramp's clothes. I admit it would have helped us to have the tramp. But it was foggy. He threw off the tunic. I went for the tunic and the man disappeared into the fog. It could have happened to anyone.'

Dr Pervoyedov frowned at his sketch. 'What do you think of that? Have I rendered the stains accurately?'

Virginsky gave an impatient jerk of the head in begrudging assent.

'Now all that remains is to ink in the sketch.'

'Can you not do that later? I do not have all day.'

'No, I must do it now, so that you may witness the accuracy of the finished figure with your signature.'

'Very well, though it is hardly convenient for me to wait on you. I am not even assigned to the Polenova case. That, I believe, is at the root of why he wishes to punish me. I have been assigned to the case of a missing boy. Indeed, I have been told that my participation in that case was specifically requested by an interested party. That seems to have put Porfiry Petrovich's nose out of joint. I would not be surprised if there is not some element of professional jealousy involved here. But really, he has no grounds for complaint. He brought it on himself. He failed to investigate the case when it was first brought to his attention – by me, I would have you know. Now she has chosen me and he doesn't like it.'

'She? Who is this *she*?'

'It doesn't matter. The thing is, it was while I was doing the rounds of the hospitals that I encountered the tramp wearing this tunic. A pure accident. Porfiry Petrovich should consider himself fortunate to have even this. But no, he wanted the man wearing it too.'

'He can be a very demanding taskmaster, I'll grant you that. There. I have finished the inking. A tolerable rendition, I dare say. If you would be so good as to sign it, we may proceed with the analysis itself.'

While Virginsky signed the diagram, Dr Pervoyedov took a scalpel to the cloth of the tunic.

'It seems to me that you have never forgiven him for the prank he played on you here in this very room.'

'You call it a prank? To confront me without warning with the severed heads of two of my friends!'

'It was designed to disorientate you. You might even say, to unhinge you a little.'

'Is that not sadism?'

'Not sadism, no.' Dr Pervoyedov extracted a small square of stained cloth from the tunic with a pair of fine tongs. He held the sample up for scrutiny. 'If this is blood, it should dissolve in distilled water – although that is not the ultimate test, of course.' The doctor dropped the swatch into a glass retort containing clear liquid. 'He did it because he believed it was necessary. To break down whatever carapace you had erected around the truth, so that the truth might seep out, whether you would or not.' Dr Pervoyedov peered at the retort as whorls of pink began to form in the water. 'But tell me, what's this about a missing boy?'

'A young factory worker – a labourer at the Nevsky Cotton-Spinning Factory. He is one of several now who have gone missing. All of them connected with a school that has been founded to bring the benefit of education to such children. I started with the hospitals in case he had been the victim of an accident.'

'Did you try the Medical-Surgical Academy?'

'Why would he have been admitted there?'

'He would not.' Dr Pervoyedov shook the retort to hasten the dissolution.

'Then why suggest it?'

'At least, he would not be admitted there alive. However, the Medical-Surgical Academy is very interested in acquiring unclaimed cadavers.' Dr Pervoyedov drew off a small quantity of the pink liquid with a pipette.

'I don't understand. From whom do they acquire them, if they are unclaimed?'

'There is an unofficial trade carried on between the Academy and . . .' The doctor released a drop of the liquid on to a glass slide. The minuscule mound stood proud above the polished surface. 'The police.'

'The police sell corpses to the Medical-Surgical Academy?'

Dr Pervoyedov slipped the prepared slide into place in the stage of the microscope. 'It has been going on for generations.'

'The police trade in dead bodies?'

'The practice was prevalent when I was studying at the Academy.' The soft shush of a Lundström match being struck, the delicate flicker and glow of a newborn flame, held the two men rapt. Virginsky breathed in the wheedling scent of red phosphorus, and felt the kick of something deadly spur his heart. He watched Dr Pervoyedov light the wick of a kerosene lamp on the bench and place it inside the arc of a concave reflector. The light from the lamp was directed towards the base of the microscope, where the mound of liquid was held.

The doctor gestured towards the spectroscope eyepiece. 'Would you care to take a look? It is a revelation. A small revelation of one of the wonders of science.'

Virginsky held up a palm in a gesture of deferment. 'It is an outrage. It is an abuse.'

The doctor shrugged. 'A policeman's wages are paltry. You cannot blame them for wanting to supplement their income.'

'But the bodies are not theirs to sell. And the Medical-Surgical Academy is equally at fault for creating the demand.'

'But without fresh corpses to practice upon, how can you expect medical students to acquire the knowledge they need to become doctors?'

'You cannot condone this vile traffic!'

'Without such training, I would be little use to you. Besides, as I said, the bodies are unclaimed.'

'And, I dare say, they are without exception the bodies of paupers.'

'Invariably so. Which is why I suggested you make enquiries at the Academy. Tread carefully though. If you go in blazing with indignation, you will surely fail to secure their co-operation. In short, they will deny everything. *Everything.*' At last Dr Pervoyedov stooped to peer into the microscope. 'Ah! Now that's interesting. Very interesting indeed.' He turned to Virginsky, his face enlivened by boyish excitement. 'Are you sure you don't want to look at this, Pavel Pavlovich?'

21

Anatomy 1

Virginsky crossed the Neva by the temporary pontoon bridge at the end of Liteyny Prospekt, riding on the open deck of an omnibus. The acrid smell of the Vyborgskaya District drifted over the river to greet him. A thick ash, the noxious product of factory chimneys, settled on him like a coating of despair. Snow was no longer in the air, only this infernal negative of it. He chose the upper deck, despite the cold and the poisonous fumes, because he liked to look down on the city, or rather to feel in himself the potential for ascent.

The clop of the horses' hooves lost their resonance as the omnibus rattled off the shifting bridge on to the solid embankment north of the Neva. Virginsky gave in to a resentful despondency, as he rose from his seat. No one, it occurred to him, ventured into the Vyborgskaya District unless they had to. It was a place of sprawling factories and precarious wooden slums; between them, expanses of flat, black, toxic wasteland, littered with clumps of grubby vegetation and human detritus. At this time of the year – the damp, raw season before the big freeze set in – the largely unpaved roads were churned into seas of mud. The earth became an impediment, sucking purpose from those who sought to traverse it.

He jumped off the moving platform of the omnibus on Morskaya Street, just as the Medical-Surgical Academy came forward to dominate the view. Tucked in behind the Military

Hospital, as if these institutional outposts felt the need to huddle together, it was a neo-classical building somewhere between a palace and a temple. An academy, in fact: Virginsky had no doubt that it would have conformed to all the Vitruvian requirements of that genre of building, the architect substituting obedience for imagination, as was so often the way in Russia.

Virginsky felt a glimmer of excitement at his own small act of insubordination, although perhaps it was not so very small, after all. He ought to have returned immediately to the bureau with the results of Dr Pervoyedov's analysis. And yet, he had come here, on his own initiative – or rather, in open disobedience of his superior, Porfiry Petrovich. He could argue that he was acting in response to the lead given him by Dr Pervoyedov. However, it did not help his case that the bureau lay between the Obukhovsky Hospital and the Surgical-Medical Academy. It would have been an easy matter for him to call in on his way and share the news with Porfiry Petrovich. Virginsky smiled to himself. There was no doubt he enjoyed having the advantage over Porfiry Petrovich for once, and he would hold on to it for as long as possible. He had to admit, however, that he found it impossible to make sense of the information Dr Pervoyedov had given him. At the same time, he had the irritating premonition that Porfiry Petrovich would know just what it signified as soon as it was revealed to him.

A statue of some Roman goddess (he would never understand why a nation that declared itself Christian continued to erect these tributes to pagan deities) stood in the garden before the entrance to the Academy, with a number of benches around it. Virginsky hesitated for a moment, looking up at the lemon yellow building. Its white columns gleamed like the teeth in a monumentally gaping mouth. A group of medical students in their uniforms gave him a mildly curious backward glance as they passed him. He fell in behind them, and climbed the steps to enter.

Inside, in contrast to the classical formality of its exterior, the great entrance hall presented the worn-down eccentricity of a functioning institution. It was a place where people congregated; they had made their mark on it, chipping off its edges, treading down its pathways. It had the feel of a clannish, almost familial enclosure. The members of this community knew their place, and moved about within it with the contented confidence of belonging. When voices were raised, it was in raucous fellowship, each individual burst of exuberance adding to the strength of the corporate body. Virginsky keenly felt his status as an interloper.

He had arrived just as the next period of lectures was about to begin – no doubt the last of the morning. The corridors thronged with medical students. He noticed a number of students flocking in one particular direction. They seemed possessed by a highly animated excitement that drew him into their midst. He hurried to keep up with them, pausing only once to glance through the circular window in a closed door which bore the number 11 on a small plate. Banks of seating led down to a demonstration area. On a table, beneath a green sheet, an ominously elongated mound awaited the beginning of the lecture.

Virginsky caught up with the students. Their excitement seemed to heighten into bravado. They streamed through a door identical to the one that had given Virginsky pause a moment before. This one was designated 'Anatomy 1'. He had expected it to be another banked auditorium, but it was simply a large open room in which were arranged around twenty or so tables. Each table was draped with a green sheet, though the mounds beneath these sheets were much smaller and more spherically compact than the one he had glimpsed earlier. The students took their places, a pair to each table. Their excitement had drained from them, and from many all colour too. They were tense, though an occasional bubble of nervous laughter broke out.

A bell rang. A professor in a white coat entered and strode up to the lecture podium at one end of the room.

'Gentlemen,' he said. 'Uncover your heads.'

It had come to this again, as it always did. And as ever, it was Porfiry Petrovich who had brought him here.

*

The tables had marble surfaces. He had not expected that. The heads lolled back on them. Virginsky wanted to keep looking at the marble. He wanted to find patterns in the mineral veins. He did not want to meet the vacant eyes, and even less the tendril-trailing neck stumps of the decapitated heads.

There were too many to take in at once. Each head, each face, contended for his compassionate attention, but without beseeching, without expression of any kind. All around him, dead mouths gaped in mute chorus.

He moved unchallenged between the tables, his service uniform for the moment lending the imprimatur of authority. He estimated that of the approximately twenty heads, six were those of children.

'May I help you?' It was the professor, a sinewy man of about fifty years, wearing a pince-nez across a scalpel-sharp nose. His adam's apple was almost equally sharp.

'Yes. I am a magistrate from the Department for the Investigation of Criminal Causes. I am looking into the disappearance of a number of children. I notice that there are children's ... uhm ... remains, amongst these that the students are working on today.'

'Sadly, yes.'

'Is it usual for there to be so many children at one time?'

'I'm afraid it's not unprecedented – although, yes, we do currently have a higher proportion than is typical.'

'How did they die?'

'The children?'

'Yes.'

'In different ways.'

'But you have ascertained a cause of death for each child?'

'This is an anatomy class. We are not teaching forensic medicine.'

'But if, for example, a child had died in an horrendous accident, you would notice, would you not? There would be wounds, broken bones perhaps, even ruptured internal organs?'

'Oh certainly. We get our fair share of those. They are of limited usefulness to the students. The industrial accidents are the worst. The bones are not simply broken, but crushed, sometimes to a fibrous pulp. Picture a shredded banana skin. I'm talking about young bones, of course. The older, more brittle bones simply shatter into fragments, which become embedded in mangled tissue.'

'I trust the police make allowances for this in the price they ask for such sub-standard goods.'

The professor gave him a severe look over the top of his pince-nez. 'That does not come into it.'

'You do not pay the police for the bodies?'

'We are assured that the money goes to the families. Our payment is made in the form of a charitable contribution.'

'There are families involved? I understood that the bodies you acquired were unidentified, and therefore unclaimed. Is that not so?'

'I cannot comment. The police assure us that the money goes to the families. That is how it is put to us.'

'But wouldn't a family wish to bury its children?'

'These are very poor people.'

'But they are also Christians, are they not? And Russians?'

'Poverty compels people to do things they would not otherwise countenance. Especially if it is compounded by vice. When a mother will sell her living daughter's body to a sensualist – for the price of a jug of vodka – how can you suppose that she will scruple to sell the same body when dead to a teaching hospital? We see the ravages of venereal disease in corpses as young as ten.'

'That is indeed educational. Let us take it then that the money goes to the families. We must trust the police to pass it on.'

At that point one of the students, holding a scalpel aloft in readiness, called out: 'Professor! What would you have us do with our heads?'

The question provoked widespread hilarity.

Virginsky raised his hand in restraint. 'I'm afraid I must ask you to call a halt to today's class. These heads, the heads of the children at least, must not be damaged any further. For the purposes of identification, you understand.'

'What about the adult heads – you are not concerned with those?'

'Your students may do what they like to those.'

The professor clapped his hands. 'Gentlemen, lay down your implements. Those of you working on juveniles, please attach yourselves to another table. We will be working on adult heads only today.'

'Thank you,' said Virginsky with a nod of appreciation. 'Is there somewhere where the children's heads can be stored for the time being?'

'Of course,' said the professor. 'We have a room for that.'

An image of what such a room must be like forced itself on Virginsky. He closed his eyes to dispel it. But the image remained, together with the certainty that he would be called upon to enter it.

22

The school over the workshop

'I congratulate you on your work, Pavel Pavlovich. This could indeed prove to be a decisive breakthrough.'

Virginsky could not help taking some pleasure from his superior's approval. However, he acknowledged that his feelings towards Porfiry were at the moment obscurely complicated, and had been ever since Porfiry had returned from Kimri after Zakhar's death. If he tried to get to the bottom of these feelings, which seemed to be dominated by an angry resentment, he could penetrate no further than the image of Maria Petrovna. Somehow he had the feeling that Porfiry Petrovich was stealthily engaged in the act of taking her from him, although, of course, she was not yet his to be taken.

The door to Porfiry's private apartment opened and Slava came through carrying a steaming samovar.

Virginsky turned his incredulity on Porfiry. 'Already?'

Porfiry blinked quizzically at the force of the question. 'Slava was able to begin his employment immediately. Neither of us could see any reason to delay.'

Virginsky shook his head in dismay.

'Did I hear someone say there has been a breakthrough?' said Slava blithely, as he dropped the samovar heavily on Porfiry's desk in his excitement.

'Quite possibly,' said Porfiry, frowning at his new servant's apparent ineptitude. 'In the case that Pavel Pavlovich is investigating – the case of the missing boy.'

'I see.' Slava's voice plummeted with disappointment as he hastily poured a glass of tea for his new master. The liquid slopped onto the desk, where Porfiry's lunch tray remained. Slava dabbed at the spillage with a large grey handkerchief produced from his pocket. 'I thought you were talking about the case of Yelena Filippovna. That is the case that. . .' He seemed to catch himself in his enthusiasm. 'Everyone is interested in,' he added, more circumspectly.

'You were listening at the door,' accused Virginsky.

Slava did not deign to answer the charge.

'What we must do,' said Porfiry, taking the glass from Slava, 'is seek a positive identification of one of these corpses you have traced to the Medical-Surgical Academy. I suggest we take a conveyance to the Rozhdestvenskaya District forthwith, in order to collect Maria Petrovna. She will be able to tell us for sure whether we have indeed found the boy Mitka.'

'Maria Petrovna?' Virginsky loaded the name with challenge.

'I believe she would be the best person.'

'You would put her through that?'

'I see no alternative.'

'There is another teacher at the school, is there not? A man.'

Porfiry sipped his tea and frowned distractedly.

Slava had not poured a glass for Virginsky, and showed no intention of doing so. But neither did he seem inclined to withdraw, with or without the dirty plates. Virginsky glared at him pointedly, then, admitting defeat, helped himself to tea. It was tepid, he noted with disgust.

'We do not know that this other teacher knew the boy.'

Porfiry drained his glass in one noisy gulp. 'Perhaps the other teacher will be willing to make the identification on Maria Petrovna's behalf. Perhaps she will insist on making it herself. I rather think the latter will be the case, knowing her as I do.' Porfiry turned to Slava, apparently with surprise. 'You may clear the lunch things away now, Slava.'

His new servant made no move to obey him. 'But what about the tunic?' Slava asked eagerly. 'Wasn't he supposed to find out about the tunic?'

'Ah yes,' said Porfiry. 'Thank you for reminding me. In all the excitement, I had almost forgotten about the tunic. Well, Pavel Pavlovich? What did Dr Pervoyedov have to say about the stains on the tunic?'

'It is blood,' said Virginsky heavily.

'Yes. We expected that, I believe. And was he able to distinguish what type of blood it is? Whether venous or arterial?'

There was no doubt it irked Virginsky to have to relinquish his advantage over Porfiry before he had been able to make use of it. 'What do you think?'

'Ah no! You cannot embroil me in a wager now! Not now that you are privy to the outcome of his analysis.'

'I am not seeking to embroil you in anything,' said Virginsky with an involuntary smile. 'I do confess, it was not the result I was expecting.'

'No?'

'And I am curious to know whether it is the result you were expecting.'

'Given what you have said, I would imagine that Dr Pervoyedov found it to be venous blood. You would naturally have been expecting arterial blood, believing as you do that Captain Mizinchikov is Yelena Filippovna's murderer.'

'And you do not believe that?' The question, enlivened by delight, came from Slava.

Porfiry Petrovich rose from his desk. It could not be said that he rose to any imposing height, but the full bulk of his body was nevertheless impressive. 'It is time for Pavel Pavlovich and me to be on our way. Be so good as to bring my furs. There is a freezing fog out, by the looks of it.'

*

The school was over a carpenter's shop, surrounded on all sides by gigantic, smoke-blasted factories. It seemed as unlikely as a flower growing in a wall. Porfiry and Virginsky had driven east in a black departmental carriage, watching the quality of the fog change as they approached the heavily industrial area. Around Stolyarny Lane, the shifts of swirling grey had a wispy ethereal quality, a kind of innocent playfulness. It lifted the heart to wander through them: the squalor of the Haymarket District concealed, it was possible to imagine one's self transported anywhere. But here, in the Rozhdestvenskaya District, deep within the noose of industry that encircled the city, there was more coal ash than water vapour in the choking curtain through which they had to push. It was a relief to step inside, where the sawdust itch emanating from the workshop seemed by comparison wholesome. As they climbed the stairs, hammer blows and the wheezing of saws gave way to childish voices raised in song.

Kalinka, kalinka, kalinka maya . . .

Virginsky could hear Maria's voice underpinning their warbling efforts, deeper, steadier, leading them with unwavering clarity and strength. Her voice at that moment, it seemed to him, was the pure expression of her love for her charges.

And how earnestly the children sing! thought Virginsky. *They put their souls into it.* He could picture their faces clearly, before even he set foot in the schoolroom.

And then he remembered why they had come for her, and where they were intent on taking her.

They had reached the top of the stairs and now he could see her. The door to the schoolroom was open, the scene just as he had imagined it. She was standing by an easel-mounted black-board, pointing out the words to the song. Her hair was pinned up. She was wearing a simple grey dress with a white apron. He saw that she was utterly absorbed in the song and in the children, of whom there were barely a dozen, seated on two rows of benches, their slates on their laps.

Perhaps the song would never come to an end, and she would never look up and see them, and they would not have to take her there.

But she caught sight of them before the song was ended. Her face was instantly sapped of the energy and enrapt joy that her absorption in the music lesson had lent it. Her voice faltered momentarily, before she rallied herself to deliver one last chorus. She no longer pointed out the words but pumped her arms and stamped her feet in a stationary march. The beat of the song fell in with the hammering of nails downstairs. A beaming smile was splayed across Maria Petrovna's face. Her head turned from side to side like a mechanical doll's, driven by the song and the carpenter's hammer. Roused by her display of enthusiasm, the children strained their voices to match hers. The song ended with a resounding shout, which collapsed into a voluble babble of excited chatter.

'Silence!' called Maria Petrovna, with a finger to her lips. The children obeyed instantly, though the pounding from the workshop continued recalcitrantly. Maria softened the abruptness of her command with a smile of appreciation at their obedience. It occurred to Virginsky that if he were one of her class, he would do whatever she asked of him on the promise of that smile.

'Now then, children,' she continued. 'You see I have written the words to the song here. I have to talk to these gentlemen . . .' Twelve faces swung round as one to get a look at Porfiry and Virginsky. Porfiry raised his hand to the level of his chin and waved his fingers with a simpering smile. Virginsky frowned. 'While I am talking to them, I want you to copy down the words. Please get on with your work. I shall not be long.'

She walked the length of the classroom with brisk steps and closed the door behind her.

'You have found him? Mitka?' Her face was drained of colour, her voice breathless.

'We cannot say for certain.' Porfiry's gaze locked onto hers. She did not seek to evade those ice-coloured eyes. 'A number of children's bodies . . .'

Maria put a hand to her mouth to stifle her distress. 'A number? Oh my God!'

'That in itself is nothing to be alarmed about,' said Porfiry. 'The bodies have come to light at the Medical-Surgical Academy, which routinely receives bodies for teaching and research purposes. I am afraid to say that children die in St Petersburg all the time, for all sorts of reasons. The fact that there are a number of bodies is not significant. The children we are looking for may or may not be amongst them. We need you . . . to identify them, if you are able.'

'It doesn't have to be you,' put in Virginsky quickly. 'There is another teacher here, I believe. He could do it.'

'Apollon Mikhailovich? But he did not teach Mitka.'

'He will have seen him at the school.'

'No. It has to be me. You have come to take me there now?'

'Yes,' said Porfiry.

'But you don't understand,' began Virginsky, his face contorted with anguish.

Maria held firm. 'You must allow me a moment to inform Apollon Mikhailovich. He will be able to take the little ones.'

Porfiry and Virginsky stepped back against the wall to allow her to pass along the narrow landing to a closed door at the opposite end. There was a lull in the sounds of construction from downstairs. In the unexpected silence, they heard raised voices coming from behind the door.

Maria paused at the door. 'That sounds like Father Anfim. Apollon Mikhailovich will insist on goading Father Anfim. And sadly, Father Anfim always rises to the bait.'

She knocked and opened the door to a second classroom. A familiar looking shovel-bearded man was perched on the edge of the teacher's desk, as if to address the class, but there were no children present. Instead, an imposingly tall and grey-bearded cleric dressed in the long black robe of the Orthodox priesthood was pacing the room. The two men turned to face Maria as she came in, a look of wry amusement on the first man's face, while the priest's expression was frozen in thunderous rage. This melted somewhat at the sight of Maria Petrovna, to be replaced by reluctant contrition.

Both the men took in the presence of Porfiry and Virginsky with guarded suspicion. Porfiry narrowed his eyes at the shovel-bearded man in half-recognition.

'For goodness' sake, gentlemen. Please moderate your voices. Do you want the children to hear you arguing?'

'I apologise, Maria Petrovna, for raising my voice.' Father Anfim's face was red and strained. He stared stiff-necked at a point on the floor. 'However, I must tell you that I have been subjected to the most extreme provocation by . . . this man.'

'You are shouting again, Father Anfim,' said Maria, gently.

'It's nonsense, of course,' commented Apollon Mikhailovich Perkhotin, launching himself off the edge of the desk.

'He says he will take down the icon! And the portrait of the Tsar! He even says he will take down the map! The map of the empire, my good lady! I am here to inform you . . . it is my duty, as the representative of the Holy Synod charged with the sacred responsibility of ensuring the moral probity of the schools in the Rozhdestvenskaya District . . . if he carries out just one of these intentions, I will have no alternative . . . No alternative, I tell you.'

'But Father Anfim,' objected Maria, 'do you see the icon?' She pointed to the corner from where the icon of the Virgin Mother looked down.

'Yes,' admitted the priest.

'And do you see the portrait of his Imperial Majesty? And the map of Russian territories?'

The priest had to agree that these images were also in place.

'Well then.'

'But he says he will take them down!' spluttered Father Anfim.

'Did you, Apollon Mikhailovich?' It seemed to Virginsky that the tone she adopted was the one she would use with a naughty schoolboy.

'No!' denied Perkhotin emphatically. 'The subtleties of my position have been lost on the reverend father.'

An explosion of bluster escaped from the priest's mouth.

'Then what *did* you say?' asked Maria calmly.

'I said that there would come a day, before too long, possibly within our lifetime, certainly within the lifetime of the children we teach, when such symbols will not only be taken down, but also will be destroyed.'

'Is that what you are teaching?' screeched Father Anfim. 'It is revolution!'

'Nonsense. In the first place, I do not teach it. The inevitable cannot be taught. One may as well attempt to teach the tide to come in. Whether one likes it or not, these things will happen. And to observe as much implies neither approval nor its opposite. It is morally neutral.'

'There!' cried Father Anfim triumphantly. 'Condemned by his own words . . . Morally neutral! It is not your place to be morally neutral, sir. It is your place to teach loyalty to the Tsar . . . and devotion to God, while you're at it.'

'But what about the principles of science?'

'The principles of the One True Church. That is your priority. You are producing the Tsar's future subjects. It is your duty to impose most emphatically upon them . . .'

'To impose what, father?'

'A sense of their place in his empire whilst assuring them of his fatherly love for them.'

'Is it a father's love that condemns them to a life of hellish drudgery and back-breaking toil out there?' Perkhotin waved sweepingly at the casement window. The lights of the surrounding factories glowed dimly through the smog.

'A father's love may at times appear distant . . . his visage stern. But if those children place their trust in him . . . they will find . . . he will not let them down! Indeed, he is their best hope for protection. Was it not this tsar who lifted the yoke of serfdom? Even you must admit that! Well, now, he applies the same zeal . . . the same loving diligence . . . to, to, to . . .'

'To what?'

'To the question of factory regulations.'

'Another commission that will come to nothing, its findings hidden away in some dusty departmental cupboard.'

'The Tsar will consider its findings carefully, as he always does.'

'Before giving his order: *Bury it!* As he always does.'

'Please, gentlemen,' broke in Maria Petrovna desperately. 'This is fruitless. Father Anfim, you have my assurance that I will never consent to the removal of the icon.' She spoke at a racing lick, her fluency inspired by necessity. 'The same goes for the portrait of the Tsar and the map. Not only that, I can assure you that Apollon Mikhailovich agrees wholeheartedly with me on this. Is that not so, Apollon Mikhailovich? *Is that not so, Apollon Mikh—?*' The final, repeated question fell away into tears.

'Maria Petrovna! Whatever is the matter?' Perkhotin took her hands in his. 'If I have caused you any distress by my ill-judged remarks . . .'

'My dear lady!' cried Father Anfim, who appeared almost panic-stricken as he pressed in on her. The priest and the teacher jostled to assert their solicitude. 'Do not upset yourself. I . . . I . . . Given your assurances regarding this individual . . . I accept unreservedly.'

'Thank you, my friends.' Maria Petrovna pulled her hands free from Perkhotin's. 'I must ask you to forgive my outburst. I assure you, it has nothing to do with either of you. It is simply that I must go with these gentlemen. They are magistrates. They have something they want me to look at.'

'What's this?' Something sharper than concern, a look almost of cunning, pinched Perkhotin's features as he considered Porfiry and Virginsky.

'It's to do with the children. The ones who went missing. There is the question of identification.'

'I see.' The words rasped at Perkhotin's throat.

'Oh my dear, how terrible for you. May God give you strength.'

Virginsky felt impelled to speak up. 'Of course, there may be a way to spare Maria Petrovna from this ordeal. If either of you gentlemen would be willing to make the identification in her place? That is to say, if the children were known to you.'

'They were my pupils,' insisted Maria. A desolate calmness had entered her voice. Her eyes were fixed on a distant point.

'It's the boy, isn't it?' began Perkhotin hesitantly. 'Mitka? I know him. I could identify him, I believe.'

'There are other children missing too, whom I do not think you know.'

'I would know their faces, Maria Petrovna.'

'No!' The force of her objection shocked them all. 'I mean to say, yes, you would know their faces, I'm sure. But I cannot ask you to do this. No one knows these children as I do. No one else can do this for me.'

'But there is something you should be aware of,' said Virginsky, with a desperate look to Porfiry.

Porfiry shook his head warningly.

'What? What is it?' Her words came constricted by fear.

Virginsky fixed his gaze on Porfiry. 'We told you that the bodies were received by the Medical-Surgical Academy, for the purposes of teaching. The students have been at work on them.'

'What do you mean?'

'The heads have been removed.'

The sound was something more than a groan. It was the throbbing churn of her living flesh.

'I'm sorry,' continued Virginsky. 'There was nothing we could do about it. It was part of their studies. It is important, however, that you are prepared for what is to come. To expose you to this without warning would be cruel.' He cast a significant glance towards Porfiry Petrovich.

'I will not permit you to subject yourself to this,' said Perkhotin grimly. Then, as if he sensed her inevitable intransigence, he added: 'Or at least allow me to accompany you.'

'No.' This time, she uttered the word of rejection softly, and Virginsky marvelled at how quickly she had regained her composure. 'Though I thank you from the bottom of my heart for your offer. You must stay here for the children. And for me. I need you to take my class.'

'Then *I* will come with you,' said Father Anfim, drawing himself up to his full height.

Maria Petrovna rewarded this quixotic offer with a smile of unbounded gratitude. 'It will not be necessary, dear, kind Father Anfim. I will have these gentlemen with me. As well as being magistrates, they are also my friends, or so I consider them. I hope I am not wrong to do so.'

Absurdly, Virginsky felt himself blush, though whether it was out of pleasure at the favour shown him, or resentment at being grouped together with Porfiry Petrovich, he could not say.

23

A basement room

'It is as well your colleague came when he did. I was about to set the students the task of removing the facial epidermises.'

The professor, whose name, it turned out, was Bubnov, led the way by candlelight through the dark corridors of the basement, which like every basement in St Petersburg was permeated with the cloying smell of damp rot. His remark, intended for Porfiry Petrovich, was made a little too volubly. It drew a gasp from the darkness behind Virginsky. He turned and waited. Maria Petrovna's face appeared, wraithlike. She seemed hardly there, the flickering intimation of a presence in the shifting darkness. Virginsky reached out a hand to console her, but lost faith in the gesture before it was completed.

Virginsky ran two steps to catch up with Porfiry. 'Porfiry Petrovich,' he hissed through clenched teeth. 'We cannot, in all conscience, subject her to this.'

'It's all right, Pavel Pavlovich.' Maria's voice came deep and firm, as if something of the darkness had entered it and given it strength. He thought of her singing in the schoolroom. 'I must do it.'

'But you don't know what it will cost you. You will never be the same after this. What you are about to see, it will enter you and take hold of you, and *never* let you go.'

'You wish to spare me. I understand. But I do not wish to be spared.'

'Pavel Pavlovich.' Porfiry's voice was stern as he cut in. 'You must not presume that everyone will be affected in the same way that you were. Now, please calm yourself. This discussion is not helpful to Maria Petrovna.'

Maria's presence faded momentarily as she reeled back from their attention. It was as if she could not bear even the feeble glow of the candlelight on her. The force of their dispute, and that she was the subject of it, seemed also to weigh heavily on her.

'I just want to . . . get this over with.' Two bright points glittered in the darkness, then flickered uncertainly before disappearing.

'Take my arm, Maria Petrovna.'

The glittering points came back, their gleam directed at Porfiry Petrovich. He held out his forearm receptively. Her hand, like a timid creature venturing from its hiding place, bobbed tentatively towards it.

Virginsky felt the pivotal roll of defeat inside him.

*

As they entered the room, the smell of damp intensified, or rather it was overlaid with another smell in a similar register, but sweeter and somehow more insinuating. Professor Bubnov touched a taper to the candle flame and lit an oil lamp suspended from the centre of the ceiling. Its spread of yellow light seemed to take them all by surprise.

There was a glacial chill in the room. The floor was of trodden earth, the walls exposed brick, apart from one wall which was taken up with rows of small, square doors of varnished wood. These doors were numbered from one to twenty four, and had been constructed, Virginsky noted, with evident care and craftsmanship, to precise specifications. The polished brass hinges and fastenings gleamed. A folded stepladder was leaning against this wall.

'This is where we keep the body parts,' said Professor Bubnov, placing his candle on a long table in the centre of the room. Virginsky noticed that the surface of the table was stained with blood. 'Complete cadavers are kept elsewhere. As you may have noticed, the temperature here is several degrees lower than in the corridor, on account of the ice, in which the parts are packed.'

Porfiry addressed himself to Professor Bubnov. 'We are looking for a boy of about ten years of age. He would not have come to you before, say, the thirteenth of September.'

'We do keep a record of when we take possession of our cadavers.' Professor Bubnov took up the candle again and crossed to a desk against one of the brick walls. There was a lamp on this too. He removed the cylindrical glass and lit the wick with unhurried methodical care. Replacing the glass seemed to take an age. At last the professor sat down at the desk, then opened a drawer and took out a ledger book. With the same slow meticulousness, he turned the pages, running his fingers along rows of numbered entries.

Virginsky craned his neck to peer over Professor Bubnov's shoulder. 'Does it tell you from whom the bodies were acquired?'

'As I informed you this morning, we receive them from the police. There is no need to go into any greater detail than that, as all the bodies come from the same source.'

'Of course,' granted Virginsky, frowning enquiringly at Porfiry Petrovich. Porfiry smiled and nodded approval.

'We did receive such a body, number four three six one, a

boy, estimated to be around that age. Received, let me see, on the twenty-third of September.'

'And these letters here,' said Virginsky, pointing to a column in the entry Professor Bubnov had his finger on. 'I. P. S.? What do they signify?'

'Do you wish me to show you the head of this boy?' There was a note of aggression in the offer. 'You will be interested to know that it was one of the heads the students were to have worked on this morning.'

'I see each entry has a set of similar letters in the same place,' persisted Virginsky. 'I. I. D., P. P. Ch., S. D. L. They look like initials to me. Some of them occur more than once. This I. P. S., for example, occurs here, here and here.'

'It is nothing.'

'But it must mean something.'

Professor Bubnov closed the ledger. 'I had the heads from this morning's class placed in compartment seven. The head of four three six one should be with them.' He turned sharply away from the desk, consigning the ledger and its contents to the past.

Porfiry treated Virginsky to a significant blink. 'My dear Professor Bubnov,' he began smoothly. 'It really would be most helpful for us to know the meaning of those letters. Perhaps you are embarrassed because you do not know.' This time, his facial contraction was without doubt a wink. Professor Bubnov's eyes darted slyly, as he calculated his position. 'Yes, that must be it,' continued Porfiry. 'I cannot believe that you would deliberately withhold information from the judicial authorities.' The professor looked down in embarrassment. 'In that case, if you need to consult with the person who entered these letters in order to learn from them directly what they signify, and then pass on that information to us later, that would of course be acceptable. Do you not agree, Pavel Pavlovich?'

'It will be acceptable,' said Virginsky.

'And now, professor, if Maria Petrovna is ready . . .'

Maria Petrovna bowed her head in heavy assent. Her face was ashen. Her lips were compressed and colourless.

Professor Bubnov rattled open the stepladder and positioned it alongside compartment seven, the first from the left on the third row. He climbed to the second step of the ladder and reached out to turn the brass handle. As the door swung open, Virginsky saw that the back of it was lined with a dull grey metal. A wooden panel came half way up the aperture of the door: the front of a deep drawer. A brass handhold had been inlaid into it. Again Virginsky marvelled at the care that had gone into creating these holding bays for dead matter. Above the drawer front, an impenetrable blackness squatted. It seemed to be an entity released by the opening of the door. But it did not burst out with boundless energy; rather, it began a slow, seeping infiltration of the room.

The professor took hold of the brass handle and pulled. An enormous drawer came out smoothly and easily on a well-oiled sliding mechanism. The black entity shrank back with a grumbling murmur.

The tray of the drawer extended more or less the length of a grown man into the room, supported on iron rods along its bottom edges. The professor lifted the long side nearest him, which turned over and dropped, giving him easier access to the contents: six wooden crates, which could easily have contained the lovingly packed-up possessions of a family removing to their dacha for the summer. The boxes possessed the insolent neutrality of inanimate objects. For it seemed a provocation that anything in the universe could remain unmoved by what Virginsky knew those crates in fact contained.

'Four three six one, here we are,' said Professor Bubnov, taking hold of the second crate. 'May I pass this down to one of you gentlemen?'

Virginsky stepped forward to receive the crate. His heart raced as he took it. He felt also the hot blush of shame. What on earth had impelled him to put himself forward with such unthinking alacrity? Whatever else he might argue, he knew that he had wanted to feel the weight of the crate in his hands. He knew also that this was something he couldn't blame on Porfiry Petrovich.

The box was heavier than he had expected, so much so that it almost slipped through his fingers as the professor released his hold. *How heavy could a boy's head be?* flashed through his mind.

'Be careful with it,' warned Professor Bubnov. He scuttled down the steps to share the load, or rather to hover his hands in a precautionary manner close to the box as Virginsky carried it. 'On the table, please.'

Virginsky slid it into the centre of the table. It gave a protesting screech. Professor Bubnov lifted the lid, which was only loosely in place. Virginsky peered in. To his disappointment, all he could see was tightly packed crushed ice. He felt a tap on his arm. Porfiry signalled for him to move back, inclining his head at the same time towards Maria Petrovna. Virginsky remembered himself with a grimace; his head hung as he backed off.

Professor Bubnov laid the lid upside down on the table, revealing that it too was backed with lead. He began to transfer ice from the crate to the lid. Virginsky wanted to look inside to see what was being uncovered, but it was not his place to do so. At last, the professor nodded to Maria Petrovna. She stepped forward and stooped over the open crate, as if somehow she was readying herself to dive into it. Indeed, at one point, she seemed about to fall forward. She was forced to take hold of the sides of the crate to steady herself, giving the impression that she was drinking up whatever was contained in that bland cube.

Now, now was the time to look into her face. He might tell himself that it was his official duty to look there, simply for confirmation of the boy's identity. But he knew that he was looking there because he was guilty of every charge he had laid against Porfiry Petrovich – of a kind of emotional sadism, in fact.

Even so, that self-realisation did not prevent him from looking.

Maria Petrovna closed her eyes, squeezing them tight over the terrible sight within the box. A sob broke from her. Her head nodded forwards once. This movement set in train a spasm of nodding. 'Yes, yes,' she gasped. 'It's Mitka.'

It was Porfiry who took hold of her, gently, with infinite delicacy, and guided her by the elbows away from the table.

Virginsky stepped into her place.

The boy was looking up at him, his head surrounded by a halo of ice fragments. His face was tinged with blue, eyes almost the same blue, wide open, in boyish wonder and excitement. His lips were parted, in a lung-bursting gasp.

'Shall I put it back?' asked Professor Bubnov.

'No, thank you,' said Porfiry. 'Please leave it on the table. I will need to examine it more closely in due course. You may replace the lid, however – for now, that is.' Porfiry turned his attention to Maria: 'How are you, my dear? Do you wish to sit down? Pavel Pavlovich, that chair, please.'

Virginsky fetched the chair from the desk. Maria sank into it gratefully. She covered her face with one hand, fingers spread as if to catch her pain and squeeze it into nothing.

'There are other children missing.' Porfiry's voice was low, a husky whisper, awed at its own temerity.

Maria nodded.

'They may be here.'

A wince as though of acute physical pain contorted Maria's face.

'Would you be willing to look at the other children here, to try to identify them too?'

'Porfiry Petrovich!' cried Virginsky.

Porfiry was ready for his protest. 'Surely it is better to face it now, once and for all, and never to have to return to this room?'

'Porfiry ... Petrovich ...' Her voice, though faltering, compelled their attention. ' . . . is right.'

Porfiry nodded decisively to Professor Bubnov, who mounted the steps again.

Five more crates were handed down, with Virginsky and Porfiry taking it in turns to receive them. They placed them side by side on the table. Then Professor Bubnov climbed down the steps to remove the lids. Still wearing the black rubber gloves, he began to scoop ice out of the first of the crates. His hands plunging into the ice made a brittle hawking sound.

There was something hypnotic about his execution of the task. His slow methodical movements seemed to create a haven in time, which would serve to postpone indefinitely the dreadful spectacle to come.

He moved along the row of crates, clearing ice. Each time he worked with the same unhurried persistence.

Eventually, he came to the end of the last crate. He straightened himself above it and turned to Porfiry with a grim dip of his head. Porfiry reached out a hand to Maria Petrovna. Her face was stricken, nauseous. She was shivering, her teeth clattering violently.

She said nothing. Virginsky watched as Porfiry took her hand. He imagined the cold frailty of that hand. All her vulnerability and courage seemed to be concentrated in it. He wanted to be the one who was enclosing it in his own firm hands.

Maria rose shakily from her seat.

She stood over the first of the crates. An inarticulate cry, a gurgle of horror and grief, vibrated in her throat. 'Lana!' she cried. 'That is Lana!'

Porfiry steered her on to the second crate. Maria shook her head, as she did over the third and fourth crates. The fifth crate, however, produced a gasp and a name.

'Artur.' She looked up, first into Porfiry's face, then into Virginsky's. Her gaze was searching. He felt her trying to look beyond his face, beyond his humanity even, for some explanation of what she had been shown. 'They were my children,' she said at last. 'They came to my school.' Her eyes narrowed as she processed a difficult thought. 'Is that why they are dead?'

Virginsky and Porfiry exchanged a brief, almost guilty, glance, but neither answered her question.

24

Strange marks

At Porfiry's instruction, the three heads were taken out of their crates and laid side by side on the table. Additional lanterns were fetched, their light reflecting garishly back off the livid flesh, lending it the illusion of animation as each lantern was swung into place.

Porfiry looked down at the children. Mitka, Svetlana and Artur. He tried to imagine that they were lying in a big bed, asleep. But their eyes were open, and that horrific emptiness beneath their necks mocked any attempt to take refuge in a sentimental fantasy. Their faces were united by death and childhood, but Porfiry made an effort to appreciate them as individuals before he hardened himself to the task of assessing their remains as evidence. Mitka's features were elfin, his head coming to a delicate point at the chin. Svetlana, pale and blonde, appeared younger; her features less mature, her nose a mere button, her chin hardly there at all. Artur was the oldest. His features had begun to coarsen, his nose outgrowing the rest of his face. His hair was dark and wiry, and the faint smudge of his first moustache shadowed his upper lip.

Porfiry heard the door close behind him. He half-turned to acknowledge Virginsky's entrance.

'How is she?' Porfiry asked, stooping again over the children.

'How do you think?'

Porfiry twisted his head in Virginsky's direction, then quickly faced back towards the table. 'My dear Pavel Pavlovich, I cannot help remarking a strange, strained tension in your demeanour towards me. One might even call it resentment. May I ask what I have done to cause offence?'

Virginsky seemed to weigh up his options before replying. He gestured towards the heads. 'You would have sprung this on her, as you once sprung a similar shock on me.'

Porfiry stood up to face Virginsky. 'I did not want to warn her at the school, that's true. I saw little point. I wanted to spare her the anguish of imagining this, at least for the duration of our journey here. However, I would have told her before bringing her into this room.'

'I see,' said Virginsky stiffly. It was evident that such a consideration had not occurred to him.

'It makes little difference, I suppose,' conceded Porfiry. 'The anguish of imagining such a prospect, which was all I sought to mitigate, is nothing compared to the horror of seeing it.' Porfiry widened his eyes, inviting a response from Virginsky.

But Virginsky withheld his thoughts.

'Is there no other reason for your constraint towards me?'

'I am not aware of any.'

'So, how do we stand now? Now that I have explained my earlier prevarication. Does my explanation satisfy?'

'It does.'

'And may I once again count upon your friendship, as well as your professional assistance?'

Virginsky drew breath noisily before replying: 'Yes.'

'A hesitation!'

'No. That is to say . . . if I am honest . . .'

'Why should you not be honest?'

'That man. Slava. I confess I do not like him and I fail to understand why you have taken him into your employ. His interest in our cases strikes me as entirely inappropriate. To be frank, Porfiry Petrovich, I do not trust him.'

'My goodness, Pavel Pavlovich! But he has the most glowing references, albeit from deceased individuals. Tell me, of what do you suspect him?'

'I really cannot say.' Virginsky glanced down at the disembodied heads, as if he believed them capable of eavesdropping. 'Perhaps he is a spy.'

'A spy?' Porfiry's face opened in what appeared to be genuine surprise. 'That is an original suggestion. For whom do you suspect him of spying?'

'You must remember your encounter with the gendarme at the Nikolaevsky Station. I told you at the time that it does not pay to cross those people. One hears of the Third Section attempting to infiltrate other arms of the state machinery, particularly the police and judiciary. There is someone in the Third Section who has every reason to take an interest in the conduct of this case in particular.'

'You are referring to Maria Petrovna's father, are you not?'
'I am.'

'But if he wishes to know details of the case, he has only to come into my chambers and ask me. There is no need for any subterfuge.'

'You forget, Porfiry Petrovich, subterfuge is in the nature of these people. They know no other way of operating.'

'But it is really rather subtle of you to suggest this, Pavel Pavlovich. After all, Slava gives the impression of not being at all interested in this case, but somewhat more interested in the murder of Yelena Filippovna.'

'It is what I believe is known as misdirection. A classic trick of such people.'

'I see.' Porfiry blinked out a display of innocence. 'How very cunning.'

Virginsky regarded him with narrowed eyes. 'You knew, didn't you? That is to say, you suspected the same thing? But why would you employ him, believing him to be an infiltrator?'

'Let us assume you're right. He is a spy. Now that we know he is a spy, he cannot hurt us. We are fortunate that he is a very bad spy. If I had not employed him, they would perhaps have sent along a better one. Besides, we have nothing to hide from them. Our conduct of the case will be exemplary, that is a given. It does no harm to play along. Consider it a game.'

'I thought you employed him to keep me on my toes.' Virginsky's pronouncement had the cadence of a confession.

'That is what I wanted *him* to think.'

Virginsky gave a reflective wince. 'You know, Porfiry Petrovich, such misunderstandings between us would not occur if you confided in me more.'

'I fear I do not have a confiding nature.' Porfiry looked back at the table impatiently, as if he had been torn away from dinner with friends. 'Now. Come. Help me. Look at these heads and tell me what strikes you.' He made the invitation with the excited zeal of an enthusiast sharing his passion.

Virginsky approached the table. Porfiry studied his face keenly as he scanned the heads.

'The bruising,' said Virginsky at last.

'Yes! Good man. The bruises around the neck. Strikingly similar, are they not, in every case?'

'The children were all strangled.'

'It would appear so,' said Porfiry thoughtfully. He leaned over to peer at Mitka's neck, pivoting backwards and forwards to find his focal point. 'These damned eyes! Would you be so kind as to lift down one of those lanterns, Pavel Pavlovich?'

Virginsky unhooked a light from the ceiling and brought it towards the table.

'Thank you. There is something here, I'm sure of it. Look! This mark, here just to the right of the larynx. Do you see it, or are my eyes deceiving me?'

Porfiry pointed to a small intense burst of purple almost in the centre of Mitka's throat, a pinpoint darkening in the general discolouration at his neck. The mark was complex, though what drew the eye to it was its strange, almost perfect symmetry. It was a bifurcation of tiny hooked blobs around a central stem.

'Yes. There is something there,' confirmed Virginsky.

Porfiry now transferred his attention to the same area on Svetlana's neck. 'And it is here too, on this one.' A quick glance at the third head confirmed his suspicion. 'On Artur too. They all have it.'

'What does it mean?'

'Come here, Pavel Pavlovich.'

Virginsky took a hesitant step closer to Porfiry, his face creased with confusion.

'If I may for a moment borrow your neck.' Porfiry raised his hands to Virginsky's throat and applied a gentle pressure. When he took his hands away, he kept them splayed in the shape they had attained around Virginsky's neck. 'Point to the part of the hand which cuts off the air supply.'

Virginsky touched a finger to the tautly stretched tendon

between Porfiry's thumb and forefinger, first of the left, then the right hand.

'Yes. That is precisely the point that would close down the wind pipe. It would naturally touch the centre of the larynx. This mark . . .' Porfiry released his hands from the strangler's grip and gestured vaguely towards the table, . . . would appear to be caused by some hard protrusion, just to the right of the fatal point.' He held up his hands again to study them. 'It is nevertheless a point at which we would expect considerable pressure to be applied, and whatever caused this mark will have facilitated the constriction of the windpipe.' Porfiry squeezed closed his thumbs, slowly, tensely. He then clutched the base of his left thumb with the fingertips of his right hand, rotating the hands together. 'Something here,' he murmured thoughtfully.

'A thumb ring.'

The two men were silent in the aftermath of Virginsky's idea. They seemed reluctant to meet each other's eye, as if an exchange of looks would lend substance to their private suspicions.

Then Porfiry suddenly released his thumb, as if he did not wish to be caught holding it. When at last he spoke up, his voice was startled and distracted. 'I will have to make sketches of these marks.' He touched his lips and nodded. 'And later we will send a photographer. It is essential that we have an accurate reference to work to. There can be no room for mistakes. We must be certain. We must base our conclusions on precise measurements.'

'Is it possible though?'

The two men finally dared to look one another in the face.

'Anything is possible, Pavel Pavlovich,' said Porfiry, and as if to prove his point he held his stare without blinking until, in fact, Virginsky was compelled to look away.

25

A mysterious communiqué

After the night's cold snap it did not surprise Porfiry to find ice on the inside as well as outside of his window in the morning. Through the refractive filter of the frozen layers he had an impression of whiteness and movement outside. He tipped himself up on to his toes and squinted through a patch of the window where the ice was thinnest. Snow fell with determined haste, as if it didn't know how long it had.

Was it winter already? he wondered.

He wondered too what he could expect from the day and what the day would demand of him. His dreams had taken him so far out of the immediate context of his life that he felt himself bereft without them. He had dreamt of his father, he remembered that much. Then it came to him more specifically that he had dreamt of his father and his father's younger brother, Uncle Prokofy. In fact, he now remembered, his dreams had been crowded with relatives, the living and the dead. In one, a host of them had been crammed into his apartment for some kind of party. It was clear that the celebration had been in Porfiry's honour. Was it a birthday party? No, it had not been that. Nor his name day. Strangely, the reason for the party had not been alluded to in the dream, as if out of tact. Only as the dream approached its climax did Porfiry realise that a terrible mistake had been made, *and it was all his fault.* His relatives were assembled there, he realised, to celebrate his wedding party, and the peculiar delicacy that seemed to affect his guests was due to the fact that so far there was no sign of a bride. Somehow, inadvertently, he had led them to believe that he was marrying Maria Petrovna. But carelessly he had failed to broach the subject with her; hence her absence.

The scenario of his dream was extremely painful to him, both at the time he had dreamt it, and now as he recalled it. He remembered that the tension of the dream had eased suddenly as his sleeping mind had caused all his relatives to disappear, all apart from his cousin Dmitri Prokofich, who had then acted as his manservant. The recollection of the humiliating role in which he had cast his good-hearted cousin provoked a surge of embarrassment in Porfiry. He was ashamed to realise that he had not seen Dmitri Prokofich for many years, indeed not since the affair of the student Raskolnikov, whose friend Dmitri had been. He resolved to look him up at the soonest opportunity, but then remembered the reason for their estrangement. Dmitri Prokofich had married Raskolnikov's sister.

As far as Porfiry was concerned, that was no grounds for awkwardness, but he had always sensed on Avdotya Romanovna's part a reserve bordering on aversion. It was clear that even if she did not hold Porfiry responsible for her brother's fate, she at least found his presence in her home painful, serving as it did to remind her of those difficult times. Not wishing to be the cause of anguish to a blameless woman, he had, over a period of time, slipped out of his cousin's life. The fact that the affable Dmitri Prokofich had allowed the distance between them to grow confirmed Porfiry's fears. His cousin's spirit was so generous and forgiving that he had continued to consider Raskolnikov a friend even after he knew the horrific nature of the student's crimes. He had continued, in short, to believe in Raskolnikov. And, it seemed, he could not forgive his relative Porfiry Petrovich for his part in bringing Raskolnikov to justice.

Such was human nature, reflected Porfiry. He could not find it in himself to blame Dmitri Prokofich, although he wondered whether his cousin's servile status in the dream was an attempt on his part to exact revenge. He did not care to pursue this train of thought. The dream did him no credit at all, but that was often the way with dreams.

The sound of someone moving about inside his apartment brought him back to the awoken reality of his life. With a lurching presentiment of doom, he remembered the man he had employed as a servant – almost as a joke, one of his characteristic pranks. But against whom was the prank directed, if not himself? He had brought into his home a stranger, a man he could in no way trust, whose life was now entwined with his own. What if Pavel Pavlovich was right, and Slava – if that indeed was his name – was a Third Section spy?

'Speak of the grey one and the grey one heads your way,' said Porfiry as Slava came into the room bearing the breakfast tray.

Slava looked about uncertainly, as if he expected to see someone else in the room. 'You were talking about me? To whom?'

'Only to myself. Thinking about you, that is to say.'

Slava laughed nervously.

'I was merely wondering what on earth possessed me to employ you!' Porfiry's face expanded with delight. He began to laugh and could not bring himself to stop laughing for some time.

Slava's discomfiture intensified. For one moment it looked as though he might drop the tray and bolt from the room. A metallic shudder convulsed the silverware. But he regained his composure quickly. 'Have I failed to provide satisfaction in the execution of my duties?'

'Good heavens, what a question!'

'It is a simple enough question, I believe.'

'Ah, but it begs another question, does it not? And that is, to whom do you owe those duties?'

'I don't understand. To whom else but you?'

'Who else indeed!'

'Are you suggesting that I serve two masters?'

Porfiry raised his hands in a pantomime of shock that was overdone even by his own standards. And then he winked at Slava.

'Do you wish to terminate my employment?' asked Slava tersely.

'Do *you*?'

'There is the question of my honour.'

'Is there really? Could you explain that to me?'

'You have impugned my honesty ... ?' But Slava did not seem at all certain that this was in fact what Porfiry had done.

'In that case, you must do whatever you deem necessary.'

'I'm sorry?' Slava's face was furrowed in confusion.

'Apology accepted. Let us say no more about it. I am so glad we have had the opportunity to clear this up. Now, if you would be so kind as to deposit the tray on the table, you may then go about your other duties.' At this, Porfiry winked heavily several times.

Slava regarded him warily, as if he were an unpredictable dog given to biting for no reason. He kept as much distance as possible between himself and Porfiry as he placed the tray down. He backed out of the room, flashing uneasy glances as he went.

Porfiry smiled to himself. But the smile drained from his lips when he looked down at the breakfast tray. His familiar silver-plated coffee pot stood as if it were turning its back on him. Four curly sausages huddled together conspiratorially on their plate, their curved shoulders excluding him. The thought occurred to Porfiry that if he could not trust the man who had brought him this food, how could he trust the food?

He told himself he was being ridiculous. The Third Section wanted to keep an eye on him, they did not want him dead. But what if Slava was not an agent of the Third Section, but represented far darker and more dangerous forces?

His dream came back to him. Perhaps he had been wrong in his interpretation. He had not wished to punish or humiliate his cousin. It was more complex than that. He now saw the dream as an expression of regret. He longed to replace his intimate reliance on this stranger, who had suddenly appeared in his life like a cuckoo chick, with the simple but lost love of his family, as represented by Dmitri Prokofich.

He remembered too that Maria Petrovna had figured in the dream, but as an absence not a presence. He sensed that there was something significant in this, but did not care to grasp it.

*

Porfiry lit a cigarette and turned his attention to the pile of correspondence on the desk before him. He chose to open first an envelope which bore the official stamp of the Obukhovsky Hospital. It was written confirmation from Dr Pervoyedov of the results of the blood analysis from the mirror, ring and tunic. Porfiry put it to one side. Next he opened a bulkier package, which turned out to contain the latest edition of a journal to which he subscribed. He began to browse the pages, but in a distracted manner, looking up eagerly at a knock on the door.

Virginsky came in, holding up a small cardboard box, which Porfiry recognised as the sort used to hold evidence. In his other hand, he held a police folder.

'What have you there, Pavel Pavlovich?'

Virginsky crossed to Porfiry's desk, where he lifted the lid of the box and tipped out its contents, a silver ring. 'I took the liberty of retrieving this. It is the ring that we found on Yelena Filippovna's thumb.'

Porfiry made no move to pick the ring up, as if he believed that to do so would take them one step closer to the unthinkable.

'You will remember,' said Virginsky, picking up the ring himself and almost thrusting it in Porfiry's face, 'the emblem of the house of Romanov – the imperial symbol of the double-headed eagle – embossed on the face of the ring.'

'Yes,' said Porfiry. 'I remember it well.'

'It is the same size, is it not, and approximately the same shape, as the strange bruise we found repeated on each of the children's necks?'

'I would need to take precise measurements to be certain.'

'I have already done so.'

Porfiry met this statement with a sceptical start.

'The Romanov symbol on this ring is one fifth of a *vershok* in height, by one tenth in width. Almost precisely the measurements taken by you yourself from the necks of the dead children. Furthermore, the similarity between this motif and the mark is striking.' Virginsky opened the folder and shook. It was almost as if the contents were reluctant to come out into the light of day. Porfiry saw that the folder contained photographs. They stuck together, hiding one behind the other, shy, awkward, out of place. Ruthlessly, Virginsky prised them out and laid them side by side on Porfiry's desk.

Porfiry knew the subjects of these photographs well. He had spent hours studying the luridly coloured three-dimensional objects now represented in flat monochrome. And yet the images still shocked him. He might have expected the mediation of photography to soften the horror, rendering the blood and bruising of the neck stumps in various depths of grey. To some extent that was true. But this neutralising effect paradoxically also added to the power of the images. The shock was one of intense pathos, rather than pure horror. For a brief moment, he could almost believe he was looking at studio portraits; that he saw in the eyes of the three subjects the earnest innocence of children looking forward to their lives, trusting, hopeful, and slightly overawed. But eventually his own eye tracked down to the abrupt line and the inky void at the end of the truncated neck.

Porfiry sighed out a cloud of smoke.

Neither man spoke. Porfiry went back to opening his mail as if Virginsky had said nothing remotely of interest to him. Virginsky returned the ring to its box and replaced the lid, though he left the photographs on Porfiry's desk. He then took out from the inside pocket of his frock coat a folded sheet of paper. 'I have written my report, based on these findings.'

Porfiry nodded.

'The burden of my report,' continued Virginsky, 'is that circumstantial evidence strongly suggests the possibility that

Yelena Filippovna Polenova murdered Dmitri Krasotkin, Artur Smurov and Svetlana Chisova.'

'For what motive?'

'I do not speculate as to her motive. That must remain closed off from our enquiry. She is after all dead. And you know the saying, the soul of another is like a dark cellar. However, I would suggest that the deaths of these three children are not unconnected to her own death, and in fact provided her murderer with his motive.'

'Which is?'

'To prevent any further killing.'

'You are suggesting that Yelena Filippovna was subject to uncontrollable murderous impulses and that the only way to curtail her homicidal activities was to kill her?'

'You may put it like that, if you wish. Mizinchikov loved her but somehow he found out about her crimes. Perhaps she told him herself, to taunt him. Or perhaps this is what lies behind the fact alluded to in Prince Sergei's testimony, that Yelena Filippovna sought her own death. Guilt, and a horror at her own actions, prompted her to make that grotesque demand. And consider what effect this revelation would have had on Captain Mizinchikov's mind. To be confronted with such horror, to discover that the woman he loved was a monster. Rage, perhaps, played a part in it. Fear, too. And love. He would not have wanted this horrific truth to get out. Killing her was one way to keep her secret safe. She would never be in a position to reveal it herself, at least.'

'But why would she kill the children? That is the point past which I cannot get,' protested Porfiry.

'I don't know,' admitted Virginsky. 'But I fear that it may have something to do with Maria Petrovna. She is the connection between Yelena Filippovna and the dead children. Did not Prince Sergei say that Maria Petrovna's school was a cause close to Yelena Filippovna's heart? Perhaps it held a special place there, but not in the way that Prince Sergei imagined.'

'All this is dependent on a colossal supposition – no, worse than that, *two* colossal suppositions. First, that the distinctive marks on the children's necks were caused by the impression of a ring. Second, that the ring responsible is that worn by Yelena Filippovna. You realise, Pavel Pavlovich, that if either of these suppositions is false, then the flimsy construction of your theory will collapse.'

'*My* theory? All I have done is put into words what you yourself suspected when we first saw the marks on the children.'

'Be that as it may, whoever is to be credited with this theory, it remains unproven, and, frankly, incapable of proof.'

Virginsky appeared sanguine in the face of Porfiry's objections. 'For the time being, yes. But as soon as we find Captain Mizinchikov, he will be able to confirm it.'

'If he chooses to co-operate,' said Porfiry dubiously. 'It is conceivable that he would deny such a construction of events, in order to protect the memory of Yelena Filippovna.'

'But it places his own crime in an entirely different light. You know the way our Russian juries are. Excitable, and sentimental. Above all, inexperienced. No Russian jury would convict him. He will be seen as a saviour of children. If he could be persuaded to see the affair in those terms, with the promise of an acquittal, he may be willing to co-operate.'

'You have just reminded me of the third questionable supposition upon which your theory is constructed. That Captain Mizinchikov is Yelena's murderer.'

'You no longer consider him a suspect?'

'The bloodstains on the tunic do not condemn him.' Porfiry waved Dr Pervoyedov's report. 'The blood on the tunic did not come from a pumping neck wound. It is far more likely to have come from a lacerated cheek.'

'But blood from his own face would not have made that pattern,' insisted Virginsky forcefully. 'And so much else certainly incriminates him.' Virginsky paced the room impatiently as Porfiry looked on amused. 'We need to talk to Mizinchikov!'

'But we do not have Mizinchikov!'

'He must be persuaded to hand himself in.'

'And how do you propose to achieve that desirable goal?'

'Through the newspapers. If we were to release an account of our discoveries, intimating the nature of consequent hypotheses, hinting too at the leniency that Yelena Filippovna's murderer may expect . . .'

Porfiry contracted his lips distastefully as he stubbed out his cigarette. 'No. Out of the question. It would be utterly irresponsible to publicise such wild and unfounded speculations. I forbid it. Do you understand me, Pavel Pavlovich? I absolutely forbid it.'

Virginsky seemed taken aback by the strength of Porfiry's reaction. 'But why? Surely we must use whatever means we can?'

'And if this theory turns out to be mistaken? Have you stopped to consider what damage may be wrought by the release of such a story, not only upon the reputation of a dead woman, but also on the state?'

'What has the state to do with this?'

'The murder of factory children by a woman of high birth?

258

Can you imagine anything more provocative . . . more inflammatory?'

'But if it is the truth?'

'If it is the truth, that would be a different matter. However, until we are in a position to prove or disprove these allegations against a woman who cannot defend herself, we must maintain the most scrupulous discretion. No good can be served by seeking publicity at this stage of the investigation.'

'I beg to differ,' said Virginsky stiffly.

Porfiry lit another cigarette and glared at his junior colleague warningly. He held the look for a moment and then turned back to processing his correspondence.

'You cannot hold back the inevitable,' said Virginsky darkly.

But Porfiry had not heard. His attention was held by the letter in his hands, hands that were now shaking. A precarious column of ash toppled from the burning cigarette he held between his index and forefinger knuckles. He made no move to clean it up. As he had unfolded the letter – a single sheet of crisp white paper – he saw a length of red silk fall weightlessly onto his desk. Porfiry felt the muscles of his heart contract. There was only one line of writing, a flow of red ink that seemed to be a second thread, cleverly lain on the page. He read: *For every child killed by the oppressive machine, we will take the life of one member of the enslaver class.*

'Pavel Pavlovich.' His voice came thickly, as if it cost him much effort to produce it. 'You must look at this.'

26

At the *banya*

'Slava! Slava! Where is that man?'

It was Porfiry's turn to pace the room. His steps were short and agitated. His eyes flickered with wild excitement.

He went to the door that led to his private apartment. As he opened it, his eye was caught by the tail end of a movement. It could have been a trick of the light, a shifting shadow created by the opening of the door. Or it could have been another door closing, carefully, noiselessly. A moment later, the door in question – the one to Slava's room – opened and Slava came out, his face blandly expectant.

'You called?'

'Yes. Please fetch the samovar.'

'I am to serve you in your chambers?'

'Yes. Bring glasses for myself and Pavel Pavlovich. With lemon. And sugar.'

Slava nodded sharply, then turned towards the kitchen door.

Porfiry waited till he was out of sight before closing the door.

Virginsky was still studying the note, as if it were crammed with words, instead of bearing just a single line of text.

'It changes everything,' said Porfiry breathlessly. 'You have to admit it, Pavel Pavlovich.'

'If it is genuine,' said Virginsky, turning the sheet over as if he expected to find evidence of trickery on the reverse.

'Of course it's genuine! The thread! Who knew about the thread? Other than you and I – and the murderer?'

Virginsky wrinkled his face sceptically. 'It could be a coincidence.'

'Are you mad?' Porfiry began pacing again, impelled by indignation. 'One does not encounter coincidences such as this! A red thread found on a murder victim – a red thread sent by someone claiming responsibility for that very murder!'

'Very well. I accept it is not a coincidence. However, it is possible that this has been sent to us by the murderer in order to mislead. To lend the crime a political aspect which it does not in truth possess. Mizinchikov—'

'Mizinchikov did not write this.'

'But if he did, it would be a way of deflecting suspicion from himself.'

'No, no, no – you have it all wrong, Pavel Pavlovich. Let us say, for the moment, that Captain Mizinchikov did kill Yelena Filippovna. You will concede, I think, because you have said as much yourself, that his crime was . . . well, if not a crime of passion, then something very akin to it. Either he killed her out of jealousy, as we first believed, or out of horror, as your most recent theory speculates.' Porfiry broke off pacing and narrowed his eyes in concentration. He unconsciously tapped his breast pocket for his cigarette case. Once the ritual of taking out and lighting a cigarette had been completed, he seemed calmer, more reflective. 'And not simply horror, perhaps. Compassion, too. For her, and for her future victims. But as we have already had occasion to note, those who are driven to such crimes do not normally engage in such evasive strategies as this.' His eyes darted towards the note that Virginsky was holding.

'And so you are minded to accept this note at face value?'

'I am certainly inclined to take it very seriously indeed. I intend to consider its implications as fully as possible.' Porfiry cocked an ear towards the door to his private apartment, behind which the approaching rattle of the samovar could be heard. 'Not here, however.'

Porfiry sprang to open the door, blowing smoke back over his shoulder, courteously away from Slava's face. 'Ah, there you are. I am afraid that Pavel Pavlovich and I have been urgently called away. You may drink the tea for us, if you wish.'

Suspicion compressed Slava's face. 'But you have only just asked for it.'

'Such is the nature of our work, I'm afraid. Now be a good fellow and take it back to the kitchen, where you may drink it at your leisure.'

'Where will *you* be?' To soften the peremptoriness of his demand, Slava added: 'Should anyone ask, that is.'

'No one will ask,' said Porfiry flatly. 'And if they should, you are at liberty to say you do not know.'

Slava hesitated, apparently reluctant to go back into Porfiry's apartment as he had been instructed. He seemed to fear it would place him at a disadvantage.

Porfiry made a shooing gesture with both hands.

Slava closed one eye, sighting Porfiry with the other. At last, he began to back away, though without turning his back on the magistrate, all the time viewing him through a single eye.

'Good man,' said Porfiry cheerfully, as he closed the door on him. He then hurried back to his desk and swept the note, the thread and the photographs into a green case file. 'I think perhaps we should put this beyond the reach of prying eyes.' He placed the folder in a drawer in his desk, which he locked, pocketing the key. Next he replaced Yelena's ring in its box, which he held out to Virginsky. 'Now, Pavel Pavlovich, if you would be so good as to return this ring to the police evidence room, I shall meet you back here in five minutes. There is something I must retrieve from my room before we go.'

*

This object turned out to be a curious conical hat made from beige felt, decorated with appliqué flowers. It was now the only item of clothing that Porfiry was wearing, apart from a pair of hemp sandals and a simple wooden crucifix around his neck.

He made the sign of the cross with the clump of leafy birch twigs in his right hand and stepped into the steam room. He felt his skin liquefy immediately. The wall of heat was almost impenetrable. He had to push himself into it, his whole body rebelling against the madness of that intention. The kick of his heart quickened alarmingly; each pounding thump another moment of his life ticked off. He looked down at his body forlornly. His chest sagged and the skin of his belly strained under the pressure of his paunch. Sweat clung to the translucent down of his body, made visible against the vibrant pink glow of his skin. He turned his head towards Virginsky. Nudity revealed the younger man's latent athleticism. He was taller, leaner, physically stronger than Porfiry had ever been.

The steam room was quiet but not empty. Porfiry indicated a corner as far away as possible from any others.

They laid their hired towels out on the tiled bench that ran around the wall and sat down at right angles to one another.

'Why are we here, Porfiry Petrovich?' Virginsky posed the question with wry indulgence.

'To sweat.' Porfiry blinked rapidly. The sweat was flooding his eyes. The hot steam, too, made it difficult to see. 'The salutary properties of the *banya* are well-known. I myself particularly value the steam vapour's efficacy in clearing excess catarrh from my chest and nasal passages. At this time of year, I am prone to pneumonia. Only the *banya* can keep it at bay. In addition, the heat is cleansing spiritually as well as bodily. I feel the pores of my soul opening up.' Porfiry closed his eyes and inhaled deeply through both nostrils. 'Ideas and influences flow more freely through me. And, of course, there is the fact that one is naked. As a newborn babe.'

'In a pointed hat.'

'Ha! Naked, one is more aware of one's humanity.' With a grunt of exertion, Porfiry cracked the birch whisk down across his distended belly. The pain of the blow melted into the pain of the heat. He felt the boundary of his body open up even more, in an almost transcendent sense of physical dissolution. His wince relaxed into a blissful smile. 'One feels the dirt and detritus of everyday life slip away. The mind is freed. The body restored. On top of all this, I find it has a palliative effect on my haemorrhoids.'

Virginsky gave a sly smile. 'So . . . it was not to get away from Slava?'

Porfiry's lips puckered out to kiss the steam. He licked the sweat dripping from his upper lip. 'I can think here,' was all he conceded. He laid his head back against the wall, eyes closed as he flicked his shoulders lazily with the whisk.

'Do you not think, Porfiry Petrovich, that the arrival of the note obliges us to involve the Third Section? It does, after all, give the case a political aspect.'

Porfiry's eyes flashed open. He shook the birch twigs towards Virginsky, striking him lightly on the chest.

'Well?' insisted Virginsky, evidently not satisfied with Porfiry's response.

'In my experience, the Third Section needs no invitation to involve itself in cases. We will be hearing from them soon enough. If Slava is indeed a spy, he will already have alerted his superiors to all that he knows – and possibly more. He suspects that I am excluding him now from our deliberations. This will provoke a change of strategy from them. I expect an overt intervention. We have come here to buy ourselves a little time.'

'Do you not ever ask yourself whom are we fighting, Porfiry Petrovich?'

'I am not fighting anyone,' said Porfiry. There was a note of wounded innocence in the assertion. 'There is a lot to consider here, Pavel Pavlovich. Are we really prepared to accuse Yelena Filippovna of murdering three children to whom she has the most tangential of connections, on the flimsiest of circumstantial evidence?'

'You saw the marks. You saw the ring. It is not fanciful. That bruise is a precise imprint of the emblem on her ring – which she wore twisted round in such a way as to inflict just such a bruise.'

'But the woman is dead. She cannot defend herself against the charge. And as yet, we have no motive.'

'We must ... speak to Maria Petrovna.' Virginsky's eyes darted uneasily, as if even he shrank from what he was suggesting.

Porfiry sighed. 'Even to voice such allegations to someone who was a friend of the deceased is brutal.'

'Frankly I am surprised at your fastidiousness, Porfiry Petrovich. You have never baulked at brutality before.'

Porfiry met this accusation with a look of mild rebuke. 'But she is dead, Pavel Pavlovich!' he insisted.

'What difference does that make?'

'She cannot be saved. We can only pray for her soul.'

'With all respect, it is not *our* job to concern ourselves with saving people, Porfiry Petrovich. We must only uncover the truth and set in motion whatever judicial process arises from that truth. We are not concerned with souls.'

'Perhaps you are right.' Porfiry felt suddenly light-headed. 'But what if she is innocent!' He made the cry plaintively. 'The note does not accuse her directly.'

'Now it is you who are making a specious assumption, Porfiry Petrovich. You are assuming that whoever wrote the note knows who killed the children. But we cannot even be certain that they are referring to the same dead children. The note speaks only of children *killed by the oppressive machine*. That could just as easily refer to children dying of malnutrition, unnecessary disease, or factory accidents.'

'If whoever wrote the note fulfils his promise, we are facing a bloodbath – in which all the victims will be highborn.'

'A revolution, in other words.'

Porfiry stirred the vaporous air in front of his face with the birch whisk, as if to see more clearly.

'If Yelena Filippovna did not kill these children then someone else did. Someone wearing a Romanov ring. Possibly – it is not beyond the bounds of possibility – a member of the Imperial Family. Perhaps you now regret allowing the Tsarevich the opportunity to make his escape to the Crimea?'

'No!' cried Porfiry. 'Will you go from accusing a dead woman to making unspeakable allegations against the Tsarevich?'

Dim shapes stirred in the hot mist. The murmurs of outrage and excitement were audible.

'Our first loyalty is to the truth, Porfiry Petrovich. Now, thanks to the Tsar's own reforms, no one is above the law.'

'But it always comes back to this question of why. Why would the Tsarevich murder these children?'

'I do not insist that it is he. It could be any member of the family.'

'You will exclude the Tsar, I trust!'

Virginsky rippled his brows. 'To come back to your question – why would anyone? Perhaps there are some crimes concerning which the question of motive is irrelevant.'

'Not satisfactory, I'm afraid, Pavel Pavlovich. There is always a motive, however twisted, petty, or tenuous. The motive never justifies the crime, never fully explains it. And we may divine something else at work within the criminal's mind, whether it be sickness or . . .' Porfiry looked away from Virginsky. 'Some other influence,' he added reticently, almost sheepishly. Virginsky narrowed his eyes, noting the evasion. 'But the criminal himself will always provide a motive, in which he believes, categorically.'

'Is it not sometimes the case that a criminal will provide more than one motive, and that often they are contradictory?'

'Sometimes the criminal is the last person to understand his own motivation. However, that does not mean that we, as investigators, must forego the attempt to understand. If we give up insisting on a motive, then . . .' Porfiry stared into the steam. He had the fleeting sense that it swirled in an infinite abyss, that there was nothing behind it, and therefore nothing behind anything.

'Then what?'

Porfiry's expression as he sought Virginsky's eyes was despairing. 'Then we have opened the door to moral chaos.'

'That door is already open,' answered Virginsky glibly. 'You know as well as anybody that man is an irrational creature.' When Porfiry made no reply but stared in mute indignation, Virginsky added: 'And evil. You were going to say the word yourself, were you not? You drew back at the last moment because you understood that it undermined your argument.'

'What do I care about arguments!'

– 'In that case, you were afraid.'

'No!'

'Well then, it was to maintain your position. You do have your position, Porfiry Petrovich: that man, even the vilest criminal, is capable of salvation. You cannot allow that there may exist a man who is irredeemably evil. A man, for example, who would kill children just for the sport of it.'

'On the contrary. I know such men exist. I have met them and talked to them. And listened to their motives.'

'Did you manage to save any of them?' Virginsky could not keep the sarcasm out of his question.

Porfiry closed his eyes and shook his head minutely.

'No,' confirmed Virginsky, relentlessly. 'If you accept that such men exist, then logic insists that they may be found within any social class. Within any family. You can hardly believe that the propensity to evil may be contained by social boundaries.'

'Enough!' Porfiry began to thrash himself energetically with the birch whisk.

'What do you intend to do?'

Porfiry Petrovich lifted the conical hat from his head and looked inside it, as if he expected to find the answer to Virginsky's question there. 'We must do our job. That is to say, we must slowly and methodically gather evidence.' He restored the hat to its former position and met Virginsky's challenging look blankly. 'As far as the deaths of the children are concerned, we have hardly begun to scratch the surface. It is certainly too early to jump to conclusions.'

'You think that is what I have done?'

Porfiry held out the birch whisk, as if it were an olive branch. 'I think you are in need of this.' When Virginsky did not take it, Porfiry shrugged and settled back into the heat.

*

After losing himself in the melting heat of the *banya*, the subsequent plunge into an icy pool restored the edges of his being with the vicious shock of a thousand slaps landing simultaneously. Once again his heart hammered out alarm. There was something reckless, almost self-destructive, about the rate of its pummelling. Porfiry felt the stab and twist of new pains. He tasted his own mortality. More than that, he sensed his heart at the edge of capacity. And yet, strangely, it seemed to gain strength from this forcible reminder of its own frailty.

Drying himself briskly with the threadbare towel, Porfiry acknowledged a new energy in his muscles, a lightness to his bones, and a mental clarity that he had not experienced for a long time. He felt almost sorry for Virginsky at the sight of the

269

younger man's sullen, graceless movements. His limbs seemed to be weighed down with unhappiness.

'Who are *you* fighting, Pavel Pavlovich?'

Virginsky gave Porfiry a guarded look as he held his towel in front of himself defensively.

'Did you not ask me that question earlier?' explained Porfiry. 'I am intrigued to know how you would answer it.'

'The criminals, of course,' said Virginsky.

Porfiry laughed appreciatively. 'Correct answer! Well done!'

Porfiry continued to pat himself dry. 'There is much work still to do. Difficult work. This is a murky business. And it is set to become even murkier. Other agencies and interests are sure to get involved, if they are not already. We need to know who our friends are, for it will be far from easy to discern our enemies.' Porfiry sensed Virginsky shrink back under the force of his scrutiny. 'I need to know that I can count on you, Pavel Pavlovich.'

Virginsky's mouth tightened pensively. Neither man said a word as they dressed.

*

Back in his clothes, Porfiry's skin felt not just cleansed but renewed.

They took a carriage north along Liteyny Prospekt. There was a moist chill to the air, which was heavy with the threat of snow. But their naked exposure to the extremes of the bath house had fortified them for whatever shocks the climate held. Both men fixed their gaze on the District Courthouse as they rattled past it. The solid square building, with its high arched windows, like wide-open eyes searching out the truth, seemed to be the physical embodiment of an ideal.

Porfiry caught the challenge brimming in Virginsky's look. 'We must place our faith in it, Pavel Pavlovich,' he said gently.

Virginsky blinked and shook his head as if he had been roused from a deep reverie. His brow contracted into a questioning frown.

'Progress,' continued Porfiry, 'the progress of Russia, is taking place in there, through the exercise of legality. The judicial process, Pavel Pavlovich, the open examination of evidence, the presenting and arguing of cases, without prejudice or fear ... progress. Adversarial dispute ... progress. Cases heard before a jury ... progress. And we – you and I – we are the agents of progress. Simply by doing our job, by investigating crimes, gathering evidence, pursuing leads, interviewing suspects – in so many ways are we taking Russia forward. We do not need a revolution, Pavel Pavlovich. The change you desire will come about simply by virtue of us doing our job.'

'That is what *you* believe.' Virginsky's emphasis sought to distance him from Porfiry's optimism.

'Yes.'

'But the tsar who gave this licence may just as easily take it away.'

'He cannot. Besides, he does not want to.'

'Perhaps not now, not today, not this tsar.'

'Is that what lies behind your suspicions of the Tsarevich? Fear of a reactionary backlash?'

'Do you consider me so naïve?'

'It is not naivety, Pavel Pavlovich. On the contrary, it shows a sophisticated understanding of the power with which our office is invested. However, to bring a charge against an individual for political reasons would be an abuse of that power.

Anyone who did so would be guilty of perpetrating an injustice. I trust you would agree with that?'

Virginsky grunted his reluctant assent.

'You cannot bring about a just society through injustice. In the same way that you cannot reach the truth through lying – though many are seeking to do exactly that.'

The carriage drew up outside the Surgical-Medical Academy just as the first fine particles of snow began to swirl in the grey.

'By doing our job, Pavel Pavlovich. Carefully, meticulously, patiently.' With that Porfiry forced himself out of the carriage, like a cork popping from a bottle.

27

I. P. S.

'You have come back?' Professor Bubnov held the expression of distaste that he had worn all the way across the foyer.

'Yes,' said Porfiry, his eyes flickering coyly as though he believed Professor Bubnov's exclamation had been prompted by irrepressible joy. 'We went away. And now we have come back.'

'I see.' Professor Bubnov touched the tip of one finger delicately to his lips. 'This is about the initials.'

Porfiry gave an unconvincing performance of surprise. 'Ah yes, the initials! How kind of you to remind us. Have you had any success in interpreting them?'

'I know nothing about the meaning of any initials.' Professor Bubnov seemed to be picking his words advisedly. 'However, there is a man here who may be able to shed some light on them.'

'Where is this marvellous luminary? You must take us to him immediately.'

'He is not a luminary. He is a very lowly individual.' If Professor Bubnov understood Porfiry's pun he gave no indication of enjoying it. 'Smerdyakov is a porter of sorts. It is his job to receive the bodies from the police.'

'Then he truly is the man to clear up the mystery.'

They were taken to a large storeroom at the rear of the academy, with wide double doors of an unloading bay open to the elements. A cloud of tobacco smoke hung over a screened-off area in one corner. Professor Bubnov approached the screen, seemingly to converse with the smoke. Eventually, a man dressed in a peasant's belted shirt and high boots, with a pipe clamped between his teeth, stepped out of the booth. He had a lean, strangely bent face, his long jaw being at an angle to the rest of his head. His eyes were pinpricks of cunning. He took a moment to get the measure of Porfiry and Virginsky before approaching them.

'You want to talk to me?'

'You take receipt of bodies that are brought here by the police?' Smerdyakov flashed a glance back towards the professor, who was in the process of vanishing beneath Smerdyakov's smoke trail.

'A-aye?'

'Could you explain to me what happens? The police bring the bodies here . . . ?'

'A-aye?'

'And you record the receipt in the ledger book?'

'No.' Smerdyakov was startlingly emphatic in his denial. 'I am not the one who writes in the book.'

'But you do make some kind of record?'

'I fill in a chit.'

'I see. And the chit goes with the body to the morgue?'

'A-aye?'

Porfiry experienced a strange surge of gratification at the return of the equivocal refrain.

'What details are recorded on the chit?'

'You know. The standard ones.'

'Please be more specific. I'm afraid I don't know at all.'

'Sex. Age.'

'You are qualified to determine the age?'

'I have a go.'

'What else?'

'Date. Time.'

'And the details you put on the chit are subsequently entered into the ledger book?'

'A-aye?'

'Who is responsible for that?'

'Who?'

'Aye. I mean, yes.'

'Not me.'

'No. Very well. What about the initials?'

'Initials?'

'Each entry in the ledger has a set of letters in one column. Professor Bubnov was not able to tell us the meaning of those letters. He rather thought you would be able to.'

There was a stirring in the smoke. Smerdyakov determinedly refused to turn towards it. 'Did he now?'

'Yes. Are these letters taken from your chit?'

'Maybe they are.'

'I see. And if they were, what possibly could they mean?'

'That's who we got it from. For settling up, you see.'

'Who you got it from? You mean to say they are the initials of the individual policeman supplying a particular corpse?'

'A-aye?'

'And the payment is made to the individual policeman, not to the force as a whole, or the station from which he comes.'

'A-aye?'

'Who pays them? Not you?'

'No. Not me.'

'Who, then?'

'The bursar's office. The chit goes to the bursar's office. They present themselves for payment.'

'It's all very organised.'

'It has to be.'

'You receive a lot of bodies in this way?'

'The students must have their corpses.'

'The policemen who supply the corpses are all known to you?'

'Maybe?'

'If we were to get the ledger now, you would be able to tell us the identity and station of every officer entered in there?'

'Ah! If I may intervene here.' Professor Bubnov stepped forward from the cloud of smoke that half-enshrouded him. 'I am afraid to say that the ledger has gone missing.'

'Missing? How can this be?'

'We have searched everywhere for it. I fear . . . it may have been . . . stolen.'

Porfiry's rage expressed itself in the mute and frantic snapping of his eyelids. 'But why?'

The professor gave a forlorn shrug.

'I will tell you why. To prevent the information it contains coming into my hands. By God, I was a fool not to take the book when I had a chance. I misjudged you, professor. I thought I was dealing with a decent man, a man of humanity and compassion. I believed if I gave you a little latitude you would do the right thing. How wrong I was! My God! Do you not realise? This is murder we are investigating – the murder of three innocents – and all you are concerned about is protecting your sources of supply!'

'But I know nothing about the disappearance of the ledger,' protested Professor Bubnov lamely.

'I know nothing, I know nothing! It's always the same with you moral cowards. Be under no illusions, I hold you responsible for this, sir.'

'We have turned the Academy upside down.'

'You were the last person to have the ledger in his possession. You knew the importance of the book to the investigation. Don't think you'll get away with this. If the book does not turn up, you may face a charge.'

'I cannot produce the book, sir. It is out of my hands.'

'I want a name. Tell him to give us a name, or you will be arrested.'

'But you don't understand. It was the police. The police themselves came for it.'

Porfiry's eyes widened as he took this in. After a moment his expression contracted into a threatening glower. 'That will not help you. Let me explain something. I am independent of the police. The police cannot protect you from me. From the law. My God, how it shames me as a Russian to be having this discussion. Tell him to give me a name or you'll suffer the consequences.'

Professor Bubnov bowed assent.

'You, Smerdyakov,' snapped Porfiry. 'I. P. S.? Who is I. P. S.?'

'That'll be Salytov. Lieutenant Ilya Petrovich Salytov. Of the Haymarket District Police Bureau. The one with the face.'

Porfiry placed a hand over his eyes, as if to still their frenzied blinking, and groaned.

28

A representative of the Third Section

The St Petersburg Gazette, Thursday, 17 October 1870
Investigators examine link between murders
Dead beauty suspected of horrific crimes

Magistrates investigating the disappearance of three child factory workers, Dmitri Krasotkin, Artur Smurov and Svetlana Chisova, are considering the possibility that they were murdered by the society beauty Yelena Filippovna Polenova, herself the victim of murder, as reported in these pages on the 2nd instant.

The outlandish theory hinges on the discovery of mysterious bruises on the necks of three juvenile remains, which have been positively identified as belonging to the missing children. Magistrates are of the opinion that these bruises correspond closely in shape and size to the design of a ring worn by the dead woman. It is supposed that, for reasons known only to herself, Mademoiselle Polenova strangled the children to death, and in the process of so doing, left the imprint of her ring on their innocent necks.

As of yet, no one has been charged with the murder of Yelena Filippovna, although magistrates have appealed for Captain Konstantin Denisevich Mizinchikov, a deserter from the Preobrazhensky Regiment, in whose apartment an incriminating razor was found, to come forward and give an account of his conduct, at the Naryskin Palace, on the 1st instant, being respectively the location and date of Mmelle Polenova's demise.

A source at the Department for the Investigation of Criminal Causes has revealed that whoever killed Mmelle Polenova may have done so to prevent the slaughter of future innocents. If this is indeed the case, it is to be expected that such an individual would be treated with great sympathy by investigating magistrates. We urge the killer to hand himself over to the authorities, not only for the good of his own soul, but for the peace of mind of the entire city.

*

Ivan Iakovich Bakhmutov slammed the paper down on the boardroom table.

'Bad, very bad,' snarled von Lembke, through teeth clenched around a cigar he was in the process of lighting.

Prince Naryskin took the paper. 'What?'

'There!' Bakhmutov jabbed the offending article with a finger.

'My God! It cannot be true?'

'Of course it's not true,' declared Bakhmutov, pacing the room restlessly.

'Then why print it?'

The naivety of Prince Naryskin's question drew an ugly guffaw from von Lembke.

'Our enemies are behind this,' said Bakhmutov darkly. 'They seek to ruin us.'

'I thought you had friends on the *Gazette*.' Von Lembke's tone was mocking. Bakhmutov did not deign to answer the remark.

'But I do not see what this has to do with us.' Prince Naryskin looked up pleadingly at Bakhmutov.

'It brings her name back into the public mind.'

'She was his mistress,' said von Lembke flatly. He was surprised to see Prince Naryskin blush.

'Not only that, it associates her name with the most despicable crimes. At a time when we are seeking to capitalise on your involvement with the bank. They mention the Naryskin Palace, I see. And so they sully your name as well as hers.'

'This is insufferable!' protested Prince Naryskin.

'Question is, what to do about it?' Von Lembke's thin smile closed tightly shut. He studied his cigar intently, casting occasional sly glances at Prince Naryskin.

The prince felt himself the object of Bakhmutov's attention too.

'My dear friend, I think the time has come to discuss the terms upon which the board would be willing to consider the cancellation of your debt. That is something you desire, is it not?'

But there was something about Bakhmutov's smile that made the prince question whether this was as desirable an outcome as he had once imagined.

*

'What is the meaning of this?' Porfiry threw the newspaper at Virginsky as he came in for his morning briefing. The pages fell apart in a flurried panic, littering the surface of Porfiry's desk.

'I beg your pardon?'

'Do I not have enough to contend with? A servant who is a Third Section spy. Salytov carrying on an illicit trade in the bodies of murder victims. And now this. You. Talking to the press when I had explicitly forbidden it.'

'But I know nothing about this,' said Virginsky, retrieving the scattered newspaper sheet by sheet.

'Again, *I know nothing!* Are you a moral coward too, Pavel Pavlovich? Do you refuse to take responsibility for your actions?'

'I did not speak to any journalists.'

'This is not helpful.' Porfiry shook his head darkly. 'Who knows what it will unleash. There are consequences here that you cannot conceive of.'

Virginsky put the paper back together carefully and folded it as neatly as he could. 'I swear to you, Porfiry Petrovich, I had nothing to do with this.'

'We will just have to deal with whatever comes our way. In the meantime, where is Salytov?'

'You do not believe me.' There was a deadened fatality to Virginsky's tone.

'I have no time to consider the question now. We will inquire into this in due course.'

There was a brisk rap at the door.

'At last, Salytov. Come in!'

The fact that Porfiry had been expecting Lieutenant Salytov made the appearance of the man who did come through the door especially mystifying. His face was somehow familiar, and yet, as Porfiry strained his memory to place it, all recollection of the man's identity eluded him. He knew him from somewhere. But where? There was something not right about the man, or perhaps he was sensing some fundamental change that had taken place since the last time he saw him that made recognition impossible. He was dressed in a dark frock coat.

The more Porfiry looked at this item of clothing the more certain he was that here was the source of the mystery. The man held a charcoal grey bowler in one hand; between the thumb and forefinger of the other, he twirled the apex of a waxed blond moustache.

'Good day, Porfiry Petrovich *Razumikhin*!' His voice sank to a conspiratorial whisper on the last word.

As soon as he heard the voice, he knew where he had seen the man before. 'You're out of uniform.'

'I am not obliged to signal my presence with the uniform everywhere I go, although it is sometimes useful to don the sky blue – when one wants to make an impression.'

'Was it for show then, your exercise in the Nikolaevsky Station?'

'Not at all. We were in earnest.'

'Did you catch your man?'

'Murin? No. He still evades us. But I believe we are closing in on him. It is to be hoped that we will catch up with him soon. He is a very dangerous individual.'

Porfiry nodded his head, almost in admiration. 'Evidently you have discovered my family name.'

'I did not know it was a secret.'

'Perhaps you would be so good as to reveal yours?'

'I am not bound to.' The visitor renewed the energy with which he rolled his moustache and smiled. 'However, I am here on official business, so there is perhaps little point in concealing it. I am Major Pyotr Afanasevich Verkhotsev.'

'You are Maria Petrovna's father!' exclaimed Virginsky.

'And you are Pavel Pavlovich Virginsky,' said Verkhotsev, facing Virginsky with a polite bow. 'Now that we are all friends, perhaps I should reveal the purpose of my visit. I have here . . .'

Verkhotsev withdrew a sealed paper from inside his frock coat '. . . a warrant issued by Count Shuvalov, whom you will know as the Head of the Third Section of His Imperial Majesty's Chancellery.'

'Yes, yes. Quite.' Porfiry broke the seal and studied the document Verkhotsev had handed to him.

'You will see that it is quite in order. It requires you to share with me all the evidence you have gathered so far in the investigation into the murder of Yelena Filippovna Polenova, as well as all evidence relating to the murders of Dmitri Krasotkin, Artur Smurov and Svetlana Chisova. As you will observe, the warrant has been countersigned by Count Konstantin Palen, the Minister of Justice, and General Trepov, the Chief of Police. The Chief Superintendent of the Haymarket Station, your very own Nikodim Fomich, has also initialled it to signify his approval.'

'You are taking over the investigation?'

'No, no, no! Only a very vain or foolish man would remove the greatest investigator in St Petersburg from a case in order to take it over himself.'

'You flatter me. For my part, I will say that you are welcome to it.'

'Really? Why do you say that?'

'I hope you will not take this the wrong way, but, in my experience, as soon as the Third Section becomes interested in a case, I myself lose the will to continue with it.'

'I am sorry to hear that, Porfiry Petrovich. Mortified, even. May I ask why?'

'Things become unnecessarily complicated.'

'Ah, now – if I may be permitted to correct a misapprehension on your part?'

Porfiry nodded for Verkhotsev to continue.

'It is not that things *become* complicated with our involvement. It is rather that we reveal how very complicated they were right from the beginning. Things are always complicated, Porfiry Petrovich. Invariably so.'

'But they acquire a degree of complication that makes it impossible to get to the truth.'

'There is nothing I desire more than to get to the truth. Especially in this case. I think you will understand that this is a case that concerns me personally. Pavel Pavlovich has already alluded to my daughter Masha's involvement. In addition, an account in today's *Gazette* has alerted us to the wider implications of these cases. By the by, I might ask, Porfiry Petrovich, why did you decide to release the details of the case in this way?'

'It was not my decision,' said Porfiry sourly, blinking aggressively towards Virginsky. 'I did not authorise it.'

'The *Gazette* speaks of a source at the Department for the Investigation of Criminal Causes. It was not you?'

'Of course not.'

'Then who?'

'I cannot say.'

'Do *you* have any suspicions, Pavel Pavlovich?'

'I am as much at a loss as Porfiry Petrovich.'

'I cannot believe the great Porfiry Petrovich is ever at a loss.'

'Please, I really would prefer that you did not flatter me in this way. It is rather unnerving to be flattered by a representative of the Third Section.'

'Ah, but it is not flattery.' Verkhotsev now did something that almost scandalised Porfiry: he blinked. He blinked excessively and rapidly, in a manner Porfiry could only think of as his own. And how provoking it was to see the coyly feminine gesture mirrored in another's face! He had the distinct impression that the man was mocking him. Either that, or Verkhotsev had arrived independently at the same mannerism. It was certainly an uncomfortable spectacle to behold.

'At any rate,' continued Verkhotsev. 'The article makes interesting reading. Do you really suspect Yelena Filippovna of murdering the children? She was at school with my daughter, you know.'

'The distinctive bruises on the children's necks are very suggestive, but not conclusive. In addition, some new evidence has come to light which rather militates against one of our theories – that Yelena Filippovna was murdered to prevent her from killing any more children.'

'Indeed? May I see it?'

Relieved to have something to do, Porfiry retrieved the key to his desk from his pocket and unlocked the drawer. He opened the green case file and handed the anonymous note to Verkhotsev. 'This arrived yesterday. A length of silk thread was enclosed with it.' Porfiry rolled his thumb and index finger to lay a trail of red on to his desk, as if he were sprinkling magical powder. 'You should know that a similar thread was found on the body of Yelena Filippovna.'

'How interesting.'

'If her murder was political, as the note suggests, then she was chosen as a victim purely on the basis of her status as a pampered society woman. That does not disprove she was the children's murderer, of course, although it would be a colossal coincidence for the revolutionary assassin to have picked her, of all the women he could have picked.'

'Unless he knew, of course.'

'But if he knew, why not make it explicit in the note? And besides, killing the specific murderer rather undermines the political point the sender wishes to make. Such a killing has no wider societal significance. The meaning of the note, as I understand it, is that women like Yelena Filippovna, who live as parasites on the labour of children like those murdered, are guilty by their very style of living – not because they have actually strangled anyone. The sender of the note wishes to equate such a life with the most heinous of crimes.'

'Yes. I see your point,' said Verkhotsev. 'But as you conceded, we cannot rule out a coincidence here. There have been no more children found since her death?'

'Not as far as we are aware. However . . .'

Verkhotsev had become distracted by the open file on Porfiry's desk. The edge of a photograph was visible. 'What have you there?'

'These are the photographs that show the bruises on the children's necks.'

'May I see them?'

'Please.'

'This is the mark that has aroused your interest?'

Porfiry's chair squealed sharply as he rose from his desk to join Verkhotsev. 'Yes. You will see that it is found in each of the photographs.'

'And the ring? May I see the ring?'

'Pavel Pavlovich, would you be so good as to fetch it?'

Virginsky nodded sullenly and left the room.

'An interesting young man, your Pavel Pavlovich. Is he entirely trustworthy, do you think?'

'Entirely,' replied Porfiry without hesitation.

Verkhotsev raised both eyebrows sceptically and returned

the photographs to the folder. 'I am glad you have chosen to co-operate.'

'I was not aware that I had a choice. The number of signatories on your warrant is overwhelming.'

Verkhotsev waved a hand dismissively. 'Ah, but a person may still be obstructive. And you have chosen not to be. I am grateful to you for that. As a father.'

'You are here as a father?'

'In part. Of course.'

'Did Maria Petrovna ask you to involve yourself in the case?' Porfiry could not keep the disappointment out of his voice. Had he failed her?

'Masha? We discussed it, naturally. I am pleased to say I have an open and trusting relationship with my daughter. It is not always the case these days between parents and their children. The next generation is a great cause for concern, do you not agree?'

'I do not care to make sweeping generalisations about anyone. I prefer to judge individuals on an individual basis.'

'You are quite right. However, the young are subjected to so many alarming influences. One cannot help but be frightened for them. Take this note, for example. There is a seductive logic to it, do you not think?'

'Logic? Surely you mean false logic?'

Verkhotsev raised his palm in demurral. 'You do not have to pick your words carefully in front of me, Porfiry Petrovich. I am not here to trip you up. Logic is pitiless. That is why we cannot build a society on logic alone. Therefore I do not indicate my approval of such a declaration by referring to its logic. Nor am I trying to entice you into doing so. Yes, it is logical. But it is also insane. Man is not an organ stop to be pushed in or pulled out for a prescribed effect. You know what I am talking about? The young are seduced by such ideas. I know. I was young once. When I think about myself as I was in my younger days – my idealism and passion – I find I am moved by a protective tenderness. That is all I am trying to do, Porfiry Petrovich. To protect the young from themselves. I am driven by compassion for them. And yet they see me as their enemy.'

'Whereas you see yourself . . . ?'

'As their saviour, of course!' Verkhotsev grinned ironically.

'Perhaps it is your methods that they hate.'

'And yet they would willingly throw themselves at the feet of a monster like Nechaev!'

'True.'

'This note. Was it written by Yelena Filippovna's killer?'

'I believe so.'

'Captain Mizinchikov?'

'I am not so sure. The only thing condemning Captain Mizinchikov is his flight from the scene of the crime. There may yet turn out to be a reasonable explanation for that.'

'But what of the razor found at his apartment? Not to mention the bloodstains on his uniform?'

'As for the razor, it proves nothing. A man may keep a razor. It cannot possibly have been the murder weapon. It is true that it was found in an unusual place – one does not normally keep one's razor in a desk drawer – and that it was found together with some letters that seem to suggest a motive.'

'So it could be significant? The newspapers certainly considered it incriminating.'

'I do not direct my investigations according to what is printed in newspaper editorials.'

'Quite right. But the blood?'

'It does not appear to be her blood, as far as we are able to tell.'

'You can tell this?'

There was a knock at the door. Now, at last, Lieutenant Salytov presented himself. Porfiry judged the impact of his entrance in Verkhotsev's eyes, which flickered with interest as he took in the other man's damaged face.

'You wished to see me?'

'Shall I wait outside?' suggested Verkhotsev with disarming discretion.

'No. This pertains to the case.' Porfiry pinched the bridge of his nose as he bowed his head, before turning abruptly to Salytov: 'On the twenty-third of September, you sold the body of a male child to the Medical-Surgical Academy on Morskaya Street. Do you deny it?'

The expression of Salytov's melted flesh was one of perpetual surprise. But it seemed possible that he was genuinely surprised to find himself summoned to the investigating magistrate's office to answer not questions but allegations, and in the presence of a stranger. He regarded Verkhotsev haughtily. 'Who is this man?'

'That need not concern you,' answered Porfiry quickly, cutting off Verkhotsev before he could introduce himself. 'Just answer the question. Do you deny that you traded in the body of a dead child?'

'I do not deny it.'

'By what authority?'

'I beg your pardon?'

'Who authorised you to make the sale?'

'No one. That is to say, I did not need any authorisation.'

'Where in the police code does it say that officers are entitled to sell for their own gain whatever bodies they happen to come across?'

'I cannot point to the specific article of the code, but the practice is widespread and allowed.'

'Allowed? Oh no, my friend, it is not allowed! Did you not consider that you had a duty to report the body and investigate the death?'

'What's the point? There was no way of identifying the body. No one came forward to claim him.'

'Did you advertise the discovery of the body?'

'N-no,' admitted Salytov; for the first time a note of uncertainty entered his voice.

'Then how can you be surprised that no one came forward?'

'No one ever does. He was a street child, most likely. Left for dead by his family. They could not care for him in life. What did they care about his death? His parents, if they are alive, and if they did not kill him themselves, were probably in a drunken stupor the night he died. Even now, I dare say, they do not realise he is missing. Or if they do, they are glad. It is one less mouth to feed. Certainly, he is more use to society dead than alive, if his body can be used to train future doctors.'

'You knew nothing about him. Your assumptions are incorrect. He was not a street child. He was a factory worker. An orphan.'

'Well then. There you are. No one to care. No one to grieve. And more importantly, no one to pay his funeral expenses. I certainly wasn't going to.'

'He was murdered. A crime had been committed. You are a policeman. You had a duty.'

'Don't lecture me about my duty. How do you think I got this?' Salytov jabbed a waxy pink hand towards his glistening face. Porfiry sensed Verkhotsev flinch.

'I know how you got that, Ilya Petrovich. But I fear that the bomb blast disfigured more than just your flesh. Was your soul, too, blackened by the flames? The Lieutenant Salytov I knew before that outrage would never have contemplated this evil trade.'

'Wrong! You are wrong about that, Porfiry Petrovich!' jeered Salytov.

'But you have children of your own. Were you not moved as a father?'

'My children are nothing to do with that sort.'

'What do you mean by *that sort*?'

'The poor.'

'Are you not ashamed to hear yourself say such things? You are a Christian. You are a Russian!'

'The poor will always be with us. So it says in the Bible.'

'That is not a licence to profit from their deaths.' Porfiry pushed a hand back through the colourless stubble on his scalp. 'Where did you find him?'

'Who?'

'Mitka! The dead boy!'

'I . . . don't remember,' Salytov answered evasively.

'What is this? You don't remember! My God, man! Is the discovery of a dead child now such an insignificant event that it fails to register on your memory? I would have thought that the circumstances would have been etched in your mind.'

Salytov considered Porfiry in silence for a moment. 'Before you condemn me out of hand, there is something you should know. Your friend, our esteemed chief, Nikodim Fomich . . . a father himself . . . he knows about this practice and has even, in his time, engaged in it.'

'That is a lie! A slanderous lie!'

Salytov angled his head provokingly. Something like a smile of triumph contorted the permanently contracted muscles of his face. 'No,' he said calmly. 'It is the truth. The salaries of policemen are pitifully inadequate, particularly for men like myself and Nikodim Fomich. Fathers, that is to say. It is accepted that we may exploit certain opportunities that arise in the exercise of our duties to supplement our income. It is the way things are done. It has been since time immemorial. Your good friend, the very civilised gentleman, Nikodim Fomich, is no more immune to the way things are done than I am.'

'Nikodim Fomich is a decent man. I cannot believe . . .'

'Now then, as for the boy,' continued Salytov, with the tone of one pressing home an advantage. 'I do not know where he was found because I did not find him. It was one of my men.'

'I don't understand. If that is the case, then why were your initials entered in the ledger at the Medical-Surgical Academy?'

'All the transactions go through me.'

'I see. A picture is *indeed* beginning to emerge.' Porfiry gave the neutral remark a bitter emphasis.

'I will not be judged by you.'

'You were so eager to get your hands on your cut,' continued Porfiry hurriedly, 'that you did not ask even the most rudimentary questions of the man who brought you the body. You are worse than a Jew!'

'Be careful what you say.'

'No Jew was ever so rapacious that he would sell the body of a child.'

'I warn you.'

'Who was it? The *politseisky*?'

'You will not hear his name from me.'

'Wha-at?'

'I take full responsibility for the disposal of that body.'

'Don't you understand? It is not a question of that. We are investigating a murder here. It is vital that we know where the body was found and in what state. We have only a head to work with now. The rest of the body was dismembered by students. I must talk to the policeman who found him.'

'I will not betray one of my men.'

'This misguided honour beggars belief! Your first loyalty is to the truth, Ilya Petrovich.'

'And I tell you, Porfiry Petrovich, no good will come of investigating this. I advise you to drop it.'

'I cannot drop it, even if I wanted to. It is in the newspapers now.' Porfiry pointed to Verkhotsev, who had been following the interview with a wry expression. 'The Third Section is involved. I would not be surprised if the Tsar himself has taken an interest in the case.'

'I will speak to the man and report back to you. If there are to be any disciplinary repercussions from this affair, I will bear the full brunt.'

'Oh, you are very noble now! Tell me, how much do they pay?'

'What has that to do with anything?'

'It may provide a motive! Do you not see? We have before us a case of multiple murders. Three children so far. That is to say, three that we know of. Who profits from the deaths of these children? Why, you do, Ilya Petrovich! That gives you a motive. You may consider yourself a suspect!'

'You are not serious.'

'Am I not?' Suddenly Porfiry could not suppress the full force of his rage any longer. '*How much did they pay you for Mitka's body?*' The shouted question snagged abrasively on the muscles of his throat.

'Five roubles.'

'What is your cut from that?' Porfiry made an effort to calm his voice. The question came in a tremulous whisper.

'If the Tsar does not wish us to engage in such enterprise he should pay us a living wage in the first place.'

'How much?'

'Four roubles. And fifteen kopeks.'

'What a strangely precise figure! No doubt that beguiles the poor policeman into thinking that his takings are impeccably calculated.'

'Will that be all?'

'No, I am not finished with you yet. Have you had any recent communication with the Medical-Surgical Academy?'

'Recent?'

'They did not inform you of our inquiries there?'

'I do not . . . believe so.'

'And you know nothing about the removal from the academy of a ledger detailing all the bodies received from the police – the ledger in which your initials were entered?'

'The book has gone missing? Then you have no evidence against us?'

'Do not celebrate too soon. A witness has named you as the policeman responsible for selling Mitka's body.'

'Witnesses may be mistaken.'

Before Porfiry could give full vent to his exasperation, Virginsky returned. He held up and shook the small box containing the ring.

'You have taken your time,' snapped Porfiry.

'They could not find it at first. It was not where it should have been. However, we turned the evidence room upside down and it came to light.'

'Thank God for that. This case is slipping through our fingers as it is. I could not have borne it if we had lost another piece of evidence.' Porfiry waved abruptly to dismiss Salytov, though he could not bring himself to look at him.

29

The enemy within?

'An ugly business,' winced Verkhotsev when the policeman was gone.

Porfiry frowned at him. It was easy to forget that he was a senior officer in the Third Section, such was the impression of affability and sympathy that he was able to create. And, of course, he was Maria's father, Porfiry reminded himself. 'You asked to see the ring,' he said, nodding to Virginsky, who handed over the box.

Verkhotsev turned the ring in his fingers. 'I am pleased that you kept the details of the design out of the newspaper. This is highly incendiary, of course. You realise that.'

'I too am relieved that the design was not published, but I can claim no credit for it.' Porfiry could not prevent himself from glancing at Virginsky.

'You are sure that this corresponds to the marks on the children's necks? You have taken your measurements carefully? A lot may come to hinge on those measurements.'

Porfiry's mood was not improved by Verkhotsev's labouring of the point. 'You may rest assured that in this department we are scrupulous in the gathering and recording of evidence.'

'As I am sure you realise, this evidence is highly circumstantial. If it comes to constructing a case around it, there must be no discrepancy. Otherwise your case will fall apart.'

'I am grateful to you for the benefit of your counsel. I had not realised that the officers of the Third Section placed such store in the integrity of forensic evidence. Is it not more usual for you to proceed on the basis of hearsay and informants' testimony?'

'Our methods are not the issue. You and I are both agreed that what is needed here – for the good of the state, I might add – is for the judicial process to be open and above board. All eyes will be on the conduct of this case, from the very highest to the lowest in the empire. There will be those who will seek to use the outcome for their own purposes. There must be no clumsy mistakes, and in saying that I am pointing the finger not at your department but at my own section. I will be frank with you, Porfiry Petrovich. There are some amongst my colleagues who would seek to control the outcome of your investigation from the very outset. It is simply too dangerous, they would argue, to allow you to discover whatever is there to be discovered. But I am of a contrary opinion. Such tactics are in the long run counterproductive. Besides, I have my daughter to think of. The truth, Porfiry Petrovich – we must set our sights on attaining the truth. Nothing less will do.'

Verkhotsev closed the lid on the evidence box. 'Please ensure that this is returned to its proper place.' He gave the box a deliberate shake, causing the ring to rattle inside, before relinquishing it to Virginsky. 'I thank you for sharing it with me.'

'Not at all,' replied Porfiry. He watched Virginsky go. 'Perhaps I may beg a favour in return, a reciprocal display of trust. Now that we are to be openly working together, I wonder if you would be so good as to call off your spy.'

'My spy?'

'Slava. The man the Third Section sent to be my personal

servant. He is, in fact, a poor servant and a poorer spy. He serves neither of us very well.'

'I know nothing of any spy.'

'Come now, there is no need to maintain the pretence.'

'It is not a pretence, I assure you. We have not sought to spy on you.'

'Then who is he? He is some kind of infiltrator, I feel sure, if only for the way he has sought to involve himself in our investigation. I admit that I was amused at first. I thought that his presence here might even prove useful to me. It was, after all, a way of communicating with the Third Section.'

'Which no doubt you would exploit to pass on disinformation,' chided Verkhotsev wryly.

Porfiry pursed his lips and blinked ambiguously. 'But he no longer amuses me. Especially if, as you assert, he is nothing to do with you. I shall dismiss him immediately.'

'No. Do not do that. He may yet prove useful. We must ask ourselves who would benefit most from knowing the progress of your investigation.'

'*Cui bono*? Curiously, that is the principle he himself advised me to apply.'

'Well? Where does it lead us in this instance?'

'You are suggesting that he is something to do with one or other of the crimes I am investigating? That he may be a *murderer*?'

Verkhotsev shrugged. 'It is a brilliant and bold masterstroke, is it not? Where better to go to ground than in the apartment of the man set to hunt you down? He can keep a watchful eye on how you are faring in your enquiries, thereby ensuring that he stays one step ahead of you at all times. If he gains your trust he may even be able to direct your investigation away from himself. And if he discovers that you are closing in on him . . . why, he is perfectly placed to take evasive action. Or – we must admit the possibility – to terminate your investigations in a manner appropriate to his criminal nature.'

Porfiry looked with alarm towards the door to his private apartment. 'That is not a very comforting supposition.'

'It is better to be prepared. In any case, you must not arouse his suspicions. If he imagines that you are on to him, he may feel himself backed into a corner. At the same time, if you simply dismiss him from your employ, we will lose him for good. No, you must keep him close to you.'

'That is all very well for you to say.'

'There is no need to be unduly afraid.'

'Really? And what, I wonder, do you consider to be a due proportion of fear?'

Verkhotsev made no attempt to answer. 'There is another possibility we must consider. He may not himself be guilty of any of the crimes under investigation. He may simply be acting on behalf of the person or persons who committed them. The communiqué you received suggests a revolutionary grouping. There have been cases of such groups seeking to infiltrate government departments in order to further their anti-state goals. This would simply be a variation of that tactic. We have had intelligence that one such grouping is seeking an exemplary assassination. A notable investigating magistrate would make an admirable target. Your man Slava may have been sent for that purpose. You say he is a poor servant. Our revolutionaries are invariably upper-class gentlemen. Servility does not come naturally to them.'

'This hypothesis is no more comforting than the last. I am at a loss to know what to do with all this shocking information.'

'Nothing, for the moment. As I have said, on no account must you arouse his suspicions.'

'I am afraid it may already be too late for that. His meddling in the case became intolerable. I had to do something.'

'What did you do?'

'I went to the baths.'

Verkhotsev rolled his moustache thoughtfully. 'I see.'

'That is to say, I removed myself from my chambers to discuss the case with Pavel Pavlovich free from Slava's intrusive presence.'

'That in itself may not be fatal. Your work requires you to absent yourself from your chambers from time to time, I dare say. He may have thought nothing of it. Or it may have made him wary without forcing his hand. Certainly he has made no move as yet.'

'As yet. No.'

'And we can do nothing until he does.'

'You almost sound as if you want him to strike.'

'I would not have him strike until we are ready for him. However, we will reach a point at which it will become necessary to provoke an attack if one has not already occurred.'

'I see. So I am to play the part of a sitting duck?'

'In all probability, there is nothing to fear.' Verkhotsev gave a less than reassuring smile. 'We may be wrong in our suppositions. This fellow Slava may simply be what he appears to be . . . a bad servant. However, to proceed on the basis that he represents a threat to your person enables us to take certain precautions. It is unlikely that he will attack you in your chambers. To do so would be to expose himself to unnecessary risk. After all, he shares your apartment, does he not? Therefore, he has access to you when you are at your most vulnerable, and when it would be easiest for him to effect his escape. That is to say, at night, when you are asleep. If he is going to strike, that is when he will do it.'

'And how am I to protect myself against nocturnal attack from this enemy within?'

'Don't worry, I shall think of something. However, it will be difficult without positioning a guard in your bedroom, which I fear would only discourage Slava from making an attempt.'

'Heaven forbid that he should be discouraged.'

'Of course, if he is associated with the group that sent you the communiqué, it is possible that you are intended to be their next victim. In which case, it is reasonable to suppose that an attempt would definitely be made on your life should another child be found murdered. There is a certain logic to this. You are a gentleman. A magistrate. You could be said to be – what was it? – "a member of the enslaver class". Furthermore, you are known to be investigating Yelena Filippovna's murder. Indeed, my daughter tells me that you were most zealous in pursuing that investigation whilst neglecting the investigation into the deaths of the missing children. That could count against you in their eyes.'

'At the time we had no bodies. We had nothing to go on. No evidence of any crime!'

'My dear friend, you do not need to explain yourself to me. And I fear that it will be useless to attempt to do so with them. To go back to Yelena Filippovna's murder, it may be that a similar strategy was used there. One of their number – if not the very same individual, this Slava – may have infiltrated the Naryskin Palace as a servant in order to be in place on the night of the gala to commit the murder.'

'A witness who saw Captain Mizinchikov flee the scene also mentioned seeing a number of servants about.'

'Of course. It is the perfect cover, allowing access to every part of the palace without arousing suspicion. Furthermore, his incompetence as a servant would be less noticeable in a larger household.'

Porfiry Petrovich placed a hand to his neck and rubbed distractedly, as if to soothe a wound that had not yet been inflicted. 'I pray to God that we do not find any more dead children.'

'Of course,' said Verkhotsev. 'Although that would rather clear Yelena Filippovna's name, would it not?'

30

The dead come back to murder

A sky of beaten metal pressed down on the sprawl of the Baird plant. Inside Shed 3, tiny figures scaled the tiers of gantry stairs lining the walls: insects, or so they seemed to Fedya Mikhailovich Shatov as he approached the shed along the embankment. In a matter of minutes he would be one of them. But for now he paused to watch them teem over the giant shell at the centre of the workshop. He was late already; ten kopeks docked from his pay for sure, a few minutes more would make no difference. He was certainly in no hurry to enter that deafening hell, despite the shelter that it offered from the cold.

From this distance, the scale of the ship was monstrous. He could feel it weighing down on him, like the formless mass that oppressed him in his brief, exhausted dreams and kept him pinned to his bed every morning. At 57, Fedya was finding it increasingly difficult to rouse himself from the narrow board he slept on. The mornings were getting darker, perhaps that had something to do with it. It was as if night were spreading into day, and more and more he wanted to cast in his lot with night and let the day go to the devil. At those moments, he didn't care what happened to him, just so long as he could be allowed to keep his head down for another five minutes. His mates had given up trying to rouse him with pinches and slaps. They knew he would get up in his own good time, and if he did not, it was his look-out.

Deep down, Fedya knew that it was something other than the morning gloom that kept him in his bunk longer than his fellows. The darkness around him was mirrored by a deeper darkness inside him. He knew his body. He knew his bones. Something had taken root there. Something that pulled at his lungs with hooks and turned the screws on a bench clamp fixed to his spine. His days in the workshop were numbered, he knew. And, much as he hated it, if he had no place there, he had no place anywhere.

He was worn out. He was dying.

Loose bundles of mist rolled and disintegrated over the black river, the Bolshaya Neva as it was called at this point. Fedya hawked and spat into the water before continuing his reluctant slouch towards the shed.

At first sight, it looked like a bundle of rags had been discarded in the lee of the shed. But no, he knew that it was not that, even as he willed his perception towards such an interpretation. Straightaway, the sickening lurch of his heart informed him: it was a body. The body of a child, judging by its size. A child discarded as carelessly as a bundle of rags. The head was towards him, the face hidden by a piece of sacking, but Fedya could see the child's hands, the fingers curled into tight blue fists. He lurched towards it, his own hand trailing along the wall for support. He slumped down and lifted the sacking. His heart pounded wildly at the first shock of what was revealed. The eyes stared horrifically, the pale blue irises surrounded not by white, but by an intense blood-filled red. It seemed like a devil was staring out at him from inside that dead boy. Unable to look into those eyes any longer, Fedya closed the lids with his fingertips. And in the cold touch of death, he felt his own future. With his eyes closed, the boy's humanity was restored

304

to him. He was no longer a devil, just a child, a fellow worker, judging by his clothes, a brother. Fedya saw that the boy was about the same age that he had been when he had first been put to work in the Carr and Macpherson plant on Vasilevsky Island.

Perhaps the boy was better off dead; he had been spared a life of misery and toil, that much was certain. Things were supposed to be better now; the Tsar had made them all free men. But such freedom meant little when you were enslaved by poverty.

And yet something within Fedya rebelled against these thoughts. He looked again into the face, and again touched the cold flesh, laying his hand against the boy's cheek.

'Poor bastard.' He wheezed the eulogy hoarsely and shook his head.

*

'Do you see the marks, Pavel Pavlovich?' Porfiry was squatting on his haunches over the dead boy. As he leant back to allow Virginsky a clear sight of the neck, his body trembled violently, apparently with the strain of maintaining his balance in an awkward position.

'Are you quite well, Porfiry Petrovich? You seem a little shaken.'

'No,' answered Porfiry tersely. 'The marks, Pavel Pavlovich,' he barked to Virginsky. 'Concentrate on the marks. They are the same as the others, are they not?'

'They appear to be.'

Porfiry held up a hand to Virginsky who hauled him to his feet. 'Are we to infer that Yelena Filippovna is the murderer of this child?'

'That is patently absurd.'

'It is at least unlikely. We have not yet ascertained the time of death, but from the state of the body it does not seem that the boy has been dead long. Certainly Yelena Filippovna has been dead longer.'

'I accept that Yelena Filippovna did not kill him.'

'But the marks? The marks correspond to the motif on her ring, do they not?'

'There is no need to be facetious. I understand the point you are making well enough. If she did not kill this boy, as she clearly did not, then there is a possibility that she did not kill the others.'

'It is to be regretted that an account has already been published contradicting that possibility.'

'How many times must I tell you, Porfiry Petrovich, that I had nothing to do with the release of that information?'

'It was not information. It was speculation.' Porfiry's face was stern. He looked away from Virginsky, as though dismissing him.

'You are angry with me, but it is unfair of you.'

'For God's sake, Pavel Pavlovich! There are more important matters to attend to than your hurt feelings.' Porfiry gestured down to the dead child. 'Do you realise what this means?'

'Yes. That Yelena is not the killer.'

'But what else? Remember the note. "For every child killed by the oppressive machine, we will take the life of one member of the enslaver class." Is this not another child killed by the oppressive machine?'

'You think that a revenge murder will follow?'

'We cannot keep *this* out of the newspapers. Too many people have seen the body.' Porfiry watched a *politseisky* handle a group of labourers whose curiosity had drawn them out of the shed. Fear made them compliant and the single *politseisky* easily kept them back. A superstitious awe required them to crane their necks past him for a sighting of the body, but that seemed to be enough for them. It was as if the prospect of death sent them back to work rather than the intervention of the policeman. 'Besides, news of this murder may not need to find its way into the *St Petersburg Gazette* for the sender of that note to know about it.'

'What do you mean?'

'Major Verkhotsev assures me that Slava is not a Third Section spy. He suggests a rather less pleasant possibility.'

'Which is?'

'He may be a member of a revolutionary grouping that is intent on carrying out a conspicuous assassination. Possibly he is connected to whoever sent the note.'

'Why do you not arrest him?'

'The Third Section is involved now. Major Verkhotsev will not allow me to terminate Slava's employment, let alone arrest him. He is anxious that we do not arouse his suspicions.'

'But in the meantime,' said Virginsky, hotly, 'as soon as Slava finds out about this latest victim, your life is endangered. We must keep the news from him.'

'I am rather afraid that Major Verkhotsev would have us do the opposite. I believe he wishes to provoke Slava into making an attempt. Until he does, we have no evidence against him.'

'But what if he is successful?'

'I am touched by your concern, Pavel Pavlovich. However, I would ask you not to give the matter another moment's thought. It may turn out that Major Verkhotsev is entirely mistaken. It certainly would be a bold assassin who dares to strike against an investigating magistrate in his own place of residence. You have met Slava. Does he strike you as one capable of such a *coup*? I think not. If he impresses one at all it is only by virtue of his ineptitude. Now, let us put these thoughts behind us and find out what we can about this poor unfortunate.'

Porfiry approached the *politseisky* who had been controlling the crowd. 'You were the first officer on the scene, is that correct?'

'Yes, your honour.'

'Who is he, do we know?'

'One of the foremen identified him as Innokenty Zimoveykin, your honour. Patronymic unknown, most likely on account of him being a bastard. He was a worker here at the Baird plant.'

'Age?'

The *politseisky* shrugged. 'Who can say? Twelve? Thirteen at the most, I would have thought.'

'I see. Very good.' Porfiry called to Virginsky: 'We have a name. That is something.'

A sudden harsh shout drew attention to an auburn-haired man in a black tailcoat who was striding towards them wearing a stovepipe hat. His short legs pumped out like pistons encased in tweed. 'You men, back to work. I don't pay you to stand around gawping all day.' His face was set in an angry scowl that was not softened by a set of stiff mutton-chop whiskers. 'You!' he barked at Porfiry. 'I take it you are in charge here. How much longer do you intend to allow this macabre sideshow to continue? Cannot you see the disruptive effect it is having on my workforce?'

Porfiry bowed in a conspicuous display of courtesy. 'To whom do I have the honour of speaking?'

'My name is Smith, Charles Smith. I am the director of the Baird plant.'

'You speak Russian exceedingly well, Mr Smith, if I may say so. Without a trace of an accent.'

'That's no compliment. I was born here and brought up speaking it. My mother is Russian. My father English. That's by the by. Who might you be?'

'I am Porfiry Petrovich, Investigating Magistrate. This is my colleague, Pavel Pavlovich Virginsky. You will be aware that we are investigating the murder of one of your employees.'

'Murder? You have determined already that a murder has been perpetrated?'

'I am at a loss otherwise to explain the marks of strangulation around the boy's neck.'

'Marks?' Smith looked darkly down at the dead boy. The truculence had gone from his voice. He sounded almost cowed. 'Just like the other children.'

'That is correct,' said Porfiry. 'The marks here are similar to others we have found.'

'I thought she was dead, the woman you suspected of killing them. That's what it said in the paper.'

'Was the boy known to you?'

'I employ eight hundred and fifty-nine workers. I cannot be expected to know them all personally.'

'But he was very young, was he not? Surely he must have been one of your youngest labourers?'

'What of it? I assure you he is legally employed. I know my obligations under factory law.'

'Of course. I do not doubt it. I merely meant to suggest that his extreme youthfulness would have rendered him conspicuous. Unless it is the case that you employ many as young as him.'

'No, not many. We don't have much use for the really young ones, unlike the textile factories. They lack the strength to operate the heavy machinery our industry requires. However, it is useful to have a number of agile shrimps about the place. They can get inside the machines for cleaning and oiling and such like.' Smith looked down at the bundle of interrupted childhood. 'I dare say I have seen his face about the place,' was all he was prepared to concede.

'Do you concern yourself at all with their education?' It was Virginsky from whom this question came, his voice bitter and accusatory.

Smith turned his head sharply from the dead boy and took in the junior magistrate with a coolly assessing glance. 'They receive all the education they require on the job. What's the point of teaching them the extent of the empire when all the empire they will see is the inside of the workshop?'

Virginsky seemed stunned into silence by the answer. A flood of colour rushed into his cheeks. Porfiry resumed the questioning, adopting a light conversational tone. 'I have heard of some factory owners building schoolhouses for their child labourers. That has not been a course of action that the Baird plant considered?'

'You are right.'

'May I ask why not?'

'I am not aware that we are obliged to.'

'Some owners go beyond their obligations,' suggested Porfiry, with a strained smile. He sought to keep his composure by a flurry of blinking.

'I am not the owner. I am answerable to the board. I could not build a schoolhouse even if I wanted to – if the board did not agree to it.'

'Has such a proposal ever come before the board?'

'No, it has not. We limit ourselves to the discussion of strictly business matters.'

'You do not consider the education of your workforce to be a business matter? Might it not have a beneficial effect on productivity, for example?'

'Quite the contrary. It would only foster discontent and agitation. We have enough trouble with agitators as it is.' Smith turned sharply to address a fresh cluster of workers who were gathering to view the body. Their faces were pinched with fear. 'Nothing to see here. Back to work.' Smith swept his hand upwards to shoo them. Their fear sharpened into hostility but they backed off, albeit slowly, as if making a point of going in their own good time. 'The more that lot are taught their letters,' confided Smith to Porfiry, 'the more of them can read those infernal pamphlets. *Destroy everything!* That is the latest clarion call, I believe. Have you ever heard anything so ridiculous?'

'And yet,' answered Porfiry thoughtfully, as if he were speaking the words as they occurred to him, without fully grasping where they would lead him. 'And yet . . . a society founded on the wilfully maintained ignorance of its largest constituent class, the class on which it depends for its material well-being – such a society, surely, is doomed to failure?'

'I do not concern myself with society. I concern myself with output,' answered Smith emphatically, and with a certain grim pleasure. 'And, frankly, I am surprised to hear you, a magistrate, an upholder of the Tsar's law, mouth such imbecilities. Why, you are talking like a nihilist! Like a student!'

'I am surprised to hear it myself,' admitted Porfiry, with a questioning look towards Virginsky. 'But there is something about the sight of these dead children that stirs these sentiments to the surface of my consciousness. All the victims have been child factory workers like him. Indeed, is it not true, Pavel Pavlovich, that all were employed by foreign-owned – or substantially foreign-backed – factories?'

'That is true,' confirmed Virginsky.

Porfiry turned a mildly reproving gaze on to the factory director. It was met with an indignant glare. 'Is that what lies behind this? An attempt to blacken foreign capital? Someone would seek to turn the Russian public against honest men like me?'

'It is another connection. All such connections are inevitably suggestive to the investigator. I fear it will be suggestive to the public too. It is almost as if the mighty industrial machine that powers the empire demanded their deaths. Poor Innokenty was sacrificed to feed the demon.'

'Fanciful nonsense,' barked Smith. 'Worse than the other bilge you spouted.'

'Why, then, *were* they killed, Mr Smith? Can you tell me that?'

'Agitators. It's all the work of agitators, I'll wager. Now then, if you have no further questions for me, I will leave you to your ... investigations. I have a factory to run.' With a terse nod, he turned on his heels and stomped away.

'A charming example of the modern capitalist,' observed Porfiry.

'I believe we will make a radical of you yet, Porfiry Petrovich.'

Porfiry sighed as he took out his enamelled cigarette case. 'More and more, Pavel Pavlovich, I find myself longing for the quiet life. That's all.'

'Oblomov.'

'Perhaps you are right.' Porfiry lit a cigarette. He watched his exhaled smoke rise slothfully, wisps of pale grey merging with the heavier grey of the sky. All around him, the factory chimneys churned out plumes of black smoke from the furnaces of the plant. He had the sense of the world burning itself up in a frenzy of production and consumption. He turned the cigarette in his fingers and studied it, as if the solution to the crimes he was investigating was contained within its burning paper. 'Miller brand,' he observed. 'Didn't one of the children work at the Miller tobacco factory?'

'Yes. Svetlana,' confirmed Virginsky.

'Perhaps I should change to a Russian brand. I used to smoke Russian cigarettes but the manufacturer went out of business. We Russians are not natural entrepreneurs, I fear. We lack the necessary energy, perhaps.'

'We are a nation of Oblomovs, sleeping our way to ruin.' Virginsky's tone was condemnatory. 'Do you now believe there is a political aspect to *these* murders, too?'

'It would help us to know where the other children were found, in relation to their workplace. Damn Salytov and his venal fellows. I hope to God there is nothing more than illicit profiteering to their involvement in these cases.'

'How do we proceed?'

'I fear we must make enquiries at the Rozhdestvenskaya Free School.'

'You believe Innokenty was a pupil there?'

Porfiry threw down his cigarette, although it was barely halfway smoked, and ground it into the frozen earth with his heel. He turned and walked away without answering Virginsky's question.

31

The *Kammerjunker*

'I have a fearful presentiment.' Maria Petrovna's voice was bleak, her face drained of colour. She closed the classroom door as a wave of volubility crashed over the handful of children arrayed on the benches. 'Your appearance is always associated in my mind with the most dreadful of sights. I pray for once that you have come with good news, or simply out of friendship.'

Porfiry winced and Virginsky bowed his head, but neither found the words to disabuse her. She was determined anyhow to forestall them in the delivery of their message. Her eyes glistened and a sudden fire rushed to her cheeks, a bitter recollection all at once chasing out any friendly sentiments. 'I read what they said about Yelena in the newspapers.' Her voice was grim and recriminatory now. 'Do you really believe that? Are you honestly accusing her of murdering those children? You did not know her as I did! Is it not enough that she has been cut down by an assassin? Now you must destroy her memory with these vile accusations! How convenient for you, to blame those crimes on a dead woman, who can no longer defend herself and has no champion to protect her memory. Now you can declare your case closed without the necessity of having to prove it. How convenient – and contemptible!' Maria Petrovna trembled with the force of her anger. And then, suddenly, it seemed to leave her. Her head sagged, as a violent sob convulsed her frame. 'I'm sorry,' she relented. 'I know you must have your reasons. The news came as a great shock to me. That she could have committed such terrible crimes. She must have hated me very much. I can think of no other reason why she would have attacked my children.'

'Maria Petrovna, I for one do not believe that Yelena Filippovna killed the children. That account does not represent the official position of my department. I cannot say how it found its way into the newspaper. I can only say that I regret it very much.'

Powerful, conflicting emotions pulled at the muscles of her face, leaving them ravaged. 'Then it is not over.'

'No,' said Porfiry. 'We have found another child. I am sorry, but we have to know whether he was a pupil here.'

The cry came from deep within her, a throbbing shift of anguish painfully disgorged. 'You want me to go with you . . . to see!' Her face was taut with horror.

'No,' said Porfiry gently. 'That will not be necessary in this instance. We already have a positive identification of the body. All we need to know from you is if the boy was a pupil here. His name was Innokenty Zimoveykin.'

'Innokenty?' The wild careening of her eyes was all the confirmation they needed. 'Why are they killing my children? It is because of me, isn't it? I am to blame. I am to blame for all this. If I had not started the school, none of this would have happened. If they mean to hurt me, why don't they just kill me? Perhaps they will. When they have killed all the children, they will come for me.'

Her voice had risen to an almost hysterical wail. The door to the second classroom opened and Perkhotin emerged, his face drawn with solicitude. He took in Porfiry and Virginsky with a quizzical frown. His fingers pulled anxiously at his great shovel beard, which seemed to have gained in mass since the last time Porfiry had seen it. 'My dear Maria Petrovna, whatever is the matter?'

'Innokenty,' sobbed Maria. 'Innokenty is dead.'

Perkhotin's face was instantly drained of any remaining colour. His eyes stood out in shock. 'No, that is not possible. I mean to say, how can it be? I had read in the paper that the police suspected Yelena Filippovna.'

Maria jerked her head violently in denial. 'Yelena . . . is innocent.'

'Is it the same as the others?' Perkhotin demanded of Porfiry. 'I mean to say, was he strangled? Were there the same marks?'

'Yes. So far as we know, the details are the same in this case as with the other children.'

'How extraordinary. We had hoped it was all over. It was shocking to read the charges against Yelena Filippovna, but at least it meant an end to it, or so we hoped.'

'I'm sorry,' said Porfiry. 'You taught Yelena Filippovna too, did you not? At the Smolny Institute, I believe.'

'Yes, that's true,' confirmed Perkhotin.

'And her sister Aglaia?'

'Yes. How is Aglaia?'

'She suffered a terrible shock which her nervous constitution was not strong enough to withstand. It seems to have induced an onset of epilepsy. Added to that, she reacted adversely to the medication her doctor prescribed and sank into a coma from which she only periodically emerges.'

'They have suffered so much, the sisters.'

'You are referring to the deaths of their parents?'

'Yes.'

'What happened to them, do you know? It is unusual for both parents to die prematurely.'

'Their deaths are related, tragically. The father killed himself over some scandal. He shot himself, I believe. He was a military man. And then, I'm afraid to say, the mother also committed suicide ... whether her heart was broken or her mind unhinged, I cannot say.'

Porfiry was unable to quell a fit of startled blinking. 'That is an extraordinary tragedy.'

Perkhotin nodded his agreement gravely.

'One cannot help wondering what effect it had on the girls. There were no other siblings?' wondered Porfiry.

'No.'

'And what ages were they when their parents died?'

'I cannot say for certain . . .'

'Yelena was sixteen,' cut in Maria. 'Aglaia must have been fourteen, or perhaps fifteen.'

'You were closest to Yelena?' Porfiry narrowed his eyes into what seemed a calculating expression. His voice was compassionate though.

Maria nodded wordlessly, her lips pressed tightly together, as if she feared what she might say.

*

Soon after returning to his chambers, Porfiry was visited by Lieutenant Salytov, his blasted face shadowed by something that might have been contrition. He was not able to meet either Porfiry's or Virginsky's gaze.

'There has been another child found, I hear.'

'Yes,' answered Porfiry. 'Fortunately, the first *politseisky* on the scene was an honest man. It did not occur to him to seek to profit from the discovery. Do you have any information for me?'

'Yes. I have spoken to my man. The boy Mitka was found on the Yekaterininsky Canal embankment, near the Kammeny Bridge.'

'Very well. You may go.'

Lieutenant Salytov clicked his heels and spun around.

'This muddies the waters, Pavel Pavlovich,' said Porfiry as soon as Salytov was out of the room. 'Kammeny Bridge is over two *versts* from the Nevsky Cotton-Spinning Factory.'

'What of it?'

'Innokenty was found at his place of work. I had hoped for a pattern to emerge.'

'They were both pupils at the school,' offered Virginsky.

'Yes, that is something, I suppose. But the discrepancy in the location of the bodies, one killed and left where he works, the other transported halfway across the city, is troubling.'

'Perhaps it was simply a question of circumstances. The children were killed as and when opportunity allowed, the bodies discarded in a similar manner, according to opportunity. It may be wrong to read too much into it.'

'That is our job, Pavel Pavlovich. To read too much into everything. We must operate on the assumption that everything is significant. Unfortunately, we do not have sufficient information about the location of the other bodies to determine whether there is a pattern to their disposition, and whether Mitka's body or Innokenty's is the exception to it.'

The door to Porfiry's chambers opened and Slava came in bearing Porfiry Petrovich's lunch tray. Porfiry and Virginsky exchanged a significant glance.

'What is this?' said Porfiry, as the tray was set in front of him.

'Your lunch.'

'Yes, I see that. But what is it?'

'It is a meat pie. I would have thought that was evident.'

'A meat pie? I cannot eat a meat pie.'

'Why ever not?'

'Today is Wednesday, a fast day. I am allowed only bread, vegetables and fruit.'

'No. Today is Thursday. I brought you your fasting meal yesterday.'

'No, yesterday you brought me a meat pie, which I ate. So even if today is Thursday, I will forego this meat pie as a penance. Take it away.'

'Very well,' said Slava uncertainly. 'Am I to bring you some bread and fruit instead?'

'There is no need to bring me anything.'

'But you must eat.'

'Do not concern yourself.'

'You have stopped confiding in me,' observed Slava darkly as he lifted the tray.

'It is not a question of that. You are my domestic servant. It is inappropriate for you to involve yourself in my investigative work.'

Slava looked ominously from Porfiry to Virginsky, as if he suspected them of a conspiracy. 'You will regret excluding me in this way.' With that he pushed the tray back through the door, disappearing into Porfiry's private apartment.

'Good heavens, Pavel Pavlovich! Was that a threat?'

'Do you really think he is dangerous?'

'I do not know what he is.'

'He seems so . . . ridiculous.'

'It would be easy to underestimate him.'

Virginsky smiled to himself. 'That is what is said of you, Porfiry Petrovich.'

'Really?'

'But how long can this go on? It is intolerable having him under your roof.'

'If Major Verkhotsev is correct, then this issue will come to a head sooner rather than later, now that another child has been murdered.'

'And has Verkhotsev come forward with any plan to protect you?'

'He rather vaguely intimated that he would think of something.' Porfiry positioned a sheet of Department-headed paper in front of him and charged a pen with ink. 'I shall inform him of our most recent discovery. In the meantime, I must rely on myself. I cannot expect my personal safety to be as urgent a concern to others as it is to me. And merely pointing out a danger does not oblige the major to preserve me from it.'

Porfiry began to write. *To my esteemed colleague, Major Pyotr Afanasevich Verkhotsev . . .*

'You seem remarkably sanguine,' observed Virginsky.

'I suppose I am safe as long as Slava does not know about the latest murder.' Porfiry recharged his pen, then pointed the nib accusingly towards Virginsky. 'That is to say, until the newspapers get hold of it.'

Virginsky's indignation flared momentarily at the provocation. And yet he evidently decided not to rise to the bait: 'As you yourself observed, a great many people saw the body. Word is bound to get out.'

'Yes, you're right,' said Porfiry, acknowledging Virginsky's restraint with a smile. 'Nonetheless, we must be careful of what we say in front of Slava. If we are able to keep him in the dark at least until tomorrow's editions, I may increase my chances of surviving the night. Besides, it will buy us a little time in which to further our investigations.' Porfiry put down his pen distractedly. 'There is someone whom I am most eager to interview.'

*

As Porfiry Petrovich well knew, achieving an audience with the Tsar of all the Russias was not simply a matter of presenting one's self and one's visiting card at the Winter Palace. There were official channels to go through. His superiors would have to sanction the interview, which would require Porfiry to enter a formal written submission detailing his reasons for disturbing the autocrat's serenity. To have the gist of such a submission be 'because I suspect a member of the Imperial Family of the murder of innocent children' would not go well with those it was intended to win over.

It was clear that if he were to go ahead with a formal submission, he would need to exercise a degree of circumspection, not to say deception, in its wording. However, entering a specious reason – for example, to say that he wished to divulge to the Tsar information of a politically sensitive nature fit only for his ears – would not necessarily result in the outcome he desired. His ruse was likely to be seen through by those whose place it was to process such applications. Either his request would be denied, without explanation or appeal, or he would be called before a hearing to give an account of himself. In that event, if convinced by his arguments, others would take upon themselves the role of intermediary, seeking to gain for themselves the Tsar's approval, and his plan would be frustrated. And if he failed to convince, he would succeed only in drawing over himself a cloud of distrust greater even than the one in place already. In addition, to go through official channels would waste valuable time, which Porfiry could ill afford given the potential danger hanging over him.

There was another avenue open to Porfiry: Verkhotsev. Porfiry assumed that his new friend in the Third Section had access to the Tsar. Of course, it had to be borne in mind that Verkhotsev might prove reluctant to share his privilege with another. If Porfiry were to disclose the full extent of his suspicions to Verkhotsev, the danger was that the Third Section would take over the investigation, or, more probably, bury it. What were the lives of a few factory children compared to the honour of the House of Romanov? However, Porfiry had to remind himself that Verkhotsev was Maria Petrovna's father. He had declared himself to be on the side of the truth. At the same time, he had admitted the existence of elements within the Third Section who, it was to be presumed, were less concerned with the provision of that elusive commodity.

What Porfiry least expected as he chain-smoked his way through one side of his cigarette case, while struggling over the wording of his note to Verkhotsev, was to achieve his goal without doing anything. It seemed that his own desire to see the Tsar was matched by a reciprocal desire on the part of the Tsar. A middle-aged *Kammerjunker* wearing the order of St Stanislav visited Porfiry's chambers to present him with a folded paper sealed with the Romanov seal. Porfiry's heart raced as he studied the familiar double-headed eagle imprinted in the shiny red wax. The precise and sharp-edged image bore little resemblance to the vague blurs that they had seen on the necks of the children. He wondered now if they had been mistaken. True, there did seem to be a certain consistency in the shape and size of the repeated bruise. However, its definition was compromised by the leeching of ruptured capillaries under the skin, a spidery halo disrupting the line. Was it indisputably the impression of the Romanov signet ring, as the imprint before him now so clearly was? Or had he succumbed to the influence of Virginsky and fallen into the old trap? *What you go looking for, you will find*, as the saying had it.

'Will you not open it? Your instructions are on the inside, you know.'

Porfiry looked up at the *Kammerjunker*, whose aristocratic features were set in an expression of indulgent good humour. 'Come now, the Tsar doesn't like to be kept waiting.'

Porfiry peeled the brittle encrustation of wax off the paper taking care not to break it.

'You are like me,' said the *Kammerjunker*. 'Frugal. Why buy sealing wax when you can re-use the Tsar's?'

'Indeed,' said Porfiry, as he opened the document. He read that he was commanded to return forthwith with Prince Shchegolskoy – evidently the gentleman who had delivered the summons – to the Winter Palace for a private audience with Tsar Alexander II.

'I have a carriage for us outside,' advised Prince Shchegolskoy. Porfiry slid the detached imperial seal into a drawer, then rose to his feet with a nod of obedience. He would finish the note to Verkhotsev when he returned.

*

Inevitably, the black-lacquered carriage bore the Romanov crest on its doors. The insistence of the design was beginning to haunt Porfiry.

The liveried footmen must have had to cling on for dear life as the carriage thundered beneath the arch of the General Staff Building into Palace Square. Whether it was the ruddy hue of the low October sun, or the sanguinary cast of his own thoughts, Porfiry could not help but see the great red-painted palace as stained in blood. He shook his head to dispel the fanciful idea, recognising once more Pavel Pavlovich's influence.

Prince Shchegolskoy had kept up an affable patter throughout the journey, playing the part of the professional courtier, at ease with any individual into whose company his emperor's command thrust him. Possibly not a very bright man, thought Porfiry as he listened to his prattle, he was without doubt happy with his lot, which was little more than that of a glorified messenger boy.

Steering a course through the centre of the square, and thereby almost skimming the Alexander Column, the driver urged his team to a final burst of speed. The horses' hooves clattered over the swirls of paving stones; Porfiry saw the sparks in his mind's eye. He noted with alarm that they were galloping towards a closed wrought iron gate in the central arch of three. Prince Shchegolskoy was surely also aware of this circumstance but seemed unperturbed. At the last moment, the gates swung open, operated by unseen hands. Porfiry found himself inside the courtyard of the Winter Palace.

'I thought it was usual for members of the public to enter the palace from the Neva side,' Porfiry observed to his companion, as the carriage decelerated sharply to the restraining shouts of the driver.

'That is only in the case of state ceremonials. You are here on private business. The Tsar's private apartments are best approached by this entrance.' Prince Shchegolskoy smiled and added an afterthought: 'There are over one thousand and fifty rooms in the Winter Palace. One can waste a lot of time if one does not choose one's entrance advisedly.'

The carriage came to a halt. The door was opened and the steps pulled down by a footman. Prince Shchegolskoy gestured for Porfiry to lead the way.

As he climbed down, Porfiry glanced about to take in his surroundings. A cluster of denuded trees in the centre gave the courtyard a desolate air, although unusually for a St Petersburg building the inner walls maintained the columned and corbelled grandeur of the façade. In the great Winter Palace, it seemed, there was to be no discrepancy between outer and inner glory.

Prince Shchegolskoy steered him towards a high arched doorway in the nearest wall. A rifle-bearing Cossack stood to one side at the prince's nod.

They crossed the threshold into a grand entrance hall, littered with marble and emblazoned with gilt mouldings on white. Porfiry looked up, his gaze drawn by towering columns, and saw a magnificent frescoed ceiling. Celestial beings peeped out through pink clouds fixed to a sky of Mediterranean azure.

'One thousand and fifty rooms?' whispered Porfiry, though the echo of his voice cascaded back to him louder than the original. 'Are they all on this scale?'

The prince merely smiled in reply.

A massive double staircase ahead of them folded itself around a triple arched passageway. The prince led Porfiry up the left arm of the stairs. Porfiry was cowed by the echoes of their footfalls. It seemed that the palace was a giant sounding box, amplifying everything that happened within it.

The landing at the top led on to a long hall. A river of ultra-marine carpet flowed over the parquet floor, until it was dammed by a closed door in the far distance.

As they walked along the gallery, Porfiry's eye was drawn by one or other of the paintings, which seemed to provide glimpses into other worlds, worlds of strange, classically attired heroes in highly charged poses, or of mysterious landscapes, or lifeless still lives. The surfaces glowed with intense colour. They both seduced and repelled him. What had these scenes to do with the Russia that began outside the palace walls?

They reached the door at the end of the blue carpet, which opened on to a second identical gallery.

'Are you sure we chose the most convenient entrance?' asked Porfiry.

'Oh yes!' replied the prince delightedly.

Beyond that gallery was a staircase that led down to a vast circular room over which an immense rotunda ceiling floated. Light filtered in through a central round window of frosted glass. A colonnade ran around the periphery of the room. Here Porfiry got his first sight of other people: two men in military uniform, generals, were engaged in a hushed, bowed confer-ence by one of the blood red columns. They broke off and watched in silence as Porfiry and the prince crossed the great marble-tiled floor.

There were doors all the way around the circumference. Porfiry heard one close somewhere to his left with a reverber-ating click. The door the prince selected led to a shorter enfilade gallery, at the end of which was a brass-lined door guarded by two Cossacks.

'His Imperial Majesty's private apartments begin here,' said Prince Shchegolskoy.

*

The man whom Porfiry knew as Svyatoslav Andreevich Tushin, or Slava, stooped to press his ear to the connecting door between the magistrate's private apartment and his chambers. He heard no sound. It was possible that the magistrate was working alone, in silence. Slava tapped gently on the door. When no response came, he tentatively pushed the door open and stepped through.

The room was empty but still he would have to act quickly. The magistrate might return at any moment, or the self-important clerk Zamyotov might come in with correspondence.

He dashed across to the desk and tried the drawers. Locked. As they had been the last time he had tried them. It really did seem that the magistrate was wise to him.

The green desk leather was clear of all clutter, apart from a writing set and a single sheet of official paper, placed at an angle to the edge, as if abandoned in a hurry. Slava picked it up and read:

To my esteemed colleague, Major Pyotr Afanasevich Verkhotsev,

I am writing to inform you of a further tragic development in the case that concerns us both. The body of another child was discovered this morning at the Baird Shipbuilding Plant in the Kolomenskaya District of St Petersburg. The child in question was a worker at the factory, a boy, aged approximately 13 years, by the name of Innokenty

Zimoveykin. The distinctive mark which we discussed at our last meeting was in evidence on his neck. Clearly, Yelena Filippovna cannot be his murderer. Moreover, it is my belief that this new circumstance further calls into question her involvement in the earlier murders.

The draft ended there but Slava had read enough. He placed the sheet back on the desk and tiptoed back towards the door that led to Porfiry Petrovich's private apartment.

32

An audience with the Tsar

The accommodation on the other side of the brass-lined door was on an altogether more human, and even intimate, scale. Porfiry had the real sense of entering living quarters, that is to say, within which memories accumulated, ordinary human complications were created and tidied away; a place where fires were lit against the cold, meals eaten, naps stolen, where arguments stormed and doors were slammed. It could have been the St Petersburg apartment of any well-to-do gentleman, although perhaps the floors were polished, the dust chased away, the carpets beaten more frequently than in most.

Prince Shchegolskoy's fist was poised inches from the surface of a door panelled in two colours of wood. What seemed to give him pause was the sound of raised voices – or rather, one raised voice – from within. A moment later the door flew open and Porfiry was surprised to see a man he recognised as the elder Prince Naryskin flee the room, his face flushed and drawn. Prince Naryskin seemed equally surprised to see Porfiry there. He met the magistrate's questioning gaze with a look of startled outrage, and then brushed past without a word of greeting.

Prince Shchegolskoy's knuckles now fell superfluously against the open door. 'Your Majesty, I have the magistrate Porfiry Petrovich to see you.'

That sense of intimacy was even more in force in the room

Porfiry now entered. The Tsar's study was crammed with a very particular kind of clutter: the photographs and portraits of the people who made up his life. A multitude of faces looked out from every square inch of the wall, frames butting against frames. There were even portraits hung on the back of the door, which Prince Shchegolskoy now pulled behind him as he left. Heavy green drapes were suspended above a pair of alcoves; Porfiry noticed paintings of battle scenes hung within them, as well as a sideboard piled high with folders and official papers: the glories and burdens of state stashed together.

The Tsar sat behind the furthest of the desks, his uniform dripping with braid and medals. Enormous epaulettes squatted on his shoulders. A broad sash of lustrous turquoise silk ran diagonally across his chest. Despite these trimmings of power, the face that looked up at Porfiry was remarkably human. This was just a man, a man like any other, struggling to comprehend and control the world around him. To bolster his confidence he had surrounded himself with images of his family and friends. To inspire the awe of others, he had dressed himself in an imposing costume. But Porfiry was struck most by the thought that his head was slightly small for his body, although not to the extent that Peter the Great's had been. He also found himself unduly fascinated by the Tsar's moustaches, which were kept long. They curled away from his face with a kind of unruly waywardness, as if – for all the things this man could bend to his will – his own facial hair refused to do his bidding. Porfiry was reminded of Gogol's tale of the nose.

'What are you smirking at?' The Tsar asked the question uncertainly, looking down at himself to check that every detail of his personal appearance was perfectly in order.

'I beg your pardon, Your Majesty. I was not aware of . . .'

'You were undeniably smirking at something.'

'I am sorry. I cannot explain it. Except to say that for some reason I found myself thinking of one of Gogol's stories.'

'They tell me you are the most brilliant investigator in St Petersburg. You seem to me to be something of an imbecile.'

'The truth, I dare say, lies somewhere in between, Your Majesty.'

The Tsar's face remained fixedly blank for a moment, then opened up into abrupt laughter. The laughter somehow failed to touch his eyes, which seemed infected with a perpetual wariness. 'Well, we will have to make do with that, I suppose. Do you smoke?'

The Tsar opened a jewel-encrusted box on his desk. Porfiry breathed in the heady waft of dormant tobacco suddenly released.

'Yes, thank you, Your Majesty.'

'Good man.' The Tsar sat back as he breathed in the first draught of his own cigarette. 'You may sit down.'

The study was filled with a profusion of empty chairs, as if the Tsar preferred the possibility of company to the reality of it. However, there were no doubt times when this room was crowded with ministers of state, jostling for a seat.

Porfiry bowed his gratitude and took a seat on the other side of the Tsar's desk.

'You are investigating the murders of those unfortunate children.'

'That is correct, Your Majesty.'

'I know it is correct. I am not in the habit of uttering statements that are not correct.'

'I beg your pardon.'

'This is a case that touches me deeply.' Here the autocrat

struck his chest with one clenched hand. 'As head of state, I am father to all the empire's children. Indeed, I look upon all my subjects as my children. Can I not protect my children? That is what they will say about me now.'

'Your Majesty, I am sure that no one would dare—'

'Oh, they dare!' His head shook in a tremor of self-right-eousness. 'Now they dare to say anything of me. I can do no right by them. Of course, to continue the analogy, fathers are always misunderstood by their children.' The Tsar paused to reflect on this, then burst out bitterly with: 'What do they want from me? Did I not free the serfs?'

'The noble act of a generous heart.'

'And what were the thanks I got? I didn't go far enough, said the radicals. I went too far, said the conservatives. And the nihilists started shooting!'

'I fear, Your Majesty, that discontent is the natural state of mankind.'

'I am not free! I am not content!' There was a note of personal hurt in the Tsar's voice. His eyes for a moment lost their wariness and became wistful. 'But do you hear me complaining?'

Porfiry suppressed the urge to answer in the affirmative. He bowed his head solemnly instead and said nothing.

'And then there are the law courts. You're a magistrate. You know what goes on there. Every trial is reduced to an indict-ment of the state, which is to say of me, because I *am* the state. It is not poor Ivan's fault he stole the loaf of bread, it is the Tsar's for making him hungry. That's what they do with the freedom I gave them! I have a good mind to take it back.'

'I am afraid, Your Majesty, you cannot take freedom back once you have given it.'

The Tsar regarded Porfiry with a steady, dangerous gaze. 'And now this. These children. I will be blamed for this, without doubt.'

Porfiry took a moment to hold and savour a lungful of smoke, which saved him from the necessity of speaking.

'How is your investigation progressing? You suspected that woman, I believe. Yelena Filippovna, was that not her name?'

'No, no, no. I never suspected her. That was an erroneous story that somehow found its way into the newspapers.'

'Really? How extraordinary. How on earth did that happen, do you know?'

Porfiry raised both arms in a despairing shrug. 'Tittle-tattle. It may have been something that was discussed. All sorts of theories are discussed in the course of an investigation.'

'Yes, but there must have been something linking Yelena Filippovna to those children? Something that led you to consider her as a possible murderer?'

'There were a number of things, in fact. But everything linking her to the deaths was highly circumstantial.'

'Please be more specific. It is essential I know everything about the case.'

'It is?'

'Yes. I intend to take over the supervision of the case personally. You will report to me. Is that clear?'

'Your Majesty, surely you have other more pressing duties?'

'There is nothing more pressing than the welfare of my children. When this case is solved and the perpetrator brought to book, you will let it be known to what extent I aided you in its solution. Until then you will say nothing of our meeting to anyone, in case . . . you are unsuccessful.'

'You wish to take over the investigation?'

'Not at all. I merely wish to take credit for it. It is not quite the same thing. Everything, of course, relies on a successful outcome. I am relying on you, Porfiry Petrovich. My children are relying on you. You must catch this monster before any more are killed.'

'That is my earnest desire, Your Majesty.'

'So, what led you to suspect this society woman?'

Porfiry had the sense that he was being tested. Perhaps the Tsar knew more than he was letting on. He felt the need for caution. 'Before I answer that question, Your Majesty, I would be grateful if you would answer one from me.'

'What's this? Are you interrogating me, your tsar?'

'This is a delicate matter. I merely wish to be sure of something before I proceed.'

'I don't like the sound of this. Very well. Ask your question.'

'Did you know Yelena Filippovna Polenova?'

'Did I know her?'

'Yes.'

'Am I somehow now a suspect in your investigations? Do you realise how impertinent your question is?'

'As I came in, Prince Naryskin was leaving your study. You will know that Yelena Filippovna was murdered at the Naryskin Palace.'

'And so I am implicated? I was not there!'

'You were not, although your son was.'

'What has this to do with the children? I brought you here to discuss the children.'

'One of the things linking Yelena Filippovna to the murdered children was a ring she wore on her thumb. We found marks on the children's necks that correspond to a design embossed on the face of that ring.'

'Yes, I have heard of this ring.' The Tsar missed a beat, before explaining: 'They mentioned the ring in the newspaper.'

'The newspaper did not mention that the design in question is the emblem of the House of Romanov. The double-headed eagle.'

This information did not seem to surprise the Tsar. His response to it came quickly, without undue thought, as if rehearsed. 'I know nothing of the existence of this ring.'

'But what of your son? Might he have given the ring to Yelena Filippovna?'

'I cannot speak for the Tsarevich.' The Tsar crimped his brows angrily. 'This line of investigation will not result in the desired outcome, that is to say, the discovery of the children's murderer. I command you to abandon it. Besides, as you have now admitted, you no longer suspect Yelena Filippovna. And so her possession of this ring is irrelevant. You must concentrate your efforts on solving the murders of these innocents and forget all about this ring. I would not be surprised, in fact, if the ring was not what you imagine it to be.'

'I don't quite understand, Your Majesty.'

'Anyone may make and sell a ring bearing the emblem of a double-headed eagle – it implies no direct contact with myself or any member of my family.'

'Very true, Your Majesty. However, I fear that the symbolism may still have a bearing on the case. The latest victim bears the mark too. He cannot have been killed by Yelena Filippovna. But indubitably he was killed by someone. Either by someone who inadvertently wore a Romanov ring, not realising that it would leave an imprint. Or by someone who wishes to generate a rumour that a series of children have been mercilessly killed by a Romanov. In short, Your Majesty, the case may yet prove to have a political aspect.'

'There will be no rumour. You will see to it. If I do hear of any rumour, I will hold you accountable.'

Porfiry felt the tightening of a vice around his heart. 'Naturally I shall do all in my power to keep the specific design of the ring out of the newspapers, while continuing to pursue a vigorous investigation. However, it is in the nature of rumour—'

'Do not seek to make excuses in advance. Oh, I understand your trepidation. You are right to feel it. You will incur my most violent displeasure should this detail find its way into common currency. I understand too that you are concerned because – by your own admission – there is one in your department privy to the secrets of the case who is in the habit of talking to newspapermen. A loose tongue is more danger-ous than a loose cannon. I warn you, your toleration of this person reflects badly on you, Porfiry Petrovich. If you have any suspicions as to who it might be, I advise you to come down heavily on them. Crush them, if necessary. There are rooms in the Peter and Paul Fortress where such a disloyal individual may be held indefinitely, at least until you have solved the case, free from their destructive involvement.'

'I confess that I have no clear suspicions at this moment.' Porfiry did not look at the Tsar as he said this.

'Then form some. It cannot be so difficult. Your suspects are limited to those who know of the distinctive bruises on the children's necks and also of the ring found on Lena's thumb.'

'Lena?'

'Yelena Filippovna, I mean. I am beginning to think quite fondly of her now that I know she is not a murderer.'

'But you did not know her when she was alive?'

The Tsar gave no indication of hearing the question. 'I shall help you if you like. Let us run through the names of your staff and you will provide me with character sketches. I will be able to tell, I am sure, who is the most likely to betray the confidence of your office.'

Fortunately for Porfiry Petrovich there was a knock at the door. He had no wish to engage in this tedious exercise with the Tsar, and besides, his suspicions, he always felt, were his own affair.

Prince Shchegolskoy poked his head around the edge of the door. 'The Foreign Minister is here to see you, Majesty. The situation in the Balkans requires your urgent attention.'

'Ah yes, of course. I am afraid, Porfiry Petrovich, that I cannot offer you my assistance, after all. Affairs of state, you understand. If only my detractors could see how hard I work, would they attack me so? There is not a man among them who would willingly shoulder the burden I bear. My life is not my own.'

Porfiry gave a tense smile, which he hoped expressed his sympathy.

'And remember,' continued the Tsar, bringing his fist down heavily on his desk. 'Clamp down and crush the snake in the grass. A room in the Fortress awaits. It may just as easily be put at your disposal if you fail to find another to occupy it.'

'I will bear that in mind, Your Majesty.' Porfiry stubbed out his cigarette in a heavy onyx ashtray on the Tsar's desk and rose to his feet. 'I am grateful to you for the condescension you have shown in assisting me in my enquiries. May I ask one final question, Your Majesty?'

The Tsar looked uncertainly towards Prince Shchegolskoy. 'Please be so good as to ask the Foreign Minister to wait.'

'Very good, Your Majesty.' The prince backed out of the room, bowing as he went.

The Tsar turned expectantly to Porfiry Petrovich.

'How am I to communicate with you, Your Majesty? You said that you wish to supervise the conduct of this case. If you are to do so, you must be kept informed.'

'You are to present yourself here at this time every day to brief me on the progress of the case. Prince Shchegolskoy will supply you with a pass that will allow you access to the palace and my private quarters.'

'There may be times when we are required to act quickly. Given your many duties it may prove impossible to attain your approval for a decisive course of action.'

'In that eventuality, you must do what you judge best, and answer for the consequences later. This murderer must be brought to book. That is my first command to you. Everything else is subordinate to that and must work towards its execution. If it is necessary to act decisively, you must act decisively. Do I make myself clear?'

'Pre-eminently so, and I am grateful to you.'

'Till this time tomorrow then.'

'If I may just impose on your indulgence for one moment longer, Your Majesty.'

'Good heavens! You really are an exceptionally trying individual.'

'Forgive me. But it appertains to the case. There is one other thing linking the dead children to Yelena Filippovna – and, incidentally, linking them to one another. They were all pupils at a charitable school – the Rozhdestvenskaya Free School.

338

Yelena Filippovna was taking part in a fund-raising gala at the Naryskin Palace the night she was murdered. The Tsarevich was in attendance, as I have already intimated.'

'You are determined to bring the Tsarevich into your investigation, I see.'

'I am afraid to say that he brought himself into it.'

'My son and I do not see eye to eye on many things. When I am dead, and he is tsar, you may be sure that his very first act will be to undo as much as he can of my life's work. My rule has been based on a belief in the necessity of reform. Much good it has done me personally, but still ... I have come to realise that the only way to ensure the survival of the Russian monarchy – indeed, of Russia – is to grant the people as many of their aspirations as is safe and reasonable. The path I have set out upon is one that leads eventually to democracy, I know. Better a managed and measured approach to democracy than its alternative: revolution. My son would have us turn back. In fact, he would rather we had never set foot on this path. To cede one inch to the democrats is to give up everything, he says. The Russian people are not ready for democracy. More than that: they never will be. It is not in their nature. They crave a strong leader. A father. He says that I have failed the Russian people with my weakness. When he is tsar, he says, they will feel again the firm hand of a stern father. No doubt he is impatient to begin. Every day that I am on the imperial throne weakens the power that will come to him – or so he sees it. In our family history, it is not unheard of for such generational differences to be resolved through bloody violence. Fortunately for my son, there is no shortage of individuals ready to do his dirty work for him without his even having to ask. What he fails to understand is that the same individuals will be on hand to mete out the same fate to him once he inherits. Unless, that is, I succeed in removing all vestige of popular support for these terrorists by giving the people what they want. What need for revolution when there is nothing to revolt against? But my son is not very bright. Even the slightest paradox baffles him. Certainly the notion that to hang on to power one must cede power is beyond his comprehension. He is driven by instinct, appetite and passion, rather than by intellect. That will make him a dangerous autocrat. But does it make him a child murderer? I do not believe so. Do not allow misguided ambition to lead you into making a monstrous mistake, Porfiry Petrovich.'

'May I not at least speak to him?'

'No, you may not!'

Porfiry bowed his head meekly in the force of the Tsar's reaction.

The Tsar softened his tone to say: 'But *I* will talk to the Tsarevich. If anything arises from our conversation that I feel concerns you, you may rest assured that I will bring it to your attention.'

'You will have my sincere gratitude, Your Majesty.'

'And now, I really must not keep my Foreign Minister waiting a moment longer.'

33

Justice is delivered

That night was not a restful one for Porfiry. His note to Verkhotsev, which he had completed and dispatched upon his return from the Winter Palace, had prompted a laconic and not particularly reassuring response: *You are safe for now. He will not strike yet.*

Perhaps Verkhotsev was right, although Porfiry struggled to understand on what evidence he based the assertion. Perhaps it was simply the fact that Slava had not acted so far and, being as yet oblivious of the latest body, had no fresh pretext for an attack. It was reasonable to assume that he would continue to bide his time.

Even so, it was hard to relax.

Porfiry had considered confiding his fears to Nikodim Fomich, who as chief of the Haymarket District Police Bureau would have been in a position to make arrangements for his safety. However, since Salytov's disclosures, Porfiry had sensed a distance grow in his heart between himself and his friend. He could dismiss Salytov's allegations as malicious slander, prompted by a desire to bring others down with him. But still, suspicion lingered.

At the same time, Porfiry was inclined to see Verkhotsev's eagerness to provoke an attack as foolhardy in the extreme. It was now clear that the Third Section officer was acting according to his own agenda, and could therefore be added to the growing list of people Porfiry could not trust.

He slept fitfully, sitting bolt upright at the slightest noise. He had never realised how voluble his apartment could be. Like unseen nocturnal creatures, the cooling pipes and contracting boards stirred into querulous life with a chorus of cracks and clicks. From the adjoining apartments, both those above and those around his, came answering sounds, even more obscure and disturbing, the susurrations, shuffles and thumps of one part of the darkness calling out to another. As he drifted in and out of sleep, these sounds looped into the anxious thoughts that his mind turned over endlessly, providing a dark, sub-musical overture to his dreams, which that night were of hidden figures moving about in impenetrable blackness.

Was it in a dream or in a wakeful moment that he first heard the footsteps? As soon as he heard them he was alert, his whole body strained to listen. There was a curious duality to the tension that wracked him. Release would only come when he heard the footsteps again; their erratic suspension became unbearable. At the same time, their recurrence would signal the fulfilment of his fears. Someone – Slava? – was moving against him.

There it was again, distinctly, unmistakably, the clip of a shoe heel followed by the prolonged groan of a floorboard. But if Slava meant to creep up on him, why was he wearing shoes? Another footfall followed the last, and then another. Porfiry was able to place them as coming from Slava's room, the room from which for so many years Zakhar's snores had emanated. It seemed Slava was pacing his room. Perhaps he was simply an insomniac, who needed to wear himself out with exercise before he could think of lying down. If so, it was strange that Porfiry had failed to notice his servant's night-time habits before now.

Porfiry eased himself up slowly, careful not to set the bedsprings quaking. But even the creaking of his bones sounded deafening. He cocked his head, staring into a particulate swirl of darkness, as if he expected something of it. And then it came. The click of Slava's bedroom door opening.

Porfiry felt his heart make a bolt for it, only to crash into the restraining cage of his ribs.

He heard Slava's door grumble and yowl. The footsteps now were on the landing.

Porfiry was suddenly a child again, lying in the dark listening to the relentless thud of Baba Yaga climbing the stairs. He could not say what age he was when he had finally realised that Baba Yaga's footsteps were nothing more than the pulse of blood beating in his ear.

But the footsteps he heard now were not a trick of anatomy. There was a real man, a man he believed was intent on harming him, stalking his apartment. The footsteps approached his door. Porfiry counted them. One, two, three, four. A pause. Then came steps five and six.

Slava was standing right outside his door now. Porfiry held his breath. He heard the twisting grind of shoe leather on wood. The footsteps receded, one, two, three, four, five, six – stronger, quicker, without hesitation. They carried on the length of the hall, to the front door, the public entrance of Porfiry's apartment that gave onto the communal stairs. He heard that door open and close. Slava's footsteps on the stairs resonated through the slumbering building as he bounded down, then burst out into the night.

Porfiry breathed out noisily and lay back down. Who was this man he had admitted into his life?

Somehow, against his will, he fell asleep.

Next morning, the *Gazette* carried the following account:

Fourth child murdered
St Petersburg, Thursday
The body of Innokenty Zimoveykin, 13, was discovered
within the precincts of the Baird Shipbuilding and Machine
Works, where he was employed as a labourer. This brings to
four the number of child murders perpetrated in the city in
recent weeks, death in each case being rendered by
strangulation. All four children were pupils at the
Rozhdestvenskaya Free School. A source within the
Department for the Investigation of Criminal Causes has
revealed that investigators have now discounted the theory
that the crimes were carried out by Yelena Filippovna
Polenova, herself the victim of a murderous attack, and
confess themselves baffled by the presence of the same
distinctive mark on the latest victim's neck as found on the
necks of all the previous victims.

'A shabby piece of reporting,' adjudged Porfiry, folding the
newspaper down onto his desk. He had one eye on Slava who
was clearing away his empty coffee pot. He had breakfasted in
his chambers, ostensibly to get an early start on the day's work,
but more truthfully because his apartment was suddenly alien
and inhospitable to him; overnight he had become the
outsider in it. Perhaps unwisely, he had eaten the breakfast that
Slava had put in front of him. But exhausted and hungry after
his troubled night, his body's needs had taken over and he had
forgotten that he no longer trusted the food Slava brought

344

him. Besides, if Slava really was a revolutionary assassin in waiting, it was unlikely that he would choose such a cowardly means of dispatch as poison. The point of a political murder, surely, was that it should be bloody, bold and spectacular. Cold comfort perhaps for Porfiry, but at least it meant that he could eat heartily until the blow was struck.

Porfiry's suspicions must have shown on his face, for he noticed that Slava flushed under the magistrate's steady gaze.

'Why do you say that?' said Slava antagonistically. 'Is it not factually correct?'

'It claims that we have confessed to being baffled. I have made no such confession. In fact, I strenuously refute it.'

'So, you know who killed these children?'

'Ah, to say that we do not yet know who killed them is not the same as to say we are baffled. We are pursuing a line of investigation that I am confident will result in the arrest of the murderer.'

'May I ask on what you base your confidence?'

'No you may not. May I ask you where you went last night, and in the middle of the night to boot? I heard you leave the apartment.'

'I could not sleep. I thought a walk around the block would settle me.'

'And did it?'

'Yes.'

'I am glad. However, I must tell you that your pacing kept me awake.'

'I'm sorry. I thought you were already asleep. It was very quiet in your room. But that perhaps should have alerted me.'

'What do you mean?'

'Well, I should have known you were awake because I could not hear you snoring.'

'I do not snore. Zakhar was the one that snored.'

'I must inform you, Porfiry Petrovich, that you do.' Slava's smile was retaliative. 'Furthermore, your logic is at fault. The presence of one snoring man within a household does not preclude another – or indeed, any number of others.'

Porfiry was denied the opportunity of replying by the eruption of shouts from the main hall of the police bureau. The commotion seemed to be rolling towards him like a thundercloud borne on fast-moving air currents. The door burst open and Nikodim Fomich rushed in, immediately followed by Virginsky.

'Porfiry Petrovich, something extraordinary has turned up.' Excitement raised Nikodim Fomich's voice to a shout. 'You must come!'

'What? What is this?'

'Outside. You must see for yourself.'

Behind Nikodim Fomich, Virginsky nodded his head energetically in affirmation. Porfiry cast an uncertain glance towards Slava, only to be met with a blank, uncomprehending stare. Slava seemed to be as much in the dark as he was.

Porfiry touched his desk with the pads of all his fingers, as though to push himself to his feet.

*

'Daring! Most daring! To do it in broad daylight. And here, outside a police station.'

'Do we know how it got here?'

'A peasant's cart was driven past. At a fair lick, by all accounts. According to witnesses.'

'There were witnesses?'

'Yes. A number, including some of our men. They saw two men in the back of the cart.'

'Do we have descriptions?'

'Their faces were covered with mufflers.'

'I see. How were they dressed?'

'They were dressed flashily.'

'Flashily?'

'One in a ginger suit, the other was in green. As criminals are wont to do.'

'Our criminals wear only green or ginger suits? That is indeed considerate of them. It should certainly make our investigative work easier. I wonder that we have any unsolved crimes on our books when all we need do is round up all those in green or ginger suits.'

'Don't be obtuse, Porfiry Petrovich. You know very well, there is a class of criminal who takes pleasure in affecting a certain dandyism. They are the peacocks of the underworld. They may not always wear green or ginger suits, but they do favour sartorial ostentation.'

'And the driver?'

'The driver was in peasant's garb. A kaftan over a belted smock.'

'Was he masked too?'

'We may presume so.'

'Presume? My dear Nikodim Fomich, I do not wish to presume anything.'

'His face is a blank to the witnesses. Whether that was because he was masked or because their attention was held by the extraordinary actions of the extraordinary men in the back of the cart, I cannot say.'

'That is understandable, I suppose.'

'Of course it is! These men were standing in the back of a racing cart.'

'How many horses pulled the cart?'

'Porfiry, please! You want to know about the horses now!'

'You describe the cart variously as "racing" and going "at a fair lick". I merely wish to establish how quickly it could conceivably have been travelling. One horse or two will make a difference.'

'But your questions are interrupting my narrative! Can you not allow me to get to the end of my account and then put your questions to me?'

'Well, no. That is not how I like to proceed when I am conducting an interrogation.'

'But you are not interrogating me! I am a policeman, not a criminal!'

Porfiry gave one slow blink. 'I would be grateful if you would confirm the number of horses before continuing with your account.'

'I don't know! No one has remarked on the number of horses. How many horses usually pull a cart?'

'Most usually, I would say one, although the number may be dependent on the weight of the load and the wealth of the peasant.'

'Well then, one. That was why it was not commented on. It was not worthy of comment.'

'I do not see how a heavy cart carrying three men and this load – effectively four men – could achieve the speeds suggested by your terminology when drawn only by one horse.'

'Very well, it must have been two horses.'

'But if there were two horses, would not the witnesses have remarked upon that circumstance?'

'You may question them more carefully about the number of horses yourself. What has it to do with anything?'

'Because if the cart was drawn by one horse, it cannot have reached such a great speed. Certainly it would not have gone so fast that your men could not have given chase.'

'But why would they give chase? They were not in a position to interpret the meaning of the singular occurrence that took place before their eyes. They were, in a word, astonished.'

'What was the nature of this singular occurrence?'

'A sack was thrown from the back of a hurtling cart.'

'The cart is *hurtling* now?'

'At any rate, before they had time to comprehend what had taken place, the cart had disappeared around the corner. In the meantime, their natural instinct was to examine the sack. In which they found . . .'

'The body of this man.'

'Yes.'

'The large wound on the right side of the head, surrounded by blackened, burnt skin and scorched hair, suggests death was caused by a gunshot to the temple, the barrel of the gun being placed against the head. This smaller wound, at the other temple, is where the bullet exited.' Porfiry looked down at the violently disrupted flesh he had just described.

'But you have not commented on the sign.'

The body lay on the pavement, still partially contained in the large hessian sack in which it had been deposited. Only the man's head and shoulders had been exposed. His face was drawn, as if the fatal assault had caused him to suck his cheeks in. In truth, he appeared to be an emaciated and ravaged indvidual. His clothes were those of a workman, coarse, worn and grubby. Around his neck, a white cardboard rectangle was hung by rough twine. The following legend had been scrawled on the cardboard with a blunt pencil.

This is the child murderer what you are looking for. His name is MURIN. He confessed to a fellow. There is honour amongst thieves. This man is scum.

'Well?' said Nikodim Fomich.

'He appears to have been executed.'

'Yes.'

Porfiry, who was squatting on his haunches, worked the edge of the sack down. The man was big-framed, but undernourished so Porfiry was able to manoeuvre him without too much difficulty. Soon the man's hands were exposed. They seemed disproportionately big, at odds with his scrawny physique, as if they had somehow been attached to the wrong arms. The fingers were chubby. The thought struck Porfiry that they had somehow been fattened on all the nourishment the rest of his body had been denied.

An inverted gold ring cinched the little finger of his left hand. Porfiry tried to rotate it on the finger but it refused to move. He turned the hand over, the touch of the cold dead skin sending a stab of revulsion to his heart.

On the face of the ring he saw the double-headed eagle of the House of Romanov.

34

The Tsar will be content

'And so, Porfiry Petrovich, you have your murderer.'

Porfiry regarded his blue-clad visitor with astonishment. 'I see that today you have chosen to appear before me in your gendarme's uniform.'

Verkhotsev bowed.

'And with reinforcements,' added Porfiry, staring pointedly at the other two gendarmes accompanying the major. 'Is there some significance to your choice of apparel?'

'Murin. We have come for Murin.'

'But he is *my* murderer, or so you have declared.'

'Ah, but he was my agitator first.' Verkhotsev smiled winningly, and twirled his moustache. 'Besides, you do not need him any more. You have enough to write your report. Do you not have an appointment with the Tsar this afternoon? Imagine how pleased he will be to discover that you have solved the case.'

'I have not solved the case!' protested Porfiry. 'The body of an escaped political prisoner was dumped outside the head-quarters of the Haymarket District Police Bureau. If Murin is indeed our child-murderer, and we have only the supposed allegation of anonymous criminals to suggest that he is – if he is, then his identification as such owes nothing to me. I had not begun to suspect him. Indeed my suspicions were directed in an entirely other direction.'

'It is perhaps just as well that his body turned up when it did.' Verkhotsev charged his words with dark significance. 'Otherwise you might have made an embarrassing blunder, Porfiry Petrovich. At any rate, whether you claim the credit for solving it or not, the case is closed. You must be thankful for that, as well as relieved. Now you are free to concentrate your efforts on bringing Yelena Filippovna's murderer to justice.'

'Perhaps I will be presented with her murderer in a similarly miraculous way,' remarked Porfiry with bitter irony. 'But I am frankly astonished to hear you say that the case is closed. How can the delivery of a corpse outside a police station signal the end of our work? Surely it is merely the prelude to further investigation?'

'You are not seriously intending to go after Murin's killers? The criminal fraternity has, in this instance, done us and the whole city of St Petersburg a great service. They have delivered justice. Rough justice, admittedly, but justice all the same. And we should be thankful that that depraved individual can no longer harm our children.'

'I confess that I am mystified by this outcome, and by your acceptance of it,' Porfiry countered with force. 'I had understood that Murin was a political agitator. Why does a political agitator engage in child murder? Especially when his victims are drawn from the class whose interests he purports to further?'

'Is it not obvious? The ring is the key. His aim was to incriminate the regime. He would have us believe that a Romanov was behind the crimes. And admit it, he very nearly succeeded in convincing you, Porfiry Petrovich.'

'You must be aware that yours is not the only interpretation

352

that the facts permit. But even if what you say is true, I was not aware that the Tsar put his legal reforms in place only for us to surrender the judicial process to criminals. For whoever has murdered this man is a criminal, Pyotr Afanasevich. Be in no doubt about that.'

'But you have no hope of finding his murderer,' said Verkhotsev flatly. 'You must see that. The criminal fraternity will close ranks. There will be no witnesses. There will be no leads.'

'You speak with remarkable confidence.'

'This man Murin is no ordinary criminal. He is a revolutionary. As such, he has placed himself outside all society, even the society of criminals. He has no friends amongst them. He is looked upon with contempt – disgust even, considering the foul nature of his crimes. In addition, when all else is taken into account, our criminals – our ordinary criminals – always remain Christians. It is natural that they would look upon the slaughterer of children with the greatest revulsion. In them there is a fundamental decency beneath the layers of acquired dishonesty. How could they tolerate one such as Murin? I vouch you will not find one among their number prepared to assist you in the execution of your justice when they have already meted out their own.'

'It is not a question of *my* justice. There is only *justice*. And it is certainly not dispensed by criminals.'

'Our spies in the underworld inform us that criminal society is highly organised. You may be assured that he was tried and found guilty in one of their courts. And that his sentence was duly executed.'

'So, is that the justice you defer to? Because I do not.'

'But the Tsar will be content. St Petersburg will be content.

The murderer you have been hunting is disposed of. I urge you to be content too, Porfiry Petrovich.'

'*He confessed to a fellow!* You expect me to be content with, *He confessed to a fellow?*'

'I grant you it is somewhat lacking in style.'

'It is not the lack of style that concerns me but the lack of substance. Allow me to present my alternative interpretation of the facts, Pyotr Afanasevich. The four children were not murdered by this Murin. But by someone else. A person whose identity is as yet unknown to me, but whom I presume to be in some way associated with the house of Romanov. Perhaps this individual has been prevailed upon to desist from his murderous activities. And in the meantime this Murin has been delivered up to us. My murderer. Your agitator. It smacks rather too much of killing two hares with one shot, does it not?'

'What are you suggesting, Porfiry Petrovich?'

'Oh, come now, sir! Surely you do not need me to spell it out for you. You gentlemen of the Third Section are more subtle than that. A man who can put on and take off a uniform at will does not need things spelled out for him.'

'I almost feel you are insulting me.' Verkhotsev made the remark lightly, almost delightedly.

'You came here pretending to be Maria Petrovna's father!'

'I *am* Maria Petrovna's father!'

'In name only. You claimed to be interested in the truth. And yet you have colluded in a charade. This man Murin was not executed by common criminals.'

'And what makes you so certain of that, Porfiry Petrovich?'

'I am not certain of anything. I admit it. That is the way of the Third Section. In the end, no one can be certain of anything.'

Verkhotsev gave a half-apologetic shrug.

'Your daughter is distraught. She thinks that whoever has been killing those children will come after her.'

'She has nothing to fear.'

'You will tell her that? You will take her hands in yours, look into her eyes, your own daughter's eyes, and tell her that her fears are at an end?'

'Without hesitation.'

'But how can you be so sure? Do you not at least want to talk to this *fellow* to whom Murin supposedly confessed? I warn you, Pyotr Afanasevich, if Murin is not the killer, if there is some other person being protected, then there will be more bloodshed. No matter what assurances have been given, such an individual cannot be contained, however watchful his custodians, however noble his family.'

'You are once again venturing into dangerous waters, Porfiry Petrovich. Why, you talk as if you almost wish it were a Romanov who had committed these crimes!'

'That is not true. But I do know that you cannot sweep these things under the carpet.'

Verkhotsev took a moment to consider Porfiry's words. 'Let us talk openly, man to man.'

'There is nothing I would like more.'

'You suspect the Tsarevich, why not say it?'

'I certainly would like to put some questions to the Tsarevich, but so far that has not been possible. I was granted an audience with the Tsar, however. That was a gracious condescension on His Majesty's part, for which I am grateful, but perhaps it served a purpose of his own.'

'Which was?'

'To impress me. And thereby to control me.'

'You are too modest. I am sure the Tsar knows you are not a man to be controlled.'

'He said he found me something of an imbecile.'

'Ah! A certain bluntness of discourse is one of the more regrettable aspects of autocracy, even amongst its most liberal examples. I am sure you were soon able to convince him of your mental acuity.'

'I cannot say. But when I brought up the question of the Tsarevich—'

'You brought up the Tsarevich?'

'Naturally. That was primarily my purpose in seeing the Tsar.'

'Your purpose? My good fellow, the Tsar summoned you.'

'Ah, but I wanted to see him too.'

'Well, go on. What did he say?'

'He expressed the opinion that the Tsarevich was more likely to kill *him* than anyone else. At any rate, he quite firmly blocked my request for a meeting with the Tsarevich. He said he would speak to his son himself.'

'Murder has certainly been a Romanov family tradition, I grant you that. But only ever as a political tool, limited exclusively to family members to ensure a desired transition of power. His Majesty is surely right. There has never been any precedent for the random murder of innocent children.'

'But what if it is not random? What if it is political?'

'Then we come back to Murin!'

'What if it is an attempt to undermine the Tsar? To show him as incapable of protecting his children, no longer the Father Tsar?'

'We are agreed! That is indeed how I see it. Murin!'

'No. It is not Murin who is behind it. It is . . .'

'The Tsarevich? But that is absurd! Why does he need to bring down his father? He knows he will inherit the empire one day. All he has to do is await his father's death.'

'But by then it will be too late. His father will have taken the country even further along the path of reform, towards full democracy. He will have surrendered the autocrat's power before his son had any chance to wield it.'

'But upon what are your suspicions of the Tsarevich based? The fact that he was at the Naryskin Palace the night Yelena Filippovna was murdered? At a gala event in honour of the school the victims attended? It is tenuous in the extreme, Porfiry Petrovich. Were there not many other people there too? Will you suspect them all?'

'The ring.'

'The ring! Murin had a ring! Yet it is not enough to persuade you that he was the murderer. I take it you have measured the motif on the ring?'

'Yes.'

'And?'

'One fifth of a *vershok* by one tenth.'

'Is that or is it not an appropriate size to cause the marks on the children's necks?'

'It would be. However, the ring was on his little finger! A ring worn on the little finger would leave no mark on the children's necks!'

Verkhotsev was visibly thrown. He turned to glare angrily at his subordinates, each of whom, in turn, shifted disconsolately under the force of his disfavour. 'He . . . must have moved it,' Verkhotsev offered weakly to Porfiry, without meeting his gaze.

'It would not fit on his thumb. It barely fitted on his little finger. Must have been quite a struggle to push it on – eh, gentlemen? It was not his ring, after all.'

'Now, now. You have no grounds to make such an assertion.'

'You handled Yelena Filippovna's ring! You must have somehow taken it and substituted it with another.'

'That is a very serious allegation. I examined the ring right here in front of you. Will you honestly say that you saw me substitute it?'

'No, I did not see that. You're right. But there is something you are withholding from me. I know it. That is what I don't like.'

'Very well, I will tell you something about Yelena Filippovna's ring, and perhaps then you will trust me more. The Tsarevich is involved. You are right to suspect him of something, although not of murder. He gave Yelena Filippovna that ring. She had a habit of demanding a ring from each of her lovers. Yes, the Tsarevich loved her, quite hopelessly. And she did not love him back – can you believe that? So, there you have it. The one thing, perhaps, that you did not suspect him of, love. That is why he fled the Naryskin Palace after her murder. He was heartbroken. Simply heartbroken.' Verkhotsev's voice grew choked with emotion. Then a sudden pragmatic clarity descended. 'And of course he wished to avoid a scandal.'

'It is a strange kind of passion that is so careful of its reputation,' observed Porfiry waspishly.

'You forget, he is next in line to the imperial throne. He is not free to love as other men may.' Verkhotsev ran a finger along one of his moustaches. 'So, what will you say to His Majesty?'

'I shall simply and factually report what has occurred. That a body has been dumped—'

'You will use that word?'

'Discarded, then. I have made a note of the wording on the sign. I shall be interested to hear what the Tsar has to say about it. His Majesty has personally taken over the supervision of the case, you know.'

Verkhotsev allowed a wry smile to flicker on his lips. 'There is nothing exceptionable in that. We are all his servants, exercising his will, agents and instruments of his authority. If he should deign to involve himself directly in our activities from time to time, it is merely to make manifest the truth behind our own illusions of power. It is not ours, but his.'

Porfiry blew out his cheeks.

'And if the Tsar should decide that the case is closed, will you remonstrate with him as you have with me?'

'One does not remonstrate with the Tsar.'

'You are wise to take that view.'

Porfiry shook his head impatiently.

'There is one other matter that I wished to speak to you about, Porfiry Petrovich. The matter of your own safety. I take it that the individual we were discussing did not make an attempt against you last night?'

'As you see, I passed the night unharmed.'

'I am glad to hear it, though if you remember that is as I predicted. Now that the news of the latest child's murder has been reported, I fear that the danger against you is heightened. I would urge you to take all precautions. With that in mind, I have brought something for you. Consider it a gift.'

Verkhotsev nodded to the gendarme on his right. The officer looked into a dispatch bag that he was carrying and retrieved a parcel wrapped in brown paper and string, which he handed to his major. Verkhotsev in turn passed it to Porfiry, who rose from his seat with a bow to receive it. It was about the size and weight of a small dish. Before Porfiry could unwrap it, the door to his private apartment opened and Slava came through. Major Verkhotsev raised an enquiring eyebrow and Porfiry nodded. Verkhotsev gave a warning shake of the head over the parcel and even went so far as to lift his hand to signal restraint.

Slava appeared taken aback by the sight of the gendarmes. It seemed for a moment that he was going to turn on his heels and run, but he held his ground. A sullen cast fell over his features, however.

'What is it, Slava?' demanded Porfiry.

Slava frowned as if he were puzzled by the question. 'Oh . . . did you want anything?'

'Did I want anything?'

'I'm your servant. I was merely trying to . . . serve.'

'No.'

Slava sucked the nail of his right index finger and nodded pensively.

'Now, I really must . . . go,' said Porfiry, utterly bemused by Slava's display. 'I am late for my appointment with the Tsar.'

'You're going to see the Tsar?' blurted Slava.

It seemed for a moment that he was about to ask if he could go with Porfiry, but, to everyone's relief, even he drew the line at that.

*

As a room that was used for the processing of tragedy, the main hall of the Haymarket District Police Bureau was inevitably the scene of emotional disruptions. The station served one of the poorest areas of St Petersburg, though there were pockets of poverty throughout the city that could rival it. Those who were driven to the limits of existence would find they had nowhere else to turn but to crime. Whether they sought to alleviate their lot through prostitution or larceny, these accidental criminals would sooner or later find themselves rounded up and herded into the gas-lit gloom of the main receiving hall. The police who brought them there abandoned them. The clerks who were to process them ignored them. And yet, of course, they were not allowed to leave. Some ventured in voluntarily: the victims of crime, or more rarely its witnesses; sometimes the relatives of those who had gone missing or those who had been arrested.

Exceptionally, there appeared someone whose presence there, at least at first sight, simply could not be explained; nor could it be ignored.

The woman clearly fell into that category. Porfiry saw her immediately as he came out of his chambers. She was dressed in male working clothes, several sizes too big for her: the sleeves of the corduroy jacket flapped uselessly over her hands and she continually tripped over the trailing trouser legs. Her hair had been roughly cropped and her face was smeared with soot. There would have been something stagey, almost comical, about her crude attempt to pass herself off as a man, had it not been for the desolate detachment of her eyes and the wild, harsh keening that vibrated in her throat. It would not have been true to say those eyes took in nothing of their surroundings. But it seemed as though she saw the world as something to which she could not be reconciled.

'Who is she?' Porfiry asked of Zamyotov.

The clerk at his desk half-turned towards her disdainfully. 'God knows. Some specimen of riff-raff. The tide of human misery washes up all sorts in here. Ask Pavel Pavlovich. He takes an interest in such cases.'

Virginsky was indeed watching the woman with keen interest, at the head of a small huddle of officials – policemen, magistrates and clerks – who seemed drawn to her distress but unsure of how to react to it. Without doubt it was a disturbance and therefore needed to be curtailed. Compassion for the woman, too, may have stirred in the breasts of some of those watching and that perhaps should have been enough to prompt one of them to intervene. And yet there was something compelling about the spectacle that made them reluctant to end it. At the same time, there was a raw power to the emotion on display that commanded respect. The feeling seemed to be that it had to be allowed to play itself out.

The first of them to approach her was Virginsky. He did so not in a movement of restraint, but of consolation. His face seemed to implore her, for mercy's sake, to spare herself. An arm was extended, ready to reach protectively around her shoulder. But the woman backed away from him, her eyes glaring with terror and distrust. Her gaze darted frantically about, seeking a bolt hole. But instead she caught sight of something that only added to her agitation. Her eyes now had the wild panic of a trapped animal. Her keening rose to a sharp shriek of negation. She thrust out an arm in front of her, the drooping cuff of the jacket hardly mitigating the undeniable accusation in the gesture. Porfiry followed the line of her arm. She was pointing out Verkhotsev and his fellow gendarmes, conspicuous in their sky-blue uniforms.

Verkhotsev's face was grim. He seemed shaken by the

woman's attention. His companions, however, affected what seemed to Porfiry to be a cynical hilarity. The gendarmes had not been part of the group watching the woman, but had been making their way across the hall, having left Porfiry's chambers moments before. Something had made them glance towards the woman just as she found them and pointed them out. And they, for some reason, were held frozen by the trajectory of her accusation.

While the woman was distracted by the gendarmes, Virginsky was able to make his move. He closed in on her, stepping to the side and coming back in from behind. His arm was on her shoulder now and his head was close to hers, his mouth whispering comfort into her ear.

She broke off from her wailing; her arm fell lifelessly. She twisted to face Virginsky, at the same time working herself free from his hold. Her lips began to move steadily, releasing a low torrent of speech. Porfiry could not make it out from where he stood but he could sense the force and mettle of her words, each one a gleaming hard bullet of bitterness. The volume of her speech, in part lament, in part complaint, rose until she was declaiming to the whole hall.

'They killed him. They waited for him and took him away and killed him. My Grisha, my dear sweet Grisha. What did he ever do to them that they should kill him? What did he ever do to anyone? He submitted a petition! That's what! That was his crime! He submitted a petition on behalf of his fellow workers, requesting, politely – respectful, too, so respectful you would not believe it . . . yes, requesting that the factory fulfil its legal obligations. The Tsar himself required the factory to put in place the improvements. But they failed to do it. So my Grisha submitted a petition. And this, he was told, was a crime. This, they said, was political agitation. They took him away. He was sent to the mines in the Olonets region. To Petrozavodsk. Torn away from his family, his four little ones. I was left alone to bring them up. They took a father from his children because he submitted a petition! That was ten years ago. Last month, our youngest died. I managed to get word to Grisha. He ran away from the mines. He should not have done it but his child was dead! He came back to Petersburg. He waited and waited before coming to see me. But *they* were watching for him all the time. They did not relent. And all because he submitted a petition! At last he could wait no longer, though I urged him through friends to stay away. Not because I didn't want to see him. It was what I longed for more than anything. It was for his sake I told him not to come. But he needed to see me. He needed to hold his children again after all these years. He would not be kept away. He could not come so far without seeing us. But they were waiting for him. And they took him from me again. And they killed him. And now they say he is a murderer. That he killed those children. But why would he kill children? He loved children. He was a child himself when he entered the factory. Thirteen years old. He had never hurt anyone in his life. He was a gentle soul. The gentlest. They called him a criminal, a political, but the only crime he committed before he ran away from the mines was to submit a petition. He was only asking them to fulfil their obligations. And for that, they killed him!'

Her arms swept out towards where the gendarmes had been but they were gone now. Her voice had reached an unsustainable pitch. The only place she could take it was once again into the keen of pure suffering.

Porfiry approached the woman. Virginsky, who was again

trying to encompass her grief with his arms, turned to him with an accusatory glare. 'And this is the justice we serve!' he hissed between clenched teeth.

Porfiry widened his eyes in warning. 'Take her into my chambers. See if you can get anything like a statement from her. I'll see you here later.' And with a tight-lipped smile, Porfiry bowed his tense farewell.

35

The Tsar commands

'Are you content?'

The Tsar's expression in answer was clouded and pensive. 'Content?' He gave a half-laugh, not quite bitter, but certainly regretful. 'That is not a question *I* am often asked, Porfiry Petrovich. It is assumed that I must be content. I am the tsar, after all. How can I not be? But . . .' He looked down at the rows of photographs on his desk. 'Families, Porfiry Petrovich. They are a great source of discontent. And I am *pater familias* to a whole empire.'

'With respect, Your Majesty, I simply meant to ask, are you content to accept this Murin as the murderer of the children?'

'This is the view of the Third Section?'

'It is more than their view. It is their . . . invention.'

The Tsar held Porfiry with a piercing look of challenge, under the force of which Porfiry launched a volley of defensive blinking.

'What is the alternative?' asked the Tsar at last. 'What other suspects do you have?'

Porfiry bowed his head to look up at the Tsar, wincing apologetically.

'No!' said the Tsar emphatically. 'Do not bring that up again.'

'Someone sought to undermine you by these murders. The Tsarevich—'

'But it is preposterous! That he would seek to undermine me by incriminating himself!'

'No, the plan was always to throw the blame on an agitator. Fortunately, Murin was to hand, although in truth he was a sorry example of an agitator.'

'What do you mean? They told me that he was responsible for organising protests.'

'He submitted a petition.' There was more sadness than reproach in Porfiry's voice. 'His widow came to the bureau dressed in his clothes. She revealed the full extent of his crimes against the state. A politely worded petition.'

The Tsar looked away, shame-faced.

'According to this theory,' continued Porfiry, noting the Tsar's embarrassment with sympathy, 'the Tsarevich was working in conjunction with the Third Section, or factions within it. We need not postulate that he carried out the murders himself. Only that he authorised them.'

'Should I be grateful to you for this consideration? I do not need you to tell me that my son did not carry out these murders. He spent the autumn, the time during which the crimes were committed, with me in Livadia. He was not in Petersburg. And I am his alibi. As to whether he is capable of formulating such a complex and subtle plot against me, I doubt it.'

'It may be possible that such a proposal was put to him by another, and he merely gave his assent.'

'He is stupid enough for that, I warrant. Do you have someone in mind, Porfiry Petrovich, as the source of this machination?'

'Your son was seen at the Naryskin Palace with Count Tolstoy. He is well known for his reactionary views. And as the minister responsible for education, he would naturally have been aware of Maria Petrovna's school since its foundation.'

'And this is how you proceed, is it? This is your great method? My son was seen in the company of a man, therefore he is in cahoots with him too! Count Tolstoy is my minister, loyal to me! Besides, I have it on good authority that neither my son nor Count Tolstoy in fact attended the gala at the Naryskin Palace. Those who say they were there are evidently mistaken.'

'You have been speaking to Prince Nikolai Naryskin, I see. He is a very loyal friend to Your Majesty, I can vouch for that. So loyal I believe he would be prepared to perjure himself on your behalf. I wonder therefore why you were so rough with him yesterday.'

'He sought to embroil me in petty commercial affairs. I will have none of it.' Porfiry smiled in such meek expectation that the Tsar was compelled to continue: 'He has become the direc-tor of a bank. He sought to prevail on me to withdraw my approval for a rival bank. I cannot become involved in these commercial wrangles.'

'And so you sent him away with a flea in his ear?'

The Tsar bridled at the expression but made no comment.

Porfiry held himself immobile as the two men sat in silent contemplation. It was the Tsar who broke the silence: 'Cigarette?'

Released from his immobility, Porfiry fidgeted out his own enamel cigarette case. 'I wonder, Your Majesty, would you care for one of mine?'

The Tsar nodded and took one of the offered cigarettes. Porfiry busied himself with lighting the Tsar's cigarette with fussy attentiveness.

'You are ... quite ... wrong, you know,' said the Tsar languidly, between inhalations. 'The Tsarevich had nothing to do with authorising Murin's murder.' The Tsar winced away from Porfiry's wide-eyed astonishment. 'I did not tell them what to do ... the Third Section ... I merely gave them licence to sort it out.'

'Sort what out, Your Majesty?'

'She ... she was very dear to me once.'

'Yelena Filippovna?'

The Tsar nodded minutely.

'*You* gave her the ring, not the Tsarevich!'

The second nod was even more minimal, barely noticeable.

'I could not bear to see what they were writing about her in the newspapers. It could not be true. Not the Yelena I knew. We had to clear her name. We had to *make* it not true.'

'But who killed Innokenty?'

'I did not tell them what to do. I merely impressed on them the importance of clearing her name. I ...' The Tsar looked Porfiry in the eye for the first time since they had begun smoking.

Porfiry did not flinch from the autocrat's gaze. 'Obviously, if there was another murder, then it would be assumed that Yelena Filippovna was not the killer.' The magistrate blinked once, as though in mild recrimination. 'And so the Third Section killed Innokenty as well as Murin. Verkhotsev was behind that too?'

'I don't know. How can we ever know?'

'We can enquire into it, Your Majesty. You have the author-ity. You can command the truth.'

'No. The Third Section must be allowed some latitude for its operations. For the security of the state. You see that, don't you? You're a reasonable man. It's because you are a reasonable man that I have been . . . open with you. But this must go no further than this room.'

'You are asking me to be an accomplice after the fact to murder.'

'No. I am not asking you. I am commanding you.'

'And if I refuse?'

'You cannot refuse your Tsar's command.' The Tsar's gaze remained rigidly impervious for several moments, before collapsing into something more imploring. 'Do you not see, we could not allow it to be believed that a woman of Yelena Filippovna's class and rank had murdered these factory children? It would have been like pouring oil on a burning house. The divisions in society would have split asunder. I could not, in all conscience, have permitted it. There is the greater crime, and you would have had me commit it.'

'And was Yelena Filippovna killed by the Third Section, in order to prevent further murders?'

'No. That is to say, I do not believe so. She was not suspected until you found those heads. And when that story got into the newspaper, it became a matter of urgency to nip it in the bud. Did you ever find out who was responsible for releasing the story? That, you could say, is what caused Innokenty's death.'

Porfiry shook his head in angry denial. 'We cannot proceed like this! Russia cannot progress on this basis. You cannot build a future based on lies, on even the smallest lie.'

'The future has always been built on lies. He who asserts his lie most forcibly creates the truth.'

'And what of Yelena Filippovna? Were you so ready to believe her guilty? Did you not stop to think that her name, her memory, might be better served by the truth?'

The Tsar, in his agitation, began to turn the Romanov ring that he himself wore on the forefinger of his left hand. The index finger and thumb of his other hand chased each other restlessly as he rotated the ring around the base of its finger. 'There were times when I thought her capable of anything. And yet, I do not believe she killed the children. I cannot believe it.'

'Then what have you done, Your Majesty? What *have* you done?'

'It is not for you to ask me such questions.'

'If it was not her and not Murin – as it most certainly was not – then we must face the fact that the killer is still alive and at large.'

'You must track them down, Porfiry Petrovich. You must track them down and bring them to justice. That is my command.' The Tsar continued to turn the ring on his finger obsessively. Porfiry's brows came down as he watched, his distracted fascination turning to concentration.

'Thank you, Your Majesty,' said Porfiry, rising abruptly to his feet.

'For what?'

'I believe you may have just shown me the solution to these crimes.'

36

Captain Mizinchikov's confession

Virginsky was waiting at the door to Porfiry's chambers. His face showed a mixture of grimness and excitability.

'What is it, Pavel Pavlovich?'

Virginsky handed Porfiry a slip of paper.

It is my duty to inform you that General Denis Nikolaevich Mizinchikov, father of the fugitive Captain Konstantin Denisevich Mizinchikov, was today found dead at the Polzunkov apartment building in Gorokhovaya St. Dr I.P. Predposylov, the medical examiner for the Kazanskaya District, noted the presence of a contusion to the skull consistent with a blow or fall. In addition, both the deceased's wrists were broken. The cranial contusion is not held to be sufficiently severe to be fatal in and of itself, therefore the cause of death is entered as heart failure.

Lieutenant Trusotsky

Gorokhovaya Street Police Bureau

'Do you remember what you said, Porfiry Petrovich? Here is a murder waiting to happen.'

'Did I? But there is nothing to suggest foul play in the report. He may simply have suffered a heart attack and fallen. Or perhaps he fell first, and that induced the heart attack. That would explain his broken wrists. His hands went out to break his fall. Old people have brittle bones, easily broken.'

'But what if a blow was struck, and it was the blow that brought on the heart attack? Would that not be murder?'

'Whom do you suspect of striking this blow?'

'Captain Mizinchikov, of course.'

'There is nothing here to place him at the scene.'

'Neighbours reported seeing a disreputable-looking tramp force his way into the deceased's apartment.'

'This is not in the report.'

'I managed to extract the information from the clerk who delivered it.'

Porfiry cast a passing glance at his own clerk, Zamyotov, who was following the discussion with interest. 'Yes, police clerks are often a source of interesting supplementary details. Some would call it gossip.'

Zamyotov responded with a suitably indignant pout.

'There were sounds of argument,' continued Virginsky. 'Shouting. Doors slamming. Soon after, the tramp was seen to leave precipitously. The dead man was discovered by his neighbours, on the landing of a flight of stairs outside his apartment. By the time the alarm was raised, the tramp was nowhere to be seen.'

'And you believe this tramp to be Captain Mizinchikov?'

'I think it highly likely.'

'General Mizinchikov may simply have fallen. He was elderly and infirm. Falls at his age can prove fatal.'

'Or he was pushed.'

'Equally possibly, he may have been pursuing his fleeing son, and in his haste he tripped and fell, being unsteady on his feet.'

'Is that really what you think happened, Porfiry Petrovich?'

'Sometimes people just die. Especially when they are old and sick. We need not always be looking for a murderer.'

'But the tramp was there!'

'If the tramp was indeed Captain Mizinchikov, then it must be admitted that his appearance at this moment is unfortunate – for Captain Mizinchikov, that is. It may be true that he in some way contributed to his father's death, whether deliberately or inadvertently we cannot know. It makes it more pressing than ever that we talk to him. I can only hope that this latest tragedy will operate on his conscience in such a way as to persuade him to present himself to the authorities. It is, after all, one thing to flee from a dead mistress. Parricide is quite another category of transgression.'

'And so you will simply wait for him to hand himself in?'

'You may be surprised, Pavel Pavlovich, how often the conscience of a criminal has proven to be my ally in the fight against crime.' Porfiry at last opened the door to his chambers. 'Now, I have a very important call to make. Perhaps you would care to accompany me? I am going—'

But before Porfiry could reveal his intended destination, a shout cut through the hubbub of the main hall: 'Where is he? Where is the magistrate?'

Porfiry turned towards the source of the commotion. He saw a dark-haired man with a matted beard, dressed in a dirty overcoat that was more an accretion of rags and strips of cloth. Beside him, with one hand on his shoulder as if to impel him forward, was an altogether smarter young man, dressed in a plaid travelling cape hung with tassels, and wearing something like a student's cap on his head, though he was too old to be a student. The tramp stared straight at Porfiry as he fell to his knees. 'I am Mizinchikov. I have come to confess.' He bowed his head low, until he was able to kiss the floor.

Porfiry allowed himself a faint smile of satisfaction, which Virginsky received as if it were a body blow.

*

'So.' Porfiry drew deep on his cigarette as he viewed the man sitting on the other side of his desk. It really was true what they said about the men of the Preobrazhensky Regiment. Captain Mizinchikov was a most ill-favoured individual. His eyes bulged, his nostrils flared, his teeth were as irregular as the tombstones in a neglected graveyard. In addition to that, he had no discernible chin and his forehead sloped back at a sharp angle to the bridge of his protuberant nose. Admittedly, the fact that he was filthy and exhausted after weeks of living rough did nothing to improve his looks. The dirt ended in a sharp black arc below his hairline, the tide mark of his sweat. Even allowing for the ravages of his life as a fugitive, it was clear that he would never be regarded as handsome, even scrubbed and groomed. Yet there was something unassailable about him that fascinated and held Porfiry's gaze: an energy, or integrity perhaps. 'You have come to confess. We are only wondering, my colleague and I, to what you wish to confess. Shall we start with the murder of Yelena Filippovna Polenova?'

'I did not kill Lena.'

'Good. I'm glad to hear you say it. If you had confessed to that, I would not have believed you.'

'I killed my father.'

'Did you really? That's rather serious, you know. How did you do it?'

'I . . . we argued.'

'I supposed he was frail, but I had no idea to what extent.'

'It was a violent argument.'

'Ah, you struck him?'

'No blows were struck. I would not hit an old man, whoever he might be. However, I did lay hands upon him.'

'In what way?'

'I took hold of him.'

'With what purpose in mind?'

'He would not look at me. I wanted to make him look at me. I am his son.'

'How did you take hold of him?'

'I put my hands on his shoulders . . . I lifted him . . . I turned him bodily towards me.'

'I see. And then?'

'Still he would not look at me. He turned his head away.'

'And so?'

'And so I threw him away from me.'

'*Threw* him?' Porfiry's emphasis was sceptical.

'Pushed him, then.'

'Where was this?'

'In the drawing room.'

'In the drawing room of his apartment?'

'Yes.'

'What did you do next?'

'I ran. He was on the floor, not moving. I panicked. As I was leaving I ran into my cousin, Alyosha, who had just arrived from Moscow to see my father. He went into the apartment and confirmed that my father was dead. He then prevailed upon me to give myself up to the authorities, for the good of my soul. In truth, it was my own heartfelt desire.'

'Your cousin was the gentleman who brought you here?'

'Yes. He had come of his own volition to see my father. It was about the will. I was to be cut out, in Alyosha's favour. Alyosha sought to dissuade my father on my behalf.'

'And has the will been changed yet?'

'Alyosha says not.'

Porfiry and Virginsky met each other's gaze thoughtfully.

'I did not kill my father for his money, if that's what you're thinking. I did not mean to kill him at all. I wanted to be reconciled with him. I just wanted him to acknowledge me as his son. I needed my father's love. I had nowhere else to turn.' Mizinchikov looked desperately from Virginsky to Porfiry, his eyes moist with exhausted emotion. His voice was imploring. 'I could not go to my friends. I have no friends. Other than my cousin, but he was in Moscow. I tried Bakhmutov. I went to him to ask for money so that I could get to Moscow, but he set his lackeys on me. Would not even admit me. Since that night at the Naryskin Palace, I have been sleeping rough, living on scraps. I couldn't take it any longer. I wanted to talk to my father, to ask him what I should do. But even he would not look at me. You don't know what it has been like, all these weeks! I have felt such . . . despair. Such loneliness. And when my father would not look at me . . . Everything, every insult and humiliation, every bitter emotion welled up inside me. I saw a red mist, that's all I can say.'

'A red mist?'

'Yes. Quite literally. Have you ever seen a red mist? I had not believed in the truth of the expression until that moment. I felt . . . a terrible rage. I killed him.'

'But your father was found dead on the stairs outside his apartment. Not in the drawing room. I'm sorry to disappoint you, but it seems you may *not* have killed him.'

'I don't understand.'

'Nor do I, fully. But perhaps your father went after you. Perhaps he wished to be reconciled after all. His heart gave way, however, and he fell.'

'Then it is still true to say that I killed him. For if I had not laid hands on him in the drawing room, his constitution would not have been fatally weakened.'

'There is another possibility,' said Porfiry, musingly, as if to himself. 'Pavel Pavlovich, would you ask Captain Mizinchikov's cousin to join us?'

Virginsky bowed and crossed to the door.

Captain Mizinchikov's cousin came in hesitantly, his cap in his hands. He was a tall man with a wide, high forehead, which bulged at the temples. His eyes were quick and intelligent. He wore his hair long and a soft, drooping moustache partially concealed his mouth.

'You are Alexei Ivanovich, I believe?' began Porfiry.

'Yes, that's right.' Alexei Ivanovich held his head angled backwards, as if detaching himself from his surroundings, the better to observe them.

'The deceased, General Mizinchikov, was your uncle? And this gentleman is your cousin?'

'Correct.'

'Are you related on your father's or your mother's side?'

'Mother's.'

'Ah, yes, I remember the general made reference to the fecundity of his sisters. Your family name is?'

'Zahlebinin.'

'And it was you who found General Mizinchikov on the stairs?'

'That is correct.'

'He was dead when you found him?'

'Yes.'

'Are you qualified to make such a pronouncement?'

'I have studied natural science. I felt for a pulse. And found none. I saw the wound on his head.'

'And you urged your cousin to hand himself over to the authorities?'

'I did.'

'Why? Did you believe him to be his father's murderer?'

'I knew that he had attacked his father and that his father now lay dead.'

'Did you not ascertain from talking to Captain Mizinchikov where exactly his violent quarrel with his father took place?'

'My cousin was barely coherent. His account of what had taken place was confused. I limited myself to the facts, as I perceived them.'

'He does not seem confused or incoherent now.'

'He had not eaten for days. That is a circumstance that I have since rectified.'

'Captain Mizinchikov and his father quarrelled inside the apartment. General Mizinchikov was found dead on the stairs outside the apartment.'

Alexei Ivanovich seemed overjoyed by this discrepancy. 'Then Kostya did not kill him?'

'We can at least say that General Mizinchikov was alive when Captain Mizinchikov left him. Alive and well enough to walk outside his apartment to the stairs. Where he may well have suffered a heart attack or a fatal accident. Or . . .'

'Or what?' asked Alexei Ivanovich uneasily.

'Or some other person may have pushed him down the stairs.'

Alexei Ivanovich's face flushed a deep shade of crimson. 'You think I did it?'

'There is the question of the will.'

'Yes. The will. But as the will stands, Kostya will inherit his father's fortune. My uncle did not get round to changing it. I had nothing to gain from this death. In fact, it would have been better for me if he had stayed alive a little longer ... long enough to change his will in my favour.'

'Except that you did not want him to change the will. You wanted the money to go to Kostya. You took your cousin's side and you hated your uncle as any man would hate a miser and an unnatural father. So you killed him before he was able to write Kostya out of his will. You knew very well where the argument had taken place – and therefore you trusted that no charges would be brought against your cousin, once it was realised that his father was strong enough to stand up and walk away from where he had fallen. And yet you also knew that Captain Mizinchikov had to be prevailed upon to hand himself in, because as an outlaw he would not be able to access his fortune. Of course there is the matter of the other crimes of which he stands accused. Perhaps you acted in the heat of the moment, or perhaps you took a calculated gamble. You must have followed the details of the investigation in the newspapers. Taking the hint from a recent article, you believed that the authorities would be lenient in their treatment of your cousin in relation to the murder of Yelena Filippovna. There was still the charge of desertion – but a dishonourable discharge from his regiment would not prevent him from inheriting. You yourself would have been immune from suspicion – or so you believed – because of the lack of motive. I must point out to you that you were very quick to present the argument concerning the will.'

'And all this you have deduced from *what*?' demanded Alexei Ivanovich incredulously.

'From your plaid travelling cloak.'

'I beg your pardon?'

'And your student cap. And your studies in natural science. You are, are you not, a nihilist?'

'I do not accept the term.'

'Neither do you accept traditional notions of morality. You felt the injustice of your uncle's position towards your cousin, and you determined to do something about it when you had the chance. Is that not so?'

'Porfiry Petrovich?' interrupted Virginsky questioningly. 'Dr Pervoyedov wears a plaid coat. Indeed, many people wear plaid. Will you accuse them all of being nihilists and murderers?'

'We are not discussing Dr Pervoyedov. We are not discussing other people. Furthermore, no one detail is to be taken in isolation. Everything must be considered together. This may be considered a clever, opportunistic, but essentially altruistic crime – inasmuch as the perpetrator did not directly benefit from its commission, but someone else did. A selfless crime, if you like. Someone who dons the trappings of the radical youth, and is present at the scene of the crime, must come under strong suspicion.'

'But you cannot prove any of this. Is it not equally possible that the old man simply fell?'

'Oh yes,' agreed Porfiry with delight. 'Equally, eminently possible.' Noting Alexei Ivanovich's confusion, Porfiry went on: 'I'm not interested in proving anything. Only you know

381

what happened. And if I am right, you know what you must do. If I *am* right, you have this crime, this sin on your soul. It should be you who falls to his knees and kisses the ground, preferably in front of a church.'

'But I am a nihilist! Or so you claim. What do I care about my soul?'

'You may not care, Alexei Ivanovich, but I do.'

'Well, if you *are* right, and I murdered my own uncle, a man who intended to make me the heir of his fortune, does that not make me a rather dangerous individual? Can you permit me to remain at large, free to commit other crimes?'

'Are you now urging me to arrest you?'

'I don't know.' After an uncertain pause, Alexei Ivanovich added: 'I admit nothing.'

'But you are a little afraid of yourself now, aren't you? And more than a little afraid of the world you have created by this act.'

'I admit nothing.'

'Of course you don't. But that is not the same as saying you did not do it. Forgive me, Alexei Ivanovich. I do not usually conduct my investigations so directly, so bluntly, you might say. But we are in the middle of several other investigations here and General Mizinchikov's death comes as something of a distraction. It's rather inconvenient, if I may be frank. Naturally, I am pleased that it has led to Captain Mizinchikov's surrender, and I am grateful to you for engineering that. I trust that you will consider what we have discussed and do whatever you consider necessary.'

'I am free to go?'

'Do you wish to go?'

'I don't understand. This is not what I expected.'

'If you are innocent, none of this need trouble you. If you are guilty, I am sure we will meet again. Perhaps soon. I would only say, please don't kill anyone else. I would consider it rather bad form if you did.'

'This is some kind of magistrate's technique – a trick of yours!' Alexei Ivanovich's face was suddenly shadowed with anxiety and suspicion.

'No. It is simply that I am in a hurry and there are some questions I must put to your cousin. I have not the time to interrogate you properly now. Therefore I am enlisting your *conscience* in my service.' Porfiry stressed the word, as if to emphasise how much he was relying on this faculty. 'I am sure it will not let me down.'

'Alyosha . . .' Captain Mizinchikov's intervention was mild and almost wistful, but nonetheless powerful. There was the gentlest note of reproach in his voice. 'If you did this thing, if you did it for me, you must see, I cannot accept the money. I cannot benefit from this act. And I urge you, as you urged me, I urge you, to bare your soul. To confess.'

'He fell, that's all. I did not push him, I simply . . . let go.'

'You let go.' Porfiry carefully kept any note of interrogation out of his voice. He reassured rather than questioned.

'He was unsteady, unbalanced. I was holding him up at the top of the stairs. He shouted something . . . something disgusting, hateful, inhuman. It was the act of a moment – I let go. He fell. I did not push him. I don't think I pushed him. Might I have?'

'Please sit down, my friend.' Porfiry gestured to the sofa. 'Perhaps you would like to put your feet up and rest a while? Such exertions as this are invariably tiring.'

'Yes, thank you. I will.'

Alexei Ivanovich staggered over to the brown sofa uphol-stered in artificial leather – American leather, as it was called. He fell onto it and drew his knees up, turning his back on the other men in the room. He was heard to mutter, 'I admit nothing.' Seconds after, he had dozed off.

37

Playing parts

'What will happen to him?' asked Captain Mizinchikov in an awed whisper. He stared in bewilderment at his slumbering cousin.

'Don't worry about him.'

Mizinchikov turned a fearful gaze on Porfiry. 'Can you make anyone confess to anything?'

'No.' Porfiry smiled reassuringly. After a moment, he began afresh, adopting a crisp, almost officious tone that belied his denial: 'I would like to ask you about the events at the Naryskin Palace on the night of Yelena Filippovna's death. You must know that we have wanted to speak to you for a long time. It is to be regretted that you did not come forward before now, especially if, as you say, you are innocent of her murder.'

Mizinchikov glanced back nervously at his cousin.

'*Please* don't worry about him. He will sleep until he is ready to face the consequences of his act. I wish to talk about you now.'

'I had her blood all over my uniform.'

'Ah yes, the blood. Can you explain how it got there?'

'No, I cannot. One minute it was not there, the next it was.'

'Can you describe precisely what happened? Where were you when you noticed the blood on your tunic?'

'I was in Lena's dressing room.'

'Tell me what you saw when you entered the room.'

'Lena . . . lying on the carpet. There was blood everywhere. Aglaia Filippovna must have come into the room behind me. I turned round and she was there. Her face was frozen in horror. She was pointing at me. She looked as though she was screaming but nothing . . . no sound came out. I looked down at where she was pointing . . . to see fresh blood all over my tunic.'

'How close to you was she standing?'

'I don't remember. The details are vague now.'

'It is a small room. She must have been very close, if you were both in the room.'

'Yes, I suppose she was.'

Porfiry rose from his chair and walked around the desk to join Captain Mizinchikov. 'Would you care to stand up?'

The captain got to his feet falteringly.

'I shall be Aglaia Filippovna,' said Porfiry. 'Pavel Pavlovich, would you take the part of Yelena Filippovna?'

Virginsky came forward from the corner of the room where he had been standing, an amused expression on his face. It seemed that he was enjoying his work this afternoon. 'If you insist.'

'I do. Lie down on the floor there, if you please.'

Virginsky lay on his back with his arms crossed over his chest.

'No, no, no. That's not right. She didn't have her arms like that.'

Virginsky turned half on his side and disposed his limbs about him in an approximation of the cork-screwed sprawl of Yelena Filippovna's body.

'And you, Captain Mizinchikov, can you remember where you were standing in relation to the body?'

Mizinchikov stepped around Virginsky to stand on his right.

'And so, you had your back to the door, which for the purposes of our reconstruction we shall imagine to be here.' Porfiry described a rectangle in the air and stepped through it. 'I am in the room now, with you. And I am pointing at you. Is this how it was?'

'You were closer than that, I think. Your hand was almost touching me.'

Porfiry moved a step closer to Mizinchikov.

'Like this?'

'Yes, except your hand was not raised at first. I turned and saw you, then your hand went up. I looked down at where you were pointing, and the blood was there.'

'What happened next?'

'I ran from the room in panic.'

'Was not Aglaia Filippovna in your way?'

'No. She was to one side of the door.'

'Very well. You ran out.'

'Yes, and on the way out I ran into Bakhmutov.'

'There was no one else in the room?'

'No.'

'Are you sure of that? Did you look behind the screen? Or behind the door? The door opens inwards, I seem to remember.'

'I don't know. I was not thinking about the door.'

'What about the looking glass? Did you see any blood on the glass?' Porfiry pointed to an imaginary mirror.

'On the glass?' Mizinchikov looked where Porfiry was pointing as if to study the non-existent mirror, which seemed to strike him as an infinitely strange object. 'I cannot say. I did not look in the glass.'

'Did you touch Yelena Filippovna's body at any point?'

'No . . . I . . . I panicked. You should have seen Aglaia's face. Such hatred. She clearly believed that I had killed her sister. I didn't know what to do. No one knows what he will do in such a situation until . . . I ran. I ran from the palace. Someone had killed my Yelena. Naryskin. It must have been Naryskin. I couldn't think straight. I needed time to think.' Captain Mizinchikov's eyes flitted wildly, the panic still raw within them.

'Please go on.'

'Outside, I encountered a strange tramp. He accosted me. He seemed drunk. Very drunk. He was reciting lines from Boris Godunov. Or at least I think that's what it was. He wanted to know if I had seen Prince Bykov. It was dark. The man couldn't see the blood on my tunic, or he was too far gone to care. I gave him a rouble for his coat, such as it was, and swapped it for my tunic. I threw away my shako outside the palace and then ditched my sabre in the river. I don't know where I spent that first night. On a barge, I think, lying in straw. Nothing made any sense. None of it made any sense.'

'Were you aware of any blood on your tunic before you saw Aglaia Filippovna?'

'I don't know. I don't believe so.'

'Thank you. You may sit down again.'

'What about me?' said Virginsky.

'And thank you, Pavel Pavlovich. You played your part with distinction.' Porfiry walked round to take his seat again, as Virginsky stood up and brushed himself down. 'Tell me, Captain Mizinchikov, have you seen any newspapers while you have been a fugitive from the law?'

'Yes. I looked for news all the time.'

'Were you aware that Yelena Filippovna was at one time suspected of the murders of three children?'

'I saw that. It was a lie, of course. I knew it was a lie to trick me into giving myself up. I am not so simple-minded that I would fall for such a ruse.'

'Oh, it was not a ruse. A mistake, perhaps. So, Yelena Filippovna did not confess these killings to you?'

'Of course not!'

'You do not believe her capable of such crimes?'

'You need not ask that question. She was not a murderer. And she would never have done anything to harm *those* children.'

'Why do you say that?'

'They were pupils at Maria Petrovna's school, were they not?'

'That is correct.'

'Lena . . . loved Maria Petrovna. It was a special kind of love, pure, absolute, unsullied. She preserved that love as something precious in her soul, the better part of her soul, although she had not seen Maria Petrovna since they were at school together. She would never do anything to hurt her. That was why she prevailed upon all her friends to support the school.'

'The flowers,' said Virginsky suddenly. The two other men turned towards him quizzically. 'I will always love you, M. Maria was M. She was to have been the recipient of the flowers.'

Porfiry's face lit up with pleasure. He granted Virginsky a bow of acknowledgement. 'It's an interesting theory, Pavel Pavlovich.' Porfiry turned to Captain Mizinchikov. 'Or was the bouquet of white camellias a gift from you to Yelena Filippovna?'

'I know nothing of any flowers.'

'Then perhaps she meant them as a gift *for* you. Was she in the habit of giving you flowers?'

Captain Mizinchikov shook his head, bemused.

'You expressed the opinion a moment ago that Prince Naryskin may have murdered Yelena. I take it that you mean Prince Naryskin the younger?'

'The elder or the younger, what does it matter?'

'It matters rather a lot, actually. They are in fact distinct legal entities and it would be quite improper to charge one with a crime the other had committed.'

'The younger then.'

'Do you have any particular reason for accusing him?'

'He is the one I hate the most.'

'I see. I'm afraid that's not really enough for us to build a case around. Let me put it another way. What motive did he have for killing her, in your view?'

'She insulted him. Humiliated him.'

'And he struck her. Should that not have been an end to it? In striking her, he paid her back for the insult.'

'You don't understand. Yes, she goaded him into hitting her, but that blow – struck against a woman in full view of public censure – *that* was the insult. That dishonoured him. It was that for which he could not forgive her.'

'Did Yelena Filippovna ask you to kill her?'

The grime on Captain Mizinchikov's face darkened. 'Why should she do that?'

'Because she wished to end her life. And she naturally turned to a friend to help her achieve her desire.'

'It's true that she asked me. She was hysterical. She did not know what she was asking. One had to hope that it would pass.'

'You refused?'

'Of course.'

Porfiry considered for a moment. 'This matter of her requesting her own murder intrigues me. You would think – if that were the case – that she would have welcomed death when it came. And yet, as Pavel Pavlovich just now reminded me when he took her part in our little re-enactment, the disposition of her body clamoured protest. The expression of her face too, which he did not attempt to render, was not one of acquiescence. The question is, was she protesting her fate or the person who dispensed it? What would make a woman who actively sought her own death recoil so violently at the last moment?'

'That's understandable enough, surely,' said Virginsky. 'Only when it was too late did the full enormity of what she had desired strike home.'

'Perhaps.' Porfiry turned abruptly on Mizinchikov. 'We found a razor at your apartment. A razor wrapped in silk. Do you know anything about it?'

'I have no need for a razor. I have my beard trimmed by my barber.'

'Pavel Pavlovich, please ask Alexander Grigorevich to bring us the razor that was found in Captain Mizinchikov's apartment.'

Virginsky nodded and crossed to the door to pass on the request to Zamyotov.

Porfiry smiled blandly to Captain Mizinchikov. 'Perhaps it will help to jog your memory if you see the razor.'

'It is not a question of jogging my memory. I have no razor, I tell you.'

'And yet one was found in your study. Together with these

letters.' Porfiry unlocked his desk drawer and opened it, or rather attempted to open it. However, something inside obstructed the action of the drawer. Porfiry pushed it back into its housing and tried again. When the second attempt proved no more successful, he rattled the drawer in its casing, and tried to ease the drawer out. But whatever was causing the obstruction had not been dislodged. Every time, the hidden object snagged on the lip of the drawer's aperture and prevented the drawer from opening.

Porfiry's smile acquired a degree of tension. 'Please,' he said, though it was not clear whether he was pleading with the drawer or begging for Mizinchikov's indulgence. He crouched down and peered into the narrow gap created by the partially open drawer.

'Ah! I think I see what is causing it. The very letters we were talking about.'

Porfiry took the letter knife from his desk and poked it into the gap, easing the recalcitrant letters down. He beamed a smile of satisfaction to Mizinchikov as the drawer at last eased open. 'There! Nothing to it.'

He held the bundle of letters aloft triumphantly. It was as if the ribbon was not simply binding together the sheets of paper, but also holding in the secrets written on them. Mizinchikov started at the appearance of the letters. His body tensed, suddenly alert. He watched closely, his face rippling with apprehension and even horror, as Porfiry slipped the bow.

'You recognise the letters, of course?'

Mizinchikov said nothing. The muscles around his infected left eye went into spasm.

'They are letters from Yelena Filippovna. To you. Would you like to look at them?'

The twitch of Mizinchikov's head may have been an angry shake of negation, or an involuntary muscular contraction without significance. In any event, he made no move to take the letters Porfiry held out to him.

'What did you do?' asked Porfiry thoughtfully, almost seductively.

Mizinchikov's brows contracted in confusion.

'What was the shameful act that sullied you and insulted her?'

Mizinchikov's eyes squeezed out a wince of remembrance. 'I agreed to take Bakhmutov's money. I . . . loved her. But I did not see what the harm could be . . . if Bakhmutov wanted to pay me to do the very thing I most wanted to do – to marry her.' His voice became leaden. 'She did not see it like that.'

'She broke with you then?'

'Yes.'

'So you did not get the money, after all.'

'I didn't care about the money. The money was for her. But she would have nothing to do with it.'

'And so she rejected you in favour of Prince Naryskin. Some might say that would give you a motive to kill her. Jealousy.'

'If I had killed her, I would not have run away. It was only because I did not kill her that I ran away.'

'An interesting paradox. It suggests that you regret not killing her. That you saw that, somehow, as a failure.'

Before Mizinchikov could answer, the door opened and Zamyotov entered. He held the red silk parcel out in front of him, and waved it tantalisingly at Porfiry.

'Thank you, Alexander Grigorevich. Will you pass the item to this gentleman so that he may examine it?'

'Gentleman?' Zamyotov crimped his brows in a deliberate

frown and looked over Mizinchikov's head, as if he wasn't there.

'Captain Mizinchikov is a gentleman, despite appearances. Please hand him the razor.'

Zamyotov made clear his scepticism, as well as his repugnance, as he handed it over. Turning to make his exit, he noticed Alexei Ivanovich asleep on the sofa. He shook his head and quickened his step, as if to escape from a madhouse. The door closed behind him with a clatter.

Porfiry nodded reassuringly to Mizinchikov. The captain looked down at the object in his hands. He folded back the silk to reveal the sleek, self-contained implement, freighted with dire potential. Its appearance provoked no particular reaction in him, apart from a shrug of indifference. 'It's a razor.'

'You do not recognise it?'

'I have never seen it before in my life.'

'Well then, we must presume that someone placed it in your drawer without your knowing. But who? Who would have an opportunity for doing such a thing, or a reason?' Porfiry's face lit up with realisation. 'Of course! Who else?'

The others bristled with impatience as he took out and lit a cigarette.

'Don't you see, Pavel Pavlovich? What possible reason could someone have for planting this razor in Captain Mizinchikov's desk drawer?'

'To incriminate him?' Virginsky's answer lacked conviction.

'Ah, but it is a very crude attempt at incrimination, is it not? For we have already deduced that this razor could not possibly have been the murder weapon.'

'Why then?' said Virginsky irritably.

'What if it was put there not to incriminate him, but to

prompt him? To drive him to it.' Porfiry turned to Mizinchikov. 'When was the last time Yelena Filippovna visited you at the Officers' House?'

'It was the day before her death.'

'You believe Yelena Filippovna planted the razor?' put in Virginsky incredulously.

Porfiry widened his eyes, as if disbelieving Virginsky's disbelief. 'Could it not be seen as part of her attempt to goad the captain into killing her? Its proximity to her letters, so taunting in tone, is unquestionably significant.' He turned back to Mizinchikov. 'What was her mood when she came to see you that day?'

'She was in a state of terrible agitation.'

'Did she seek to provoke you in any way?'

Mizinchikov gave a bitter laugh. 'When did she ever not?'

'But more so than usual?'

'There were some new provocations that day, it's true. Of the kind that are particularly wounding to a man's pride.'

Both Porfiry and Virginsky bowed their heads in unspoken and specifically male sympathy. There was a knock at the door, to which they all turned, as if in relief. The door flew open and Nikodim Fomich burst in, followed by the severely well-groomed and upright presence of the *prokuror*, Yaroslav Nikolaevich Liputin, Porfiry's superior. The latter's step was measured: he came into the room almost reluctantly, as though he was unwilling to be drawn into whatever was taking place within. He took in the sleeping man on the sofa with a sneer of distaste, which deepened when he saw the disreputable-looking individual sitting opposite Porfiry Petrovich.

'Is this him?' said Nikodim Fomich breathlessly. 'The missing Guards officer?'

'Yes, this is Captain Mizinchikov.'

'So . . . you have his confession?'

Porfiry's expression froze into a complicated smile, fraught with irony and unease. 'He has confessed . . . to something. But not to the crime you have in mind. And he did not commit the crime to which he has confessed.'

'This is hardly satisfactory,' declared Liputin impatiently. He scowled down at Mizinchikov. 'Porfiry Petrovich, you will step outside with us for a moment.'

Porfiry bowed deferentially and rose to his feet to follow the police chief and the *prokuror* out of his chambers.

'You must get a confession out of him, Porfiry Petrovich,' commanded Liputin as soon as the door was closed behind them. 'By whatever means.' The force with which he insisted on this caused Zamyotov to look up from his desk.

'But with respect, Yaroslav Nikolaevich, what if he is telling the truth?' protested Porfiry.

'He had her blood all over him. How does he explain that?'

'He does not need to. The blood on his tunic was venous, not arterial. Therefore it did not come from her lacerated neck.'

'We need not go into these distinctions. They are too subtle for a jury to understand. Blood is blood, after all. He was seen fleeing the crime scene. All this speaks against him.'

'But a defence lawyer would tear the case apart.'

'That is why you must get a confession from him,' insisted Liputin. 'I hear that Lieutenant Salytov is particularly skilled at extracting confessions.'

'That's true,' chimed in Nikodim Fomich. Porfiry glared at him with the fury of a betrayed man.

'Presumably this Guards officer came here to confess, just like that student. What was his name?'

'Raskolnikov,' supplied Nikodim Fomich.

'That's it. It was to Salytov he confessed, was it not?'

'Yes, but—' began Porfiry.

'I don't understand you, Porfiry Petrovich. At last you have a breakthrough, and you will not push home your advantage. Imagine what the newspapers would make of this.'

'It is not so simple.'

'Make it simple. The fugitive has served himself up to you on a plate. I consider it perverse of you not to sharpen your knives. And tell me, who is that fellow asleep on your sofa?'

'That is Captain Mizinchikov's cousin.'

'Are you in the habit of allowing suspect's relatives to doss down in your chambers?'

'No, no. Of course not. But he has just been through something of an ordeal. He may have pushed his uncle down stairs.'

'I dare say that was more of an ordeal for the uncle than for him.'

'We must not underestimate the toll such crimes take on the perpetrators.'

'So, there are two murderers in the family?'

'No. That is to say, I do not believe Captain Mizinchikov is a murderer.'

'You know what they say, Porfiry Petrovich. A titmouse in the hand is better than a crane in the sky.' Liputin nodded authoritatively to Nikodim Fomich, who mirrored the gesture with approval. 'Do I make myself clear?'

'To be absolutely honest, Yaroslav Nikolaevich, you do not.'

'There is a case that can be made against this Mizinchikov. I expect you to make it.'

'With your permission, I would like to explore one other possibility first.'

'Which is?'

'The possibility of bringing to justice the actual murderer.'

The screw of distaste that gripped the *prokuror*'s face was tightened by another turn. 'Do what you must. But do it quickly.'

38

A bloody discovery

The buoyant sway of the carriage and jaunty clip of hooves indicated that they were moving, but Virginsky could see little to confirm it. The pane of glass was a milky grey square. He had the impression that the frigid, fogged air was moving with them. He was held by the blankness of the prospect.

'The fog is dense today,' said Porfiry Petrovich beside him. He too was staring into a patch of incessantly renewed grey.

Virginsky gave a minimal nod of agreement, as if he resented the distraction. It was, he realised, the possibility that one might suddenly see *something* – and that when it came this apparition would be extraordinary – that made the fog compelling. Its monotony was laden with potential.

'And yet, in certain matters, this vaporous blind enables us to see more clearly. Do you not agree, Pavel Pavlovich?'

At last Virginsky turned to face Porfiry. 'You look very pleased with yourself, Porfiry Petrovich. Do you mean to suggest that you have solved the mystery, or should I say mysteries?'

Porfiry's face sagged with hurt. 'Your words are charged with a strange, angry sarcasm, Pavel Pavlovich, which I find mystifying. Surely, with you, I have grounds to expect more than the same old jealousy that has marred my relations with other colleagues?'

Virginsky turned sharply away, looking into the fog again.

'Staring into the fog is a little like watching the flames of a fire,' continued Porfiry. 'One may project into it whatever one wishes to see. Or rather, an unacknowledged part of one's self supplies the visions for one's conscious mind to apprehend. That is sometimes how we see people too, is it not? The soul of another is like a swirling mist. Impenetrable. And so, rather than going to the trouble of discovering what really lies within it, we project our images on to its surface.'

'You know I dislike such fanciful comparisons, Porfiry Petrovich. The soul of another is like whatever you want to say it is like. And besides, why must you always be dragging souls into everything? Why bring up souls at all?'

'I am talking about you and me, Pavel Pavlovich. I fear that the unhappy antagonism which I have detected in your recent demeanour towards me is based upon some misapprehension.'

Virginsky was silent for some time. 'What are your intentions towards Maria Petrovna?' he blurted at last.

'My intentions? With regard to the investigation? Do I intend to arrest her? Is that what you mean?'

'No. I mean your . . . *intentions*. Do you intend to make a proposal?'

'A proposal?'

'A proposal of marriage.'

'Good heavens! I was not aware that I had any such intention! I am astonished by your suggestion that I should. Have I given that impression? You terrify me with your intimations. She is a witness in a current investigation. It would be most improper of me to harbour . . . intentions.'

'You do not find her an attractive person?'

'Undoubtedly. But . . . what could she possibly see in me?'

'That's not the issue. You know my father's second wife is much younger than he.'

'I know that.'

'He stole her from me!'

'Perhaps she was not yours to be stolen. I only mean to say, one cannot possess people in that way.'

'You will do the same with Maria.'

'I was not aware that you and Maria Petrovna were on such terms.'

'We are not.'

'I am glad to hear it.' Meeting Virginsky's glare of indignation, Porfiry went on: 'I repeat, she is a witness in an investigation. It would be as improper for you, as it is for me, to allow an affectionate relationship to develop.'

'And after the investigation is over?'

'That would be a different matter, of course.'

'The field would be open to both of us.'

Porfiry's face froze in dismay. 'If you wish to express it in that way.'

'So you *do* harbour intentions!'

'My goodness, Pavel Pavlovich! You have certainly followed your vocation in becoming an investigator. Your persistence is fatiguing. I am bound to say you display a talent for extracting confessions that I hope we may soon put to very good use.'

*

The entrance to the Naryskin Palace was lit up by a lantern whose beam dissipated into the fog, rather than cut through it. One by one, the caryatids of the façade began to appear. Here were the extraordinary apparitions Virginsky had been waiting for.

They were admitted by a footman, who appeared startled to see them. To Virginsky's eye, the interior splendour of the palace was strangely changed. It was almost as if its lustre had been worn away in the weeks since their last visit. When he had first come to the palace, he could not fail to be impressed by its grandeur and scale. His gaze might have been disdainful, but his was a disdain provoked by an acknowledgement of the seductive allure of money. But now, it seemed to Virginsky, the glamour was gone, and so too were the negative sentiments it had inspired. He saw it only as a cold, empty vastness. Its occupants were only to be pitied.

'Thank you, we will find our own way,' said Porfiry to the servant. 'There is no need to trouble your master. We have come only to look at the room in which the unfortunate young lady was murdered.' With that, he hurried off.

'Have you not found,' Porfiry confided over his shoulder to Virginsky as they descended the stairs to the basement, 'in your experience as an extractor of confessions, that the greater the secret to be revealed, the greater the resistance to revealing it?'

'With respect, that is an obvious enough remark,' said Virginsky breathlessly.

'Perhaps when applied to human subjects. But what about inanimate objects?'

'I don't understand.'

'Do you remember the drawer in my desk, Pavel Pavlovich? How reluctantly it yielded up Yelena Filippovna's letters.'

'There was a simple enough explanation. The letters themselves were causing an obstruction. You must not have been very careful when you placed them in the drawer, Porfiry Petrovich.'

'Ah, but I always am. I rather think that someone else has been in that drawer and disturbed the letters.'

'But how? The drawer is always kept locked, is it not?'

'Yes. And the only key is kept in my coat pocket. But that is not the issue. It is not *that* drawer that I am thinking about.'

Virginsky frowned uncertainly but resisted the temptation to question Porfiry further. He knew from experience that when Porfiry was in this mood, one wilful mystification would only lead to another.

*

The fundamental change that had been wrought in the room was, of course, immediately obvious: the body of Yelena Filippovna had been removed, as had all traces of the violence perpetrated against her. This absence was chastening. It was a reminder of how quickly the world covered over disruptions in its fabric. Virginsky felt a strange nostalgia for the blood-soaked murder scene. This prim space, scrubbed and polished, seemed almost more of an outrage.

Virginsky sensed something else different, something other than the obvious. But it was only when Porfiry pointed it out that he was able to register it consciously: 'The rug is in a different place.'

Virginsky stared at the floor and nodded, as though this was something that hardly needed saying. Inside, a heavy pendulum of disappointment swung down. He hated it when Porfiry saw things he did not.

'It's below the mirror now, there, against the wall,' continued Porfiry. 'It was over here before, away from the mirror, underneath Yelena Filippovna's body. What does that suggest to you, Pavel Pavlovich?'

'It has been moved?'

'Well, obviously it has been moved! I was hoping for something a little more insightful, if you please! Why would whoever restored this room place the rug under the mirror?'

'Because that is where it belongs?'

'That's right, well done. No need to sound so diffident. Whoever brought the rug back to the room automatically placed it under the mirror, where it belongs. Which means?'

'It was moved when Yelena Filippovna was murdered. By her murderer!'

'Not quite so fast! By her murderer? Possibly. We cannot say for certain. But it is certainly reasonable to assume that it was by someone who had a hand in her murder. It was under the mirror and it was moved from the mirror. Why?'

'Because . . .' But the promising word did not result in the hoped-for explanation. Virginsky gave a defeated shrug.

Porfiry struck a match and lit the gas. He crossed to stand in front of the large mirror, gazing into it, enraptured by his own reflection. He held up a hand as if to wave to himself. 'Remember the smear of blood on the mirror. The smear of arterial blood.'

'She was standing in front of the mirror when she was murdered!'

'Yes. Quite brilliant, Pavel Pavlovich. She was standing in front of the mirror, consulting her reflection, preparing for her performance, when her murderer approached from behind, reaching round with a razor to slit her throat. Her blood sprayed the mirror and drained on to the carpet. The carpet was moved and she was placed upon it, some small distance from the actual spot where she was killed. In the meantime, the mirror was wiped clean. Is all this the work of one person, Pavel Pavlovich?'

'Possibly not.'

'Possibly not! Of course not, you mean!'

'But why? Why go to all this trouble? What does it matter whether she is killed in front of the mirror, or a short distance from it?'

'It matters a great deal if you wish to create the illusion that she was killed in a particular way by a particular person, a person in fact who had nothing to do with her murder.'

'Captain Mizinchikov.'

'Captain Mizinchikov had bloodstains on his tunic. We know from Dr Pervoyedov's test that the blood there did not come from the wound in Yelena Filippovna's neck, as that would have produced arterial blood. If we are correct in our reconstruction, and Yelena was murdered from behind while standing at the mirror, the murderer would not in fact be sprayed with blood at all. All the blood would go on the mirror – although some perhaps could have been caught with a towel held in front of the wound. The same towel, or another one, might be used to wipe any obvious spray of blood from the mirror.' Porfiry turned abruptly to the wardrobe. 'You remember the drawer that you had difficulty opening? I want you to look in it now.'

'But it was empty. And if there is anything in it now, it will have been put there since the murder.'

'Nevertheless, pull the drawer out, if you please. Let us see if it is as troublesome to open as it was the last time you attempted it.'

Virginsky did as he was directed. If anything, the drawer was more resistant than before.

'All the way out, if you please.'

After several minutes of wrenching and manipulation, the drawer shot out, throwing Virginsky off balance. 'It's still empty.' He displayed the interior of the drawer to Porfiry.

'Yes, the drawer is empty. But look inside the casing, please.'

Virginsky felt a wave of feeling move softly through him. He could not prevent himself from smiling. They were on the verge of a discovery, he felt sure.

'There's something there.'

The towel was neatly folded. He lifted it up carefully, as if it were something precious and fragile. What he wanted to preserve was the precise configuration of the folds.

'Very interesting,' commented Porfiry. 'The towel has not been carelessly stuffed into the space, but rather, it has been meticulously folded. The evidence of a tidy mind, would you not say, Pavel Pavlovich?'

The towel appeared to have once been white, but was now partially and unevenly dyed a dirty rust colour. Virginsky allowed it to fall open, revealing the extent of the staining. With a dark sprawling star in its centre, it was like the flag of some anarchic, blood-thirsty nation unfurled.

'I knew I could smell blood,' said Porfiry quietly. He strode over to the embroidered screen in the corner of the room. It came up to his shoulders, and so he was able to peer over it. With an impassive glance to Virginsky he walked behind the screen and ducked down out of sight.

There were footsteps outside the room and a moment later Prince Sergei Naryskin burst in. He looked about, bewildered.

'Where is he, the magistrate? They told me the magistrate was here.'

'I am a magistrate,' said Virginsky, petulantly.

Prince Sergei frowned at the bloody towel in Virginsky's hands. 'No, the other one. The little fat one. I say, what do you have there?'

'Evidence,' answered Porfiry, his head popping up from behind the screen. 'May I help you, Prince Sergei?'

'Why are you here?'

'We are conducting an investigation.'

'Have you come to arrest him?'

'To arrest whom?'

'My father, of course.'

'Your father?'

'Yes.'

'For what crime?'

'Murder. He murdered Lena, did he not?'

'Did he? What makes you say that?'

'I caught him burning some letters from her. And then I heard him in conversation with Bakhmutov. My father had been Yelena's lover. He killed her to prevent her marrying me.'

'You *caught* him . . . in *con*versation . . . he *killed* her . . .'

'I beg your pardon?'

'Your stutter has gone, Prince Sergei. The act of accusing your father has cured you.'

The younger prince blinked out his bemusement. 'Will you not arrest him?'

'I cannot be as confident as you that he is the murderer. I rather find that the interesting circumstances you have just revealed provide a more compelling motive for *you* to murder Yelena Filippovna than for your father. It is also psychologically consistent that you would wish to accuse him of a crime you had committed, as you would blame him for her death, believing that he had somehow forced you to it.' Porfiry glanced briefly at Virginsky. 'My experience of such triangles is that the resentment is all on the side of the son.'

'It is not resentment. He wanted to prevent our union because it horrified him.'

'He told you that?'

'He didn't have to. Surely it must horrify any man to think of his own son lying with his former mistress. It is tantamount to incest.'

'Had you not already slept with Yelena Filippovna?'

Prince Sergei's gaze darted away.

'I see ... how unlike Yelena Filippovna. And yet ... if she had slept with your father, she might naturally hesitate to consummate her relationship with you. My dear prince, you have interrupted us at a most crucial stage of our investigations and I fear that, through no fault of your own, you have entirely distracted me from my train of thought. The information you have imparted is extremely diverting. Yes, it has diverted me from the course I was set upon.' Porfiry seemed genuinely at a loss. He cast about the room as if to get his bearings. 'Of course, our investigations are always disturbed by the unruly intrusion of events. However, increasingly, as I get older, I am finding it more and more difficult to recover from these disruptions. My mind, like my eyes, is not as sharp as it once was. Is that not so, Pavel Pavlovich?'

Virginsky blew out his cheeks in embarrassment. He looked down at the blood-stained towel.

'Ah, yes, thank you for reminding me. Tell me, Prince Sergei, is Aglaia Filippovna still a guest at the palace?'

'She is.'

'And is she still incapacitated?'

'Indeed. She is in a state of semi-consciousness most of the time. She drifts in and out of a comatose trance.'

'But she has her lucid moments?'

'I fear not. In the brief moments when she is capable of speech, she appears utterly confused. My mother has taken to sitting with her. My mother is very devout, you know. She prays for Aglaia Filippovna constantly.'

'Your mother . . . ? Of course, your mother!'

'What do you mean by that? My mother feels a great deal of sympathy for the young lady.'

'I wonder, have you discussed your suspicions regarding your father with your mother?'

'I did not wish to worry her.'

'And yet you had no compunction in making your allegations directly to a magistrate?'

'My conscience will not allow me to keep silent any longer.'

'In other words, your hatred for your father out-weighed your consideration for your mother.'

'That is a despicable way of putting it. Was it not my civic duty?'

'To betray your father?'

'I believed he was Yelena's murderer.'

'Given what you have said today, does it not occur to you that your mother too had a motive for killing Yelena Filippovna?'

'Surely not!'

'Will your mother be with Aglaia Filippovna now? Perhaps we should pay a visit on the invalid and her nurse.'

'You will say nothing of my father's affair with Yelena. It will destroy her.'

'One cannot know in advance what it may or may not prove necessary to say,' said Porfiry. He stretched up to stem the gas, plunging them into gloom. 'You will bring the towel with you, Pavel Pavlovich.'

39

A psychological experiment

The room was as gloomy as it had always been. It was lit only by the slumbering glow from the open hearth, which was reflected in fitful waves across the ceiling.

It seemed to Virginsky that Aglaia Filippovna's hair had gained in strength and substance at the expense of every other aspect of her physicality. It sprawled around her head, no longer a halo but now wild, raging flames of intense blackness. The pallor of her skin matched the luminosity of the crisp white bed linen. Her hands lying on the folded-over sheet seemed transparent. Her face grew out of the pillow that her head rested on. Beneath the covers, her body appeared thinner and straighter than ever, merely a long wrinkle in the counterpane.

Princess Yevgenia Andreevna Naryskina maintained her bedside vigil, though she was seated now. A chair had been placed for her exactly on the spot where before she had stood. Her eyes seemed deeper-set than Virginsky remembered, their hungry energy receding physically into her head. She looked up briefly at their entrance, taking in the apprehension in her son's face, and reflecting it back with a nervous excitement. The sight of the blood-stained towel added to her agitation, but she did not linger on it. It was always to the girl on the bed that her gaze returned, although the nature and intent of that gaze was difficult to interpret. The most obvious construction was that it was a look of solicitude, but Virginsky couldn't shake off the impression that she sought to hold Aglaia Filippovna captive with her gaze. Despite her son's anxieties, Virginsky doubted that there was anything that could be said to the princess that could destroy her or even surprise her. Those eyes had seen much, and foresaw the rest, it seemed to him.

'Good day, Madam Princess,' began Porfiry briskly. 'And how is the patient today?' He leaned over the bed, and in a movement that seemed almost scandalous, so unpredicted was it, took Aglaia Filippovna's hand in his own.

Princess Naryskina tucked her chin against her collarbone to squeeze out: 'The same as ever.'

'She revives occasionally, is that not so?'

'Occasionally.'

'And always the first thing she sees is your face. At the sight of which she promptly falls back into a trance!'

'It is not exactly like that. We try to get some nourishment into her. And tend to her other needs. Besides, I am not always here. I cannot say if she revives when I am not. The nurse tells me she does, now and then.'

'Of course. It has often occurred to me how easily we might have solved this case if only we had been able to get a meaningful testimony from Aglaia Filippovna before now. What keeps her locked inside this inner prison? Surely it can no longer be the action of the bromide poisoning?' Porfiry paused, his face opening up expectantly. Virginsky was dimly aware that Porfiry was all the time toying with Aglaia Filippovna's hand, his fingers moving incessantly, obsessively among hers; but somehow one did not care about this, he realised. It was Porfiry Petrovich's ice-coloured eyes, his lashes blond to the

412

point of transparency, that demanded attention. In that moment, his gaze was captivating, hypnotic.

'I wonder, madam, if you will assist me in a psychological experiment. I take it you wish to see the young lady recover from the debilitating condition to which she is in thrall?'

Porfiry's eyes held and compelled the princess.

'I have no knowledge of psychology,' she protested, though in truth it was more a surrender of will than a protest.

'There is no need to worry about that. We are all in some degree psychologists, are we not? Besides, the role I wish you to play is very simple.' Porfiry produced a folded newspaper clipping from a pocket. 'Please read aloud the passage marked, if you would be so kind.'

He passed the slip of newsprint to the princess.

Virginsky sensed that with her static demeanour and shadowy dress, she was more comfortable on the periphery of events, hardly seen, or if noticed at all, soon ignored. Perhaps this was what had drawn her to the side of Aglaia Filippovna and why she was so riveted by the girl's unmoving form. Her fascination was not without a touch of envy. To be invited now into the centre of this momentous incident – a murder investigation – to be asked to participate, and not simply witness, it was almost too much for her. Her consternation bordered on panic. She fumbled in her reticule, spilling its contents with a yelp of dismay onto Aglaia Filippovna's bed. Virginsky looked away from the spillage as though from something indecent, though he noticed that Porfiry was unashamedly goggling at the items. Such was the greed in Porfiry's eye that it appeared he longed to handle the objects. It was only his reluctance to release Aglaia Filippovna's hand that prevented him, it seemed.

413

Despite his initial tact, Virginsky now found himself following Porfiry's example. He assessed the displayed contents of her reticule dispassionately, with an almost academic interest, as though they were exhibits in some diminished museum of femininity: a tortoiseshell comb, a porcelain cologne bottle with atomiser ball, a silver compact, and a lorgnette, also of tortoiseshell. It was apparently this last object that Princess Naryskina was looking for. She scooped everything else back into the reticule, including, inadvertently, the newspaper cutting, which she then only found by once again emptying the reticule.

Prince Sergei rushed to his mother's side to help her replace the contents. 'M-mother!'

Virginsky noted that the prince's stutter had returned.

At last the princess was ready to begin the task. She unfolded the paper and held the lorgnette up to her face, moving it backwards and forwards to find the focal point.

'Before you begin, madam,' said Porfiry. He turned to Virginsky. 'Pavel Pavlovich, may I have a word in your ear.'

Virginsky stooped, allowing Porfiry to whisper something that must have been extremely shocking, to judge by Virginsky's glare of incredulity. Porfiry nodded emphatically.

Porfiry now addressed Princess Naryskina. 'Now, madam, please don't be alarmed, whatever happens. Especially do not be alarmed by what Pavel Pavlovich is about to do, which may indeed strike you as alarming.' Porfiry nodded to Virginsky.

Virginsky moved to stand behind the princess. Suddenly he stretched his arms out, reaching over the princess's shoulders, and let the towel unfurl in front of her face. He was careful not to touch her person; even so, their proximity had the awkwardness of enforced intimacy. He felt like a hairdresser might. The bloody towel added a bizarre twist. Prince Sergei stared in mute indignation. It seemed the arrangement was so outlandish it had robbed him of the power of speech entirely.

'Now madam, if you are ready, please read the passage I have marked.'

Princess Naryskina cleared her throat thickly and tucked her chin against her collarbone. Her unnaturally deep, choked voice intoned: 'The body of Innokenty Zimoveykin, 13, was discovered within the precincts of the Baird Shipbuilding and Machine Works, where he was employed as a labourer. This brings to four the number of child murders perpetrated in the city in recent weeks, death in each case being rendered by strangulation.'

It was here that Virginsky saw Aglaia Filippovna's eyes start open. As Princess Naryskina continued reading, the two intense circles of turquoise flashed towards the bloody towel. The eyes widened. At the same time, Aglaia Filippovna's hand came to life, struggling to pull itself free of Porfiry's hold.

Her eyes swivelled briefly up to meet Porfiry's.

'Aglaia Filippovna, don't be afraid. My name is Porfiry Petrovich. I am an investigating magistrate. I know everything, my dear. Everything. I am here to help you get better.' Virginsky noticed that he was still toying incessantly with her hand, in particular turning an imaginary nut around an imaginary thread at the base of her thumb.

Aglaia Filippovna's eyelids snapped to over the glorious colour of her irises, as if withholding something precious from the undeserving. The tension that had come into her body left it. She seemed to be lost to them again.

'What did that p-pantomime achieve?'

'It's too early to say for sure,' confessed Porfiry. 'You may take the towel away now, Pavel Pavlovich. And, thank you, madam, for your assistance. You have helped me more than you can know. More than even I had hoped.'

'Is that it?' Prince Sergei voiced the question that was foremost in Virginsky's mind. Porfiry's experiment seemed to have ended in anti-climax. The same soft amber ripples flitted across the ceiling. Virginsky wondered if he had imagined the colour of her eyes.

40

A game of billiards

That evening, Porfiry invited Virginsky to dine with him at Domenika's on Nevsky Prospekt. He could not face going back to his apartment. A confrontation with Slava was overdue, but Porfiry had too much else on his mind to relish that prospect. And the thought of dining alone depressed him. Besides, he liked his young colleague. That said, he was not in the mood to talk over the events of the day, and he knew that that was what Virginsky would naturally wish to do. Porfiry felt unusually on edge. He craved distraction. He had a sense of the case as a vast but fragile lattice-work. Each of the pieces that comprised it was a supposition resting on an assumption. Somewhere at the base of it, perhaps, was a firm and irrefutable kernel of evidence. But so much had been built on so little that he could not now distinguish fact from speculation. If just one piece proved to be faulty, the whole edifice would collapse. He knew that what he should do was subject this mental construction to scrutiny, to see if it held up. But all he wanted to do was eat and drink, and afterwards, perhaps, divert himself with a game of billiards. He found the clack and clatter of balls from the billiard room comforting, and was saddened when the gypsy players struck up.

'Is this a celebration, Porfiry Petrovich?'

'What do we have to celebrate?' Porfiry could not keep the weariness out of his voice as he shouted over the music.

'*I know everything!* Were not those your words to Aglaia Filippovna? So you have worked it out? You have solved the mystery?'

'Ah, but perhaps that was simply part of my psychological experiment.'

'*Perhaps?* How can you speak of your own actions with such uncertainty? Surely you know what was in your own mind?'

'Does anyone? Ever?'

'Please don't take refuge in philosophical generalisations. It is only a reluctance to share your thoughts that leads you into obfuscation.'

Porfiry smiled and felt the tension of the smile in his facial muscles. He really did not have the energy for Virginsky's challenging banter. He sighed morosely and fixed his attention on picking the bones out of a piece of sturgeon. 'But I may be wrong, you see. And to voice my suspicions when I am wrong will be very damaging.'

'For whom?'

'For the one I accuse, of course. Surely you of all people should be mindful of that.'

'You are not thinking of your reputation?'

'It's too late to concern myself with my reputation. My career is almost at an end, Pavel Pavlovich. No, there is no *almost* about it. I feel this may well be my last major investigation. It is not simply a case of physical energy, which is sadly all too lacking. I feel that my mental powers are waning too.'

Porfiry lit a cigarette to smoke as he ate.

'But you acted with such confidence this afternoon!'

'In truth, I do not know how I succeeded in summoning it. It was founded on nothing. The exercise has left me empty and exhausted. Prince Sergei was right. It was a pantomime that proved nothing. I was trying to force the issue, to bring about some decisive revelation. To shock Aglaia Filippovna into bearing witness. Instead, I merely made a fool of myself. Please, do not attempt to contradict me. There have been too many factors beyond my control in this case. You spoke of my reputation. I suspect I have the reputation of being an arch manipulator. People believe I am able to play the human soul like a pipe organ, pulling and pushing the stops to get the sound I want. But all along I have felt myself manipulated by outside forces and agencies. It has been very trying. I fear it may have forced me into making an elementary mistake. I have come to regard everything as part of one all-encompassing conspiracy. But what if it is not? What if there are merely a number of random events – or rather, events connected only by their awfulness? And what if this is an awfulness I can do nothing about? I know that Innokenty's killer is beyond my reach, beyond justice, untouchable. He is protected by powerful parties, and I am too old, too fat, too weak, too scared to take them on. You were right, Pavel Pavlovich. I *am* Oblomov.'

'No.'

'I should just take my dressing gown and retire to the country. Perhaps I should buy an estate and preside over its ruin. That is the Russian way, is it not?'

'It doesn't have to be.'

'I find all I want to do is drink champagne and play billiards. Will you play billiards with me, Pavel Pavlovich?'

'Of course. But I warn you I am very good.'

'A wager then!'

'I do not play for money.'

'Then why play at all?'

'Very well, we will play for dinner. Will that satisfy you?'

'But you are here as my guest. It was always my intention to pick up the bill. Money, Pavel Pavlovich – I want to smell your money and roll it in my fingers.'

'Why are you so determined to force me into gambling?'

'Because I never will trust a man who does not gamble.'

'In that case . . . ten roubles!'

'Paper roubles?'

'Do you have any objection?'

Porfiry shrugged. 'I just wish to make sure that everything is clear. We don't want any arguments later.'

'When I take your money off you, you mean?'

'When I take *your* money off *you*, I rather think!'

'Nevskaya rules?'

'Come, shake on it,' said Porfiry. 'And we will prevail upon one of the waiters to pull our hands apart.'

*

Virginsky won the lag for break, his ball settling less than an inch from the baulk cushion. Porfiry, who was by now well into the second bottle of Veuve Clicquot, had sent his careening wildly from end to end.

'Have you played billiards before, Porfiry Petrovich?'

'It is all part of my tactics.'

'Before you concern yourself with tactics,' said Virginsky sententiously, as he racked the pyramid of ivory-white balls, 'it would be as well to master the basic technique. I fear you are applying too much force to your cue action.'

'Nonsense!'

Virginsky broke tightly without pocketing, although the single red ball ricocheted between the jaws of the top right pocket, leaving Porfiry with an easy pot. However, he chose to ignore this, instead going for a reckless long shot that he executed with heavy-handed ineptitude, opening up the pyramid to let Virginsky in.

Porfiry watched forlornly as Virginsky played a series of skilful in-offs, repeatedly sinking the red. Porfiry was left to apply the same diligence and determination to draining the champagne bottle as Virginsky did to making shots.

In no time at all, Virginsky had potted five balls. Things were looking bad for Porfiry.

As Virginsky was cueing his sixth potential pot, Porfiry called out 'Foul!', causing his opponent to mis-cue and botch his shot.

'What foul?'

'You're supposed to keep one foot on the floor at all times.'

'What are you talking about? *Both* my feet were on the ground.'

'Both your feet? That's acceptable, is it?'

'Of course. The foul was yours in trying to put me off. I should be granted a free shot.'

'An honest mistake on my part. You cannot pelanise me for that.'

'Penalise,' corrected Virginsky.

'My shot is it?' said Porfiry nonchalantly. He placed his champagne glass on the side of the table and retrieved his cue from the wall rack. He then decided that that cue was unsatisfactory, and so replaced it with another. After considerable deliberation, moving round the table to line up a series of potential shots, he finally settled on one. He bent down to cue, miming a series of dummy shots before standing up to re-assess his choice. He decided he was satisfied with the shot after all, hunched back over his cue and made a hurried jab.

The line was not far out, but the ball failed to sink, rattling in the jaws of a pocket. Whether it was the ball Porfiry had intended to sink, in the pocket he had selected, was unclear. He remained bent over his cue, blinking querulously at the recalcitrant billiard ball. 'These pockets, are they smaller than those on the other tables?'

'All the pockets are the same size, Porfiry Petrovich.'

'But I swear the diameter of the ball is greater than the aperture of the pocket.' Porfiry blinked each eye alternately to test this theory.

'I have successfully managed to pocket five balls. And now, if you will kindly stand away from the table, I will pocket the three outstanding balls I need to win.'

'You think you will win?'

'I am sure of it.'

'Don't be too sure, my young friend. I have one or two tricks still up my sleeve.'

'Tricks? Exactly! Your only hope is to resort to trickery.'

'In my day, I was a champion of Nevskaya Pyramid Billiards. I beat all-comers. There was no challenger who could take me on. It is some time since I played, I confess. I had to retire from the game to give others a chance. I was something of a phenomenon.'

'In your day?'

'In my day.'

'May I suggest that today is not your day?' Virginsky potted the next ball with ruthless efficiency. 'Two more to win, Porfiry Petrovich.'

But Porfiry was moving away from the table, as though he had lost interest in the game. He gravitated towards a loud and very drunk cavalry officer who was berating his own opponent with a stream of obscenities. Virginsky paused in his play to watch the developing scene nervously.

'Sir, moderate your language!'

'Moderate my language? Are there ladies present?'

'Not in this room perhaps. But in the restaurant. Without question, your appalling outbursts can be heard in there.'

'No one can hear me over that infernal gypsy racket.'

'I can hear you.'

'Are you a lady? You're the ugliest damn lady I've ever seen, and believe me I've seen some ugly ones.'

'On behalf of the ladies of your acquaintance, I consider that to be an insulting remark.'

'Funny little man!'

'Boor!'

'What did you call me?'

'Boor. You are a boorish fellow. A lout.'

'A lout now, is it? I will not be insulted by you, funny little man.'

'I am not little. I have the girth of a bear. Whereas you have the mouth of a swine.'

This was too much for the drunken officer, who swung back the cue he was holding in preparation to bringing it down on Porfiry's head. Fortunately, Porfiry was pulled out of the way by Virginsky, who took the full vicious brunt of the blow on his left hand.

Virginsky gave a sharp cry.

'That's unlucky,' observed Porfiry. 'Your cueing hand.'

The drunk fell over, unbalanced by the momentum of his attack.

'I suggest we make a swift exit, Porfiry Petrovich. That

fellow has many friends here and the mood appears to be waxing ugly.'

'But the wager, Pavel Pavlovich! We will be forced to abandon the wager!'

'I cannot believe you provoked a beating in order to get out of paying me ten roubles.'

'His language was insufferable.'

'I hadn't noticed. *I* was concentrating on the game.'

'So was I, my friend,' said Porfiry with a wink, as he allowed himself to be dragged from the billiard room.

*

The swirl and dash of Domenika's were still with Porfiry as he lay on his bed. Sweat pooled at his neck. His skin there chafed but it was a discomfort he was prepared to tolerate.

The throb of the gypsy music pulsed and echoed in his ears. The oil lamp by his bedside swayed and shimmered in time with the beat.

After their flight from the billiard room, they had stumbled into a drinking den in one of those alleys off the Haymarket. He remembered that Virginsky had been eager to get him home, but he had insisted on a nightcap. It was not the kind of place that Porfiry was in the habit of entering, a dark cellar with a sticky floor and tables, frequented by low-ranking clerks and tradesmen. Its novelty inspired a strange giddiness in him, which Virginsky was at pains to quell. There was no champagne to be had and Porfiry remembered making a scene with the proprietor over this inconvenience. He winced at the recollection. Had he really demanded that the fellow scour the streets of St Petersburg, urged him to spare no expense, and forbade him from returning without the Widow? In the event, vodka had been brought, the landlord probably calculating, quite reasonably as it turned out, that a drunk would happily drink whatever was put in front of him.

Porfiry closed his eyes and lay very still, as if his own immobility could influence the objects around him. He swallowed back a liquid reflux. It felt as though the sturgeon had come back to life and was swimming around in his stomach.

He was not entirely sure how he had arrived back at the apartment, that part of the evening being somewhat of a blank. But the empirical evidence was conclusive – here he was in his bed, after all! -- and perhaps it was fruitless to enquire beyond that.

Porfiry thought instead of Princess Yevgenia Andreevna Naryskina. He felt now that he understood her strange inertia. It was a form of sympathetic magic; she sought to control through utter passivity. He thought also of Aglaia Filippovna, equally immobile. Was she held by her coma, or did she use it to exercise a hold over others? It was certainly true that it had effectively stalled his investigation.

He opened his eyes. The room was still spinning. He came to the conclusion that lying motionless achieved nothing. But now it seemed he was incapable of doing anything else.

He was about to lean over to extinguish the light, or at least to attempt that manoeuvre, when he became aware of the sounds of movement in the apartment. Footsteps. Slava. He even thought that he could hear a stifled whisper.

Now he remembered coming in. He had stopped outside Slava's room, swaying as he strained to listen. There had been silence then, though he had the sense that it was a false silence, a suspension of frenzied activity prompted by his arrival. He had an image of Slava holding his breath, waiting for his employer to move on before resuming whatever he had been doing.

The unnatural silence had struck him as ominous. He had never known Slava to hold himself so still. It came close to unnerving him.

Now, beyond any doubt, he heard footsteps outside his door. He was not afraid. He was ready for whatever might happen. Better than that, he was drunk. He twisted his torso to dim the lamp. He wanted to give the impression that he was asleep when the intruder entered.

He closed his eyes. A wave of serenity relaxed his whole being. Within a few seconds – in less time than that, in the space between seconds – pretending to be asleep had passed over into actual sleep.

His eyes shot open in panic. A shadowy form stood over him. A limb of the shadow broke out and swept down towards his throat. A glint of steel flashed in the dimmed lamp light. Porfiry's hands seemed to be made of lead. He was powerless to lift them. The flashing metal met no resistance until it struck his neck. A scream of fury and hatred and surprise and then it was all over.

41

Slava unmasked

The scream told him everything. It also sobered him up completely.

It was a woman's scream.

Porfiry propelled himself upwards at the shadow. He met little resistance. She – for it was without doubt a woman – was slight of build and entirely lacking in strength. Her weapon had fallen uselessly from her hand as soon as she had landed the blow. His hands gripped skin and bone, slippery with warm liquid. A spasm of animal tension passed from her into him and then he felt her body collapse and he found that he was having to hold her up. He pulled her to him, letting his body take her weight as he wrapped one arm around her shoulder as if in an embrace.

The door burst open and Slava came in holding aloft a candle. The woman's face was hidden against the chest of the man she had just attacked, but her hair was revealed to be an intensely black and unruly mass. Porfiry felt her frail body shake in convulsive sobs.

'Good heavens, Porfiry Petrovich, you have a woman in your room!' Slava made the observation with a salacious leer.

'There is no need to feign surprise. You must have let her in.'

'Well, yes. She assured me she was a friend of yours. You were not here. She said she would wait. She . . .' Slava hesitated, momentarily embarrassed.

'She made it worth your while,' suggested Porfiry bluntly.

'I took pity on her.'

'You hid her in your room.'

'That's true,' conceded Slava. 'She wanted to surprise you. So she said. I am not a prude. We are all human beings. Subject to human needs and urges. I take the scientific, rather than the moral, approach. I am a man of the new generation.'

'Shut up.'

'But I had to intervene when I heard the scream. The scream did not reflect well on you, Porfiry Petrovich.'

'She tried to kill me!'

'So it was your scream?'

'No!' cried Porfiry in exasperation. 'It was her scream. I dare say she did not expect me to be wearing this.' Porfiry felt at the stiff leather collar around his neck with one hand, holding his assailant close to him with the other.

'It is an unusual item of nocturnal apparel. You wear it for what reason?'

'For protection, of course! It was given to me by an officer of the Third Section, to protect me from an attack *by you*.' Porfiry gave the final words an indignant emphasis.

'By me? But why would I wish to attack you?'

'I believed you to be a revolutionary assassin.'

'But Porfiry Petrovich, that's not true!'

'Then what are you, Slava?'

'What am I? I am your manservant.'

'There is something else.'

'Is that blood? Are you hurt? Should I rouse a doctor?'

'It is not my blood. It is hers. I do not believe it is serious.

She appears to have nicked her hand on the blade of the razor when it struck the collar and flew out of her grip.'

'She has a razor? Sensational! A magistrate attacked in his bed by a razor-wielding beauty. It is even more sensational than I had hoped.'

'So that's it. You're not a revolutionary. You're not a Third Section agent. You're a damned journalist!'

'Now now. Less of the damned. That's not very nice, in front of a lady.'

'She attempted to murder me. And that is not the worst of her crimes. She had better get used to the word.'

'Who is she?'

Porfiry looked down at the crown of black hair. He leaned forward so that her inert head fell away from his chest and her face was revealed. 'Aglaia Filippovna.'

Her eyes were closed, as if she were still in the bed in the Naryskin Palace, sunk in her comatose refuge.

'You are still my servant, I believe,' said Porfiry to Slava. 'You will go into the bureau and rouse the duty sergeant on the night desk. Tell him that I have apprehended the murderer of Yelena Filippovna and the three children, Dmitri Krasotkin, Artur Smurov and Svetlana Chisova.'

'She?'

'Yes. It's true, is it not, Aglaia Filippovna? You killed the children and then you killed your sister. What's more, you tried to make it look like your sister was the murderer of the children by wearing her ring when you strangled the children.'

Aglaia's eyes opened. 'Yelena? Is Yelena here?'

'Yelena is dead, Aglaia Filippovna – as you well know. This is all play-acting. There has been so much play-acting in this case. I am worn out with it all.'

Her eyes held his for a moment. He looked into them to see if he could find any explanation for the crimes he was sure she had committed. But there was only colour, a colour as bright and alluring as a gemstone, and as remorseless.

42

The double-headed eagle

'How extraordinary, Porfiry Petrovich!' declared Nikodim Fomich. He stared at the magistrate in amazement, as if he could hardly believe his eyes. 'There's not a scratch on you! Blessed saints preserve you! There you are, sitting at your desk as if nothing had happened! How you had the foresight to wear that leather collar around your neck, I shall never know.'

Porfiry affected a look of weary disdain. 'It is metal encased in leather. I must express my gratitude to Major Verkhotsev, who had the greater foresight to equip me with it. I knew that I had delivered a shock to Aglaia Filippovna's system. For her to hear news of another child murdered in the same manner as she had committed her crimes was simply beyond her comprehension. She had successfully gained mastery over almost every aspect of her physiology, but she could not control her emotions when Princess Naryskina read out the article from the St Petersburg Gazette.'

'Which you say was written by your manservant Slava?'

'It would seem so. He was at least the source of the information. At any rate, Aglaia Filippovna's surprise betrayed her. Only the murderer of the first three children would be shocked to hear that a fourth had been killed. She opened her eyes involuntarily and was met by the sight of the towel that had been used to mop up her sister's blood. At the same time, she felt my fingers toying at the base of her thumb, at the very place where the ring would have been when she carried out her crimes. I was letting her know that I suspected her.'

'Without question, it is that that provoked her attack. You brought it on yourself.'

'It was essential to put some pressure on her, to force her into revealing herself.'

'But when did you first suspect her?' The question came from Virginsky, who was at the window, his back to the room. The day was overcast with a heavy quilt of cloud. Virginsky's voice came heavy with resentment.

'Once, when we were called to the palace because Aglaia Filippovna had come round briefly, I noticed that she toyed compulsively with her thumb, as if twisting something endlessly round and round. The gesture made no sense to me at the time as we had not yet discovered the children's remains, with the tell-tale bruises. Indeed, I forgot all about it, until the day that I was summoned to see the Tsar. I noticed that he had the nervous habit of twisting a ring on one of his fingers. Somehow in my mind, the pieces fell into place. I realised that that was what Aglaia Filippovna had been doing, although the ring itself was lacking.'

'Remarkable,' declared Nikodim Fomich, who was striding the room delightedly. 'But then to suspect her of murdering her sister! Could there be a more unnatural crime, or one more difficult to conceive of?'

'For any normal person, perhaps. But here is a girl who had already murdered her mother.'

'Good Lord!'

'Or so I believe. Her father committed suicide, without question. But the circumstances of her mother's death are less clear. It is conjecture – I accept – but nonetheless it is reasonable to believe that Aglaia Filippovna had a hand in it, especially considering her later career. Mention of her parents' deaths certainly aroused my suspicions with regard to the violent demise of her sister. To lose a father, a mother and a sister . . . one has to wonder. One often finds that a suicide in the family initiates a preoccupation with death. It is as if a door is opened. Death becomes familiar. It also gains a certain viability as a solution to one's problems. Most often, it sets an example that can be followed. In this case, I believe, her father's suicide triggered a murderous propensity. The tragic event occurred during her adolescence, a period of intense emotional upheaval at the best of times. We can imagine that she loved her father dearly, perhaps jealously. No doubt she blamed her mother for his death, and conceived a way to exact revenge.'

'Has she confessed to this?' asked Nikodim Fomich hopefully.

'No. She has fallen back on her favourite evasive strategy. She is feigning unconsciousness again. Playing dead, we might almost say. Nevertheless, even if we do not go so far as to accuse Aglaia Filippovna of matricide – a charge we will never be able to prove – even so, it is not unreasonable to assume that the double loss of her parents at such an age had a devastating effect on her young psyche. Her sister, too, was thrown into turmoil, as evidenced by her wayward and promiscuous life. We may put it this way: one sought to heal herself through excessive love, the other through excessive hate.'

'But why?' demanded Virginsky, crossing to Porfiry's desk. 'Why did she kill her sister? Why did she kill the children? Why did she do any of it?'

'I confess I do not yet have answers to all the questions that

433

this case raises. The most impenetrable question of all is *why*. I suspect it has something to do with the one individual at the centre of all this.'

'Maria Petrovna.'

'Yes. She is the link between the sisters and the dead children. I suggest we call on her at our soonest convenience,' said Porfiry, rising.

'Before you go,' cut in Nikodim Fomich, 'I have a question which perhaps you *can* answer. It's to do with Captain Mizinchikov. How did he get blood on him? Have you worked that out?'

Porfiry directed a display of impatient blinking towards Nikodim Fomich and sighed. 'That is the only question you have? You have no questions regarding the illicit trade in cadavers conducted by the men under your command? A trade I am told you condone and indeed have engaged in, and which, I might say, considerably hampered our investigation.'

'Who has told you this?'

'Lieutenant Salytov. A man you admire for his skill in extracting confessions.'

'And the primary transgressor in this affair. Did it not occur to you that he may have sought to implicate me in order to deter you from pursuing the matter?'

'Do you swear to me that you have never profited from the sale of an unidentified and unclaimed body?'

'There will be an enquiry, Porfiry Petrovich. I am confident that I will be found blameless.'

'That is not the same thing.' Porfiry's voice was leaden with disillusionment. He would not meet Nikodim Fomich's defiantly cheerful countenance.

'But what of the blood stains?' There was a desperate jollity to Nikodim Fomich's tone. He was trying to win Porfiry over by appealing to his cleverness.

'Pavel Pavlovich, do you remember the first time we visited Aglaia Filippovna, when Dr Müller lifted her nightdress and showed us the wounds on her leg?'

'Yes.'

'I believe she harvested her own blood, and somehow engineered to disseminate it on to Captain Mizinchikov, in order to incriminate him and direct attention away from herself. Nothing in a murder case screams so loudly and distractingly as blood.'

'Good heavens!'

'When Captain Mizinchikov entered the dressing room, she held out a hand, pointing at him, almost touching him.' Porfiry mimed the gesture, reaching his hand towards Nikodim Fomich. 'What if she had had something concealed in the closed palm of her hand?'

'Something? What exactly?'

'It came to me when Princess Naryskina tipped out the contents of her handbag. Although in truth, I think I had an inkling of it from the very beginning of the investigation, from that night at the Naryskin Palace. I went into the theatre and saw a woman spray herself with scent from an atomiser.'

'An atomiser?'

'The bulb of an atomiser, adapted to release a coarser jet than usual. It could easily be concealed in the hand.'

'What happened to it? Why did we not find it?' said Virginsky.

'A good question. I have come to the opinion that the emblem of the double-headed eagle has a great significance to this case, though not in the way we formerly imagined. It does not incriminate a member of the Romanov family, as you once suggested, Pavel Pavlovich. Its significance is rather more subtle and almost serendipitous. The use of this particular ring was after all forced on Aglaia Filippovna. Allowing for that, I believe it operates unconsciously to reveal the presence of an accomplice. Do you remember the anonymous note sent with a fine red thread, claiming a political aspect to Yelena Filippovna's murder? Aglaia Filippovna did not send that. It was her intention to blame Captain Mizinchikov for her sister's murder, not to credit a political tendency.' Noticing a questioning frown across Virginsky's brow, Porfiry went on: 'Perhaps to punish him for some slight or insult, we cannot know.'

Virginsky's frown dissipated into an expression of wonder. 'For loving Yelena! She was jealous of her sister, always jealous of her!'

'A very interesting supposition, my friend.' Porfiry smiled for Virginsky, in pointed contrast to the coldness of his expression towards Nikodim Fomich. 'However, be that as it may, the point is that I discern two contrary wills at work here, that is to say, two heads pointing in opposing directions. For Aglaia Filippovna, the drive to murder always originated in the personal. Her crimes were the violent eruptions of an intense emotional life. In many ways, she was the victim of her own wild and ravening ego. She wrought destruction on everything that opposed her. No wonder that she sought escape in oblivion. We must allow that she is not entirely a monster. Perhaps horror at her ultimate crime, the murder of her own sister, overwhelmed her. On the other hand, I detect in that note a more utilitarian mind at work. A mind capable of recognising the destructive capabilities of a damaged child and exploiting them for its own wider purposes.' Porfiry's head jerked sideways as if physically struck by a realisation. The colour drained from his face and his eyes bulged with alarm. 'Come, Pavel Pavlovich. I fear it is a matter of urgency that we talk to Maria Petrovna.'

*

There was no sign of Maria Petrovna at the school over the carpenter's shop. They found only one child in her classroom, a girl of about nine years, who was seated patiently on the front bench, a slate on her lap in readiness. She turned to face them with wide, wondering eyes beneath a domed brow.

'Maria Petrovna?' demanded Porfiry.

The girl gave a mighty shrug and sighed.

'Where are all the other children?'

'Gone.'

'Why then are you still here, child?'

The girl could only answer with another shrug.

'Porfiry Petrovich,' said Virginsky, pointing to the black board. On it was written *NO SCHOOL TODAY*.

'You must go home, darling. Can you not read? There is no school today.'

'She will come back. She will not leave us.' The girl turned back to face the front.

Porfiry and Virginsky exchanged a look of understanding and left her to her expectancy.

They found the priest, Father Anfim, coming out of the other classroom.

'Where is Maria Petrovna?'

'You have just missed her,' said the priest.

'And Perkhotin?'

'He has gone too.'

'Where have they gone?'

'I do not know. Neither Maria Petrovna nor Apollon Mikhailovich saw fit to share that information with me.'

'They left together?'

'Yes. I arrived for an unscheduled inspection. The two of them pushed past me on the stairs. I came up to find the children running riot in both classrooms. I have just sent the last of them home – apart from that rather simple girl in Maria Petrovna's classroom, who simply refuses to go. She is convinced Maria Petrovna will return. I never would have expected such conduct from Maria Petrovna. Apollon Mikhailovich is another matter. He is a fowl of different feathers. Him I consider capable of anything.'

'I share your fears, Father. And unless we find Maria Petrovna, I fear it may be the end for her too. Did she or Perkhotin say anything to you on their way out?'

'He told me to get out of his damn way. I told him to go to Hell. He laughed and said that was precisely where he intended to go.'

'I see. And did Maria Petrovna say anything?'

'She ... was more polite. She begged me not to be cross. Nor to be afraid, which I thought extraordinary, I must say. It had not occurred to me to be afraid. She said that something very urgent had come up and she had to go with Apollon Mikhailovich. The life of a friend depended on it, she said.'

'The life of a friend? What could she have meant by that?' wondered Porfiry.

'Where do you think they went?' Virginsky's eyes locked on to Porfiry's. There was a note of touching dependence in his voice. It really did seem that deep down he believed Porfiry capable of answering any question asked of him.

'Perhaps we will find some clues in Perkhotin's classroom.'

This answer seemed to satisfy Virginsky, or at least hold his burgeoning panic at bay. Without the animation of the children who cascaded daily into it, the classroom seemed stale as well as still. There was an air of abandonment to it. The figures in the illustrated alphabet on the wall were frozen and mute, giving the impression that the room had been locked into one moment of time.

The priest had followed them into the room and was watching closely as the two magistrates cast about, straining for a significant detail to jump out at them.

A line of text was written on the blackboard, partially smudged as if someone had half-heartedly attempted to erase it; or rather, not so much to erase the words, as to add a flourish to them.

'*Out of the . . .* something, *the* something?' read Virginsky, quizzically.

'*Out of the eater, the eaten,*' supplied Porfiry. 'You must recognise it, Father Anfim.'

'It is Samson's riddle to the Philistines,' confirmed the priest. '*Out of the eater, the eaten. Out of the strong, the sweet.*'

'Of course. You see, you needn't have worried. Your atheist Perkhotin was teaching scripture.'

'I do not believe that!' blustered Father Anfim.

'To be honest, neither do I. Do you see that, Pavel Pavlovich? The pattern made by the movement of the eraser across the board? A line moving diagonally up and down in a zig-zag.'

'The letter M! Just like on the mirror!'

'I feel certain we have found our accomplice.'

'Perkhotin?'

'We know that he taught Maria Petrovna at the Smolny Institute. He must also have made the acquaintance of the

Polenov sisters too.' Porfiry was standing in front of the blackboard, peering into its dust-smeared surface as if into a fog from which he expected figures to emerge. 'Now all we have to do is work out what he means by this. Samson fought the lion. He ripped it apart with his bare hands. A nest of bees settled inside the lion's carcass and Samson ate their honey. Is that not the story, Father Anfim?'

'Yes, that's correct. Judges, chapter fourteen.'

'You could take it as a religious text, or equally a revolutionary one. The lion is the state. Samson is the revolutionary fighter, Perkhotin in this case, who brings about a sweet boon through a cataclysmic destructive act.'

'This does not help us!' cried Virginsky. 'It doesn't tell us where he has taken her.'

'In these situations, it is imperative to remain calm. We are attempting to navigate the unfathomable pathways of the mind, and of a very peculiar type of mind too. It is possible that, like the two-headed eagle, this message has a double valence. It may be that he has inadvertently betrayed himself in writing this. Or perhaps he has left it here intentionally for us to find. It may be that he wishes to lead us to him. If I am not mistaken about his character, it is dominated by vanity. This is always the case with men such as Perkhotin. School masters, I mean. They put themselves in a position where they are cleverer than everyone around them. I feel he is testing us. Are *we* clever enough to solve his riddle?'

'I considered becoming a school master,' said Virginsky with sullen resentment. 'If my life had followed a different path – one that did not bring me into contact with you – that may very well have been the career I would have chosen. I do not consider it a profession for the vain. Humility and dedication to service are rather the qualities I would associate with it.'

'I apologise, Pavel Pavlovich, to you and all school masters. No doubt you are right. No doubt it is my own vanity that induces me to view others through the distorting prism of that defect. I will hazard that there is no vainer class of professional man than the investigating magistrate. And that is why I am determined to solve his riddle. Indeed, I feel that it is already solved in my mind.'

'So? What is the solution?'

'The children who were murdered by Aglaia Filippovna . . . what links them?'

'They were all pupils at this school?'

'What else?'

'They were all factory workers.'

'Yes. Factory workers. To be more precise, they all worked, in fact, at foreign-owned factories.'

'That is true. But what of it?'

'Samson's riddle. Why think of Samson's riddle now? Unless a certain address in St Petersburg put Samson's name into his mind and suggested the riddle, which is particularly apt to his intentions.'

'Samsonyevsky Prospekt.'

'Very good, Pavel Pavlovich. Samsonyevsky Prospekt. There is, I believe, a prominent foreign-owned factory that lies between Samsonyevsky Prospekt and the Vyborgskaya Embankment. On Samson's Quay, in fact.'

'The Nobel Factory! You think he has taken her there? But why?'

'Time is of the essence, Pavel Pavlovich. Let us find a *drozhki*. We can talk on the way.'

43

Three hundred foxes

The air was crystalline. A piercing winter clarity assailed their eyes and sharp particles of frozen moisture stung their faces. Sensing their urgency, the driver stood and whipped his horse mercilessly. The *drozhki* swung precariously from side to side, as fragile as an empty acorn shell tossed on the wind. At times it seemed to leave the ground.

Porfiry shouted to be heard over the roar of conveyance. 'News of Aglaia Filippovna's miraculous recovery no doubt reached him. He must have realised that once she was up and out of his control, it was only a question of time before we came after him. And so, perhaps, he wishes to make one final grand gesture.'

'What?' The word came out sharply and was whipped away by the wind.

'His plan was to incriminate the Tsarist regime – to make the public believe that a member of the Romanov family was capable of child murder, or at the very least to prove that the Tsar was incapable of protecting the empire's most vulnerable children, thereby propagating revolutionary sentiments to the wider populace. Aglaia Filippovna's motives may well have been different. Her action was driven by her monstrous jealousy of her sister. She wished to harm all who loved Yelena. That is why she attacked the pupils of Maria Petrovna's school. To attack Maria Petrovna, whose love for her sister was the most unconditional and unquestioning of all. And of course, Aglaia Filippovna's jealous rage culminated in her actually destroying her hated sibling. This no doubt created difficulties for Perkhotin. He was forced to help her cover up an essentially personal murder, which he attempted to pass off as political. The two-headed eagle again.'

'And so? Where does that leave us?'

'He is no fool. I imagine that he realises the game is up. He must know that his deception has been uncovered. There is little point continuing the pretence. He is exposed as a greater monster than the regime he seeks to overthrow.'

'Go on.'

'He has nothing to lose any more. He is not a man to run and hide. He is a man to go out in a blaze of glory.'

'But why would he take Maria Petrovna with him?'

'He has shown throughout his career the need to impress young women with his cleverness. There is nothing that flatters his vanity so much as his idolisation in the eyes of young ladies. Perhaps he wishes to persuade Maria Petrovna of the correctness of his actions, to justify himself to her.'

'You do not think she was involved in this all along?'

'Only unwittingly. Were she to know the truth, she cannot but be appalled at Perkhotin's part in Aglaia's crimes. Her former idol will be transformed into a monster. The effect will be devastating. Everything she has based her life on has stemmed from his teachings.'

'Why would she go with him?'

'She may have been acting under duress, though nothing Father Anfim said hinted at that. More likely, she does not yet know the full truth. Perhaps he has revealed Aglaia Filippovna's guilt, without disclosing his own role in it. She may believe that she is rushing to a meeting with Aglaia Filippovna, and wishes to persuade her to give herself up before any more innocents die. Or perhaps she does know the truth. And Apollon Mikhailovich himself is the friend whose life – or soul – she hopes to save.'

'What do you think he intends to do?'

'The story of Samson is instructive, I think. In chapter fifteen of the Book of Judges, we are told that Samson attached burning firebrands to the tails of three hundred foxes, tethering them in pairs, two to a firebrand. I always thought that rather cruel. He released the foxes into the fields of the Philistines, burning their crops in a great conflagration. I wonder if Perkhotin has something similar in mind. The Nobel brothers manufacture a diverse range of engineering products. Including armaments for the Russian state. I have read accounts of their experiments into the development of a new and highly destructive explosive material. They have successfully blown up sections of the Neva, I believe. A crude incendiary device planted in the right part of the factory would result in a far more destructive conflagration than could be achieved by three hundred blindly panicking foxes.'

Virginsky stood in the rocking *drozhki* and screamed at the driver. 'Faster! Make the beast go faster!'

*

The Nobel Metalworking Factory was a modern, and in some ways model, factory. It had been in existence for a mere eight years, and so the semi-derelict dilapidation that characterised so many Petersburg factories had not yet taken hold. The Nobel family itself, or rather the members of it who remained in St Petersburg, resided in a mansion that was inside the

444

factory precincts. In fact, their home was attached to the factory and seemed to grow out of it, as if the comfort and leisure of these few individuals was just another product manufactured there. But by choosing to live so close to the source of their wealth, they showed that they were not ashamed of it. On the contrary, it suggested that the pride they might naturally feel towards their home extended to the factory too. It could also be taken as a gesture of solidarity with their employees, or those of them who lived on site in the purpose-built workers' quarters.

The mansion presented a neo-classical frontage which, together with a stand of trees planted beside it, almost hid the grimier blocks behind. The screen was only partially successful because the trees were now seasonally denuded. There was an ornamental garden in front of it, bounded by a wrought iron fence, with a semi-circular recess reminiscent of the entrance to a park. The productive factory buildings appeared plain and functional, though well-maintained and orderly, laid out at right angles to one another. As an indication of the factory's rational design, there was only one smoking chimney tower, which peeped over the roof of the palatial façade. Perspective suggested that it was at the rear of the factory precinct, at the furthest possible distance from the Nobel family home.

It was here that Porfiry and Virginsky called, identifying themselves as magistrates and insisting that Ludwig Nobel himself be made aware of a most serious threat to his factory. All this was very hard for the maid to take in. Somewhat panic-stricken, she informed them that Ludwig Immanuelevich was currently at work in the office.

'Then take us to him, miss! There is not a moment to lose!' demanded Virginsky. 'Do you wish to be blown to atoms?'

The question galvanised the timorous girl into action. She led them at a bustling lick through a beech-panelled hall, which had a fresh but sober countenance. There was no real decline in the standard of décor as they passed into the servants' quarters. In the kitchen, it was not just the hanging pots and pans that gleamed, but every surface, even the freshly-waxed floor.

The kitchen door gave directly on to the factory yard. Now, suddenly, as that door was thrown open, the harsh world of industry clamoured to make itself felt. The day's activity was in full flow. Haulage carts drawn by teams of colossal drays rattled across the cobbles. Creaking gantries unloaded and loaded the raw materials and finished products that represented the mighty respiration of the plant. In came palettes of coke, ore, sand, limestone and paint. Out went machine parts, pipes, gates, chains, sheet metal, not to mention mysterious unmarked crates, the contents of which could only be guessed at. But this was only a fraction of the goods processed. On the other side of the main factory building was the River Neva, where barges were loaded and unloaded, ferrying goods to and from every corner of the empire. It was here that several years ago Ludwig Nobel's brother Alfred had discharged a canister containing a chemical formulation of his devising, which had resulted in the displacement of several tons of icy water and the deaths of countless fish.

To Porfiry, there was something vital and energising about all this teeming activity, something also profoundly human.

At the entrance to the office block, the maid left them in the hands of a middle-aged clerk in a black frock coat. His face was unpromisingly lean and officious-looking, and his neck raw from the abrasion of his stiff winged collar; nonetheless, he had the intelligence to grasp the urgency of the situation immediately and hurried off to fetch Ludwig Nobel himself.

'We are wasting time,' hissed Virginsky, as they waited for the arrival of that gentleman.

'You have seen the scale of the factory, Pavel Pavlovich,' said Porfiry calmly. 'We cannot possibly guess where Perkhotin might be without help from someone who knows the place well. And who knows it better than the man who built it? Furthermore, if we attempt to search the premises without the owner's co-operation we will be challenged at every turn. A few words to Ludwig Nobel will save us vital time in the long run, I am confident.'

The clerk returned, accompanied by a man of about forty years of age, with dark hair parted low on one side and full mutton-chop sideburns. His expression was careworn around his eyes, but one eyebrow was kinked wryly. The line of his mouth was grim, though not without an angle of scepticism or reservation.

'What is all this about?'

'You are Ludwig Nobel?'

'I am. And you?'

'I am Porfiry Petrovich, investigating magistrate. This is my colleague, Pavel Pavlovich. We are here because we believe your factory may be in imminent danger. Tell me, if one wanted to wreak the maximum damage through an incendiary attack, where would one launch it?'

Nobel's features contracted into a frown. He did not seem alarmed, rather he was an engineer engaged in calculating an interesting but essentially abstract problem. 'I would suggest the munitions storeroom. We store a quantity of gunpowder there, amongst other combustible and highly volatile materials. However, it is practically impregnable.'

'But if someone were to find a way to ignite it, the damage would be widespread?'

'It is built to reduce the impact of any unfortunate accident. However, the sheer quantity of material stored there would be sufficient to inflict damage on adjoining sectors of the factory.'

'I would be very grateful if you could take us there immediately.'

Nobel nodded decisively. 'This way, gentlemen.'

They crossed a vast warehouse which led to a locomotive and rolling stock workshop. They witnessed the slow rotation of a skeletal engine on a massive turntable in the centre of the floor.

'I must say, I am impressed by the diversity of your factory's output,' said Porfiry as he hurried to keep up with Nobel.

'It is the way we have always done business. The world is so rapidly changing that one cannot afford to tether one's self to any one technology or endeavour, in case it is supplanted. We are always looking for new channels of diversification. It is the way to the future.'

'And armaments are an important part of your business?'

'The Russian army is a good customer of ours. Which leads me to wonder why there is no military presence here with you, to safeguard this important source of supply.'

'There has been no time for that.'

'Are you confident that the two of you alone will be sufficient to frustrate this attack?'

Virginsky's frown echoed the uncertainty of Nobel's question. Porfiry answered both with a wince. They continued in silence.

Eventually, they entered a room in which the temperature noticeably increased. It was soon clear why: all around flames licked up from the floor. The air was thick with noxious fumes, each breath a chemical punch into the lungs. It seemed to Porfiry that they had entered someone's vision of hell. He remembered Perkhotin's words to Father Anfim.

Porfiry saw that the flames, which never exceeded knee-height, only emerged from certain points. Covered channels ran across the floor; fissures in the coverings released the flames. The heat now was oppressive.

Workmen in heavy protective clothing wielded long rods to handle a massive vat suspended on a chain. An incandescent stream of molten iron was released from a chute and flowed sluggishly into the vat. The workmen jabbed at it as if they were goading a bear. The men swung the laden vat along a gantry and then tipped it, so that the blinding surface spilled out into a heavily encrusted receptacle.

'They are skimming off the impurities,' said Nobel. 'They will use what remains to cast cannonballs.'

'Cannonballs,' repeated Porfiry, vacuously.

The engineer's frown betrayed something of the contempt a practical man feels for a theorist.

Nobel opened a door and led them outside once more. The cold wind was a relief after the heat and poisonous air of the workshop. Across a narrow passageway was a low, brick-built outhouse, entirely lacking in windows, and sealed with a single door of steel.

'As you can see, we keep the munitions storeroom heavily secured, and, for obvious reasons, at some distance from the foundry. There is no way in or out, other than through that door, which is kept locked at all times. Do you wish to go in?'

'Who has a key?' asked Porfiry.

'Myself, of course. And the director and several of the foremen of the munitions section.'

'Are they all trustworthy individuals?'

'I believe so.'

Porfiry looked anxiously over his shoulder. 'If we open the door, we may provide him with the opportunity for launching his attack. My only fear is that he is inside already.'

'Impossible,' asserted Nobel.

'You would like to think so but we are dealing with a ruthless and resourceful individual here. We have every reason to believe that he has been planning this attack for some time. He may already have gained the confidence of one of the keyholders. Apollon Mikhailovich Perkhotin can be a very persuasive man.'

'Apollon Mikhailovich?'

'Do you know him?'

'I have engaged the services of one Apollon Mikhailovich Perkhotin to teach a series of evening classes here. I met him through my philanthropic activities. I have always encouraged my workers in their efforts at self-improvement.'

'That is commendable. But now we see how it all begins to fit together. To your knowledge, did any of the munitions foremen attend his classes?'

Nobel nodded hopelessly. Suddenly the careworn slackness around his eyes spread to the rest of his face. 'Fedya Vasilevich.'

'What do we do?' The question, strained to the point of panic, came from Virginsky.

'I am consoled by the fact that he has not yet blown up the storeroom,' said Porfiry. 'However, I fear that if we go in now we may precipitate the very event we are anxious to prevent. At the same time, we must ask ourselves for what is he waiting? For an audience, no doubt.'

Porfiry put his ear to the steel door but heard nothing. He nodded to Nobel to open up.

'Porfiry Petrovich, are you sure this is wise?'

'Don't be afraid, Pavel Pavlovich. We must find a way to talk to him. We will achieve nothing, if not.'

The door slid open heavily on its runners. The smell of gunpowder rushed out as if in flight.

'Tell me, Ludwig Immanuelevich, just so that I might be prepared . . . I have heard of your brother Alfred's experiments. Are there any of the substances he has invented stored in here?'

Ludwig Nobel shrugged his shoulders. 'Alfred has returned to Stockholm. It is eight years since he successfully tested the explosive potential of nitroglycerine in the Neva. However, I cannot say for certain that he took all his toys with him.'

A glimmer of light was visible at the rear of the storeroom, shining up from behind dim shapes.

'He has taken a light in there!' Nobel's face rippled with incredulity. 'One spark from that could take the whole building up.'

'Apollon Mikhailovich!' called Porfiry through the open doorway. 'Come out. You are placing yourself and others in grave danger.'

There was a scuffle of movement, footsteps scraping. Tense hissed whispers echoed between the looming racks of massed ammunitions.

'What does this achieve?' continued Porfiry. 'Your self-destruction will not bring about a more just society. We need you alive, Apollon Mikhailovich, to help shape the future. Russia will be nothing without its great men!'

'There can be no future,' came an answering cry. 'Until we have swept away the present.'

A stifled sob broke out.

'Maria Petrovna? Let her go, Apollon Mikhailovich. I will come in in her place, and we can talk about how we can bring about the changes you desire.'

'*Destroy everything!*'

Porfiry flashed alarm towards Virginsky. 'I'm coming in,' he called back to Perkhotin. 'I only want to talk. I am alone. Unarmed. I wish to learn from you. To be your disciple.'

Porfiry held up a hand to deter Virginsky from following him. 'Close the door behind me and see to it that the area is cleared.' With a nod of resolve to Ludwig Nobel, he stepped inside.

The light expanded as Porfiry walked towards it, picking his way around blocks of darkness. As he progressed, the objects around him became more clearly discernible. He saw stacks of metallic canisters and towers of crates. As his hand groped about him, it strayed onto a bulging column of wooden barrels, which swayed slightly at his touch. A forest of similar columns receded into the darkness. These were the barrels of gunpowder he presumed. Alongside them were metal drums, racked on their sides. Beyond the drums, he saw a pyramid of cannonballs, smaller than he had expected, each one about the size of a clenched fist. Porfiry reached a hand out towards the apex of the pyramid and clasped the black sphere resting there. He hefted it swiftly behind his back in his right hand.

Rounding a corner of the maze of deadly goods, he saw the source of light directly ahead of him. Perkhotin held an oil lantern over the black circular abyss at the neck of an opened barrel of gunpowder.

452

Maria Petrovna was seated hunched on the floor, huddled into a large, heavy shawl with a plaid pattern. Next to her was a man in labourer's clothes whom Porfiry took to be the foreman, Fedya Vasilevich.

'You see how things are, magistrate.'

Maria looked up at Perkhotin's words and met Porfiry's gaze with a look of mute pleading.

'Make any sudden movement and I will let go of the lantern.'

'Teach me,' said Porfiry. 'Teach me what you would achieve by that. I have come to learn from you.'

'How did you find me?'

'You left a clue for me, did you not? *Out of the eater, the eaten.* I presumed you meant to be found, leaving such an easy clue.'

'I congratulate you. The riddle was a test. You have passed. You will be rewarded. You will be here to witness the cataclysm.'

'You will tear apart the lion of the imperial state.'

'Yes.'

'And bring forth the honey of a new social order.'

'Yes.'

'You will send out three hundred flaming foxes.'

'Yes.'

'Only one thing concerns me, Apollon Mikhailovich. How will the people be able to interpret these wonders? How will they know that the revolution has begun, that the time to rise up is here? I know this corrupt regime. I know how it works. They will merely say that there has been an accident at the Nobel Plant. They will deny your act its revolutionary aspect.'

In the lamp glow, Perkhotin's great shovel-beard was a dark spread of negativity eating away half his face. Above it, his expression clouded as he took in what Porfiry had said.

'You need a witness,' went on Porfiry. 'Someone who will be believed. Someone the Tsar dare not silence. Let her go. Her father is a senior officer in the Third Section. She is untouchable. And think what power her testimony would have.'

'No. She must stay. You may go. They will believe you. But she must stay. She must be made to understand.'

'At least let Fedya go. He has served his purpose by admitting you here. You do not need him any more.'

'His death is necessary. All our deaths are necessary. I have no choice in this. Revolution is an inevitable process. A force of nature. The innocent will die. Blood will flow. The blood of martyrs as well as of our enemies. But the process will triumph. I must not shrink from this.'

'But you have never killed anyone, Apollon Mikhailovich! You didn't kill any of the children, did you? That is not the role you play in this. You are the leader. The great thinker, originator of the masterplan. It is for others to execute it. Your disciples. You must have your disciples. Like Aglaia Filippovna. She was your instrument, your weapon. You aimed, primed and fired her. But she was not perfect. She was too wild, uncontrollable. She reduced everything to a sordid personal drama. There was no understanding, no true sense of mission. She simply killed to appease her bloodlust. A useful tool, but not a sophisticated one. How did it work? You picked out the children for her to kill?'

'No. It was not like that. At first, I wanted just to show her how the poor live under this criminal regime. To open her eyes. Her sister Yelena had a carriage, provided by that banker. She refused to set foot in it, but she let Aglaia use it. We would go driving around the worst slums and I would show her everything. One day, I recognised one of the children from the school, Svetlana, and called her over. She climbed into the carriage and sat between us. Before I could stop her, Aglaia Filippovna had strangled the girl. She said she did it out of mercy. That it was an act of kindness to kill the girl. I dismissed the driver, gave him some money and deposited him near a tavern. He knew nothing of what had happened, so quickly and quietly had Aglaia Filippovna committed the crime. I drove the carriage myself across the city, looking for somewhere to deposit the body.'

'Why did you not go to the police? I only ask because I wish to understand.'

'The *police*?' Perkhotin spat the word back dismissively. 'One cannot undo what is done. Besides, I saw that a greater purpose could be served. I had noticed the ring around Aglaia's thumb. She was in the habit of borrowing her sister's jewellery as well as her carriage. I realised I could not prevent her from killing, so I decided to take a utilitarian approach to her murderous instincts. To use them for the benefit of society.'

'And thereafter you took her out in the carriage yourself?'

'Yes.'

'But when she killed Yelena, she went too far. That was never part of the plan, was it, Apollon Mikhailovich?'

'One must be prepared to adapt one's plans.'

'You adapted admirably. But Aglaia had ideas of her own, did she not? She wanted to incriminate Captain Mizinchikov, to punish him for loving Yelena, whereas you saw that it would be another opportunity – a tremendous opportunity – to terrorise the state.'

'Aglaia knew that her sister had placed a razor wrapped in red silk in Mizinchikov's apartment, goading him to kill her. That gave her the idea of laying a red thread on Yelena's body. In fact, she laid two – she was excessive in everything she did. I was able to steal one without her noticing. I thought it would come in useful. I didn't know how, exactly, at the time.'

'It was just as well that Aglaia collapsed under the strain of her crimes when she did. She was no use to you any more. But now you can use *me*, Apollon Mikhailovich. I understand. I am almost your equal. Notice that I said *almost*. I would not dare to set myself up as your equal. But I am worthy of you, you must see that. I shall be your weapon now, your disciple. It is not enough for me to witness the beginning of the revolution. Let me initiate it. The Tsar sickens me. I have been in his company. I have listened to his nauseating self-justifications. I want only to destroy him. Let me ignite the torch that will destroy the lion. And you, you can escape. You must escape! Russia needs you!'

'No. It is too late for escape.' Perkhotin regarded Porfiry narrowly. 'Do you really wish to do this? No . . .' He shook his head dubiously. 'How can I trust you? This is some trick of yours. Some magistrate's trick. I must do this myself.'

Porfiry closed in on Perkhotin in three brisk steps, so that he was close enough to scream in his face: 'Do it then! Do it now, Apollon Mikhailovich. Release the lantern.'

Perkhotin let go. Porfiry swung out his left hand and batted the lantern away from the barrel. It smashed on the ground. The oil spread and ignited. Porfiry was standing in a pool of soft orange flame that lapped at his ankles.

Maria Petrovna leapt to her feet and in one movement drew the shawl from around her shoulders. She spread the garment out and screamed at Porfiry: 'Out of the way!' He jumped out of the flames as if he had only just noticed them. Maria Petrovna swept the shawl down to cover the fire. Fedya Vasilevich took off his jacket and threw that down too, but the flames were already out. They were plunged into darkness.

'You fool!'

Porfiry swung the hand holding the cannonball in the direction of the voice. His hand flailed uselessly through the unresisting air. The momentum of the iron weight was too much for him. The cannonball left his hand and fell, landing almost without a sound, with just a soft swallowing shift of grit. Something granular and pungent filled the darkness, a harder, denser darkness within, an acerbic, invisible mist that clawed at their eyes and caught in their throats.

It was hard to tell for certain but it seemed that Perkhotin had borne the brunt of the dust cloud sent up by the cannonball plummeting into the gunpowder barrel. He was hacking uncontrollably.

'Fedya! Can you find your way out of here?' Porfiry felt himself to be blinded. His corneas were stinging with pain. Tears streamed from his eyes. The foreman, however, had been furthest from the barrel, and besides knew the layout of the storeroom better than any of them.

'I am here,' came Fedya Vasilevich's stolid voice. 'Stick close by me.'

'No. You go and bring them back for us. It will be quicker.' The foreman's footsteps could be heard shuffling slowly away. 'Masha, are you there?'

'I am here.' Her voice was infinite in the darkness, and at the

457

same time, a tremulous vibration so frail and fine that it barely existed at all.

'Give me your hand.'

Fingers found fingers. A shock chased along the nerve endings of his skin. Their hands groped desperately, fiercely together, into an interlocking hold. He pulled her to him.

44

Porfiry surprised

Porfiry heard the door slide open on its runners. The daylight reverberated with a thunderous metallic boom, startling the contents of the storeroom with a wash of silver.

Perkhotin was bent over, coughing, a dim figure in the semi-darkness. He straightened up. A curse escaped his lips and he hurtled past Porfiry and Maria, towards the light.

Porfiry released Maria, suddenly embarrassed by the position they found themselves in. 'I must . . .'

'Yes, of course.' She looked away, abashed. The gesture was ephemeral, gone as soon as it was expressed. Porfiry felt an instant pang of nostalgia for it.

He could not look at her now. He ran towards the daylight.

Outside, he saw Fedya approaching with Virginsky and Ludwig Nobel. Perkhotin was nowhere to be seen.

The door to the munitions workshop was open.

He was just in time to see a jet of flame leap up from the floor as Perkhotin ran through it. The gunpowder dust that covered him ignited instantly. Waves of crackling fire danced over his body, chasing up his legs, consuming his torso, and covering his face.

A scream of pain and rage gurgled in his throat as he thrashed out blindly.

Porfiry called out 'No!' but it was too late; he was too far away to intervene.

Perkhotin tripped over a discarded casting mould and fell against the great vat of molten iron that had been left dangling on its chains by the evacuated workmen.

The weight of his body tilted the vat, which would have been unbearably hot in itself.

His screams now were intense but short-lived. A flood of blazing liquid fire covered his face, sending up a plume of smoke. The sizzle of cooked meat mingled with the mineral tang of the workshop.

*

Porfiry closed the door behind him. He met Virginsky's questioning gaze. 'He's dead.'

A blanket had been found for Maria Petrovna, to replace her shawl. The rigours of the experience showed in her eyes. And yet she managed a delicate, complicated smile for Porfiry.

'What happened in there?' said Virginsky, indicating the munitions storeroom. He took hold of Porfiry. There was an undoubted edge of sexual jealousy to Virginsky's question.

'I behaved rather foolishly and Maria Petrovna came to my rescue. Had it not been for her quick thinking, the storeroom would have gone up in an inferno.'

'Well, at any rate, it is over now. You are safe.'

Virginsky's dismissiveness offended Porfiry. 'If you will permit me, I wish to talk to the young lady who saved my life.'

Virginsky bowed and released Porfiry.

Her eyes darted frantically, as if they wished to escape from his approach.

'Don't say anything.' Her smile had an edge of panic to it. She seemed for a moment very young.

'In the darkness . . .' It surprised me. The strength of feeling. I think perhaps it was the effect of the darkness.'

'I beg you, Porfiry Petrovich. Say no more.'

'I have been surprised.'

'Yes.'

'We are alive! That is the thing that surprises me most.'

'It is good to be surprised by life.' At last she looked up and met his gaze. Her smile was consoling and indulgent, but still not quite all that he had hoped for.

Even so, he could not stem the flow of words. 'Oh yes, infinitely good. I have been surprised by death too often. My heart . . . I feel my heart has opened.'

And now her smile was complicated by regret.

Porfiry felt a wave of sickening disappointment. 'Apollon Mikhailovich met with a terrible accident,' he said. 'I do not advise you to view the body.' He bowed tersely and turned from her.

'Porfiry!'

He swivelled back to face her.

'Please.' Her face was crumpled in despair, slicked with tears. 'I am sorry. You must understand, it cannot be. *We* cannot be. What happened must remain back there.'

'I quite agree. You have your life. The school. The children. I have mine. My work is everything to me. Thank you for reminding me. You must find it in your heart to forgive a foolish old man. I was momentarily overcome . . . by . . . by my surprise. Good day, Maria Petrovna.' He bowed and turned from her again.

He was aware of Virginsky staring into his face, with a strange, intent fascination. And around him, the sounds of industry started up, as the Nobel Metalworking Plant returned to work.

Historical note

Alexander II came to the Russian imperial throne in 1855. In 1861, he began a series of great reforms, including the liberation of 23 million serfs and the introduction of a fairer judicial system. If the reforms were intended to win over opponents to his regime, they failed. For the radicals, he had not gone far enough. For the conservatives, he should never have started. The first of many attempts on his life took place in 1866. He was finally assassinated in 1881. The day before his death saw the finishing touches put to a new constitution which allowed for an elected parliament – a revolutionary development in autocratic Russia. The new constitution, approved by Alexander II, never saw the light of day. One of the first acts of Alexander III – the tsarevich in this novel – was to suppress it. 'Thank God, this criminal and precipitous step towards a constitution was not taken,' he noted.

Acknowledgements

Novelists occasionally have to ask stupid questions of people who have better things to do with their time than answer them. In the case of crime novelists, the questions are often unpleasant as well as stupid. I would like to thank the following people for generously giving their time to help me find answers to my questions without ever making me feel either stupid or unpleasant: Michael Heavener, Mark Budman, Professor Alan Dronsfield of the Royal Society of Chemistry, and Carlina de la Cova, Ph.D., of the University of North Carolina at Greensboro. It goes without saying that the mistakes are all my own doing.

My debt to F. M. Dostoevsky, the original creator of Porfiry Petrovich, remains immeasurable.

ff

Faber and Faber – a home for writers

Faber and Faber is one of the great independent publishing houses in London. We were established in 1929 by Geoffrey Faber and our first editor was T. S. Eliot. We are proud to publish prize-winning fiction and non-fiction, as well as an unrivalled list of modern poets and playwrights. Among our list of writers we have five Booker Prize winners and eleven Nobel Laureates, and we continue to seek out the most exciting and innovative writers at work today.

www.faber.co.uk – a home for readers

The Faber website is a place where you will find all the latest news on our writers and events. You can listen to podcasts, preview new books, read specially commissioned articles and access reading guides, as well as entering competitions and enjoying a whole range of offers and exclusives. You can also browse the list of Faber Finds, an exciting new project where reader recommendations are helping to bring a wealth of lost classics back into print using the latest on-demand technology.